THE FORSAKEN

THE FORSAKEN

A VAMPIRE HUNTRESS LEGEND

L. A. BANKS

ST. MARTIN'S GRIFFIN NEW YORK

THE FORSAKEN. Copyright © 2006 by Leslie Esdaile Banks. All rights reserved. Printed in the United States of America. No part of this book may be used or reproduced in any manner whatsoever without written permission except in the case of brief quotations embodied in critical articles or reviews. For information, address St. Martin's Press, 175 Fifth Avenue, New York, N.Y. 10010.

www.stmartins.com

Library of Congress Cataloging-in-Publication Data

Banks, L. A.
    The forsaken : a vampire huntress legend / L. A. Banks.— 1st ed.
        p. cm.
    ISBN-13: 978-0-312-35235-6
    ISBN-10: 0-312-35235-2
    1. Richards, Damali (Fictitious character)—Fiction. 2. Vampires—Fiction. 3. Women in the performing arts—Fiction. 4. Women martial artists—Fiction. I. Title.

PS3602.A64F67 2006
813'.6—dc22

                                                              2006041721

P1

DEDICATION

This seventh book in the series is dedicated to all the seen and unseen angels who battled for me when I was too weary to lift my arms; who believed for me and in me when I lost faith; who guided me when the path became unclear; who breathed for me when life knocked the wind out of me; who held me when I'd cried so much there were no more tears left; who threw back their heads and laughed uproariously with me at the craziness around me (much of which I caused all on my own); who saw beauty in the things I thought weren't; who peeled away the illusion of beauty to show me how flawed certain things are; who taught me how to forgive the person I was hardest on—myself; who pulled me into their laps and comforted me, telling me, "Shush, child, rest"; who stood and applauded when new inspiration struck in the wee hours of the morning and I thought I was all alone; who whispered in my ear and mind and tweaked a passage or created a scene I'd never dreamed I could write; who taught me to be thankful and to have a profound appreciation for the Divine in all; who served hard lessons with tough love and tender forgiveness, gently kissing my boo-boos while they repeatedly blessed me and showed me how to live and laugh and love and forgive . . . teaching me to grow. I am still a work in progress.

Through this life, so far, I've found that the greatest battle one faces is the one within, the greatest challenge to one's humanity being the ability to be humane while being flawed and human. Thus I offer you this latest installment in the long saga of this legend with this theme: *Let the angels come forth and guide us all.*

ACKNOWLEDGMENTS

Special acknowledgment goes to: my editor, Monique Patterson, the visionary, legendary lady who conceived this project and keeps breathing new life into it; the entire St. Martin's Press team that works like a diligent, well-oiled machine that continues to move the series down the right tracks; my agent who keeps me on task (wink); Pam Nelson—a dynamic angel of mercy in the flesh; the artists, project team, Webmasters, VHL Street Team, and readers, all of whom are *serious* about their fictive family; and my own family that endures it all. Ashe! Thank you!

THE FORSAKEN

THE SHIFT

The day after Christmas, a horrific tsunami hit Southeast Asia, creating a natural and human disaster of biblical proportions. Disease and destruction lay in the wake of the giant wave, flooding and taking lives in eleven countries to the scale of Noah's time. But the animals sensed it was coming and were mysteriously saved. Ancient tribesmen, observant of nature's force, also strangely avoided destruction. But the cities . . . the tourists, all lay in ruins.

Humanity is now studying the instinctual nature of the animal kingdom. Tribal elders were asked how they knew, but their simplistic answers baffled scientists until debunked.

People in the fishing villages feared to eat the sea's yield, even while starving . . . so many bodies were in the water, and they reasoned that the fish had feasted upon that which the waters took.

Beyond the human suffering of more than a hundred and fifty thousand known dead, thousands missing, and millions left homeless and destitute with food shortages and tainted water, the power of the event actually shifted the planet—the Earth's poles moved to the east by a full inch, and time stopped for several milliseconds. It moved to the east . . . to the east . . . the east . . . perhaps east of Eden.

We do not yet know how this will influence the Earth's position amongst its planetary brethren. What we do know, however, is that everything in the universe is a fragile balance, like that of an immaculately designed Swiss watch. Move one part and misalign one gear, and then what? Astrologers have yet to weigh in on this matter, nor has the traditional scientific community. They simply have no answers.

All this while in the United States, Southern California has been deluged by unrelenting rains and the normally arid region was also covered by a blanket of snow . . . over one hundred and fifty inches has fallen on the Sierra Mountains . . . snow has even covered the desert region— Nevada . . . Texas and the Midwest experienced driving snowstorms . . . the Ohio Valley was covered in ice and floodwaters, forcing evacuations . . . this after four back-to-back hurricanes just devastated Florida's coast and the Caribbean, then one came that virtually wiped New Orleans off the map. Still there were more hurricanes, floods, tornados . . . forces of nature, also known by insurance companies as acts of God.

And, yet the world is still at war. Not even these cataclysmic events were enough to give mankind pause. In the ongoing human conflict, no one seemed to remember that even *time stood still.* The planet was rocked off its axis for milliseconds, but warring factions around the globe didn't seem to give a damn. They just kept on fighting, shooting, and blowing each other up. The stern warning is not being heeded. Dormant volcanoes around the world have awakened and threaten populated regions. Aftershocks from the tsunami and rippling earthquakes can still be felt. Floods are claiming lives in Europe, while wildfires burn in Australia as day temperatures crest and exceed one hundred degrees in the shade.

Now, scientists say that this is all rather normal, to be expected. After all, they claim, the Earth is a living organism that is shifting and evolving, and these things are not new to natural, geological, and thermodynamic patterns. But all at once?

Yet there are those within the spiritual communities who say this has all been prophesized, and it is a signal that we are, indeed, in the end of days. Time stood still.

THE REALIGNMENT

To beg her husband to relent was futile. His rage knew no bounds. Lilith huddled on the searing floor of his pit and waited for the stomping to begin again. Her eyes had been ripped from their sockets and only oozed a warm jelly of torn tissue. Angry flies crowded into the openings on her face. Her nose was crushed, her mouth was a bloodied, gaping hole, her fangs gone. There was only blood-slicked pulp where her beauty once reigned.

She could feel her entrails quivering beneath her torso as she lay prone, breathing in sips, her back filleted by his massive, spaded tail. Snakes wound around the exposed bones, snapping at bits of flesh and pulling at her veins. Her legs were gone, lying in a heap across his chamber. Beetles and maggots had already begun to feed within the ragged, gruesome wounds. A month of enduring his merciless wrath and he was still inconsolable.

"You allowed my son to be baited to his death by a Neteru! *My son?*" he bellowed, causing a thunderous wind to sweep across her exposed vertebrae and ignite them in flames. Vermin that had nested in her hair squeaked at the violation of their feast. "They took Dante's head, Lilith! His head by an Isis, which means that *even I* cannot raise him from the Sea of Perpetual Agony!"

She wailed from the excruciating pain and dissolved into sobs without tears, her will to survive fractured by the ongoing abuse. His litany had been a monthlong refrain with each tail lash. Every time a cloven hoof gashed her skin and peeled it away from bone and muscle she'd beseeched him with all the guile within her, but to no avail. He slashed the smoldering air around them, and her skin began to tear in shreds again, turning her wails into shrieks of agony. The beast would not be appeased this time. In her mind she begged for him to turn her body over to the Harpies, anything but more of his torture.

"The Harpies shall not have you, for you have taken my greatest source of torture pleasure from me—*Dante!*"

She covered her head with a remaining arm and immediately felt it rip from her body; the dull thud of flesh striking the wall simultaneously with the convulsions that jerked her limbless torso.

"Husband, please. I swear to you—"

"That you had been fucking my firstborn son for years was of no consequence to me. I enjoyed watching. That you would try to create another through a stolen half-vampire, half-Neteru embryo, I found delightful, sensually ruthless. . . . I wanted to see what it would become; the experiment was intriguing. I loved how you sent a spiritual attachment to become a parasite within the male Neteru of this era, Lilith. But you failed. He prayed to warrior angels, even with your black smoke seizing his nervous system, which means you are weak! Your attempts to change history were fruitless."

"That's why I did it, my love . . . for you," she whispered, begging on a strangled swallow and choking on her own black blood. "*Anything* for you, *everything* for you, my all. I knew you would cherish the child, since nothing like it had ever been created. It was a gift, a surprise for you, darling. Please let me make it up to you, my dark essence, please. . . . Just *please* stop the torture. I'll do anything; just command it so."

"You were always my most treacherous and favorite, Lilith. How could you betray me with such a loss? Had you not set the strategy in motion, Dante would still exist." His anger seethed forth and, baring his hooked teeth, he bent down to snatch her by her throat and then held her above his head with one talon. He watched her blood drizzle down his massive curved horns to splatter his arm.

"Just give me a chance to right this error in judgment . . ." Her voice broke off into sobs and gave way to wails of utter dismay coated by terror.

He flung her to the ground like a rag, his huge, leathery wings extending to cover her in complete shadow. "But I so enjoyed watching Dante's empire grow in the darkness. . . . So enjoyed torturing his existence with the possibilities of what he could have been, but was not. I loved watching him chase after the Neterus through the centuries, hoping to break his banishment to the sunlight, and wishing that he'd be able to procreate his kind through insemination, rather than the bite. His suffering and longing comforted me, Lilith, in a way that you can never fathom. And, now, he is no more!"

Her husband's horrific roar fused with a screeching wail that bottomed out and shook all that was around them, piercing her eardrums until they bled the gray matter of her brain. Huge rocks and stalagmites detached from the walls and came crashing down with his cloven hoof to snap her spine.

"I will stomp you for this inequity until I make a blackened puddle! Then I will drink your foul essence and spew you into flames that will lick you for eternity." His voice dropped to a frightening whisper. "Lilith, do I not always demand justice . . . that I be given *my due?* What is a son worth, do you know?"

"I'm the only one left who has interacted with the Neteru males to know their weaknesses and vulnerabilities!" she shrieked, forestalling his next blow.

He paused and stared at her for long tense seconds. "Talk to me," he said, his tone deadly.

"I was Adam's first wife."

There was silence, and her mind scrambled to make her case within milliseconds.

"It was I who tricked the newest and most aggressive, Carlos Rivera, to descend to Dante's throne briefly—only I did that. I even made him ignore the warnings of warrior angels! Dear husband, please consider the possibilities as you rightfully rage against me."

A cool wind blew, and her body began to knit itself back together and heal.

"Husband, my love, I was able to act quickly and rationally at a time of great chaos to snatch the embryo from the carnage of the female Neteru's womb . . . the millennium slayer. If you let me survive, I know another way to raise Dante."

"Continue," his disembodied voice said as the Unnamed One disappeared into the shadows, considering her offer. His eyes glowed red then went black within their slits. "Bargain with me, Lilith. You know that's my favorite game. Strike a deal with me."

Hot tears coursed down her face as she tried to speak quickly to him in Dananu. "As long as Dante's firstborn male from his original bloodline exists, all that he was can be summoned forth. It's in the DNA, as always. There is only one other who can sit on Dante's throne to replace all that Carlos Rivera had the potential to be. He is Rivera's exact match, perhaps stronger."

"The one you speak of is in a place that our realms cannot penetrate." Her husband's low, growling voice thundered quietly through the darkness.

"Your month of exacting torture against me has ripped the fabric between the dimensions," she whispered, shivering and holding her arms around herself, bracing against another possible sudden blow. "The subterranean disturbance has—"

"The one you speak of still resides within a realm that we cannot breach," he said evenly. "Do not toy with me, Lilith, for if you fail, I will blot you from all existence . . . slowly . . . with excruciating horror."

She shook her head. "As I have been trying to tell you, dear husband, neither you nor I can breach that realm, but a living Neteru can. I've been around them and know their weaknesses."

Again, her proposal was met by silence.

Panic-stricken and yet filled with hope, she pressed on. "The one we seek has the mark of banishment from the One on High that we never name, but a Neteru can bring him forward through the barrier if the veil between worlds is weakened. You just did that, my beloved. You weakened the veil as you raged beneath the earth. Torturing me was wise, dear husband, and most appreciated, for it created another opportunity that we may have missed."

When her husband didn't answer, Lilith's voice became strident. "I know Rivera's greatest weakness, his insecurities, because he sat on Dante's throne. Let me go to Dante's throne and extract what we need from the residue of energy Rivera left in it. It's still there, and as a female of our kind, I can still taste that essence," she said, speaking quickly and bargaining for her life. "Therefore, knowing *his* shortcomings, I also know the female Neteru's greatest weakness as well, because they are linked at the heart chakra; they are *soul mates*. Fracture the soul mates, and you will have your revenge, which will be no less catastrophic to mankind than what happened to Adam and Eve."

The lack of response made her tone urgent as she continued to speak in a flurry of Dananu. "Husband, your righteous fury thinned the veil between worlds. Time stopped, a rip occurred; therefore I can siphon the past to the forefronts of their minds. I can delve into the darkest crevices of what they have forgotten, what has been forsaken. After that, all we have to do is sit back and watch as their love implodes, taking their team of Neteru Guardians with it. Unprecedented. Think of it. The Covenant will wobble and fall. There will be no earthly protection for humankind. The past will feel like the present, the present like a faraway thing of the past. Let me work unhindered, beloved. You have seen my best efforts, and I have only failed you this once."

Hot tears of anguish coursed down Lilith's face. "I'll make you a new Chairman, one that you have waited for since the dawn of time . . . one who is stronger than Dante ever was and no less tortured. This one won't be infertile, and can call out the others like him from the banishment realm. He will be able to walk in the daylight, and has a soul, like those around him—thus the Guardian teams worldwide will be bereft with confusion. He's *half-human*. Those with him in the banishment realm are, too. Therefore the Guardian teams must individually select those to exterminate and cannot enact a call to arms for the wholesale slaughter of the new Chairman's soldiers."

Her voice rose to a fevered pitch when her husband didn't respond. "Anything less than that will mean that the hundred and forty-four thousand Guardians' souls will be imperiled, if they make war against those entities. Think of it, my husband: compromising the entire earthly army of Guardians at a time like this . . . forcing them to commit murder."

A low, threatening chuckle filled the cavern.

She bowed and then fell to her knees, going prostrate in submission as tears of relief ran down her cheeks. "Let us turn our combined outrage to the more important matter at hand, rather than my continued torture. . . . I know and respect that you have the Armageddon to concern yourself with as a priority to your magnificent master plan. I could assist you in creating chaos among the young Neterus, so that distrust, dishonor, and fury replace their love for one another. . . . And just like the fragile balance between dimensions, permanent fissures among them will allow one of them to call your grandson from his banishment.

"The female Neteru's weakness is one of your most irresistible wiles, and it was encoded in your grandson's natural lineage. All is not lost; his torture may even be greater than Dante's. Through this new vessel, your firstborn can live again—if you allow me to correct the error I've made. It will even cause disarray among the Neteru Councils and the Covenant, which has already been weakened, and thus the angels above them, something we've never been able to achieve. Imagine how strategic that could be so close to the big war."

Silence made her swallow hard and shudder with anticipation, knowing her husband's decision could go either way.

"You were always my favorite, my most shrewd bitch."

She remained cowering on the pit floor as the slow clatter of hooves began a threatening circle around her body. Lilith closed her eyes, but dared not shield her body with her arm again. The situation had surpassed volatile; he could be thoroughly enraged that she'd devised a logical plan and he hadn't—or he could be temporarily mollified. His power charred her skin as he moved around her, thinking, but she didn't even breathe, much less cry out.

"I will install him on a dark throne," she whispered to the bloodied floor, her eyes shut tightly. "I will lead him by the hand to Dante's power vessel."

"If you fail," a low, dangerous voice said quietly, kicking up gale-force winds around her, "I will visit all the wrath upon you that was once Dante's—banishment from daylight, sterility, blood hunger, and you shall take a nonruling seat on Level Six, stripped of your powers here . . . and you will do so as a celibate, blind, ugly old crone, governing only human dark witches, without even the ability to create my most revered race of demons—vampires." He leaned down and spoke to her softly, his hot breath setting her hair aflame. "I will neuter you, seal up your pussy in stone, turn your breasts to marble, and you will know the pleasures of this realm no more. But you will hunger for it the way my dead son incessantly hungered for human blood."

"I will not fail you, will never fail you," she murmured as sensually as she could, standing and filling his embrace as his red, sulfuric plumes covered her. She petted his broad chest, trying to calm the massive beast that clutched her. Failure was out of the question. "I exist only for your pleasure."

"Yes. You do," he murmured, scoring her throat, making her shiver.

"Then seal the new bargain with a bite before you fuck me."

Eve felt it the moment the earth shifted on its axis. The Devil was beating his wife, again, but more severely than ever before. It had rained through pure sunshine, off and on for a month. It was time to take matters into her own hands. She could feel the evil plot crawling beneath her skin like vipers, even though the details would never surface on their own. What was it? She adjusted her golden armored breastplate and stood, legs wide, east of Eden, prepared for battle. This had been coming throughout the ages, and she would not be moved or denied. Aset couldn't talk her out of it, nor could Adam. Dante was dead, which gave the Neteru Councils pause enough to hear her argument. It had been decided. This was between women. That her husband still challenged her about briefly having Dante's scent on her skin made Eve clench her teeth. Lilith had to die. The young female Neteru had not taken that godforsaken bitch's head, so she would.

Rage beyond mortal comprehension filled Eve as the past tortured her mind. She was still linked to Lilith's essence by way of Adam. Men just didn't understand how long a feminine grudge could be held . . . until the end of time. Nor could she ever explain the mixed feelings that she harbored about the fact that Dante was finally gone.

The unknown but pending threat had registered in both Neteru Councils. She was the first to perceive it and was the most affected by it, though none of them quite knew why. The only conclusion both councils could draw was that whatever it was went far back to the beginning, when the first would be last and the last would be first; the act had to be swift and decisive. For centuries Lilith's haunting laughter and evil schemes had plagued her. The solution was decapitation by Isis. The pleasure would be all hers to dust Adam's ex-wife.

Memories riddled Eve as she stood on the edge of existence. Thousands of years of having her name tarnished, her motives questioned, her womanhood and that of all women misconstrued in the sacred texts of mankind . . . her children defiled and murdered, her rightful rule given to Aset . . . oh, yes, this was more her battle than Damali's. The young one, her sister Queen, was no match for this very old evil.

The argument over the viable options had raged in council for a month, until Aset had finally relented because Damali was still under a male Neteru apex haze, and oblivious. Thus the business of seasoned Neteru Queens would have to be handled by one with a long history under her broad sword belt.

Eve narrowed her gaze, tossed her immaculate Kemetian braids over her shoulder, and then opened her hand for the Isis blade to fill it. She closed her grip around the bejeweled handle of the familiar weapon, clutching it like it was a long-lost friend. Yes. This went back to the beginning. Renewed fury spiked adrenaline through Eve's system as she leaned back her head, and a battle cry filled her throat.

"Lilith! Your head on a pike!"

Instantly, Lilith materialized in black armor before her, standing a hundred yards away. The desert went dark, just before dawn. The wind rose and brought stinging particles of sand that felt like scorpions to beat against their faces. A pair of black glowing Bedouin eyes stared into unblinking Kemetian irises that gleamed silver in the eclipse.

"It's been a long time, Eve," Lilith hissed.

"Very long indeed," Eve said coolly, walking forward, too angry for any fear.

A swishing, spaded tail unfurled from Lilith's spine as her legs became granite and her gargoyle features slowly overtook her once voluptuous body and mouth. Eve watched dispassionately as she strode in a slow, methodical advance while Lilith's fangs lengthened.

"You should fear me more than your husband, who just kicked your wretched ass," Eve whispered through her teeth.

"At least mine can get it up," Lilith said, snarling with hatred. "How is poor Adam these days?"

Eve was pure motion. Her lunge came without warning, the Isis chiming in the wind, her slash across Lilith's breasts severe, missing Lilith's throat as Lilith ducked backward to avoid the blade. Black blood splattered Eve's face. Lilith's immediate return blow to Eve's jaw was temporarily stunning; her razor-sharp tail impaled Eve's thigh to the bone. In two lightning moves, the Isis quickly disconnected the combatants as Eve simultaneously severed Lilith's tail and levied a solid left-handed punch in the center of Lilith's chest to drive her backward, leaving Lilith's tail lodged in her thigh like an additional appendage.

Lilith quickly raised her arm to block a blow and to claw Eve's face, but Eve's fast reflexes knocked spit from Lilith's mouth when her fist connected with it, half-turning Lilith around. Before Lilith could respond with a black energy bolt, two swift kidney kicks, and a third delivered to Lilith's abdominal section sent Lilith lurching forward for a second and then made her fall back, lose her footing, and hit the ground. Eve advanced undaunted with broad, rage-filled Isis swings, opening gashes in Lilith's arms as she tried to protect her body.

Unable to match Eve's blows, Lilith instantly retreated from the infuriated Queen, rolling away and then scrambling to her feet. Eve raised the Isis over Lilith's head for a heart plunge, but Lilith's wings unfolded from her shoulders, and she quickly flew backward to put maneuvering distance between them. Silver-red blood ran from Eve's clenched fist where it had been torn open by a fang when she'd punched Lilith. The old warriors faced each other, breathing hard, positioning for the next attack, death strategies blazing in their eyes.

"You've only lived this long during this encounter because I'd been weakened by Armageddon negotiations with my husband, but know that I will prevail!" Lilith backed up farther, panting with fatigue and from significant injuries, eyes now black fire.

Eve screamed, running forward, anger making her entire body shake. "I will take your head *before* the Armageddon! Know that!"

Lilith disappeared, her voice a taunt. "I will not fail, again. That is what *you* must know, dear Eve. I now know your greatest weakness, now that I've spilled your blood and tasted your heartbreak curdled within it. Just like before, *this,* you cannot win!"

Whirling around in a frustrated circle, Eve shouted her complaint into the temporary darkness, brandishing the Isis. "Fight me! We do this to the death, you cowardly whore! I have wanted your carcass for centuries and will have it!"

Silence answered her. The dawn had crested. Tears of unspent rage glittered in the sunlight within Eve's eyes as she drove the Isis into the sand and walked away. "Damn you! This isn't over!"

An eerie laugh echoed behind Eve like a whisper on the wind. "No, you arrogant Neteru bitch, it's not."

ᴆ CHAPTER ONE

Gabrielle watched Rider sleep beside her in the late afternoon sun, her hand gently stroking his bare chest. Filaments of light added flecks of gold and red to his blond hair and coated his damp skin in warm hues. Jack Rider was a good man . . . a human like she was, who hadn't judged her, hadn't lied to her, but who had become her friend and lover over time, even though he couldn't bring himself to commit to loving her fully.

But he'd also been honest about that. They both knew the reason why. Tara. Oddly, she owed Tara for sparing her, when it would have been so easy for that female vampire to take her blood to survive the Level-Seven Hell onslaught visited upon Master Yonnie, Tara's new mate. Yet Tara had shown honor, and had bled out only her demon brothels to heal him. Gabrielle let out a quiet sigh. The complexity of it all was profound.

Life as she once knew it was peeling away from her; New Orleans was gone, the French Quarter and her establishments were now shambles and mud hovels. Hundreds of people had died, graves were overturned, and the spirits were restless.

It was time. Her bargain with the dark side would be a debt called in soon. Gabrielle brushed a stray lock of mussed hair away from Rider's forehead and kissed him there softly so not to wake him. He looked so peaceful when his haunted eyes were closed and his breaths came deep and slow. But she also enjoyed his ribald humor; a slight smile tugged at her mouth. Yes, she loved Jack Rider.

Ever so gently, she nestled her head in the crook of his shoulder and felt him stir to protectively pull her in beside him, and wondered what her life might have been like had she met him before she made a dark bargain. As she listened to him breathe and his heart quietly thud within his chest, she knew the answer. There would have been no coven brothels, no death, Hell, and destruction in her life. She would have stayed within the safety of this semi-jaded Guardian's arms and never let him go.

Tears of remorse wet her lashes, but she refused to cry. The forces of darkness were realigning; she'd felt it in her bones. The dark covens had surged up, briefly siphoning power from all, and then it went still in the underworld. An event had been set in motion. Something had happened, and now the aftermath would have to play itself out. It was a strange knowing, like something was gloating and watching an evil strategy take form, and it could now just confidently sit back and watch the pawns move on an unseen chessboard, but she couldn't put her finger on the source.

For a moment she'd thought this was the final hour, that she'd been called to deliver what she'd promised so long ago to the Dark Lord, but then an eerie stillness had claimed her. Temporary reprieve had been granted, a more powerful female had taken the brunt of the unseen fury. However, one day or night her turn would come due, and she wanted Jack Rider and the Guardians nowhere near that awful conclusion. She also had to protect her two young coven initiates . . . they, like her, had come into this life out of desperation, not knowing how long a dark eternity could be.

Gabrielle leaned up and brushed Rider's lips with a soft kiss to wake him, watching his eyes slowly open. "You should go home," she said quietly.

He smiled and cupped her face with his palm and glimpsed the bright sunlight. "Don't tell me I'm losing my touch, darlin'. You putting me out already?"

She forced a smile and allowed her finger to trail along the edge of Rider's jaw. "Never," she whispered. "I just have a funny feeling they're gonna need you there."

For a moment he didn't move, his smile fading into a sober expression. "Gabby, what's wrong?"

She sat up slowly in bed; he followed suit, staring at her. The hotel room felt like it was closing in on her.

"I don't know," she said quietly, "I just want you safe. Even in the daytime."

"Now you're making me nervous."

Too many thoughts crowded into her mind at once, and it took her a moment to sort them out before she could reply. Dark power was realigning, and he didn't need to be anywhere near a lightning rod—her. If the surge she'd felt was accurate, then he also needed to go back to the new Guardian compound to help protect her sister and niece and nephew. The senior members of the team couldn't be distracted during this fragile space and time.

Gabrielle gazed at Rider for a moment without speaking. Krissy, her young niece, had the potential, like her mother, Marjorie, to be a significant white lighter. Her sister, Marj, was going to need all the guidance possible to take over her role, once Hell demanded full payment. Bobby, her nephew, stood on the precipice between becoming either a wizard or warlock. Their decisions needed to be clear—go toward the Light. Bobby needed to lean wizard, Krissy and Marj toward Druid whitelighter Celtic ancestry that ran through their collective bloodlines. None of them needed to do what she'd done.

Gabrielle's eyes searched Rider's. Her family being with a Neteru Guardian team was the only thing that allowed her to sleep at night; her family had a choice that would be heavily weighted by the powerful influence of the Light. They didn't have to go out like she had, making dark and irreversible decision of black magic.

"I love you, Jack Rider." It was the first of many thoughts that leapt to the front of her mind.

He lowered his forehead to hers and stroked her hair, but didn't answer.

"No commitments, remember?" she whispered, her fingers trembling as they grazed his jaw. "I'm a big girl, and I understand."

"It's not like that," he said quietly. "It's just . . ."

"I know I'm not Tara."

He let his breath out hard in a sad sigh. "You don't have to wear lavender for me."

"I know," she murmured. "You tell me that every time. But I do it because I know you need that, even if you'd never expect it and would touch me without it. Just knowing the sacrifice you'd make to lie with me without that scent, is enough. . . . You respect me by not requiring it. That's also enough."

"It's not a sacrifice to touch you, Gabrielle. You're a beautiful woman in your own right. Gorgeous auburn hair," he said quietly, allowing his fingers to become tangled in her long, silky tresses. "Pretty face, smoky, green eyes, wonderful mouth . . . fantastic body that can stop traffic on Sunset Boulevard. Go shower and get the lavender off you and I'll call housekeeping to get the sheets changed, and then I'll show you it doesn't have *anything* to do with the lavender you wear. Afterward, you tell me if you still think it's a sacrifice for me to be with you." He shook his head in disbelief. "Is that why you want me to leave? Because if I did that to you, made you feel like that, then I'm sorry."

His hazel eyes held such gentle sadness that she almost turned away from him.

"No," she said, and swallowed unshed tears. "You didn't make me feel that . . . you never do. But you do have a way of making a woman feel cherished for a few hours in a way that I never knew was possible. I'm getting too attached to you, because of that." She forced a smile. "That's why you have to go."

"You're real easy to grow attached to, yourself, kiddo." He offered her a half-smile and took her mouth slowly.

She shivered as his rough palm slid down her shoulder and cupped her breast, feeling a renewed heat begin to warm her. But she had to remember more important things. "I'm glad you only brought Bobby to the New Orleans house once. Don't bring him to the one in Los Angeles. Promise me. He's in training and doesn't need to indulge and get his head all screwed up. As it is, my initiate, Jasmine, hasn't been able to concentrate on anything but him since he deflowered her." Gabrielle forced a chuckle. "You Guardians have a way of making a girl crazy, did you know that?"

Rider chuckled and sighed, allowing his hand to glide over the swell of her naked hip. "I don't know if that was a good thing or a bad thing, giving Bobby a onetime taste of female affection. Now that he's no longer a virgin, the poor kid is really bouncing off the walls. But, Dan, God bless him, is gonna have an aneurysm if I don't bring him to see one of your girls again soon." So much was changing, just like his beloved New Orleans. He just prayed Gabrielle would be a constant for a little longer.

She shook her head, her eyes holding a warning. "Don't. He's young, doesn't need to be corrupted, and my establishments are too dangerous—and I can't afford to lose another initiate right now." She tried to soften her warning with a smile. "If I let him have Heather, then where would this witch be? No virgin initiates to appease the beast. I don't want Dan or any of you guys fooling around with anything in my establishment that might bear fangs . . . or a human female that's got a negative aura, especially not your young guys. Not now."

Rider looked at her and stopped the lazy caress up and down her hip. "Okay . . . but he's also male, young, and a Guardian, and the Light doesn't exactly move at the speed of light. That kid could be left hanging for a very long time, Gabby. I won't let anything happen to him."

"I know," she said, gathering the sheet around herself and standing. Rider watched her cross the room.

"Okay, at the risk of divulging sensitive client information, er, uh, did one of my guys upset one of your ladies or something? Bobby being banned from your houses I can understand. Can't have your nephew thinking a certain way about his aunt—some things are just not done, and I'm glad he still hasn't put it together that where I took him that one time was under your management. But Dan . . . jeez. For crying out loud, he'll be a basket case if several years go by before he gets laid again."

Rider pushed back with his spine pressed to the headboard and a wry smile tugging on his face. "Give the kid a break, Gabby. I had to get Dan out of the house when your niece turned eighteen a few weeks back. After the little fracas the brothers had in Arizona over her, Dan's frame of mind was damned near suicidal when J.L. gave her his little jade Buddha amulet and her dad finally let the two of them *supposedly* go have a private lunch after we cut the cake."

"But—"

"You shoulda seen it," Rider said, grinning wide and cutting her off. "The girl clutched the amulet to her chest like J.L. had given her a diamond ring, and then the two of 'em went all googly-eyed to the point where her own father gave up the battle. So, if Dan came into your L.A. joint on his own and momentarily lost his mind—"

"No, no, no, it wasn't like that," she said, smiling despite the circumstances. "He didn't offend, even though from what I hear, he definitely lost his mind for a few hours."

Rider closed his eyes laughing and slapped his forehead. "My nose is never wrong. Jose and Carlos told me the same thing—the three of us got bloodhound in us, hon. That kid was so torn up by your niece, he still has to do his own laundry. Don't banish him right now," Rider pleaded with a mischievous grin as he opened his eyes. "He's a tactical, and suffering . . . your niece is flitting around the house wide-open, new sexual experience flushed on her pretty face, looking like the blond cheerleader of Dan's wet dreams *and* getting laid by a Kung Fu master, who just so happens to room down the hall from him. Gabrielle, you just don't know the house dynamics we have to cope with!"

She shook her head and fought a smile. "But I just feel that it's too dangerous. He's still impressionable, like Bobby. I allowed him to visit once after New Orleans, and then I told him that was it." She threw up her hands when Rider laughed harder. "The girls in L.A. are . . . oh, I don't know."

" 'Spectacular' comes to mind," he said with a droll wink. "That's why I took the puppy out and let him get a good hard run on. At his age, realistically, he could go three times a day, seven days a week. It was only once after New Orleans. But you know what they say, Gabby, once is never enough."

"That's the last time, Rider," she warned, still smiling and folding her arms over her breasts. "I'm glad you left him at the house today. And I don't know what you're gonna do about Bobby."

"Don't tell me, you want him to find a nice wholesome girl and settle down?" Rider slapped his forehead. "Jesus, you sound like Marj."

Gabrielle laughed. "Yes, I do, Jack Rider. I want that for both Dan and Bobby."

"All right, all right, all right." Rider stood with a grunt and crossed the room to pin her against the dresser with his body. "But for those of us already corrupted and no longer impressionable, please don't put us on newbie rations," he said, delivering a burning kiss to her neck. "Been there. Did my time. We Guardian brothers don't get out much. Just tell me we're not banned and cut off from the most basic pleasures in life?"

"Because I love you, after today, you are," she said, stroking his shoulders.

He pulled back from her to look at her. "You're serious, aren't you?"

She nodded as sudden tears filled her eyes. "I love you, Rider. I'm not supposed to fall in love with a client, much less a Guardian."

"So, now I'm just a client, huh?" There was no anger in his tone as his thumbs caught the tears that spilled down her cheeks. "I thought we were friends with a very definite understanding."

"No, you've become more than that, that's the problem," she whispered. "You were never a client, and are my friend. You just became something beyond that, is all."

He nodded and kissed her softly. "I know . . . same here. When did that happen?"

They both laughed sadly.

"That first time," she said in a far-off voice.

"Yep," he murmured against her forehead. "It's always the first time that gets you, isn't it?"

"Go home, Rider. Keep the family safe. Keep yourself safe by staying away from me until things settle down."

"The Chairman is dead, hon, last I checked. So is his replacement. Rivera took his head off with Damali's Isis. Lilith bought it on the side of a mountain in Tibet—saw it with my own eyes. Cold-seeking missiles got her and started an avalanche that I'm lucky to be here to tell you about. Our two Neterus are in union bliss, probably off somewhere as we speak knocking boots. So, what's to settle down?"

"I don't know . . . call it female intuition. Just go with me on it for now. Maybe it's nothing, but if it is, I'd rest easier knowing you and especially the younger males on your team aren't anywhere near a place that has . . . different energy. All right?" She stared up at his handsome face and set her mouth hard, resolute.

He gathered her in his arms and released a long, soulful breath. "And how am I supposed to rest easy knowing that someone very important to me is out there all by herself, dealing with the unknown? Like you said, we're friends."

She held this man who'd recently stopped drinking and smoking . . . this man who'd begun to heal in her care. His tall, muscular frame made her feel safe against everything deadly in the world. The last thing she'd do is put him at risk, yet she wondered how she'd ever get him out of her system when the time came that she'd have to.

"If it will make you feel any better," she finally said, trying to make him laugh, "I'll be on rations, too."

He smiled; she could feel his face move into the expression against the crown of her head.

"Oh, that makes me feel just peachy knowing you're somewhere as horny as me, but that I can't get to you to cure what ails ya. I'll develop a nervous tic knowing something like that."

"Call me. I do great phone sex."

They both laughed.

"Yeah, right, with seers in the house? Be serious. It's bad enough that the tacticals bristle and take a walk when the young bucks have to get the monkey off their backs solo. Now you wanna add me into their TMI schematic?"

She laughed harder and covered her mouth. "Go home, Rider!"

"I'm being serious," he said, nipping her neck and making her shudder. He pushed her hand down his abdomen. "Feel this wood, woman, and tell me you are *not* sending me home like that."

She let her hand lazily stroke him, glad that he was smiling and that merriment had crept back into his eyes. "All right. One more go 'round, and I'll send you home tired. But then you get your incorrigible self home before dark, and you stay there until my jitters pass. Is that fair?"

His eyes slid shut as he moved against her slow caress. "Oh, yeah, darlin'. That's more than fair. Just lemme return the favor in spades before I leave."

"Then definitely come back to bed, Jack Rider, so we can wear each other out."

Beverly Hills, California

Dan sat quietly on the edge of his bed in the newly retrofitted mansion, staring out the window. Seal's CD had been set on repeat, cut six, *Kiss from a Rose,* a mantra by now, something filled with hope to enter his tactical field and drown out the vibrations emanating from J.L.'s room every time Krissy was there . . . now that she was in bloom.

Yeah, it was true, just like Seal sang it—she could be compared to a kiss from a rose on a grave, and there was indeed so much a man could tell her, so much he could say. She remained his power, his pleasure, his pain. He was dying, the new mansion was his tomb, but he had to let all that go.

Celtic and Gaelic chords took him so far back into his mind that for a while he was no longer in the room. Stonehenge appeared in the mist as the strands from the song entered his daydream. . . . He was a knight, his white charger rearing, refusing to enter the circle of standing stones. She was there wearing a crimson cloak, her hood spilling forward to hide her face.... Then she reached for him. A sense of desperation swept through him as he tried to dismount the frightened horse, and as always, she began to fade into the mist just as he'd accomplished the task. All he could see was a wash of her blond hair transforming into a thicket of auburn ringlets and a flash of blue eyes becoming gray as she turned to leave him. Pain.

A silent prayer constricted his chest. Don't go. I love you. No words escaped his mouth before she vanished. The loss made Dan slowly hug himself and begin to rock slightly in agony where he sat. It was always the same sensation when J.L. loved Krissy hard. Dan dragged in a shuddering breath and closed his eyes. "Just get it over with soon," he whispered into the empty room. "Just finish, for God's sake."

He missed the old compound, the former team life when they were touring, the music was happening, and demon-hunting was a sideline venture. All the working out in the world didn't change what was, couldn't banish the dim reality from his mind as the sun began to set. He was alone.

"Not for long," a strange female voice whispered.

Dan was on his feet in seconds, had crossed the room, grabbed his nine-millimeter and a vial of holy water off the dresser, and spun to meet the threat. The moment the phantom materialized, he dashed it with the anointed water and held his gun steady with both hands. But it didn't smolder, didn't combust. The faceless female form remained placid, the water glistening silver to make her aura brighter.

"Two seconds and you're history," he said, panting from the adrenaline roiling through him.

"I'm already history and mean you no harm," she said in a gentle voice. "Daniel, please put down the gun and don't alarm the house."

"Show yourself."

"Promise not to fire. I came out in the Light, during the day before sunset. I am not a demon."

"Show yourself," he repeated, his finger trembling over the trigger in readiness to squeeze off rounds.

"If you fire, the bullets will go through the wall and could hurt one of your brethren. Disarm and I will comply."

He didn't lower the weapon, but extended his trigger finger as a compromise. Slowly a deep toffee hue filled in the glowing places where the entity's white robe revealed skin. Thick, long dark hair washed over her shoulders. Her face became recognizable, and he backed up farther, stunned, knocking over colognes and deodorant on his dresser.

"Raven . . ." he whispered.

She shook her head. "Christine. Raven is dead, and I am who I had been before I was ever turned."

"Oh, shit! Marlene—"

"It will hurt her to see me. Don't." A sad expression filled the entity's beautiful eyes. "Please."

Dan slowly lowered the weapon, but didn't abandon it.

"I cannot go to my mother without stirring up her old pain. I cannot go to Damali now, even though I owe her for the gift of release into the Light. She is in a very bad place within her mind. . . . And I cannot go to Carlos for a number of reasons. I do not know that he will ever forgive what I did to his brother and cousin or his human friends from his old life . . . or forget that I was his first sexual conquest when he first turned vampire. Too much pain." Her voice drifted around the room in a soft echo that seemed to be everywhere at once. "Sense me, Daniel. You're a tactical Guardian. Do I feel like a threat?"

Dan now held the weapon at his side. What she'd said was logical, and he felt no pending attack. Still, this was Raven. "Why me? I'm no seer. If you've got a message from the other side, then one of the older seniors—"

She placed her finger to his lips to still his argument. "I chased you when I was that which shall not be named. If I hadn't, who knows? Maybe then you might never have been inducted into the Guardian life. I owe you, and I'm trying to earn my wings, trying to clean up the life disasters my poor choices created. So, I came to you."

Dan could feel adrenaline-induced perspiration making his T-shirt cling to him. "Yeah, well, I guess it was fate. I'm here, woulda been brought in one way or another."

Her tone was so sad and her gaze so gentle that a sudden calmness filled him. The gun dangled in his loose grip by his side.

"Dan, tell me, is the Guardian life so bad?"

He looked away from her out the window, unable to immediately respond. "What's not to love? My parents think I'm in Israel on a kibbutz," he said, laughing sadly. "Rabbi Zeitloff handles the correspondence between us, and has people check on them to bring me word, sends them pictures. . . . It's all a bizarre ruse, but for their own good. They're happy, with parental bragging rights." He glanced away from the window and nervously ran his fingers through his hair. "So, how about you? How's the Light treating you?" Then he stopped and stared at her hard. "Seriously, all jokes aside, what's it like where you are?"

"Free," she whispered. "There is no way to describe the peace."

He nodded. "That's very cool and real good to know—especially since on any given day or night, any of us on this team might find ourselves over there with you. Glad you got somewhere safe. I know Mar rests better knowing that you did."

Dan's eyes held Christine's, compassion wafting through her body and covering his skin from where she drifted across the room.

"She's real good people, Rav—I mean, Christine. Is like a Mom to me, too. Really, she's like that for all of us, except maybe Shabazz. . . . You know what I'm saying, since she sleeps with him, how can she be his mom? But, I'm . . . oh, shit, I've never talked to an angel before, so I don't know what I'm supposed to say or not."

Christine nodded and her expression remained serene. Then she smiled. "I'm not an angel, just a very lucky spirit that wound up on the first ring of Light. I have so much to learn, so many things to correct, and who knows how many incarnations to go through before I get it right. But thanks for the compliment."

"Oh, well . . . that's cool, too, I guess. Reincarnation is like a do-over," Dan said, slowly setting his gun on the dresser. "Beats me why you'd wanna come back down here to check on any of us, after you got a get-out-of-jail-free card, though."

"It's because I did get one of those," she murmured, her large, luminous brown eyes pouring empathy into his. "I felt your pain, followed you here. Something happened and allowed me to come onto this side of the veil. Lopez almost followed me, but they've pulled him so high up, I don't think he can slip out without them knowing. He has a message for Carlos and Jose, but it's not time yet to deliver it. Padre has work to do, some other mission, but sends his love. You have to let Carlos know there's no hard feelings, just love here."

"Whoa . . . you saw Lopez?"

She nodded and looked away. "He's in our old line from that old existence. . . . They let you remember all so that you gain wisdom, but it doesn't hurt once you've faced it and admitted it. I'm in an atonement phase, I guess. That's why I'm here to help."

Dan shrugged and jammed his weapon-free hand into his sweatpants pocket. "Well, we did pretty good on our own in Tibet, unless you guys from the unseen side of things were in the equation, which I don't doubt."

"We were."

"Thanks," he said, smiling. He carefully put the safety on his gun before sliding it further away on his dresser. "Glad you're on our side . . . but we're cool now."

She tilted her head and glanced away. "I used to be a master vamp's lair mate . . . and, uhmmm . . . for a while, I bottomed out in the succubae realms. So can we speak freely?"

Sudden heat flushed Dan's face and he walked away from the smiling entity that glowed to brace his hands on the window frame.

"Tell me you guys don't see *everything*."

"We don't spy on personal things, no. That's unnecessary. We can feel things . . . sense the vibrations. Although we don't sashay into dreams uninvited, if that's what you're worried about. We only come when we're called, or if the person is really in trouble or upset and has a prayer for guidance in their hearts. You had one of those just now, so I came."

He let out an audible breath; her tone still nagged him. There was too much amusement in it.

"You're not trapped down here, or anything?"

"No," she said, giggling softly, "and I'll go away, if I'm upsetting you."

"It's not that I don't appreciate your looking out for me, but . . . just some things are really personal, and I'm working through it on my own, and it'll really wig me out if you just blow through my room when I don't know you're there." He glanced over his shoulder and saw her swallow away a broad smile. That was the *last* thing he needed anybody to see, those times when it was so bad he had to relieve himself just to get through another day.

"I won't do that to you. I promise. I just followed your pain trail and heard the prayer and thought you might want to talk to someone who knows how you feel."

Her voice had become gentle as she glided closer to him. She was truly beautiful and not the least bit threatening. But the things that had been on his mind weren't the sort of topic one discussed with a heavenly body.

"The truth is the Light, you know," she said with a wide grin. "I can take some of that pain away. Just take the edge off."

He backed up, rendered near speechless. "How?"

She laughed, sending the sound of tinkling bells around the room. "Not like *that*," she said, and then covered her mouth with her hand. "Oh, Daniel, it's really bad, isn't it?"

"I don't wanna discuss it, and I think you should leave before you get stuck here or something."

"I'm sorry. I didn't mean to laugh."

She came closer and touched his face. This time he didn't draw away from her. A quiet peace filled him, and the need to hug her to feel more of her calming sensation made him jam both his hands into his pockets. To his surprise, she opened her arms and embraced him. He'd expected the touch to be ghostly cold and to pass right through him. Instead serene warmth radiated against his skin like a humid summer breeze.

"Don't covet what J.L. has. . . . They're making one especially for you—and right now, we need you to be one of the voices of reason. I don't know exactly what's going on, since I'm new. But I know something is about to happen, and it's *big*. Just be careful, Dan, and don't worry about having a mate. One is on the way." Christine smiled. "Would you like to see her?"

He gazed into Christine's beautiful brown eyes, seeing through her translucent irises into what seemed like infinity. He'd heard the part about something major going down, but at the moment, his focus was on the last part of what she'd said. Then he saw her, just like in his daydream. Gorgeous gray eyes and a lush spill of auburn curls. That was all he could make out in the mist blanketing standing stones.

"Wow . . . you mean you know that they're sending another female Guardian?" His voice had come out on a choked murmur of anticipation.

"I heard them whispering that two more will be coming. The team needs that for balance. Daniel, I know you're lonely, and I know what that feels like. Just trust and know you've been heard. Yours will be exactly the right fit for you. I overheard that she's really sweet and really pretty. . . . You'll know her by her eyes . . . gray, I think?"

"Is that what you came to tell me?" he asked quietly, still gazing into the depths of Christine's limitless eyes. "It's hard to believe that they'd send a special envoy just to tell me, a new senior Guardian, anything so personal."

"They don't even know I'm here," she whispered. "I came, like I said, because I owe you, and I caught the prayer first. I've heard murmurs, plans, but I don't know the details. But if it's coming from above, it's all good. I sorta slipped out while there was a bit of chaos, but have to go back soon. Everybody was all up in arms about something, and I figured now was as good a time as any to let you know I'm available."

He paused and didn't immediately respond. It was the emphasis that she'd placed on the word *available.*

"You have to stay out of Gabrielle's establishments, though. There's dark energy passing through her houses, not that it's my business. Just a warning."

Total embarrassment made him look away with a scowl. "So, are you now like my Guardian angel? I thought you didn't spy on the living."

She smiled shyly and glanced away. "I just saw you go in, that's all. What happened inside, I can only imagine, but I didn't peek. But common sense is common sense, Dan. . . . If you need a friend until they send you a soul mate, then . . ."

He let out a sigh of frustration. "I can't have an angel for a *friend,* Christine. Not that type of friend, anyway. That much is common sense, too."

"I told you, I'm *not* an angel," she argued in an upbeat tone. "But I do care . . . and you're sorta cute." Christine's smiled widened. "No, let me be honest. Actually, you're *really* cute. Handsome. That's why I chased you into the garage before."

"You were gonna bite me, then." His smile widened to match hers. It all seemed like so long ago, and strangely the memory didn't dredge up fear like it once did.

"I know. Yeah, yeah, yeah, I was gonna bite you—so sue me. But that wasn't *all.* Some of it you might have enjoyed." She blushed and glanced away again, glimpsing him from the corner of her eye with a sly smile. "I said I was sorry."

He chuckled, very flattered, and that made her giggle, sending the bell sensation through his limbs again.

"You're blushing," she whispered.

"Yeah, well, so are you."

"Oh." She tucked away her grin, but it kept escaping.

"Are you flirting with me?"

She giggled again. He loved the sound of her voice and how it sent tingles through him.

"I can visit in dreams if you call me by name," she said, avoiding his question and glancing over her shoulder nervously. "I knew how to do that really well from . . . before. But you have to say it like a prayer now is the only real difference—really want me with all your heart to visit." He just stared at her. The proposition was outrageous. "I don't think a heavenly entity is supposed to trip over the edge of my dreams," he said, feeling his face get warm as he laughed. "Especially not the ones I've had lately."

She shrugged, but still couldn't seem to contain her smile. "Can I tell you a secret?"

"Yeah."

"Promise not to tell?"

"Like anyone would believe me. If I told my brothers, they'd say I was hallucinating. Maybe I am. But, yeah."

She leaned in close to whisper in his ear, sending a warm, sensual breath into it. "It's soooo boring. I'm not complaining. Believe me, I'm glad that the pain and horror are gone, but I liked being alive, when I could *feel* things."

"Whoa," he whispered. "You shouldn't even think that, let alone whisper it. Words have power," he added, glancing around. "You could get in trouble, couldn't you?"

She nodded quickly. "I think so," she whispered, "but I don't know. I'm not sure what all the rules are yet, and I don't wanna get put out."

"Well, then, you definitely don't wanna step into my dreams," he whispered, leaning into her and making her giggle again. A light rose scent filled his nose, and he had to pull back to remember that he was talking to a ghost. "You're really pretty, and anything could happen in my mind. Not to be disrespectful. But it's been a very long time since, you know."

"If you think about me instead of Krissy, it might make it easier to be around her and easier to not be so mad at J.L., that's all I'm suggesting. I'd be bringing, uhmmm, *team harmony*. That's good, right? We could just talk, if you feel uncomfortable about . . . thinking beyond that. It could really, really cheer you up."

They stared at each other for a moment.

"How about if I call you when I need somebody to *talk* to? I really like talking to you, Christine. You make me laugh and are already beginning to make me feel like I've got somebody of my own to hang out with."

"You do. I'll be your spirit friend. Besides, anything important that I hear from the other side, I'll bring it to you—and you can tell the others, if you need to," she whispered, cupping his cheek. "If something bad is about to happen, Dan, I promise, I'll come to you first, like I did now, if I can. Okay?"

Impulse drove him, and he quickly kissed her cheek. "Okay."

She covered the place where his kiss landed with her palm, and then just as abruptly, kissed the bridge of his nose. "Okay."

"Your aura is becoming lighter," she murmured sadly. "You don't seem as down anymore. So I did what I was supposed to do, which was cheer you up, and since you're not in danger . . . I suppose I have to leave. If they find out I visited you, at least I can say I did a good thing, brought a little joy to your spirit and made it brighter again. You have such a wonderful light inside, Daniel."

"Wait. Hang on," he said, trying to hold her ethereal body in the loose hug they'd been in, but she'd begun to dissolve. "If I'm really down in the dumps or in peril, you're allowed to come—but if I'm happy and safe, you have to stay away and not interfere with the living?"

She nodded and pouted, moving out of his embrace. "Unless you reach out in a dream . . . and I so want to be on this Guardian squad with you. On the astral plane is where your spirit and mine can dance and play. There'd be no distortion because you were in the flesh and I'm not. It's different there."

"But what if something, you know, risqué happens in the dream?"

Her bright smile caught the waning sun. "What if it does? Wouldn't be my fault. You called me. Prayed for the physical agony to stop. Plus, I'd just be cheering you up in your fantasy."

He could see furniture that was across the room through her body now, and knew she was quickly leaving. Oddly, he didn't want her to go. Moreover, he was trying to adjust to the fact he'd just been thoroughly turned on by a very sexy ghost. If she kept this up, he'd sleep all day and all night, trying to hold on to her in his dreams.

"I don't know how to astral travel like a seer. . . . I'm a tactical Guardian. Before you go, you've gotta tell me how to call you, if I have to, uh, see ya again. It's been really bad, Christine, I'm not gonna lie."

"Just dream me, and I'll do the rest. Put on the music to raise your vibrations to the love level, say a prayer for the pain to stop, call my name, and I'll be there." Her gaze held his for a moment. "The more information I get about the new Guardian who's coming, the more I can . . . sort of take on her shape for you when I visit, if you want."

Dan slowly shook his head and stared at her, imprinting her into his soul. "If you come to me like that, Christine, come as yourself. You're beautiful. Your spirit . . . your eyes, your face, your gorgeous, ethereal body, and your vibration is more than enough for me." His voice became a deep murmur of awed appreciation. "And if you're my secret friend, then . . . I'd wanna know you, not someone who's not here for me yet. I don't know her. I know you. I'll remember your energy tracer, always. Thank you for being there for me."

Christine covered her mouth with her translucent hand and briefly closed her eyes as tears brimmed in them. She let her shimmering palm fall away as she backed up farther, dissolving as she glided. "That's the kindest thing any man has ever said to me, dead or alive," she whispered. "The next time you go to sleep, call me, Daniel. I will most assuredly cheer you up."

"Would *you* feel it, though?" he asked, his tone urgent as she became harder to see. "Would you feel *whatever* my mind came up with? And, would? I mean, like you and I just felt that kiss?"

She waved and disappeared, leaving him her soft giggle to feel with her whispered answer. "Yes. Better. Just like it was real."

Yonnie opened his eyes the moment the sun went down. Tara's body instantly covered his.

"Good evening," he said with a slow smile, somewhat confused by her passionate outburst. This was not the reserved Tara he knew, their new connection notwithstanding.

Her response was a hard, punishing kiss, and then she pulled away, breathless, her eyes wild and glowing red. "I have to feed."

"No problem," he said, growing concerned as he offered her his throat. "Take what you need, baby."

She scored his throat with such wanton pleasure that it made him arch. This was no mere feeding, and that Tara had initiated it was blowing his mind.

"Oh . . . shit . . ." he groaned, presenting fangs. "Had I known you were feeling like this all day, I would have stayed awake in lair and rocked your world."

"I need a body," she murmured hotly against his bleeding jugular. "Human."

"Whoa, hold up, sis." Yonnie sat up and held her away from him by her upper arms. He stared into her eyes, reading thoughts, gaining impressions, even though her ardor had made him pant. "I thought you said we weren't supposed to go there—no human deaths so we had a chance at Light conversion—"

Her fervent kiss stopped his words, and she pushed him against the jumble of red silk sheets then covered him in a hot swath of skin against skin.

"Yonnie, I need human blood," she whispered against his throat in a hiss. "I'm losing my mind . . . I need that now—can't you feel it? The power surge from below."

Tara's caresses against him were aggressive and soon she'd lit every pulse point he owned with fevered want. He could barely keep his eyes open as she mounted him and writhed against him. The moment he'd entered her, he'd felt it. Something stronger than he'd ever known tore through him and made him flip her onto her back. His arms trembled as he stared down into her eyes, and then they both watched a black arc of energy crackle through his aura. Yonnie threw his head back and groaned.

"You want a body? I'll bring you fresh kill in a minute."

Tara wrapped her legs tightly around his waist and reached up to hold his hair in her fist. "Take me to V-Point and then feed me," she said between her teeth, digging the crown of her head into the profusion of pillows.

The feel of her was exquisite, her passion genuine, and it was something that he'd longed for and had been denied. The deep moan that traveled up from her insides created near madness. Only a flicker of sanity made him ask himself why as he moved against her in hard thrusts.

"If I take a body for you then there's no going back," he said between agonized breaths. "Is that what you want?"

Her nails dug into his shoulders as she began to convulse with pleasure beneath him, nodding. Tears streamed down her cheeks, her eyes were shut tight. He dropped down to his elbows and held the sides of her skull, his fingers splayed in her hair, needing to know. Had it been any other vamp female, he would have gladly obliged, but after all they'd been through and knowing Tara as he did, something had to be wrong.

"Baby, talk to me," he said, kissing her face, her mouth, and her throat in a fast spill. Her wails of ecstasy were slicing at his libido, and even he wasn't sure how he was able to hold on without fracturing into cellular bliss.

"You're a councilman—just do it!" she shrieked.

Yonnie stopped moving for a moment and stared down at her. "What did you say?" he whispered very carefully.

Tara came out of the pleasure haze with him still lodged deep within her. "I don't know . . ." she sobbed, her voice catching in her throat. "Why are you torturing me?"

He grabbed her jaw roughly between his fingers and turned her head to expose her throat. "No humans, ever," he whispered, feeling a new level of control simmering inside him. Something had definitely gone down.

"But why?" she moaned, arching her back to take more of him in.

"My Chairman's edict . . . unless I hear it directly from Rivera that he's changed his mind."

"He's no longer a vampire, Yonnie. He's no longer one of us." Her eyes were wild and desperate as they searched his for answers.

"He'll always be the one who elevated me—that's enough, no matter what he is now. My brother never lied to me . . . whatever's messin' with your mind I don't trust." He kissed her forehead, sensing a powerful darkness there that had been strong enough to compromise Tara's iron will. If it got to her, then whatever it was had to be serious.

"Then just do me," she said breathlessly, not sounding herself. "Forget the human."

Yonnie lowered his mouth to Tara's throat, siphoning a gasp from her as his fangs raked the fevered skin of her neck. "I won't go against our brother, or fuck up a chance to get out of Hell. But, V-Point, baby . . . any night of the week."

Lilith sat down very slowly on Dante's old battered throne, feeling it come alive at the armrests under her caress. As the red velvet fabric knitted itself together beneath her she closed her eyes, leaned her head back, and released a slow, burning breath of satisfaction. She would miss Dante sorely, no matter how insidious her treachery had been. He was special.

But that was then and this was now. She watched without emotion as the Vampire Council Chamber on Level Six began to reorganize itself and the abandoned, pentagram-shaped table slowly gurgled to life with black blood now pulsing in the veins of the marble. So much waste, so much strain on the empire . . . she well understood her husband's rage. She would not incur his wrath again with failure.

Concentrating on Carlos Rivera's essence, Lilith waited. The dark side of him that had been born from her machinations put tears of pride in her eyes—the entity had been so foul. Then the good one had killed it . . . just like the female Neteru had slain her Dante. The loss of her would-be heir, a dark Rivera, was profound, leaving a visceral hole in the evil empire—one of no less magnitude than Dante's demise.

Lilith glanced up toward the cavernous ceiling, enraged that even vampires in the new male Neteru's old family still would not submit to the lure of human blood or the temptation of an elevation, and were still loyal to the Neteru team. Guardians hadn't even been fully compromised!

Revenge gripped her and her nails grew to talons that penetrated the armrests. The Neterus would pay.

Slowly, through the haze of sudden fury, she felt it. The sensation came into her spine like a lightning strike and made her throw her head back and screech with laughter.

"Oh, Carlos . . ." she whispered, clucking her tongue. "Now I know your dirty little secret—the one thing that will fell you and will make you lose your mind. I own your greatest fear . . . and now I can turn the blade in your side, thus hers, just like she gored my womb. Wait until Damali sees *this*."

@ CHAPTER TWO

Damali stared into the bathroom mirror as she brought the towel down from her damp face. Suddenly, out of nowhere, the past slithered through her. Everything that Carlos had ever done wrong came to life within her mind like a hot coal burning the good memories away.

"You can run but you can't hide," she told herself quietly, and took her time puttering around in the tiled sanctuary with the door closed.

She didn't feel like making love to Carlos this morning. Not after what she'd finally come to understand, and not after it had had time to fully sink in. Things like this took a minute to germinate in one's soul. The awareness left her feeling like doing nothing at all. Numbness threaded through her and left her very sad. Weary. In fact, all she wanted to do was to go home—back to her own place in Beverly Hills.

The emotion had crept up on her by degrees. In the midst of battle when she'd faced her man's other half, the dark side of him, she'd seen horrible images hurling at her. But she'd paid them no mind, then. Going up against a serious demon presence would send every, and anything, into one's mind, so a sister had to be strong, ignore it, laugh at the bullshit. That's what she'd done. Then.

Once she and the team had handled their business—and thankfully all of them had made it out of that madness alive—it was about a party, a celebration of life. They'd won.

Damali peered at the shut door as she sat down slowly on the edge of the wide, midnight-blue porcelain Jacuzzi and began applying shea butter to her skin. Suddenly she wanted to cry as much as she had a fight surge roiling inside her.

After the party came a month of pure indulgence in her apexing

Neteru's arms. Heaven. Heart-stopping, mind-melting, time-altering, mad-crazy lovemaking day and night until it didn't make any kinda sense. What was there to think about, then? The powerful jolt from his sexy pheromones kept anything out of her head, except getting with him and enjoying every moment of it. She'd almost eloped with him, being so swept up in the passion of it all. They'd only waited a few so that Father Patrick could get back from Rome and they could do the thing proper with their beloved priest, who was like a real father to Carlos.

Damali closed her eyes. Tears wet her lashes. Maybe she should have just gone ahead and married him and not waited. Time was kicking her ass now. The cold light of day was real ugly and she could no longer escape the fleeting impressions that had gradually become too clear and full blown within her mental sight.

It was so unfair, and the rational part of her had diagnosed her problem with logical detachment. By all rights, she knew she couldn't blame him. He'd been under the influence. For several days she'd repeatedly reminded herself of that fact. But the emotional part of her being still had major issues. Her unspent rage seemed to come out of nowhere, which was the crazy part.

And it all happened in a slow dissolve of her reality as Carlos's apex ebbed, and the spiking hormone levels in her body dissipated to a dull roar. Snatches of information had come back to her third eye with a vengeance. Things no woman should ever see her man do, foul behavior that had been previously blocked within her head was loosed. This was worse than the were-demon incident, to her way of thinking. Oddly, she could live with that and she didn't really go there in her mind. But this thing with a Guardian sister . . . family, such as it were, was too messed up. Too close to home, literally.

The thing that hurt so much about what she'd witnessed was the fact that the only reason it had happened at all was because he'd defied a direct angelic command . . . which had tethers to the fact that he'd been so resentful of her command, her position, and the fact that for even a little while, she'd been the one in charge. *That hurt.* That was how he'd been seduced to prematurely act, contagion or not, it was at the core of his being. That was what had put him in a position of being nearly compromised beyond redemption. And once his brief possession by the unthinkable occurred, he did things under the influence that were horrible.

More than anything else, she also knew that, even possessed, the dark side worked with what was already looming within the shadowy sections of the human spirit. All it did was bring those things to the fore with a vengeance.

Carlos had been angry at Yonnie, way down deep, for making a pass at her. He'd been conflicted and upset with Tara, for Rider's sake and for Yonnie's, and all the dark possession did was elevate it and bring it out in its worst form; he'd wanted her to choose clearly and decisively to end the drama between two of his closest friends. He owed Jose and loved him like a brother, but had still been pissed off at Jose's attention, his silent love-jones, and the blanket—going after Juanita made sense while possessed. Nasty Scorpio bastard.

Most of all, Carlos had been furious with her for still being the team's most seasoned Neteru, and not wanting to get married or to conceive right away . . . so, while "under the influence," as Carlos called it, he'd set out to punish her—even though he loved her . . . even while possessed. The demon had a stranglehold on him through his deepest, darkest insecurities, much the same way a man who loves his wife beats her to be sure she stays with him. Insanity.

His twisted goal while possessed had been to break her back, spiritually. Paralyze her ego, stomp what he perceived as her arrogance, and snuff out her inner light. Making a baby with Juanita would have done that until the end of time. The more she really thought about it, that he would go there, even under the influence, rubbed a raw spot in her heart until it bled.

Damali drew a shuddering breath as she applied more cream onto her body with harder strokes. That was worse than the physical act of Juanita giving him head on her back deck, oddly enough. She could rationalize that as the actual demon, not Carlos. But what she *couldn't* forgive at the moment was that he'd had so much quiet rage toward her within him that he couldn't control the demon—hellfire notwithstanding . . . because she could. Had done it for a long time, had sucked up all his mad-crazy drama, but *never* had succumbed to doing anything, for any reason, that would have carved his heart out of his chest . . . even when she could have, even while she'd been fully infected with demonic contagion and standing on a beach in Jose's arms. She'd backed off and made a choice, and said no.

An eerie sense of betrayal had filled her. Over the last three days, nagging bouts of insecurity had coated her inner being with a new, virulent level of anger and jealousy like she'd never known. She'd found herself becoming clingy at times—something so not her that it frightened her more than any demon she'd encountered. *Her?* The Neteru? Clingy? What was up with that?

If she'd brought this to Marlene, and she never would, she knew Marlene would tell her to focus, get still, and meditate on the sensation not the incident, to see if there was some new threat that she and the team should be aware of. Marlene would also tell her that forgiveness was divine, and to pray on it. She'd done that.

Her sensory awareness didn't register any immediate pending doom. The Divine wasn't lifting the burden from her heart, either. It sat there like a dull, heavy stone, making her occasionally sigh for no reason, out of the blue. Her inner vision had become a mental torture chamber, providing no answers, just a rehashing of what had happened. What she saw instead of a demonic threat was nothing that she could kill or justifiably beat down without violating every law of Ma'at. That's when the arguments had started in earnest.

A light tap on the door made Damali jerk her focus up to stare at it. Damn straight, Carlos had better not just waltz in or blow into the bathroom on her without permission to enter.

"Yeah," she said, becoming surly at the invasion. Damali went back to applying the cream to her calves. The man needed to stay out of her face this morning, if he knew what was good for him.

Carlos peeked in and then slowly came into the large, brightly sunlit room with her. She watched him lean on the sink and send his line of vision toward nothing in particular. He had on black silk boxers. Whatever. His ass needed to get dressed. She wasn't interested.

For a moment, Carlos hesitated by the sink. He stared at Damali, seeing the light around her body as a dull, gray covering that was growing darker by the second. Pure alarm filled him. Something was wrong with his woman. Then he watched as a dark orb exited the base of her skull and dissipated. He started at the sight of it. She was looking down and furiously slathering cream on her legs. Maybe it was the final contagion purging out of her system . . . or maybe it was the final dark blockage he'd placed there leaving. It could be a good thing that it was finally gone, or a bad one—the problem was he wasn't sure. But her darkening aura couldn't be a good sign.

"You still leaving today?" he asked quietly, trying to feel her out before launching into his observation. "I can take you home so you don't have to drive."

"The road will do me good," she said, not looking at him as she put shea butter on her elbows. "Fresh air will clear my head."

He didn't say anything, and then let his breath out hard. The room seemed to be growing darker around them; hopefully it was just his imagination. He glanced out the window, quickly studying the clouds to see if that was all it was. The last thing he wanted to do was to set her off again about what had happened in Arizona, but as his mind tried to take a different path and his mouth tried to form a different sentence, the subject he vowed he'd never bring up came out instead.

"Listen, D, that thing that happened between me and Juanita in Arizona—"

"Oh, you mean that foul shit that went down in *my house?*" Her tone was salty as she stared at him hard for a moment and then went back to her original task, serving him pure attitude. "I know. You were under *the influence.* You told me, I got it, we discussed it to death. There's nothing more to say about it."

"That wasn't me—"

"Right. I keep forgetting that it was your evil twin," she said, sucking her teeth.

He rubbed his palms down his face and sighed, frustration adding tightness to his voice. What was wrong with her? What was wrong with them?

"You *know* what happened when I made that attempt to get the book. I got possessed for a few, but if that hadn't gone down, I wouldn't have . . . baby, what I'm saying is, the shit wouldn't have gotten crazy . . . and I know you're still feeling some type of way about it and—"

"Oh, yeah," she said with a brittle chuckle. "I am *definitely* still feeling some type of way."

"So am I," he said quickly, feeling his pulse race and not sure why. He glanced around the bathroom and then focused on her aura. It was now almost blackened with flecks of eerie, static-charged filaments running through it. "Baby, your coloring is off, so is the light around you. This isn't us, not how we roll. I need to get you diagnosed by Marlene, or something . . . just like you told me back then, when I had my run-in with Level Seven."

She didn't move or speak; he didn't move or speak. All he wanted to know was where this conversation was going and what the darkness was that entombed her. Okay, she didn't have a blade on her. Good. However, he could see her losing control of all reason second by millisecond. Fury radiated in her aura the longer he stood in the same space with her. It was as though black lightning was coursing through her normally silvery glow, making it take an unnerving dark turn. Her tense expression and jerky movements while applying cream to her body said everything. What had happened?

As he tried to think of what he could say to her, he knew the change within her had occurred in painful waves over a course of days. It was as though the sudden awareness hit him all at once.

At first she'd been stunned numb when the full memory came back again, and had then cried bitter tears when it all washed over her as sensations. They both did when he confessed, only after she knew for sure and wouldn't let it rest. She'd soaked in his explanation too hurt to even speak. Having to tell her something like that, and to see the look of horrified disbelief on her face, was the thing that had brought him to tears. Sobs, to be exact. She'd taken his vampiric turn better than that.

Then she became somber, as though someone had died—maybe they had. Then she asked fifty million questions, trying to understand and wrap her mind around the phenomena . . . made him relive it in excruciating detail, impression by impression until he was almost ready to walk. But he couldn't; she had the right to know. Then she had become calm and psychiatric and seemingly resigned over breakfast. He'd thought the storm had passed. Thought the poison was out of her system and the stone between them had rolled away. Thought it was over. She'd even made love to him once after that . . . he was sure, then, that she was cool . . . even though she was a little more subdued than he would have liked—which made him wary and a little nervous. But it was all too clear now, her ass was still mad as hell.

"I knew it would have to come out, surface, sooner or later," he finally said.

"You know what they say," she replied casually and still not looking at him. "A lie will always out, Carlos. The Light has a provision to ensure that happens sooner or later."

"It wasn't a lie; I just didn't speak on it because I didn't want to—"

"An omission of truth. Oh, that makes a difference." She looked up at him for a moment before glancing back down at the shea butter.

"I knew you'd have to let it run its course to get out of your system and all, and once it did we'd be back to normal. You know I wasn't trying to hurt you, baby." His voice was near pleading as he mentally fought with the harshness in her eyes. Yeah, there was something else going on than a regular argument. Had to be. Damali had *never* looked at him like that, and he'd never found himself feeling so totally unable to explain his position.

"I'd never intentionally do that, and you know it," he said after a pause to find the right words, his tone logical but containing hurt. "It wasn't supposed to go down like that. Of all the battles we've been in together, I know that more than a blade, something like this would cut your heart out and drive a wedge between us—so you know I wouldn't do that to us, boo. Right? You know that. So, this was their side just going for our foundation, our Achilles' heel, D. Don't let 'em mess with your head like that, all right?" He slapped the center of his chest to make his point. "It's me and you, baby. Always has been, right? Always will be, right?"

When she didn't answer the last and most critical questions he'd asked, he really began to sweat. "Damali, baby, listen, you can't stay mad about this forever. It was a demon transgression. You and I have a lot of road ahead of us . . . we can't be allowing nonsense to get between us like that. I didn't actually sleep with her—I mean, it was sex, but it wasn't *sex,* you feel me? It was more like foreplay, not real sex—"

"What?"

She'd looked up at him so slowly and had spoken so softly that he began talking faster and backing up.

"It wasn't the Full Monty, boo, like you know it can go down, and uh, what I'm sayin' is, *mi tresora,* you're my heart and treasure, girl, and you can't be concentrating on a lapse that wasn't really me. Right?"

"I'm cool," she said in a falsely upbeat tone. "It all checks out metaphysically. A dark entity overtook you, it was a spirit attachment, a parasite that made you do things to a lot of people you shouldn't have. The thing is over, so, hey. I'm cool."

He stared at her hard, knowing she was anything but cool. "Then why are you still leaving?"

"Because I've got things to do—like get back to my music, for one. For two, I don't live here and need to be in my *own,* unadulterated, unblemished, never transgressed by a foul deed, house. *My space.*" She set the shea butter down hard on the edge of the tub and stood, bringing her hands to her hips. "And, three, because I feel like it and I'm grown. Do I need any more reason than that?"

"The Bible says to forgive and forget," he replied quietly, pain shimmering in his tone. "Don't do this, Damali."

"Now you're going to go *biblical* on me? About this? Puhlease." She shook her head and strode toward the door. "What does it say in *the Bible* about letting some sister suck your dick on my back deck after you defied a direct order from On High? Forgive and forget? Okay. I ain't mad, and it wasn't sex—so we cool, ain't nothing to discuss. *Right?*"

He was on her heels as she shrugged away from his attempt to grab her by the elbow. "How you gonna hold me accountable for—"

"*Don't* touch me," she said quickly, holding up both of her hands and glaring at him. "Not until *I say so.*"

"Aw'ight, aw'ight," he said, holding up his hands to match her stance so she could pass. "I'm sorry. I just want to talk to you. Okay, baby? There's something dark around you that I just saw come out in this—"

"You can cut the 'baby' crap. My name is Damali."

"Aw'ight, my bad." He had to get through to her, get her mind focused on the potential threat. "Let's just talk, for real. Let's get this thing worked out, girl," he said, his voice faltering as he watched her cross the room. "I don't want you blaming me for something that I really couldn't control. You've got something trying to attach to you—been there, and I know what I'm talking about. This time, D, you need to listen to what I'm saying." Carlos folded his arms over his chest. "You have to stop blaming me, get past the hurt, and stop thinking this was—"

"I'm not blaming you," she said, snatching up her underwear and trying to step into them without removing her towel.

He just watched her. She was covering her body from him? After all they'd been through and done with each other? Now she didn't want him to see her naked? This was really bad and had kicked it up a dangerous notch. Whatever had come out of her head, had taken something with it.

"Baby, listen—"

"No, *you* listen," she said, her voice beginning to escalate. "What would happen if I had an aberrant moment and lost my damned mind, huh? What if some tall, fine, ridiculously sexy brother opened my nose for a minute while under the so-called influence, and let's say, I had sex that really wasn't sex because I didn't go all the way, but would have if I could have—and mighta gotten pregnant, too, if my Guardian brother hadn't walked up on me, and I had nearly busted a nut for him and did it in your house or *your lair,* and whatnot, and was ready to have a baby for him but didn't have time to really get my swerve on correct, so I postponed that vibe only because of time, not commitment? Feel *me?"*

"I was *possessed,* baby, *I swear,"* he said holding his hands out in front of him, imploring her to relent and to give him another chance to explain. "I just saw that dark smoke exit you, so it's got your thinking jacked! That's why I cut that motherfucker's head off, all right? I'd *never* make a baby with nobody but you, *mi corazón.* C'mon, now, D, this is me you're talking to. You sound crazy. You ain't making sense, girl; don't go there. Let's just calm down, discuss this rationally. We'll work this out, together, and go see Mar to purge you righteous, and things will be fine."

Damali began walking around the room to put the bed between them so she could yank on her jeans and shirt under the shield of her towel. She gave him her back as she pulled on her tank top and snatched off her towel in one deft move without allowing him to see her breasts. "Say he was a warlock and put a spell on me, or it was a fine voodoo priest that whipped down some dark ritual that blew my mind. Would you be okay with it when I came out of the haze?"

"Yeah," Carlos said, louder than he'd wanted, "because it wouldn't be your fault!"

"If you *saw* it, you could just shake the image out of your mind with no problem? It wouldn't take a little while for the impressions to fade, for the thing eating at your brain and your heart to go away?" She nodded and chuckled angrily. *"The Carlos Rivera* would just be smooth, wouldn't care if his woman arched her back and called another man's name? Gave up the cold-blooded puss—"

"Damali, it wasn't like that and you know it! You're not being fair."

She glared at him, wanting to just unload a full clip of verbal obscenities at him like rounds from a semiautomatic, but was so suddenly enraged that for a moment she couldn't speak. His eyes held a frantic quality that she oddly enjoyed. *Let him twist.* She knew it was sick, but hurt fury had a grip on her logic that was unraveling by the second. She wasn't sure what about any of it hurt her more, the fact that he'd ignored an angelic command and *once again* had gotten himself jacked up in a situation that they'd all had to figure out how to live with, or the mere fact that he hadn't been strong enough at the core to not do something to their relationship that would damage the one thing that had been rock solid between them—trust. Instantly she decided that it was all of the above.

"Fuck you trying to tell me about some black smoke coming out of my head. It's probably coming out of my ears, too, from being so damned mad at you, Carlos! If the same thing happened to me, you'd be off in a lair somewhere, alone, licking your male ego wounds, with me having to beg you to come back to me. You'd have me on my fucking hands and knees groveling to make it right, explaining over and over again every detail of how it happened, why it happened, swearing on a stack of Bibles that it would never, and could never, ever, ever happen again."

"No, I wouldn't," he said, now pointing at her, "because that weakness that got me fucked around in the first place is gone, D!" He stepped toward her, head tilted to the side, ready to go to war over the principle. "I know who I am now, the male Neteru." He pounded both fists against his chest. "No bullshit is ever gonna make me doubt the Light again. I'm not ever gonna be unclear about my powers, you got that? I refuse to go backward, I'm going forward, and this time there's something messing with you—but your ass is too arrogant to accept that just maybe you ain't invincible." He leaned in toward her. "You ever consider that, D? Ever think about the fact that that's how I got messed up? Your best bet is to learn from my big mistake, rather than try to rub my nose in it. I ain't no puppy, or no newbie, D."

She pointed at him and then drew her hand away quickly to press her palm against her stomach while willing her voice not to crack. "You'd be so hurt, Carlos," she whispered. "You'd wanna know, 'Baby, how'd it take your mind like that—how'd it get inside the black box of me and you?' And . . ."

Damali briefly closed her eyes and two huge tears rolled down her cheeks without her consent. "And you'd want to know what was already resident within me that would have allowed it to get its claws under the lid to lift it enough to take me there." She stared at him. "The Chairman and the Harpies couldn't get into it, because at that time, the seal was tight between me and you—unbreakable. But once you felt like I was the team leader, your ego gave the core of us right to 'em on a silver platter. That's what I can't forgive. Juanita being dragged into a trance by a Level-Seven demon using your body, nah," she added, shaking her head. "That ain't what's making me put my clothes on and leave. It's not about her; it's about *you*. Period. I don't trust how you really feel down deep. So, tell me I'm lying. Isn't that how you'd process all of this?"

When he didn't respond fast enough to her liking, her voice took a dangerously low dip as she spoke between her teeth. "And then you'd make me TWIST, *my Scorpio brother*, and you know that. Don't try to confuse the issue and get out of this by talking about some black smoke you supposedly saw in the bathroom. Be real. Things would *never* be the same between you and me again. If we both lived to be a hundred years old, you would whip out your 'right as a man,' " she added, making little quotes around the words in the air with her fingers, "to fling a transgression of this nature in my face whenever the mood hit you. It would be the perpetual ax over my head until the end of time. The blade of Heru!"

She paced back and forth in a tight line, raking her locks. "You'd be telling me that, possession or not, I shoulda loved you so hard that something like this couldn't have happened. Then you'd be telling me some male Latino-based yang about how it's different for a man than a woman, and I'd have to give you time to sort it all out. Tell me I'm lying?"

Part of what she was saying, he knew in his soul, was the stone-cold truth. But he also knew what he'd just seen. There *was* black smoke. Yet for the moment, words failed him.

She stopped pacing and looked at him hard and folded her arms over her chest, breathing in hot bursts as another fury spike jolted her system. "You *know* that's how it would go down if the shoe were on the other foot—that's why nary a female in the house—or on the planet for that matter—can just have a lapse without having to seriously think about the chain-reaction consequences to her relationship! A woman can't just claim to have been under the influence, possessed, or whatever! But a man? Sheeit. He's a man and prone to go there anyway by nature, right! A little demon topspin to make the offense allowable; a sistah should have a heart and understand, right?"

"Baby—"

"Save it!" Her arm snapped away from her body as she pointed at him so hard that her hand shook. "Women from fifteen to well beyond fifty, like Marlene, and Marj, and Tara, as well as Krissy, all know, *don't even think about* going there under *any* circumstances, unless you want your entire world to change—even if your man has taken a walk on the wild side for whatever reason! They didn't even forgive *Eve*—and that sister had encountered the fucking Duke of Darkness . . . but noooo. . . . She was wrong. She lost her career, position, powers, all sorts of jacked-up shit—they talked about her bad for *one lapse,* blamed her for misjudgment for centuries, and if you'd ever met her, she's the most refined, regal, def-defying *lady* I know! Girlfriend is awesome. But if it had been Adam, they would have said, 'Oh, he's a man—go in peace my son. You couldn't help yourself, you were possessed, tricked, lured.' Whateva, Carlos. So don't sweat me about having days or nights like this. So fuck fair—it ain't fair—and today I ain't feeling reasonable, understanding, or fair, hear me!"

"I'd forgive you, Damali," he said quietly. He didn't know what else to say. Even in her fury, her logic was indisputable, which *really* worried him. "Under those circumstances, if something stronger than you'd ever run up against got into your system, I'd have to suck it up and let it go."

She scowled at him and nodded. "I suppose you would," she said with a sarcastic bite. "Yeah, if you got to play the hero and save me from myself. Then your paradigm of innocent, helpless female versus the seductive monster that took my mind would hold up and you could live with that. Right," she said, nodding and rubbing her jaw like a man to rub her words into his open wound. "Sho' you right, man. Blow the motherfucker up, if it was on yo' woman. But if she was kinda sorta turned on and curious, then she's a whore. Right?"

She walked to the window and gave him her back, rolling her shoulders like a guy about to mix it up for a bar brawl. "I was raised by brothers; know how y'all think. Seen it in the house. It goes like this—if it was a dark entity and you got a chance to lop off its head, then cool. That would be different. Like a Fallon Nuit–type of thang."

Not waiting for him to respond, she spun on him when she heard him draw a breath to speak. "So, I guess the real problem I'm having is just pent-up aggression. I need to chill, right? Suck it up and let it go. Is that it? 'Cause I can't just cut off Juanita's head to make myself feel better, can I? The supposed one who did that was you or looked like you— and you got to kill it, not me, remember? It'll be all in my face, daily, once the team gets back to business. The only thing saving my sanity is the fact that the poor woman doesn't know and doesn't remember . . . but she *feels* it. Why?"

"Damali, baby, I'm begging you—"

"She still *feels* it because there's something still there for her subconscious to nurse and work with—within *both* of you! *That didn't die.* Never will. It's in every glance. You looking at her, hoping she doesn't recall it and wanting to protect her from sudden, brutal knowledge—because you defiled her and still love her down deep; her looking at you feeling a burn she can't explain . . . and she's more attached to you now that the old flame got fanned one mo' time. My poor damned brother, Jose, is helpless, not knowing exactly what went down and quietly praying it wasn't his worst fear . . . doesn't want to deal with even thinking about what mighta happened when the Devil's spawn was in you and his woman was by herself for too long. Hurt him, and I'll kick your ass for it!"

"Damali, do you hear yourself?" Carlos said, looking at her without blinking. "You're talking about kicking my ass over Jose . . . after what I haven't spoken on between y'all?" He walked toward her slowly, the threat in his stance implicit. "Now I *know* you done lost your mind."

Damali let her breath out hard as new tears rose to her eyes and her voice faltered. She lifted her chin, seeming not the least bit concerned about his outrage.

"Jose looks at me so hurt sometimes, Carlos, because he knows I have *fierce* second-sight, with a question in his eyes every time I see him, a question that says, 'D, we're tight, family, you would tell me if you knew, wouldn't you?' And I have to look away from those innocent eyes and play it off. I know *in my soul* that every time Juanita makes love to him she's still thinking about you! Jose's subconscious can feel it, too."

"Naw, Damali," Carlos said, dragging his fingers through his hair and shaking his head. "That's you projecting your own stuff onto them." He stared at her. "But if you think I need to talk to the brother that can be arranged. I'm tired of this bullshit anyway. Let's just clean house, say what's gotta be said, get everybody clear about—"

"Just stop it," she ordered, more tears coursing as she spoke. "When the two of you are in the same room—"

"Who, D? Me and Jose?" He walked in an agitated circle of disbelief.

"You and Juanita! Don't play me, Carlos. Shabazz bristles like an electric shock is running through him every time you two are in proximity—even though he never saw it! While you were apexing, I had to get you out of the compound! We couldn't even go over there to eat with everybody. The magnetic draw to you was too strong, woulda opened her memory banks, the sensuality oozing off of your ass was that bad. Freakin' Marlene just calmly shut down her third eye and is in denial, hoping this will fade back into the darkness from whence it came. I'm a tactical, and I can feel it all! Fuck you for this, Carlos. I need my space to get my head together, now that your apex rush is out of my system."

"So, the time you spent with me was purely carnal? Just because of my Neteru apex? Didn't have nothing to do with how much we love each other? Didn't have anything to do with the fact that I could forgive what freaked you out and sent you onto the damned beach and into Jose's arms for a minute?" Carlos folded his arms over his chest. "I was possessed; you weren't. I could understand and forgive that old emotions had been brewing for a long and quiet time, ran hot while your head was messed up and—"

"And I didn't blow him . . . when he probably needed me to do that in the worst kinda way . . . after all those years, *like you said*. Don't change the subject and play with me this morning."

She folded her arms. He looked away.

"He respected you. I respected you. Both of us always have." She shrugged. "It was a kiss. Yes. We were both infected. Yes. But even with old vibes, even with all the drama of woulda, coulda, possibly shoulda—it stopped there. Can you say the same thing?"

"That was different, Damali, and you know it. That hurt, too, because I know down deep the man loves you, and there's a part of you that loves him—always will. So a kiss meant way more than what went down during a demon possession moment. Be honest. If, with all that inside of either one of you, had you taken a tumble in a dark throne—the main one—it coulda happened. Don't act like you're so above it. So, I'ma ask you again . . . wasn't there anything to your staying with me these past weeks more than just an apex?" His eyes silently searched her for affirmation.

She looked away. "What did how much I love you mean when whatever you resented about me went with you and allowed them to open the box—*our box,* that was once lined with pure silver and filled with nothing but light?" she asked quietly.

"It's still lined with silver for you, baby," he whispered. "Still filled with pure light . . . now more than it ever has been." He moved to go near her, but her body tensed and he stopped where he stood. "I took its head off. Nothing like that can violate what we have again," he added quietly. "Nothing."

She smiled, but it was an angry, tight expression, not her normally dazzling one. "Only problem is, like I said, I can't just lop off Juanita's head. She's human, and on the Guardian team, at that. Lives in the compound house. And I still have to see her, and she still gives me her ass to kiss when—"

"She *doesn't remember* what happened, fully," he said, panic in his voice. Yes, they'd argued before, but never like this. "Baby, I've been over it a thousand times."

"If that skank reaches for you in my presence . . . if I even *sense* it, I'll—"

"She ain't gonna reach for me, D. Listen to yourself. She don't even remember what happened, and you shouldn't call her a skank. It wasn't her fault. *Like you told me,* we were all under the influence and reeling from the charge! She might be feeling some mild aftereffect vibe, but she's unaware of how deep it got, so don't call the sister a skank, all right. She's one of us, cool peeps, and took care of my moms and grandmom." The moment the sentence came out of his mouth, he knew he was in deeper trouble. He could feel turbine energy zinging through Damali as she cocked her head to the side.

"Wait. Let me get this right," Damali said coolly, quietly holding up one hand and then closing her eyes. "Are you standing here defending her in my face?"

"Baby—"

"This old lover, one that still has the hots for you, even before you got possessed, and you have the *nerve* to question me about a guy who literally saved your life, mine, and who I'd never slept with but kissed only *one time*—after *all* he'd been through?" Damali's hands went to her hips as she leaned halfway across the bed.

Carlos backed up farther in the room. "See, now, D, that's—"

"This woman," she said, her voice rising on each word until she was shouting in rapid-fire, broken sentences, "who, regardless of what she remembers or not . . . the same one who balked at my command of this team from the moment she set foot in our compound, gave me nothing but attitude way before you got possessed, and then went down on you, easily I might add, with no resistance in her. This is the chick I'm not supposed to feel any type of way about? When I could easily throw up *every one* of Jose's honorable deeds in your face, too, tit for tat, but this man never crossed the line, *never* challenged your position with me or your authority, and *never* went beyond the established limits! Even after you told him he could be with me, asked him to if you died, you selfish sonofabitch!"

"That's enough," Carlos hollered. "You need to watch your mouth and stop cussing at me!"

Damali wiped her palms down her face as rage made her body tremble. "Oh, shit, Carlos, you *did not* go there and tell me not to even talk about how I feel about her way down deep because you don't think I should? Are you fucking crazy! When conversely, she *never* respected me, you *never* demanded it from her, just let the bullshit fall where it may, *never* checked her quietly, discreetly, for the sake of Jose's pride, and left me to always have to suck it up when I should have *kicked* her narrow, disrespectful ass right after we did Philly! Oh, my God, oh, my God! I can't call this chica out of her name, even in here with you—in the bedroom, supposed to be our sanctuary—and you're defending her to me? Oh shit! I have to respect her when she's always got something snide to say to every command I give this fucking team! I'm supposed to be cool, always, not lose it, not even knowing you seduced Juanita into doing something she wanted to do for your horny ass anyway and in my house and was gonna make a—"

"Damali, sweetheart, please, for real—"

"The onliest reason I haven't yanked her out of the compound by her hair—the same hair you were running your hands all through when she was on her knees—to beat her ass in the yard is for *Jose's sake.* Every time that heifer cuts me dead with her eyes, every time she makes a side-out-the-neck sarcastic comment, every *damned* time she gives me her ass to kiss like she knows a secret that I don't, I am ready to draw blood. Do you know how dangerous this shit is and how close to the surface it is under my skin?"

Damali paced back and forth like a trapped panther, visibly so angry that a shape-shift was not out of the question. "If Hell was to snatch me now, they wouldn't have to pry to get to this emotion out of me. I'm so mad at you, Carlos, I'd slap that bullshit you just tried to hand me on the table and would tell 'em, 'Gentlemen, let's deal'—that's how angry I am! Own it! She's working my nerves, so you'd better fix this and get her straight!"

"Juanita acts the way she does sometimes, not because she remembers what happened in the house in Arizona, D, I swear," he said quickly, beginning to pace in front of the bedroom door. "It's, it's because she and I used to deal, and she's jealous of what Jose used to feel for you, maybe stills feels a little bit—plus, you got to both of us, him and me, and she's feeling—"

"*Fuck* what she feels!" Damali pulled her hair into her fists as she glared at Carlos. "She can feel any way she wants to in the quiet of her confused mind—but she's gonna feel my foot squarely up her ass if she challenges my command in front of this team ever again! Got it?"

Damali let her hair go, folded her arms, and took in deep breaths with her eyes closed. "When she's feeling scared, girlfriend is all about feelin' me out there kicking demon ass—ask her how she would feel if one night I wasn't feeling up to my Neteru self and stepped aside to let something horrible yank her ass down to Hell." Damali opened her eyes. "Ask her that for me, will ya?"

"You know that's wrong, D," he said, new worry hitching his voice. "You wouldn't do that, baby, would you? That would compromise your soul. You know that's wrong and dangerous to even allow a mind as strong as yours to think something like that."

"Then you could come down there and get my soul, if I lost it, right? Or you could go rescue her out of the jaws of a huge, dangerous, feeding Amanthra. You da man. After you saved us both, we'd be so grateful we might hook a brother up with a three-way . . . you could definitely hang, and she and I could sing two-part harmony—too bad you're not still apexing, but it would still be awesome, and then she and I could kiss and make up right there on your fucking lap," Damali said between her teeth, coolly appraising his groin for the slightest twitch of interest.

"Damali, don't even play like that. Come on now, you have to let this old relationship me and Juanita had go."

"Why?"

Carlos paused and drew in a shaky breath. "Because I let what you and Jose had blooming go, D, when you put his blanket in your cedar chest—which, by rights, you shoulda given back, but I let that go because all of us are cool now, and, see, baby . . . c'mon, now. She don't remember. She just acts funny sometimes because she's probably wondering what mighta happened if she and I coulda stayed together, or if Jose hadn't had a jones for you once, which I know she can sense, so you pop off her deep-down emotions, is all it is, and sometimes that gets the better of her, and—"

"*Total* disrespect," Damali said in a near whisper. She looked up at him, pressed both hands over her heart, and leaned forward, eyes blazing. "But I'ma let it ride. Not for you, not for her, but because *my Guardian brother* would die a thousand deaths if he knew, and the team has to function *as one.* This mess with you and her goes to the grave with me and beyond it, *for him*—not your ass. Hear?"

Oh, he'd heard her all right, and her tone scared him. Everything between them now hung in a fragile balance, and he didn't know how not to trip over the thin filament that was wired to emotional C4. Yeah, he knew *exactly* where she was right now. The problem was, he didn't have an answer or any smooth bullshit to tell her to bring her down, and all her points hit too close to home. Plus, it had been confirmed in his mind, something more than Damali's temper was at work here.

"It was out of my control, something had me, baby," he said, fatigued. "I don't know what else to say to make this right."

"Then if I ever go there, and tell you something had me, and it was out of my control, then this conversation will be moot—since you've been here *more than once.* Since I've sucked it up, *more than once.* And if I ever happen to accidentally get myself into a compromising position, you'll be able to forgive and let live, like nothing ever happened, right?" Damali's hands were on her hips again as she nodded and went back to staring out the window. "Okay. Fair exchange is no robbery. Duly noted, Mr. Councilman. Peace."

"I wish you wouldn't call me that," Carlos said in a quiet, urgent tone. "I'm not in that life anymore, and I'm a Neteru with just a little of the old vamp in me, but not like before. I work for the Light, and we're on the same team."

"Yeah, right," Damali said flatly.

Her words trapped him in the bedroom; he might as well have been hanging on the Chairman's torture wall getting his guts ripped out. "You know I love you, girl."

"And what dat mean?" She walked a hot path before the window. "Oh, you love me. Wasn't thinking about that when Juanita was on her knees between your legs, did ya? Oh, you love me. Didn't think about that shit when you lured her to my house. Did ya? You *really* didn't think about that when you asked her if she wanted to make a baby, did you?"

If Damali would just take a breath and stop . . . He began gesturing wildly as he tried to say what needed to be said. "No, baby, see, I didn't lure her to the house. She was still feeling the charge from the night before when I'd just come back up from the pit—and, what had happened was—"

"But you love me. Right. All right. Then I love you, too. I guess she's also still head over heels, *literally,* even though she doesn't know why. I got it." Damali's hands went back to her hips as her gaze narrowed on him. "I'm cool. It's squashed."

"If, if—listen—if there's anything still resonating in her, it isn't from that—it was from before when I was with her and human." For all the fluent, smooth vamp still lingering in him, or just general regulation street smarts, as a man he knew inherently within his soul that no male entity on any level could go up against and come out on top of a female verbal beat down. He'd almost started stuttering as he'd spoken, which wasn't him at all under any circumstances.

"Her recall had been erased when it went down—in fact, it's not her fault at all. For real, D. Don't carry that back to the house and start no mess with 'Nita—"

"Oh, so now she's 'Nita, not Juanita. My bad. I stand corrected. Why don't you just call her your boo from now on? You can tap that ass whenever the mood strikes you, and I won't have a problem with it. Bite her, too, for all I care. Serve her two inches in the jugular and let Mar purge her after you're done. We ain't married. Right? The vamp bond don't count in the Light, so hey. What it mean?"

He could feel beads of sweat begin to form on his brow. His palms felt moist. "The girl was under the influence, like I've been trying to get you to understand. She's only human, and—"

"Well so am I!" Damali shouted, losing it as new tears of rage formed in her eyes. "I might be a Neteru, but I'm also human. *And female.* That shit keeps replaying itself in my head, Carlos. All I can see is the chica giving you a blow job on the porch of *my house.* Fuck all this Jerry Springer shit, demon-inspired or not. I'm out."

ℚ CHAPTER THREE

Beverly Hills, California

It frustrated her no end that the heated exchange with Carlos had gotten way off the primary subject and had devolved into a stupid argument about Juanita—a chick that clearly didn't have a clue. What he failed to realize was that it didn't have a thing to do with that heifer!

Damali nearly screamed in the car as she drove. He was so blind! This was about trust, his previous lack of respect for and acceptance of her role as a Neteru—his copartner . . . and that he'd allowed some old, archaic, man-woman double-standard nonsense to compromise the foundation of what they had, as well as jeopardize the overall safety and well-being of the whole family behind his ego. It was unforgivable. *That's* what had cut to the bone, not his old flame. Him thinking it was about his so-called *'Nita* was again nothing but Carlos's male ego in full effect!

But how the mess got off onto a stupid tangent was still a mystery. Damali blew a frazzled lock up off her forehead and continued to drive away from Carlos's place like a bat out of Hell. He didn't get it; the fact that he didn't made her want to snatch every hair out of his thick head by the roots. It was so basic! Heaven help her get this point across to that man!

They were supposed to be fighting evil as one, be the vanguards of justice, not arguing about the ridiculous. And, yet, she was only human. This shit with Carlos hurt so badly she couldn't breathe. She needed a day or two to chill. Time. A minute to pull it together. If time could just stop for a few to allow it—but she was supposed to be taking the newbies through their paces this afternoon. Oh, God, if time could just stop . . . where were her other stones? No new insights, no new powers—and now this! Life needed just to slow down

"A prayer said in anger," Lilith whispered, cupping her hands around the black, smoldering orb in her palms. She blew a cool breath on it and brought it into Lucifer's dark chambers. "My prince of the airwaves, I have an intercepted gift for you."

He looked up from his contemplation of the world, his dark gaze leaving the swirling globe before him, his hands a tent before his mouth. All was gargoyle stillness about him. Not even solicitous Harpies dared to scamper at his feet. The cavern was pitch-black, the only light emanating within it came from the model of the earth before him, and the gleaming blackness within his goat-eye-shaped irises.

Lilith hesitated, her line of vision darting between each darkened mark he'd made on the blue-and-white marble that slowly turned on a broken axis in the center of his single throne room, and then him. It was nearly impossible to see his form in the overwhelming shadows, but she could feel the power of his presence enveloping her as she struggled with speech.

"As you know, Lilith, I am always busy. Be swift, as my patience wanes. What is this gift?"

Lilith swallowed hard as the thunderous voice rumbled through her. "A Neteru going dark and praying for vengeance . . . wanting to hurt her soul mate as much as he's hurt her."

Lilith watched her husband arch his brow and then give a satisfied half-smile.

"You would never tease me with such a gift, would you, my dear? I thought you knew the extent of my wrath when displeased."

His voice was low, sensual, and dangerously melodic, sending a renewed shiver of terror through her. Yet his form had normalized, and he seemed relaxed and in quiet repose on his black marble throne. Lilith squinted through the darkness that was so complete that it even shielded him to her night vision. She released small sips of air when he gave her a knowing smile and relented, allowing her to witness his handsome self. She almost wept with relief at the sight of him cloaked beneath his large, raven-black, fallen-angel feathered wings, rather than the leathery ones used for battle.

She opened her hands and the snatched thought orb hovered above her palms for a moment before she blew her icy breath against it to send it toward him. He caught it with one fist, and then rolled it against his cheek and laughed.

"For as long as I've known you, Lilith, you always manage to delight me." He shook his head, causing his flowing jet black curls to cascade over his broad shoulders. "All right, my very bad girl . . . go ahead with your plan to release the forsaken." He laughed low and deeply and in earnest. "*This* I have got to see."

Damali had tried to rush in and out of the compound in a flash, not trusting herself to stay longer. All she wanted was to borrow Dan's car—a ridiculous two-seater, drop-top, red Porsche racer treat to himself that had absolutely no usefulness in battle. But it was fast. She and Dan were both adrenaline junkies in that way—speed demons. Damali laughed just thinking about it.

Marlene had given her the eye, as had Shabazz, but who cared? She'd agreed to go through some battle paces with the group, but her goal was singular: to go out hunting tonight *alone.* Right now that goal was coming true. She was out in the night air, "Gold Digger" blaring from the radio, Kanye was kicking it, and just remembering what it felt like to perform live on stage was threatening to give her the blues.

She needed to kill something, find a demon; any kind would be all right with her. In fact, the old vamp club where Carlos used to operate his best game was calling her. Since he and Yonnie had abandoned it, the place was probably infested. Good.

Just one vamp, maybe a werewolf. She felt dangerous tonight. Even her clothes were dangerous and not fit for battle. Damali laughed as the wind caught her locks while she sped along the old roads she knew by heart. It wasn't about listening to Inez or anybody who could talk her out of where she was headed. She didn't want to hear another thing from another living soul. She wanted to kill or be killed, and had zoomed home to throw on a red leather mini and the wildest pair of hooker boots she could find in her closet. She was gonna eat, drink, and be merry—and kick some ass—then come home to sleep it off. That would get her straight. Old times. When life was simple. Yeah.

"Thanks for the heads-up, man," Carlos said quietly, too humiliated to stare at Yonnie directly.

"Weird energy is going down, brother. I ain't in your business, but a Neteru blazing silver-and-black aura makes me nervous . . . especially when it's my boy's woman and she's walking the alleys in vamp territory by herself. Even though there's only lower-level gens inside, if enough of 'em rush her, she could get herself in a jam." Yonnie leaned against the Porsche with Carlos and nodded toward the darkened alley behind the club. "In that getup, girlfriend don't look like she's hunting . . . used to seeing D in leather pants and Tims, ya mean?"

"Yeah, I hear you," Carlos said, trying to keep a low growl out of his throat. He was damned if he went in there after her, damned if he didn't. So rather than get into an all-out public brawl with Damali, he focused his attention on Yonnie for the moment. "I felt her drawing to our old joint, man, but like you said, there's some serious weird energy out here."

Yonnie nodded. "Thought for a minute I was a damned councilman, bro." The two men stared at each other. "For a half a minute, Tara asked me for a human near V-Point, and I almost messed up."

"Tara asked you for what?" Incredulous, Carlos pushed away from the vehicle.

"You heard me, so watch your back," Yonnie muttered as they saw Damali stroll past a Dumpster to place her hand against the brick wall, sensing for dark energies. "She's got the Isis on her, man . . . but . . ."

"Yeah, I know," Carlos said, internal worry colliding with rage. Damali looked fabulous, but the outfit was a little too revealing and way over the top for a sister about to throw down in battle. "I got this, man," he finally muttered to his friend, hoping Yonnie would take the hint and mist off. The last thing he needed was a hot argument to be seen by the family.

Yonnie just smiled, shook his head, and offered Carlos a fist pound. "I don't know what you gonna do with that," he said as they watched Damali lean into the bricks spread-eagled, close her eyes, and release a slow groan. "But my suggestion is that you handle your business." Then just as suddenly as he'd appeared, Yonnie was vapor before Carlos could form a response.

Complete outrage made Carlos begin to walk forward against his better judgment. What had gotten into her? Sensing was one thing, baiting the hook to this degree was another—especially when there weren't that many entities in the region still foolish enough to try her. As he approached, his footfalls made her look up and push away from the wall with a scowl.

"What's your problem?" she said, gripping the Isis tighter than was necessary.

Carlos looked her up and down, assessing her revealing outfit with disdain. "I was about to ask you the same thing. If you wanted to go out hunting, I thought it was the house rule to do two-by-two detail from now on?"

"Puhlease. I wasn't going anywhere with you tonight."

"I didn't say it had to be me," Carlos shot back, "just another Guardian, at least."

Damali put her foot against the wall and began tightening the laces in her boot. With the mini and her pose, she was serving all thong, and had no modesty about it whatsoever. He could only assume that she was trying to really piss him off, and it was working.

"Look, I don't know what you're trying to prove out here," he said, crossing his arms, "but—"

"I don't have to *prove* anything, Carlos. This place drew me, had some crazy energy, but I went through the entire club and couldn't even get a good beat-down going." She dropped her foot to the ground and then began working on the other laces. "If you would stop being so *muy macho* and feel the wall, you'd see what I'm talking about."

Angered by the charge she lobbed, he walked over to the wall, spread out both palms, and tried to focus. *"Nada."*

"Figures." Damali cut him a glare, sheathed her Isis, and began walking toward Dan's car.

"What's that supposed to mean, *'figures'?*" Exasperated, he walked in long strides to catch up to her, and grabbed her arm, forcing her to stop.

Damali looked down at his hand until he removed it. "You didn't feel the bodies . . . the faces . . . the hands on that wall pushing like they were caught inside and trying to get out of it? It wasn't a pure demon presence, or a vamp or werewolf sensation." She sucked her teeth when Carlos looked back at the wall. "Like I said. Figures. You're so worried about your so-called woman doing whatever, and dressing however, you can't focus on the real."

"That's bullshit," he muttered, walking toward the wall and opening his hands against it again. "And if it was all that you said, what the hell is wrong with you, getting all up on it until you knew what it was?"

She arched an eyebrow and gave him a wicked smile. "It felt good. What can I say? I'm going home."

He whirled on her as she jumped over the door and slid into the driver's seat. "Just like that—no, 'Baby, you need a ride?' "

"Just like you blew in here, now that you can do transport with accuracy, you can take your own ass home. I drove because I wanted to feel the motion and keep my mind occupied with some music, okaaay? If that's all right with you."

He stood in the darkened alley listening to air-conditioning compressors and club music thudding through the walls as she turned on the engine and careened away.

Something was so wrong with his baby that he could only look up at the full moon and stare. Fury was spiking through him so hard that it almost stopped his pulse. About to leave, Carlos turned as he felt it, or rather, felt *them*.

Twenty very foolish, lower-level male vampires eased into the alley with smug expressions. Carlos just stared at them. They had *no idea* how badly he needed to kill something to vent the bubbling rage within him right now. Every chest before him had a bull's-eye on it.

"Where's your shield, Neteru?" the boldest one in the group said, stepping forward. The blond vampire chuckled as the others began to fan out in a semicircle around Carlos. "What . . . ain't got no blade?" The vampire shook his head. "A dark alley is a *real bad* place for an ex-Councilman to be caught solo."

Carlos rubbed his jaw and smiled, appraising the biker-looking vamp with a bad mousse job on his spiked platinum blond hair. Skinny motherfucker was gonna get his heart ripped out. The Goth crew with him, serving hard-dyed black-and-red punk-style haircuts with black lips and nails, made the muscles in his forearm twitch. "I'm not in the frame of mind," Carlos said in a quiet, lethal tone. "Just be advised." He looked around. "Damn . . . this used to be my club, too."

One copper-coiffed, very high vamp giggled in a squeaky-pitched tone. He adjusted his twisted nail-and-leather dog collar and then opened his black leather vest to stick out his bony, naked chest at Carlos in a dare. "He's claiming old territory, fellas—is gonna hurt something with no fangs and no blade. Oh, I'm soooo scared! He used to hold check here, yeah, I remember, just like he used to hold check on his woman, but don't now."

The high vampire glanced around smiling a snaggletooth grin as all twenty vampires suddenly bulked to bodybuilder proportions. "Just like his lady came out here for a fight, was gonna hurt somethin'. Oooohhhh . . . Sends chills down my spine. Makes my dick hard, just thinking about it."

That was it. Slow rage set off something crazy within Carlos that had no limit. It was all the excuse he needed to kick some ass, and he surveyed the group deciding which one would die first.

"Yeah, she was gonna hurt something all right," another vamp said from the sidelines, taunting Carlos. "The outfit was killer, for sure. But at least she had sense enough to bring her blade—unlike this dumb bastard."

Carlos didn't even turn as they fully encircled him. He kept his eyes on the ringleader and released a very slow breath. This was just what he wanted, and he could actually feel an invisible block break his contact with Yonnie and Damali. The threatening sensation crackled through his aura as though a black net had been dropped around him. Good.

"Thank you," Carlos said evenly. "Tonight I really needed this one-on-many beat down. . . . Y'all just don't know."

"Be cool, man, his boy is a Master and might come back—or that bitch with the Isis could," a smaller vamp warned the group in a low, nervous whisper. "Just 'cause Yonnie ain't in good standing, don't mean he can't get in it, feel me?"

Carlos looked at the lead entity and spoke in a calm, deliberate tone as he began to slowly walk forward. "You ain't gotta worry about my boy . . . you need to worry about what you just called *my wife*."

"Chivalry is not dead, huh?" the platinum blond said with a snarling laugh. "But it will be soon."

It just took a glib second. The moment the vamp before Carlos briefly turned his head to gain another round of laughter from his friends, eight inches of battle-length fangs instantly filled Carlos's mouth. He bulked to stand six-foot-eight, towering above the six-foot-two blond, and had reached in for a snatch so quickly that the entity before him just stood there for a moment, dazed, chest cavity cleaned out, organ gone. Carlos had yanked it out so fast that the vamp's lungs and esophagus dangled from his fist still attached to the severed heart. The copper-haired one that was talking trash instantly lost his throat all the way down to the bone, causing his head to drop back, hanging by only the thin ligaments and tendons that still kept it attached to his shoulders.

"Oh, shit!" a vamp beside the blond shouted as their leader dropped to his knees with a thud, then keeled over and torched beside the smoldering vamp with no throat. "This motherfucker still got fangs! Still got the speed snatch—get him!"

Carlos left the ground before their muscles could react to send them airborne. Heart tissue and an Adam's apple squeezed between his clenched fists like oozing black mud. The punch that he landed on the vamp that had just spoken disconnected his jaw and sent it skittering under a Dumpster. The deadly group lunged in a blur, and Carlos pivoted, slammed his fists through two chests, coming away with spinal columns and then used them like bloody chains to bullwhip around throats and lacerate once-smug faces.

"I told you I was not in the frame!" Carlos shouted, disemboweling four entities in a windmill rake as he spun then kicked several back, his black Timberlands connecting to temples, noses, and cheeks, and coming away with fangs in the sole of his shoe. "But you kept fucking with me tonight!"

Three half-wounded vamps tried to scramble up the fire escape, and Carlos grabbed the bottom rung of the iron bar, flipped up above them, crouched low in a saliva-dripping growl, and then lunged. Throats were between his jaws like old times. Adam's apples were summarily crushed, then gone. He glanced up with silver gleaming eyes and burned right through a beginning swirl of bats, then leapt off the fire escape right into the fray of nine remaining attackers.

He came away with a thigh bone, and plunged it into a chest, breaking it off and leaving part of it planted in a screeching vamp that became cinders. Noting the short bone dagger in his hand, eight vampires backed away but were too injured to propel themselves away to escape.

"What are you, man!" one screamed, holding where his arm had been, black blood gushing everywhere.

"I'm the brother who *told your ass* that I was not in the frame," Carlos said through a snarl, then instantly lunged and sliced through the entity's windpipe with the bone dagger.

Bloodlust and moonlight madness filled him as the entities tried to flee. Their backs were a target, that was all he could see, the place where their skulls ended and their spines began. He claimed that anatomy with sudden, ruthless fury, two at a time, leaving quivering, twitching forms on the dank alley ground and using the gore to strangle another that fell gasping.

"Take it back," Carlos said in a low growl, standing up from the lifeless form beneath him that he'd beheaded with vertebrae. Leaving smoldering ash at his feet, Carlos advanced to where three remaining vampires cowered behind a Dumpster and snarled with a spit of fury against the ground.

"Okay, okay," one called out. "She ain't no bitch!"

"Then what is she?" Carlos yelled, overturning the Dumpster and watching his burning gaze sizzle against the speaker's chest. "Tell me!"

"She's a queen!" the entity screamed, trying to put his hands in front of the smoldering area, which only ignited his arms and hands.

"Do I look like I need a fucking blade or shield?" Carlos shouted, sending a silver bolt of energy to fillet the entity's chest and expose his heart, searing away skin and snapping back breastbone and ribs one at a time. "I'm just coming out of an apex, motherfucker—do you know who I am?"

"Naw, man, shit . . . you don't need nothin'. . . . You da weapon, boss," another one said, breaking down into sobs. "We was just playing, man. Ease up. We ain't know you was still holding Council powers!"

"I'm holding a lot of deep shit," Carlos whispered, his tone deadly. "Got a lotta pent up aggression tonight. You wanted to play . . . let's play."

"Neterus ain't supposed to be able to do that shit, enjoying it, too!" the other said, covering his head as the two vamps huddled against the wall watched their howling comrade's heart burn.

Carlos tore a metal panel away from the Dumpster and folded it over into a wide, sharp-edged instrument of death. "A lotta shit ain't what it's supposed to be these days or nights," he said evenly, then hurled the metal like a discus, severing two heads against the wall.

The alley became eerily silent, save the hum of compressors. Carlos rolled his shoulders and spit on the ground again, still too hyped to normalize. A Level-Seven pulse was in the air. He could feel it, taste it, knew it like he knew his name. The bodies around him had slowly combusted into cinders one by one after each death blow had been dealt, and he stood wide-legged surveying the carnage of splattered guts and ash, a strange sense of satisfaction overtaking him.

"Anybody else feel like playing tonight?" Carlos asked the darkness, hoping a werewolf pack or something stronger might lunge at him while the rush of adrenaline was still coursing through him.

Yonnie slid out of a corner, and Carlos whirred on him breathing hard. "Yo, yo, yo!" Yonnie said quickly, holding up two hands in front of his chest. "It's me—drop the silver shit before you torch a brother."

Carlos rubbed the back of his neck and spit, trying to get the taste of sulfur off his palate and sending his gaze elsewhere.

"Felt good, didn't it?" Yonnie said with a sly smile. "Got the juices flowing."

"Like old times," Carlos muttered. "Nothing like it."

"Yeah, well . . . I was gonna double back and get in it, but figured you needed this."

Carlos gave him a sidelong glance and a half-smile. "I did, man."

Yonnie nodded. "Cool." He began walking though the piles of ash, chuckling. "Damn, man . . . but lemme ask you this—did you feel a communications dropout between us for a minute, or was it me?"

The two friends stared at each other for a moment.

"Naw, man, I felt it, too," Carlos finally admitted. "Maybe 'cause I was spiking pure Neteru fury, you couldn't pick me up . . . or maybe 'cause I really needed to do this myself?"

"Yeah, maybe," Yonnie said with a concerned glance as he stared at the remnants of the battle. "But like I said earlier, there's some real strange energy out here. Soon as we broke connection, I doubled back just to check on a brother. Feel me?"

Carlos nodded. "I hear you." He let out a hard sigh. "Just wish there were some Masters left to keep it interesting. This wasn't shit."

In an odd way, he could understand where Damali was at. There was nothing left to kill, nothing of real consequence left to fight. He could only hope that's what was making her battle herself—a worthy adversary. Maybe that had something to do with why she was battling him. There was too much to think about. Right now, he was simply out for blood.

Yonnie calmly stepped back and became very still. "There is one left," he remarked calmly. "Me. But you ain't going Neteru *loco* on me, right? We still cool, man, or did something change that I need to know about?"

Carlos gave his friend a sidelong glance and smiled with battle-length fangs still in his mouth. "C'mon, brother. What kinda question is that? You family. We peace til the end."

Yonnie straightened the lapels of his black Armani suit. "Just checking, 'cause twenty-to-one as a ratio . . . hey . . . they mighta been lower-gens, but that's still some shit to consider. Major props." He gave Carlos a once-over. "You'd better have Marlene purge all them nicks, man, I'm serious. You got cut up pretty bad."

Carlos smiled. "I'ma show you some Neteru shit I ain't even showed D, yet," he said with a wink, extending his arm that was badly lacerated. "Check this out . . . male Net purge."

Yonnie stood where he was, not moving, and gazed at Carlos's ripped chest, his torn, bloodied jeans, and then focused on the gashes in Carlos's arms. But he didn't speak as Carlos closed his eyes and the blood running from the wounds suddenly went silver.

"Oh, shit," Yonnie said, gagging and backing away while covering his mouth. "Smells like pus to me, man. I don't know how you deal with it!"

"An hour in a white bath, a half a gallon of holy water to wash it through my system, and a brother will be good ta go."

"Nasty . . . holy water . . . you gotta *drink* that? Damn!" Yonnie shook his head and looked like he was about to dry heave. "That's deep science, man," Yonnie said, going to the alley exit and then taking a deep gulp of fresh air. "But you're gonna have to whirl your own ass home. You my boy, and all, but I can't touch you with the silver leaking like that. Don't even pound my fist with that shit on you."

Carlos nodded, looking up at the beauty of the night sky, remembering and then jettisoning the thought. After a battle like this, if his woman would just be halfway reasonable . . . show a brother a little affection. Then he remembered they weren't speaking.

"It's cool. It's all good," Carlos finally said, grabbing the invisible edges of the darkness around him and enveloping himself with it. "Need the air, got some soul-searching to do, anyway. Catch you later."

"Later," Yonnie said, and then hocked and spit. "Crazy-azz Neteru."

With effort, Damali finally pushed the argument with Carlos out of her consciousness, telling herself that she refused to let negativity rule her. Later for that. It wasn't about allowing perpetual man-drama to take her off focus and away from her inner light. Juanita had always been a nut case anyway, Guardian or not, so what else was new? There was no stated rule that she had to like everybody in her Guardian family. Just like any other family, there were those who were favorites, those most cherished, then folks who simply got on your last nerve.

The drive had cleared her head. Her mind was on creative fire. Maybe it was the welcomed proximity to a club. It didn't matter. Lyrics, harmonies, keys between keys practically sizzled within her—something that hadn't freely occurred in almost a year. Conceiving new music was the closest thing to natural conception that she'd ever experienced. It felt so good, so comforting, so real that it produced a heady, natural high.

She couldn't wait to be alone, quiet, and cloistered, so that she could release the building creative flood of composition within her. This was so much more productive than staying enmeshed in anger. Developing artistically blocked pain, even if surreal emotional trauma often inspired it. That made sense to her way of looking at things. Most artists' best works had come from bone-deep pain or knowledge from hard-learned experiences, sometimes both. She certainly had enough to give her music a razor's edge for years. She'd use that and work with that—a much better option than cutting out Juanita's and Carlos's gizzards.

Music was the answer. She reminded herself of that as she went into the house. This outlet was from the strong side of her being, rather than the weakness that took root in rage and jealousy. And there was something about the artistic process that was so intensely private that this part of who she was couldn't even be shared with Carlos. He was many things, but an artist he was not. He couldn't take *that* from her. Damali smiled and sighed. *This* gift was *hers.*

By mutual respect, before the Juanita thing went down, they gave each other space when she was grooving on the universe like this, even though it had taken many conversations and heavy negotiations to bring about that understanding and change. His resistance to her need for a creative envelope had initially evoked a reaction from him at a level of jealousy that was nothing short of primal. *That,* she'd never understand, but had agreed to let it rest when he'd relented.

Come to think about it, there were a lot of things about this brother that irked her, but she'd let them all ride—up until now.

Damali closed her eyes and lolled her shoulders, dropping her clothes in a lazy trail as she walked across her bedroom. Peace filled her and made her contented, relaxed, and balanced in spirit. For the first evening in as long as she could remember, she was home, in her own space, *alone.*

After a half-day of training newbies, a four-hour, hard physical workout of putting the team through its paces before she could get Dan to part with his ride, but not before spending more time than she probably should have first thing in the morning arguing with Carlos, she was finally able to enjoy the meditative solitude of silence.

Her music was crying, begging for her to return to it. Tonight she would. A white bath soothed her frayed nervous system as she slid into the large oval tub and sank into the healing salt water. Music swirled within her at the cellular level, and she hummed softly as the water buoyed her creative purpose. Oh, yeah, she had enough pain to create something really deep tonight. *Wounded lover . . . let me explain how this all went down . . .*

Incense leaked from Tibetan pots, the smoky trails quietly infusing the healing mint-hued sanctuary with calming aromas. Long white tapers added gentle illumination to the room burgeoning with ferns. Prayers protected her like silent sentries. Starlight and a full blue moon sparkled through the stained-glass skylight, sending prisms of color all around her. Heat emanated from the bath's surface, covering her body in a blanket of wet warmth. She thought of Jose's color-splashed quilt, now languishing in her cedar chest at the foot of her bed. Tonight would be the perfect night to pull it out and wrap it around her. *Wounded lover . . .*

Life was good. Yes, there were horrible struggles still battering the world. The earth was weeping. She'd prayed for the healing of the planet and all who faced any pain on any level before she gave homage to her inner song spirit. But for this momentary slice of time, it was as though she could slip between the dimensions of it to make reality cease for just an instant, a fraction of a second, to allow her to experience stillness. In that regard, life was good . . . the water was warm, her family safe, and her man was a pain in her ass but alive. These blessings and more she cherished as she quietly dozed in light mediation, whispering to her muse to please return.

It wasn't about stressing over the need for another CD, or the demands of her profession as an artist, or even as a Neteru . . . no. Not tonight. Pure music, the healing balm for the soul, was where she'd reside. Total appreciation for every gift she'd received, every lesson learned, even the hard ones, the extraordinary ones, became her inner mantra, for there was only now, this moment—no past or future when time stopped like this for the birth of new music.

"I agree," a low, gentle, male voice said. "And that's a beautiful gift, too. Embrace it."

Peace instantly evaporated. Damali struggled to sit up, but her limbs were sluggish. Then she remembered that she'd been dozing in the tub. Common sense told her that she was thoroughly protected by every conceivable white-light barrier, but still, the sound of a male voice in the bathroom with her had shot panic through her.

No weapon on her, her mind began to process a thousand variables in lightning synaptic waves: the portals had been closed, all major vampire threats had been wiped out, all were demons had been sealed away, incubi didn't have enough power to encroach, she'd barred herself from astral plane projections . . . the voice was unfamiliar. Male. The imperative was immediate: *Get out of the tub.*

"Time stopped," the voice said in an easy manner. "You called for your muse. So, let's talk."

Bullshit. Her muse, if there was such a manifestation, *had* to be female, just like her Neteru Council. War swept through her bones. Her senses immediately keened. But oddly, the hair wasn't standing up on her neck. She wasn't bolting out of the tub, either. Nothing Neteru within her sounded an internal alarm, and there wasn't anything natural or supernatural that was registering as a threat.

"Show yourself," she said, sitting up in the tub unconcerned with her nudity. If there was a fight to be had, saving her life was way more important than that.

A form slowly took shape at the foot of the tub. She studied it, nearly squinting as she tucked her legs beneath her and prepared to defend herself. She watched the air move in heatless waves as something stepped between what appeared to be folds of invisible fabric. She wasn't sure what she'd expected, but it definitely wasn't an older, extremely handsome male being.

He sat down on the side of the tub with a casual smile, but his dark eyes burned with intensity as they roved over her damp breasts. A slight blue-white electric charge ignited the surface of the water, producing a tingling sensation across her skin.

Sudden modesty failed her. She couldn't take her eyes off him to even cover herself. His skin was the color of deep copper. Within his strong features, she could see many nations, and his ethnicity was impossible to judge. His hair was a jet-black profusion of thick curls interspersed with waist-length locks and a bit of silver gray that seemed to kiss his temples. His jaw was square, solid, and her eyes carefully appraised it for the slightest trace of fangs, but her assessment came away wanting. He wore a long white cotton robe, as though just coming off a pilgrimage, and his feet were bare. His body was so symmetrically toned that the word *perfection* came to her mind. And his voice was smooth . . . easy, melodic, and didn't inspire fear. The sound of it continued to ripple through her gently as though it were water. He was an enigma; she didn't know what to make of him.

"Say the Twenty-third, or you're outta here," she demanded, testing him.

"As you wish. I know it by heart," he murmured, and then indulged her, not taking his eyes from hers.

When he concluded, she immediately covered herself, not sure what else to do. If he could say biblical prayers, he definitely wasn't anything she'd encountered before . . . instinct kicked in, telling her it could be a guide, an angel, a Heaven-sent spirit . . . then her eyes became wide enough to split at the corners. "You're . . . you're not . . . are you?" She almost fell as she stood, clumsily hiding her body and grabbing a nearby towel.

The entity before her tilted his head, gave her a surprised look, and then burst out laughing. The sound of his mirth coated her insides, and her sudden arousal from the rich timbre of his voice caused her to clutch the towel around her more tightly.

"No," he finally said, recovering slowly from deep, booming chuckles. "I have been mistaken for a lot of things and a lot of people, but certainly not Him. I love you, Damali. You tickle me. Always have. But I have so missed communing over your prose and lyrics. We must do better at staying connected."

Damali was breathing hard as she bound the towel around her more firmly, got out of the tub, and quickly walked to stand by the door, ready to bolt toward her Isis. Panic and curiosity had become united, but she was still no fool. Something had manifest in her bathroom!

"Okay, okay," she said, regulating her breaths as she spoke. "I'm not asleep or on the astral plane. But you're from the spirit realm and are in my condo—how'd you get here?"

"You asked for your muse, stilled your mind, and stopped your time . . . just like the earth wobbled on its axis and time stopped within the earth's universe, you stopped time within your own universe, stilling the bands of matter around you." Merriment filled his eyes, making them crinkle in the corners. He shrugged and offered her a dashing smile.

When she didn't budge, he stood and she gazed up at his six-foot-five frame that moved like living fluid beneath his robe as he calmly approached her. "I have been waiting so long for you to learn how to do that." He closed his eyes and inhaled deeply. "But tonight, I am here just to talk . . . at your request."

Dazed, for a moment she didn't move. Not because she couldn't, but because in this stopped slice of time, she really didn't want to. Pure sensuality oozed from this being in a very disturbing way. And yet there was also something familiar about his features . . . he was more than handsome, there was a stillness, a settled beauty that glowed from just under the surface of his burnished skin. He also looked so much like an older, wiser version of Carlos that she almost reached out to touch his face, just to be sure she wasn't hallucinating.

"I'm not him, either," the entity before her murmured in a low, sensual rumble. "Trust that to be true."

Damali backed up so far so fast that she bumped into the bathroom door. Sure, entities had chased her, frightened her, scared the mess out of her, but this one . . . shit.

"Uh, listen, I was speaking metaphorically about a muse. I know there are angels and spirits that reside over the arts, and I was—look, I'm not ready to deal with this, okay? I need more information about what you do, how and where you came from before I just get all happy and think I've rubbed the genie in the lamp. I need—" Words were failing her, causing her to stop and begin her sentences in jags. "I may be a lotta things, but crazy ain't one of them." There. It was said. He had to leave.

His laughter was so deep and rich and resounding that she found herself smiling with him, despite the circumstances. He walked away from her and again sat on the edge of her tub, shaking his head. But when he finally looked up at her, the expression of pure desire on his face momentarily burned the saliva away from her mouth.

"Sweetness . . . I'm no angel . . . but if you want me to be a genie tonight, name your wish."

"All right, you're out!" She made a beeline for her Isis on the dresser, unsheathed it, and came back into the bathroom feeling much improved.

The fact that she couldn't focus enough to zap it into her hand really bugged her out.

"Put it down," he said, practically trembling as he stood. "We're not allowed to use that on each other."

"Who said?" Incredulous, she held the blade so hard it bounced.

He turned around, and she could see him take in a deep, steadying breath. He'd actually turned his back on an armed Neteru? Either this brother had a death wish or he might just be the baddest mutha in the valley.

"Level Seven? Speak to me! Answers. Now!" Her heart was thudding hard enough to crack her breastbone, and she couldn't breathe. The freakin' Devil was in her house? "Oh, shit! Father God protect me from all that's unholy. If—"

"Beauty of the Universe, put it down," the being urged with his back still turned to her. "Please," he whispered. "I'm not him, either."

The tone of his voice was so low and sensual that it ran through her, lighting pulse points that had once belonged solely to Carlos. The sword almost fell out of her hand, but she renewed her grip. If whatever it was could exude that much power, wreak that much sexual charge, it was a definite threat and had to go. Panicked, she lunged. He turned, side-stepped her, and unsheathed a blade too similar to hers.

Leveling his blade at her, he spoke in a low warning. "Put yours away and I will put mine away. You want to speak of the mysteries of music and harmonics, then I will teach you all that I have come to learn. It is inspired mathematics. But you must put the blade away, before I forget why you called me here tonight." Breathing hard, he sheathed his blade beneath his robe down the center of his spine and walked deeper into her bathroom, giving her his back to stare at again.

"You have no right—"

"I have every *right*," he said, his voice thundering. "*I* was there when they made you. I was there when you scribbled your first pain-filled poem in a schoolgirl's notebook!" He whirled on her, his eyes filled with anguish. "Do you think I would hurt you? *You?*" He sucked in a deep breath and let it out slowly through his nose. "Your first impassioned song . . . I was with you the whole time, bringing the high notes, the low resonance, the timbres of sheer ecstasy that stopped time for *millions.* Sound, Damali. Sound. That upon airwaves is in my DNA, and you have stopped time for me since you whispered your first echo into my world."

"Where *the hell* are you from?" Her voice was so quiet that she barely heard it herself. Still unconvinced that he wasn't the one who would remain nameless, she clutched her sword tighter, her pulse strumming through her limbs, muscles tensed for the brawl for it all. Her brain screamed an SOS to any Light-bearing receiver that would hear her. Reality was making her hyperventilate. She was possibly in the midst of something she was *not* ready for. *Lord Jesus, help me, Lord Jesus, help me, I can't go up against this one all by myself. The Armageddon is supposed to be the whole host of Heaven, the Forces of Light . . . Lord Jesus, don't leave me in here with . . . oh, my God, nooooo . . .* She stopped breathing.

He closed his eyes, walked away, and placed his hands on top his head, lacing his fingers together and then took several deep breaths.

"It looks like Eden in here. Why do you *do* that? None of us can go back there. Leave it. That is the past. Bless Eve. And then you call me here like this for a Neteru-to-Neteru challenge and expect . . ." He spun on her, raked her with a hot gaze, and pointed toward her blade. "Put. It. Down. Now."

Her blade lowered to her side. "Neteru to Neteru?" She was speechless.

"I told you what I was not. You never gave me allowance for what I might have been. But do not *ever* again make the comparison to the one who I never name. *Not in my presence* or I refuse to be in yours." He ripped his robe from his thick shoulders, exposing his massive chest. The shredded fabric pooled at his feet. Sudden rage made the muscles beneath his damp brown skin expand and contract, as golden-silver threads began to overtake his irises. She stared at his eyes and watched his breath hitch at her visual invasion. Hers matched the pause, and then her eyes followed the silvery mark that covered his heart. It was all she could do to tear her sight away from his sculpted, naked torso and bring her line of vision back up to his handsome face.

"No demon can reproduce one of those," she whispered. "Not even in illusion."

"No. They cannot. Not even at the bottom of the realms." His statement came out on a ragged breath. "I am the second male of our kind ever created," he added proudly, "and I function from a place of honor." He straightened his already perfect posture, still seeming indignant from her previous assumption of who he could have been.

For a moment, only their shallow breaths were heard echoing within the now-too-constricted confines of her spacious bathroom. Her brain scrambled to assimilate the information. Second male Neteru ever made? If this was a fact, he was a seriously older being . . . had to be spirit . . . and if this was what was guiding her music, Lord have mercy.

"Where did you come from?" Her tone had mellowed in the wake of pure awe. Curiosity and something else she wasn't prepared to name strangled her reason.

His gaze caressed hers. "From the Land of Nod."

She stepped forward, the pain within him drawing her closer than advisable. The reference dangled within her overloaded mind, but she couldn't geographically place where he meant. Slowly, the earthy, alluring scent of him wafted toward her, causing her lids to become heavy. This was the sexiest entity she'd ever encountered in her life. She had to remember that she wasn't supposed to allow her brain to go anywhere near there. Before she knew it, she heard her Isis clatter to the tile floor, abandoned. "What *is* your name?"

He shook his head and looked away. "It will make you pick up your blade again, and that cannot happen. Suffice it to say that, this time around, I am my brother's keeper. His will be done." He chuckled sadly, walked toward her, and then reached out an unsteady hand to touch her cheek with the tips of trembling fingers. "Oh, Damali, I have learned, and time teaches with a hard rod. Love, if I could save you time and turmoil, I would. But it is not my place, but if it were . . . if only it were."

She almost closed her eyes and fought within herself to back away a bit. The light touch burned where it fell. The level of pent-up need beneath it transmitted right into her skin and fused with the shiver he'd sent down her spine. "Then how did you get in here as a spirit?"

He stepped closer. "I'm both spirit and flesh," he murmured. "There was a time when I could . . ."

"Don't come closer. Explain." She needed distance, battle space, if necessary, but definitely a moment to get her head together. This being was setting off erotic depth charges within her that had awakened her body to a level of desire that was only supposed to be experienced with the one man she'd committed herself to.

"My apologies," the entity said quietly, but his eyes told her he was anything but sorry. "I may have been abrupt in approaching you in this manner . . . but I was so moved." He lifted his chin, the muscle pulsing in his jaw, and crossed the room. "An explanation is, indeed, in order."

"Thank you," she said, able to catch her breath only once he'd crossed the room.

"You feel guilt because you have committed to another in the flesh. I understand."

They stared at each other. She wasn't sure where this was going, and knew in her soul she shouldn't inquire more . . . but . . .

He nodded. "I was your first lover. Do not forget that."

"Okay, now you're tripping." She forced herself to chuckle, but her laughter faded as she stared at his intensely serious eyes. It was hard to laugh off a warm-bodied, fine, very naked spirit entity that was sculpted to perfection, standing in her bathroom with an erection that wouldn't quit. She had to get him out of her house, *now.*

"During your first yearnings, I was there. I came through your music. I, alone, was with you during your first Neteru ripening." He drew a long, shuddering breath, and sent his gaze beyond her window, and then closed his eyes. "You wanted to be loved so badly it came through your music. The moment of conception of each line . . . sweet agony."

As she stared at him, he began to slowly pace back and forth at the far side of the room wearing only a Neteru blade harnessed down the center of his back, and leaving her trapped between feeling horrified, flattered, violated, and extremely turned on. His primal male scent filled the room in indigo spires that ransomed her senses. She couldn't help but stare at the sculpted symmetry of his back, watching a labyrinth of steel-cable sinew work under his polished copper skin all the way down to the dip that created a valley in his spine and gave rise to a tight, muscular ass . . . and thighs . . . and calves. He was a gorgeous male specimen if ever there was one.

Swirls of color began to fill his aura as he made a tent with his long graceful fingers in front of his mouth and collected his thoughts, his body-light literally beginning to fuse with the multihued prisms coming through the stained glass. It was the most sublimely erotic thing she'd ever witnessed as his skin absorbed and reflected the light. Then he suddenly stopped, turned, looked at her hard, and opened his arms.

"Damali, *I am apexing.* For an *entire year* you left me—for him! You married him in a realm that is not even to be spoken of, and your loyalty shunned me for that. If you have so chosen to be his wife, *then be his wife in the Light.* Make it a legitimate bond from the high realms so that I may not cross to you again, but as long as there is ambiguity, you torment me!" he shouted. Tears filled his eyes and his voice became gravelly. "I could take it, before. Before the veil between our worlds had been pierced and I was mere spirit, I could take it! But I cannot take it as flesh."

"I didn't know, I never knew—"

"Tonight, you wanted to be alone with me, on this summer solstice eve, *while I am apexing* . . . while I need you now more than you can comprehend . . . after a year of abstinence from you, your body quivered for the touch of creative conception." He pointed toward the filled bath. "Salt water carries a charge, a *current*. Your voice carried the caress directly to me. Your spirit opened the door and willed me through it. Your skin ignited the tub, and if I were a younger man without some measure of will, I would have become manifest right in there with you when you opened your beautiful legs to the suds! Why do you haunt me so?"

She opened her mouth and closed it. Watching his desire build fed hers until she almost couldn't stand. Damali reached out her hand to lean against the door frame. "Listen," she said, her words coming out in a breathy pant, "I . . ."

He walked to the foot of the tub and snatched up his torn robe. "And you now have extreme carnal knowledge to add to my misery? Before you knew, when you were still a virgin, even then I could withstand . . . but after, I will never rest!" he said, briefly closing his eyes. "Your music is different, deeper, huskier, sultrier, and builds on experience to crescendo in a way that only a woman with such knowledge could make happen. Mercy. I implore your compassion."

He looked up toward her skylight, as though addressing Heaven as he continued to speak. "I was to learn selfless sacrifice for my offenses. I did that. Eons of what you call lessons are only masqueraded torture for me. And this last trial is beyond my endurance—I cannot teach her and remain distant! It is her choice; free will. We must all abide by that."

His eyes lowered to meet hers, his voice a hoarse whisper of want that radiated in heat waves throughout the semilit room, making the candles sputter. "Damali, my love, there have been nights when I have wanted to take my own blade to my throat." His voice faltered, and he pulled on the ragged garment. "Do you not understand the relationship between creative conception, sound waves, and emotion? We were lovers. Oh, yes, Damali, and I loved you well," he whispered, "and the things you did to me are beyond compare."

Her jaw went slack. His impassioned confession was turning her legs
to jelly. He'd already caused her to swell and slick moisture to build between her thighs. Her nipples stung so badly that it was all she could do
not to cover them with her hands.

"Tonight, after your panic, whereby you thought I was what shall not
be named, your lover will come to you, and he will benefit from this
conversation." He looked at her, not allowing her eyes to leave his. "I
have accepted that. You should as well. There is no guilt to be had in
such things. Your body requires it, and my desire is that you never suffer
want. But do know that just as he has provided for you, *so have I*. Do not
diminish my value or my commitment."

She raked her fingers through her locks. Her brain was screaming. "I
can't be with him and be with you at the same time. I can't think of you
while I'm making love to him. What are you saying?" She clutched her
hair as the renewed horror of it shot through her. "That isn't right."

His eyes glittered with a level of knowledge that she couldn't fathom,
and his lush mouth offered her a sly, primal, sexy smile. "Damali," he
breathed, "every high note you've hit belonged, in part, to me."

"No, no, no no, no," she said, beginning to frantically pace. "There
were times when it was just him and me and no music in the mix.
Most times. Only on occasion was I composing in my head while with
him. No."

"Oh, yes . . ." he said, the bass in the tone of his response bottoming
out at the pit of her stomach, causing it to clench. "You compose your
best music when you are making love. I will admit that there were times
you denied me. I acknowledge his private possession of you with the utmost respect." He nodded and gave her a slight bow with a disarming
smile. "However, just before and just after, you are *always* mine. When he
was not there, and you needed to be touched, I was *always* there. He is
not the only one that produces delirium . . . or gives you white knuckles as you clench the sheets. Do be honest with yourself, if not with me."
He inhaled sharply, and let the thought fester between them for a moment. "When you are—"

"Stop," she murmured, holding up her hand.

"Why?"

She stared at him for a moment.

"Because."

He nodded. "I understand that, as well." He waited a beat, his devastating smile drawing her eyes to his mouth. "When you thought he was dead, and you ripened alone . . . lover, I was there for it all. Thank you."

"Don't," she said, and gathered her arms around herself, closing her eyes against her will. "Too raw."

"Yes. Very. And Jose became superimposed on that urgent impression because he felt every shiver in your music . . . he, too, is an artist, and could appreciate the depth of the emotion in your creation. He didn't just hear it, like me, *he felt it*, and it spawned his own creation amid the torment." The entity released a long, steady exhale. "I cannot fathom how he lived in the same house with you, in the flesh, and remained faithful. I must study that further, and meditate upon it for my own strength. But, then, he is also not a Neteru, thus, perhaps his torment was more manageable? However, when you sing, your voice still slaughters him. You might as well be making love to the man."

"I know. Leave Jose out of this discussion," she whispered, not looking at him. She couldn't. She wanted to fill his arms so badly she was almost rocking.

"For a long time, even some nights, you have haunted him. Is that why you do not create with the group now? Are you afraid of what could manifest?"

Damali simply nodded.

The being sighed and nodded. "Misplaced guilt. You must correct that error within your mind. You will no more cross that unspoken boundary than he will. You each are grounded and tethered to others within this incarnation—but you must deal with it, or you are bound to repeat it."

Her eyes sought his, holding a plea. "I can't go through this again. Everything I've been through. No."

"Then address whatever you must address, now." The silver within his eyes flared slightly with an inhale that made his nostrils follow suit. "I have been doomed to repeatedly incarnate until I have mastered this last lesson of selfless sacrifice. This is why I implore you to learn your lessons well during this gift of human experience." He smiled sadly. "You are my greatest challenge, yet."

"I don't want to kick up any mess on the team, or do anything that could—"

"All artists feed off each other," he said flatly. "Inspired works in one dimension ignite inspiration in another, an unending fractal of pure light, combined thought . . . energy cells splitting and forming something new. Do not fear your art. Do not give it away or close it off, no matter where it takes you. Abandon it not. No more than you would give away your Isis for fear of how it cuts; your music is a part of your soul. No husband should make you fear its genesis or revelations. That is your alpha and omega within this life—not your lover. Not flesh."

Again, she nodded but refused to meet his eyes with her own. "Which is why waves of similar songs, books, films, and three-dimensional art often seem to be born in the same eras?"

His low gasp cut through her skeleton. "Yes, oh God, yes."

"Your voice, I can't . . ." she admitted. "Resist."

"Nor I, yours," he said. "Not when you are learning, creating, building to a crescendo of pure knowledge, thought. I have all but surrendered to it." Urgency filled his eyes as they searched her face. "Just tell me yes . . . permit me, just once, to hear it with you, now, in the flesh. Speak to me as I love you in total."

Her lips parted as he walked toward her. She could feel the warmth oozing from his skin, capturing the light off the floor, adding to the pure sexuality he radiated. "I can't."

He stopped, but his breaths dragged in and out of his chest like a man drowning. "Then create for me . . . your most desire-filled work. Tonight . . . *please.*"

She nodded. "This feels like I'm having an affair." She smiled weakly.

"You are. Surrender to it."

Again, only silence and a very small portion of bathroom tile stood between them. Guilt clawed at her insides, leaving her conflicted by the pure want that had overtaken the whole of her. "Carlos did a lot of shit, but doesn't deserve that."

He nodded. "My condition makes me irrational." The being sighed and walked away from her. "Then, perhaps," he murmured, keeping his back to her, "you might compose a very heart-wrenching selection of what it is like to burn for something you should not have?"

She nodded. "That you have inspired, for sure."

"Anything," he whispered, "will devastate me now." He turned slowly, a sensual smile gracing his beautiful mouth. "There is always a way for us to be together, within the limits of righteousness."

She chuckled to break the tension. "Now you sound more like a male vampire than a male Neteru."

He laughed low and deep and sensually, and shook his head. "I am *everything* that you have experienced . . . and most assuredly male." Again, his smile faded to burn her with an expression of unfulfilled want. "Admit it, if not to me, then to yourself. You want to fully know me in the worst way, right now."

She couldn't, or better stated, wouldn't answer the charge. Not while wearing a towel, him half-naked, and this much heat radiating between them. All she had to do was think about the music that swept through her while she grieved Carlos, or to remember the lusty nights of splendor in his arms that gave birth to her best work. Days of laughter, jamming with Jose, endless moments alone, doodling in her journal, sparking ideas, working out lyrics, getting in touch with every emotion that had ever filled her. Her eyes locked with his as a hard shudder ran through him.

"You know me, Damali. I am no stranger or violator."

"I know," she whispered. "Thank you for always being with me." She swept her hand down her stomach. "I just can't sync up the physical manifestation with the spiritual. As long as you were the spirit of creativity, I could cope."

"As could I. But all that has changed."

"What do we do about it?"

"You tell me?"

She looked away. "I don't know."

"We have more in common than you will admit."

She chuckled. "You're working me, brother."

"Yes, I am." He smiled. "But I have also been honest about my condition."

"True," she said, no judgment in her tone. The thing that was still blowing her mind was the fact that an apexing male spirit Neteru was in her bathroom. How in the . . .

"Do not ask me again, please." His voice was an urgent whisper. Palpable desire made the colors on the floor around him shimmer brighter. "To revisit that just runs through me like a river."

His hands found her upper arms and delivered a firm yet gentle pull toward him. Her first instinct was to resist, but what was that now, she wondered? The moment her body fused against his, the moan he released set off a tremor through her womb that parted her lips.

A hot mouth covered hers and the sweetness contained within it was like pure narcotic. His tongue ravaged the soft tissue of hers, gliding against her teeth, finding the roof of her mouth, and then deepened as the pressure of his hold increased. His kiss of life created a tremor that stirred a bubbling whimper that made her nearly faint. Music tore through her, blinding her mind with its intensity. Colors shot beneath her lids and buckled her knees. The sound he emitted inside her mouth fractured her conscience, and produced a vibrating echo in her lungs, dredging up a low moan from her that should have never been released. The next thing she knew, her towel was on the floor. A strange new pair of male hands covered her back like hot wax, melting her beneath them with every stroke, and her returned kisses were harder than they ever should have been. The song roiled inside her, quickly escalating from a sultry slow pulse of bass to implode with a demanding staccato fusion treble. Acapella agony changed key, bridged to punishing instrumental, and ended on a long mental carry near a soprano shriek that she delivered right into his mouth.

"Your voice," he gasped, breaking the kiss to breathe the words out against her neck. "That is my river. My weakness. Your mind, my undoing. Damali, let me love you hard, right here, right now, in this key." His damp forehead dropped to her shoulder. "For the love of God, do not deny me."

"We can't do this," she said, practically losing consciousness in his hold.

"Then give yourself to him tonight, like this, with me in your mind. Just call me."

When he dragged his jaw along her throat and bit her, she literally saw stars. But that's when she also held him by the shoulders and put an inch between them. He dropped his hold on her, ran his fingers through his hair, and walked to the far side of the room.

"I'm sorry," he said quietly. "That was never supposed to happen. You're already marked, and I know that." He was panting, beginning to walk in a circle, the level of agitation and frustration making several candle flames dance wildly before going out. "The Neteru mind lock is . . . Damali, I have to go." His eyes held a quiet plea. "I have been with many women and have had many wives over decades of apexes, but never . . ." He stopped, swallowed hard, and leaned on the far wall with one hand, staring at the floor, steadying his breaths. "You will make me sire in the flesh, and that also cannot happen. With you, it is forbidden."

Still breathless from the near miss, she hunted him for an explanation with her eyes. "What is your name?" she asked in a gentle tone that made him close his eyes and swallow hard again. "If you're Heaven sent then you're safe." Immediately, she shook her head. "What am I saying!" She snatched up her towel and wrapped it around her body with precision. "I've lost my freakin' mind."

He nodded, winded, and kept his gaze to the floor until she was covered, and then closed them again to stem the pain. "So have I." When he opened his eyes he simply stared at her. "No. I'm not safe. But now I truly understand so much more." His gaze searched hers. "The conundrum is neither are you, detriment of my soul. I must leave."

"No, wait," she heard herself say while her mind yelled the central question: Was she crazy? But she had to know what had just happened in this very insane moment. "I have so much more to ask you," she whispered. "You've been just the music before. I don't understand how you could have materialized like this."

"You loved it so hard, and it was the only way I could love you in return. Through sound. We have just crossed a barrier that should not have been trifled with, all emotion notwithstanding." His chest was heaving as he spoke. "I want to fill you with living music so badly right now that I cannot summon reason."

She stared at him, a hundred new questions slamming into her mind as her gaze locked with his dark, intense eyes. There were times when it felt like the music was literally making love to her . . . in her mind, inside her spirit, releasing her soul . . . something so profoundly intimate as it was being created that not even her living lover could fathom from whence it came.

As the awareness filled her, the being shuddered, shut his eyes tightly, and turned his face away as though she'd slapped him.

"Yes . . . and I have told you, that was when it was only the two of us," he whispered, breathing out the words.

The pull to this unnamed male being was so intense that she had to redouble her efforts to keep her feet firmly planted where she stood. He'd actually let his head drop back, exposing his throat, and the urge to score his jugular made her tremble.

"If you do that which you are battling not to do," he said in a low warning, looking up slowly, "we shall be lost. Score me, and it will be

all over. No going back to what was only spirit. *Then* you *will* have to
tell him." He began to move toward her again, raw lust making his
strides long and slow. "Or, if you find that too daunting, I can tell
him?"

"I'm committed, have a person who . . . I didn't mean to manifest . . . and I also didn't mean to bring you pain, in any way. I can't do
this to him, but I have to be able to sing, do my music, work." Tears were
brimming in her eyes, the frustration to go to him more acute than anything she'd ever experienced. She let out a breath of relief when he
stopped advancing. The sound of her voice had become so strident it almost shattered the windows. Pure panic swelled within her as she fought
her own emotions. "I don't understand this male Neteru stuff, you being
one in spirit, but also being a muse . . . are you from the Male Neteru
Council? I don't know what they have on their side, his side—but you
can't come to me like this again, it's too . . ."

"*Intense,*" he murmured, slowly bringing his gaze up to decimate her.
"Like nothing I have *ever* encountered."

He stared at her and stroked her neck with his thumb by merely
touching his own. She covered his hand by hiding the phantom-caressed
place that burned against her throat and stopped the sensual invasion that
caused a near gasp. Her Sankofa tattoo was burning up, sending waves of
desire up her back. She watched him place his hand over his heart, as
though trying to stop the burn tormenting the angry, silver symbol lit
beneath his palm. The moment he touched it, her head dropped back
from the shudder it released within her.

"Oh, God . . ." The words pressed past her lips on an elongated gasp.

"Damali, you have to work without me. I cannot withstand this any
longer." He brought his hand away from his chest trembling, the fabric
covering his symbol smoldering.

"I know." But she didn't move away like she knew she should have.

Again, his gaze flowed over her and came to rest at her mouth. "If I
stay much longer, I promise you I'll break my younger brother's
heart . . . and that will ultimately kill him . . . which will be my second
offense of a similar nature. I need to go. The music between us will keep
for another night when we can handle it."

"Who is your brother?" Quiet panic knotted her stomach. He was
becoming mist and the frustration of not knowing felt like a stab

wound. "Please, if you don't share anything else, at least tell me that."

"Carlos," he whispered, then was gone.

Damali walked back and forth between the door and the far wall, punching the door each time she passed it. Oh, shit, oh shit, oh fucking shit!

Her head jerked up when she heard pounding on her front door. She knew who it was, and it was the last person that needed to be there—even though her SOS had probably summoned him.

"What's wrong?" Carlos yelled, materializing inside her bedroom and crossing the room in battle mode.

Damali closed her eyes and picked up her Isis. What was she gonna tell him?

"Where is it? Level Seven—baby, get out of here, now!"

"It wasn't what I thought it was," she said carefully.

Carlos stopped, looked around the bathroom and at her blade, confusion glittering in his eyes. "You put out an all-points bulletin. You were mentally shouting—"

"I know, I know, I know—"

"Guardians are on the way and the Covenant is mounting up. Baby, if who we think blew through your bathroom did, then—"

She shut her eyes, held up her hand, and couldn't look at him. "I wigged. I was in here composing, dark thoughts, uh, I thought, listen, I'm cool."

He blinked twice and stared at her. "You're lit up like a Christmas tree, girl. Got a fucking Isis blade in your grip and you're squeezing it so hard the metal is digging into your fist. Now, I may be many things, but stupid ain't one of 'em."

Carlos walked around the bathroom, inspecting. He looked at the white bath and the dead candles and inhaled. "Something male came in here and freaked you out. If you were in a white bath and it manifested, then you need to give it to me straight, give the team a full breakdown of what could have made you bug like that, feel me?"

She nodded, too ashamed to speak. What was she going to say, I almost laid my muse, and what's in here is the sloppy aftermath of a musical tryst that went carnal? "Baby," she said, unshed tears catching in her throat, "I love you."

He pulled her to him hard with possessiveness and crushed her head to his chest. "I love you, too, girl. I'm not gonna let anything happen to you, no matter what."

She hid her face against his T-shirt and breathed in deeply, a repressed sob making her body shake. "I know." She could feel Carlos's gaze scanning the room.

"Like I said, whatever it was, it was male, with high sexual charge on the shit, too. I can feel that rippling over my skin, and the motherfucker wanted you bad, baby." He pulled Damali away from him and stared at her, his eyes glowing solid silver. "Did it try to violate you? Tell me, and I'll take its head off."

That's when the tears started flowing in earnest. What was there to say? Yeah, true, he'd had near misses with were demons, female vamps, even Juanita and probably a bunch of shit she'd never know about . . . but, still.

"I knew it!" he yelled, not waiting for her answer. Carlos stalked away from her, punched the door, and stalked back to her. "Damn! That's it, no more arguments, you're moving in with me—period."

She just stared at the man. How in the hell was she gonna move in with him, now, and risk a possible catastrophe? It was that, or abandon her muse forever, which, strangely, she wasn't exactly ready to do. However, Carlos's deadly accurate male instinct unnerved her. She picked at a lame excuse and offered it to him slowly. "Let's not jump to conclusions, baby, we should—"

"No, Damali!" he hollered. "I have *never* heard you put out a fear SOS like that since we've been together. Ever! That shit ran all through me, you were pleading with *Jesus* to save you, girl. You and I have been to Hell, done master vamps together, freaking demons from every level, and you were never cold-bloodedly afraid, like *that*. So, whatever blew through here had to be serious. It had to be something you and I have never dealt with, right?"

"It was," she said quietly, and went to the tub to calmly let the water out. Man, if this was what he felt when he'd almost gotten with that Amazon, or got temporarily freaky with 'Nita, she would never say a mumblin' word to the man for his past indiscretions. She vowed from this point forward to live in the moment, no signifying, no mild references, *nada*. Cold busted. All she could think of was what would have happened if a few more moments had passed, if she'd totally just lost her mind . . . for him to walk in on *that* . . . there would be no words. Humiliation made her face burn.

"Then my point remains."

She nodded and kept her back to Carlos, watching the water swirl down the drain and all her dreams along with it.

⊘ CHAPTER FOUR

A war party had convened in her living room. Damali sat on the large, overstuffed African-print chair by the window studying the texture of threads in her jeans. The fabric of her light cotton T-shirt felt like sandpaper against her skin. The noise level was deafening as her people argued about what could have possibly invaded her home.

True, she had been the one to accidentally send an SOS, but it still didn't seem to warrant all of this. She was emotionally exhausted and could now only imagine how Carlos must have felt trying to explain the inexplicable to a whole squad of amped warriors, especially about his many highly personal transgressions.

She cringed as the misinformation ricocheted around the room and her people formed flawed theories about an incident too delicate to fully disclose. Her body was still on fire. She needed space, time to mull over what had happened privately. Part of her just wanted to blurt out the truth and send everybody home; the other part of her just wanted to crawl under the rug. Now, with a full-scale investigation underway, their concerns led to queries that bordered on what felt like an inquisition.

Ironically, Carlos had been the one to show her how to totally detach and mentally distance herself from probing questions. She'd seen the brother do it a hundred times. He'd just get silent, look off in the distance, and set his jaw hard. When he went there, nobody could break through, not her, not Mar, and not even Father Pat. There was a certain level of compelling wisdom in saving one's personal sanity at a time like this. Dang!

The song that had blistered her mind continued to pop and sizzle within her brain. The voices of her team were becoming very far away.

Stanzas opened up a sanctuary for her to escape through, and put up a wall blocking anyone's invasion. A sassy, irreverent little tune threatened to make her smile as she abandoned the sad one for a more upbeat melody to make herself feel better.

Damali kept her gaze on the threads in her jeans, focused on the varying hues of blue. The entity that visited her had that same color running through his aura. She was almost humming. She could visualize herself strutting across the stage, finger wagging to an up-tempo beat, telling some phantom brother off. She really wanted to laugh.

> *Just because I can*
> *Don't mean that I should.*
> *Just because I wanna*
> *Don't mean that I would.*
> *I'm not the kinda girl who'll let you play with her mind . . .*

"Damali!" Carlos was in her face. "You act like you ain't even in the room. Marlene has a valid point."

Damali jerked her focus away from her jeans and stared up at Carlos. Her glance shot between him and Marlene, and she felt like she was back in school, not paying attention to the teacher, and was now called on to answer some question she hadn't even heard.

"Marlene is very wise," she said, covering her lack of involvement. "Mar, take it from the top, slowly, so I can really think about it in another light."

"The girl's in a near-trance," Shabazz said, standing. "It might still be in here."

Marlene simply stared at Damali for a moment, but was gracious enough to oblige her request. Both women knew the deal, she hadn't been listening.

"Did it physically manifest and contact you audibly in any way?" Marlene's penetrating gaze locked with Damali's.

It took Damali a moment to respond. This was the moment of truth. Was she going to give up the tapes, or not? Not.

"Like I told you, I just felt a presence," Damali said as calmly as possible. "A current rippled across the surface of the water and blew the candles out. That's when I wigged, jumped out of the tub, grabbed my blade, and sent a premature SOS. That's all."

Although her story was plausible, the eyes around the room didn't seem like they were buying it. Father Patrick's voice broke through on the speakerphone, adding to the challenge.

"The current, child," the elderly priest said through the technology, his tone strained, "was it a dark one, or blue-white in nature?"

"Blue-white," Damali said quietly. "It was all good."

"Yeah, darlin', but what made a battle-seasoned vet like you wig from blue-white light?" Rider asked, his eyes holding both sadness and worry.

Damali shrugged. "I was tired, not prepared for a guide or any spiritual anything. I just wanted to relax in the tub and chill. So, when whatever it was tried to contact me, I sorta lost it."

Jose nodded. "Been there. Look y'all, maybe this was just a fluke. Seriously. D's been through a lot, like we all have. Everyone of us is gonna have nightmares and day jitters from time to time."

"Post-battle stress syndrome, most likely," Big Mike concluded, and relaxed. But he gave Damali a look as though he'd heard a lie in her voice.

"Well, I for one think this poor girl has been through enough to turn her hair white," Marjorie agreed. "If I see a shadow in my own closet, I'm ready to jump out of my skin."

"You sure you wanna be over here by yourself, kiddo?" Berkfield asked, his tone concerned and parental. "We've got a coupla extra suites in the house, and you can always come home for a few, just until the heebie-jeebies wear off."

Damali let her breath out hard. "No, y'all. I'm all right, and I apologize for the alarm. I'll be cool here."

"I don't know, D," Jose hedged. "We know you need your own space, but sometimes a dose of family is good for the soul." He stood and began to pace. "I know it's hard to create in the household chaos, but the studio is soundproof. We all miss you, maybe think of it as a week's vacation and just play it by ear for a short visit?"

"Jose has a point," Carlos said, nodding as he went toward him to pound his fist. "My joint is too far from the group, and even though I don't think anything would be stupid enough to try to roll up on me in it, there could be times when you'd be in there by yourself. Somebody is always home in the house."

"Right, D," Inez said, throwing her two cents into the pot. "Girl, listen, I'm still not right with all this mess we're living with. I wouldn't mind being your shadow."

"Me, either," Krissy said, glancing at J.L.

"Think about it, D," J.L. said, leaning forward with his hands open.

"If anyone would know, Father Pat would know," Bobby said, raking his hair.

"Father Pat," Dan said, looking at the speakerphone. "What's your take?"

"I agree," Father Patrick replied, his gruff tone more of a command than a simple affirmation. "Better safe than sorry. Something within you sensed a Level-Seven vibration. I'm still a little jittery from it myself."

"Then it's settled," Carlos announced, folding his arms over his chest and looking at Damali hard. "Pack some—"

"It's not settled until *I* say it is," Damali said very quietly, very firmly, and never blinking as she stared at Carlos. When was this man going to learn that she was grown and not his property? She could feel the old resentment from earlier that day creeping back into her and firing up defiance. If she'd just flowed with her emotions, she would have laid the entity in her bathroom and this conversation wouldn't be taking place!

"Damali is grown," Juanita said, coolly entering the fray. "If she feels comfortable here, so be it."

Damali stared at Juanita. Of all people, Juanita was the *last* person she'd expect to have her back—albeit for her own selfish reasons. But Juanita didn't need to say a word to her. Fight adrenaline brimmed within Damali as her gaze narrowed by a hair. Yeah, that heifer didn't want her anywhere near the group house. There wasn't enough room in the mansion for the both of them; that was a fact. And Juanita would be sweating her and Jose while they were trying to work. Jose knew it, too.

New tension riddled the group, keeping everyone quiet for a moment. Before she could form a snappy comeback, a slow awareness dawned within Damali.

How many times had Juanita or Carlos broken up the groove on a jam session? How many times when she and Jose were fusing, rockin', creating the most awesome sounds, did one or the other of those two nonartistic types have an issue, or try to sabotage the connection by creating drama, and pulling them away from what they were doing? And, perhaps more importantly, how often did she and Jose allow it? Suddenly her muse's complaint began to make a whole lotta sense.

"You might have a point, Jose," Damali said, ignoring Juanita and giving crisp credit to the only person in the room who'd asked her without commanding her. She held Jose's line of vision, totally cutting Carlos out of her gaze as though he wasn't in the room. It grated her the way Carlos came at her, demanding. Fuck all that, she was her own woman. "A week, jamming, having some free mental space to create, get my head back into my music, might not be a half-bad idea."

Jose smiled. "Take it a day at a time, D. No pressure. You get back into the studio, start working again, soon you'll get caught up in that, focused, and your nerves will calm out. That's probably all that's wrong with you . . . I know I need to do that, too. Been away from my music for too long."

"Yeah," Damali murmured. "Me, too. Thanks, Jose."

Nervous glances passed around the group. Rider pushed off the wall, his gaze sweeping between Carlos, Damali, and Jose. "We'll get a room together for you. It's already set up, actually. All you have to do is bring some clothes, and we can wait here while you throw some stuff in a bag."

Shabazz exchanged a look with Rider and Big Mike. "Carlos, man, you might wanna consider crashing with us, too, for a coupla days. If something untoward went after one Neteru, it might come for the other one—you. Not that anybody is saying you can't handle your business, but like Father Pat said, better safe than sorry."

She watched Carlos bristle at the suggestion. *Yeah,* she thought, *so how do you like feeling boxed in? Ain't fun, is it?*

"There's three extra suites in there," Damali said, now looking at Carlos. "One in each wing, plus a guest room on the third floor for when the clerics roll through. You can have your space; I can have mine. You take whichever one you want."

For a moment, he just stared at her. She didn't care; she wanted it on record that she wasn't living with him. She wasn't cohabitating in his suite. He wasn't running her under any roof, especially not within the compound. He needed to know that just because she was taking a few clothes home to recharge her batteries, that wasn't a green card to invade her space, get in the way of her creative process, or to otherwise be a pain in her ass.

"I think that is a wise suggestion," Father Patrick said over the speakerphone. "That way, at the very least, we'll all sleep better at night."

"I'll go with you on this one, Father Pat, only because *you* said so, and your instincts are usually dead on." Carlos glared at Damali. His tone was salty. He shot a glance at Shabazz. "Good lookin' out, man."

The situation had disintegrated to a point beyond her endurance. Damali abruptly stood and walked out of the room. The meeting was over. She needed to throw a few clothes into a duffel bag to deal with the inevitable. Why Carlos was irking her, she wasn't sure. Yeah, they'd had a fight, but he had come when he thought something was seriously wrong. She kept weighing the two extremes, vacillating between being moved and enraged. If she could just forget about his most recent walk on the dark side with Juanita, she knew she would have mentally filtered his response an entirely different way.

All she knew right now was, for some unknown reason, he was working her last nerve. She didn't feel like playing twenty questions. She didn't feel like mind locking to get to the root of some unknown source of visitation. She didn't feel like being smothered by his overprotective presence. She didn't feel like having him all up on her and in her world. Right now, all she wanted to do was pick back up on the strand of music that was splitting her skull. There was a sultry sound within her that had become her pulse, and that demanded a response. She sought sanctuary in her bedroom.

Yanking her dresser open, she dug into it and found some T-shirts and jeans, and then pulled out her underwear drawer so hard it almost fell. Marlene's quiet presence made her look up, and she watched Marlene calmly shut the bedroom door behind her. Marlene slowly walked across the room, stood next to her, and placed a gentle hand on her shoulder.

"I know how you feel," Marlene murmured. "Every time you get out of the house and on your own, some crazy mess happens that sends you back into the family clutches."

Damali stopped rooting in the drawer and closed her eyes. She took in deep breaths, surprised to find herself on the verge of tears. "My art is suffering, Mar," Damali whispered on a mucus-filled swallow. "I need to get back to my music. A year away from it has been too long. I haven't even collected any new stones or anything spiritual lately—not even when we went to Tibet. Tibet!"

"Yes, it has," Marlene said quietly, referring to her music and not commenting on the stones. "There have been a lot of distractions."

Damali nodded, sniffed, and opened her eyes. "Tell me about it."

Both women looked at each other and a silent understanding bonded them.

"Have you ever felt like this, Mar? Like every time you carve out some quality private time just for you, something comes crashing in on it?"

Marlene smiled and then chuckled, pulling Damali into a brief, warm embrace. "Baby . . . oh, Lawdy. I have stories for you."

The gentle communion and gracious validation made Damali smile and then chuckle, too.

"Damali, girl . . . just like children, a man can soak up the universe, it seems. He can expand, take up space, and move your planets out of alignment. That's all that's the matter. You are demanding your own orbit, and he's fighting you with all the gravitational pull of a jealous male." Marlene laughed softly, shaking her head. "He thinks he's the sun and everything should revolve around him. They all do. When we get home, me and Marj will teach you a few little tips on how to relegate him to just being the moon."

"Why do they do that shit?" Damali said through her teeth. "He goes off, does his thing, runs with his boys—and like what? I'm supposed to be on his schedule, his timetable, ready to stop, drop, and roll when he's ready to hook up? Puhlease."

"I know, chile," Marlene said, her eyes twinkling with mirth and the magic of hard-learned wisdom. "You have to train him to your schedule. Make your music a nonnegotiable thing. You can have both, namely, your craft and him, too. But you have to put boundaries around your art, give it the same level of importance that he gives the things beyond you in his life."

Damali nodded, the validation coating her with a sense of peace and making her lower her defenses. Oddly, that was just what her muse had said—give him his due.

Marlene sighed and released Damali from her hug. "Girl, they act like you have another man when it comes to your career or creative solitude. My momma used to say my daddy acted like that about her church, was as jealous of her time there as if she was out having an affair with another man. He used to—"

Damali snapped her head up and her eyes got wide. The reference to an affair pulled the muscles in her back into a tight chord. "For real? He was jealous of *church?*"

Marlene gave her a curious look and measured her words. "Yes . . ." Marlene's smile faded to a tight line and she dropped her voice. "Let's go into the bathroom. Just me and you."

Damali shook her head no. "Mar, listen . . . uh . . ."

"No," Marlene said in a tense whisper. "You listen. Been there, too. I don't even have to remind you of that drama that went down in Brazil and Arizona when my skeletons jumped out of the closet."

Both women giggled as Damali closed her eyes and Marlene pressed on in a private whisper.

"Now, honey, I'ma say this once. All that glitters ain't gold. Carlos is all male, typically so, and at times, a natural pain in the butt—however, he loves you and you love him. Work it out. One night on the wild side isn't worth losing everything you've built. And none of them are perfect, so, just because he did some mess, doesn't mean you have to retaliate to show—"

"I'm not retaliating. Mar, he's the only guy I've ever been with and now he's talking marriage, permanent lockdown. Sure, he's ready, cool with it, because he's been around the block enough times to make your head spin, but I never even *allowed* myself to sorta look around, and check out the horizon . . . what if I'm missing—"

"You do the testing and trying on new shoes *before* you find *the one.* After you've found him, it's the rare male animal that can accept that you've tried on another pair *after* him. Before is hard enough for them to swallow—*after,* it's not done."

Marlene's gaze was firm but nonjudgmental. "This Richards-Rivera pair is a perfect fit. You mighta spied some shiny new red stilettos in the window, girlfriend, but before the night is over, they might hurt your feet and might not be practical, no matter how good they look in the store. Got it?"

Damali chuckled and began rooting in her drawer again. "But they was a *fine* fly-ass pair of shoes—da butta."

"How fine?" Marlene asked with a smirk.

"Oh, girl . . ." Damali whispered, her eyes holding Marlene's with mischief.

They both covered their mouths and laughed hard behind their hands.

"This fine," Damali said, finally recovering and letting her voice dip to a sexy, sensual octave, before throwing her head back and crooning in a low whisper.

Lover . . . just love me hard and tender.
You asked, and I surrender.
Don't forget, when stars are falling
Your colors make me blind.
'Cause, see, lover . . .
Tonight I'm where I'm not supposed to be.
Not sure where that is or where you're from . . .
But lover . . . I'm about to, oh, yeah . . . lover . . .
Just breathe and I'll answer.
This thing is beyond right, but is it wrong?
When the moment is what it is . . .
The solstice burns the night to cinder,
Cuts hot gold and sends wet shivers
Lover . . . I'm trying to tell you . . .
Your whisper melts . . . my . . . yeah, my mind . . .
C'mon lover . . . don't play with the divine.
I ain't right when you stop time

"*That* is *dangerous,*" Marlene whispered hard, shaking her out of the song.

"Marlene, Marlene, Marlene . . . the brother stepped out of the astral plane, or some-danged-where, six-five, carrying a gold blade, older . . . a little silver at the temples, built like a brick-shit-house, and packing enough iron to make you squint—and is *a musician.*"

Marlene shook her head, let out a silent whew, and ran her palm over her locks. "Chile, please, be careful. Ask yourself if you're ready to risk the loss, because that's what it will come down to, a permanent decision based on your actions—you're in control of this dance. *Always* remember that. They don't have the emotional makeup to take it, if what I think mighta happened almost did. Don't do nothin' crazy, hear?"

"What are you, psychic now?" Damali said, chuckling at her own bad joke.

"Yeah," Marlene said with a conspiratorial smile. "So, talk to me. Who is this guy that had you calling on Jesus for help, huh?" Marlene smiled and closed her eyes. "Girlfriend, that was real bad form. Coulda caused a cosmic standoff."

Damali laughed quietly, wiping her eyes. "He was so fine and so smooth, he scared me, Mar. I ain't never had one roll up on me like that, I swear. I didn't know what to do."

"Who is he?" Marlene asked again, this time her tone carrying more concern.

"I don't know, but dayum!"

"Okay, sister. Pull it together. At least give me a name to run through my mental database and black book."

Damali stared at Marlene for a second and then burst out laughing. She covered her mouth and shook her head. "I don't know," she mumbled.

"You don't *know?*" Marlene was incredulous.

"I don't know his name," Damali said, wheezing through a sudden case of the giggles. "Didn't need it. If you'd seen him, you wouldn't have been focused on the details, either."

"Oh, Lord," Marlene said, placing her palm over her forehead as she stared at Damali. "Markings, description, something so I know not to flat-out ice this brother if he rolls up on you quietly in the compound."

Damali glanced around the room as though someone else might be there, and she leaned in to Marlene so closely that their noses almost touched. Her voice dropped to a hissing whisper. "Mar. He's a Neteru!"

"What!" Marlene said louder than she'd intended. "Oh, shit." She yanked Damali deeper into the room and then dragged her laughing into the bathroom and shut the second door. "You have *got* to be mistaken. Get out of here!"

"For real," Damali said, her gaze leaving Marlene's to scan the abandoned tub. "Girl, he had this sexy Neteru tattoo on his chest, eyes blazing gold *and* silver. Stepped out of nowhere, apexing, chile! Soaked up the colors from the light on my bathroom floor, and busted a move on me like . . . I get the shivers just telling you." Damali began walking in a circle as Marlene opened her mouth but didn't close it. "But I had enough sense to tell him to back up, I didn't know him well enough yet to jump into anything too wild, and . . . but, shit, he was apexing, and—"

"On the summer solstice? And you're a Leo—a child of the sun . . . ooohhh . . . shit!" Marlene ran her fingers through her locks and also began walking in a circle. "Chile, now you listen to old Mar, hear? This is nitroglycerine. Waaaay too volatile a situation to be joking around and playing with. Carlos, God bless his soul, will freak. Do you hear me? And, by rights, I need to diplomatically get up with Father Pat to find out when and where a second male Neteru could have been made. That's not even supposed to happen." She looked up at Damali with pure terror in her expression. "Unless we're at the *exact* end of days and Heaven is opening its gates."

"For real, Mar?" Damali said, new realities killing her mirth. "This is it?"

"How else would another one have gotten made?"

"He said he had to incarnate for this one last time to learn the lesson of selfless sacrifice, and I was going to be his biggest challenge yet." Damali was breathing hard and fast as she spoke in run-on sentences. "He said he could deal with guiding and teaching me, as long as he was in spirit, but the moment he came into the flesh, he was losing it. I mean, you should have seen this brother—but, but, I thought Nzinga was my guide, my Neteru mentor off the female council. How did he get to be my mentor, Mar? How come he's my music muse?"

"What!" Marlene nearly shouted again, and then clasped her hand over her own mouth for a second. "*Your muse?*" She grabbed Damali by both arms and her voice came out in a fast, rushing hiss. "Muses are supposed to be spirit-manifested inspiration, not flesh!"

"I know, I know," Damali whispered quickly. "He came to me while I was mentally composing in the tub!"

Marlene's eyes darted around the room. "He pierced the veil? Shit! Music is the most sensual . . . girl . . . oh, Lawd. Listen, sweetie—"

"Mar, he gets turned on and turned out every time I compose. How the hell am I gonna work, now?" Damali's voice had become a fervent plea. "He said I'd had him in abstinence for a year, hadn't communed with him, feel me? You should have seen him. Said, and I quote, 'detriment to my soul, I need you now.' The brother was begging so hard and so smooth . . . I almost fell on the floor. Then, then, Mar, he kissed me, sent a sound wave inside me that blew my freakin' mind. He was so upset he walked across the room, tripping, talking about how he had to go, wasn't supposed to be all in my face, but I guess since I'm at the apex of my craft, he's apexing within me, or connected to me, or some wild mad-crazy drama . . . and I have to create, have to sing, have to compose, that's as much a part of my life as fighting evil, but if my muse just up and manifested into rock-hard flesh—Marlene—he was hung like a damned Georgia mule!"

"I don't know, I don't know," Marlene whispered, swiftly spinning around to look over her shoulder. "We have to send him back, close the hole in the universe. This is a good entity, but you can't do him. It's like . . . like . . . sleeping with an angel—not done! If he gets put out of his realm, and if he rules music, music could die!"

Damali covered her mouth and silently screamed behind her hands, eyes wide. "When I hear music in my head, creating my own, it's like elongated foreplay for him." She finally breathed out, closing her eyes. "When I sing, this brother is *liquefied*." She gulped and grabbed Marlene by both arms, shaking her. "Are you hearing me? He kissed me and I gasped, and I thought it was all gonna be over. He almost had a—you know what I'm saying, just from my voice—it was the sexiest shit I've ever seen in my life! The rapture was all over his face. The shit was so intense I lost my towel, dropped my freaking Isis blade—didn't care, girl! I just wanted to *create*."

Marlene's eyes were so wide that tears had formed in them. "All right, let's get rational—we need a plan."

Damali's head bobbed as she released Marlene and wrapped her arms around herself.

"First off, we have to get a bead on what shifted things in the universe to pierce the veil."

Damali nodded, hanging on Marlene's every word as though she was listening to a doctor explain cancer. "He said time stopped." She shook her head. "Sho' he right!"

Both women looked at each other and spoke in unison. *"The tsunami."*

Marlene closed her eyes. "The Earth wobbled on its axis, it happened in the east—the lands of deep cultural expansion and the earth's clock is off by milliseconds."

"He walked though an invisible fold in the air like a curtain had parted. Said I was alone, calling him with composition. And, when I think back on it, I did mentally say, 'Muse, baby, where are you?' as I was trying to figure out chords and melodies for a new song that was taking shape in my mind. But I thought a muse was a metaphorical thing, and *female*, okaaaay? Not some fine-ass, six-five entity or deity that would rock my daggone world!"

Marlene stared at Damali. "Bingo." She let out a quick breath. "Okay. Then, he's not likely to manifest unless you're alone . . . we hope."

"We hope," Damali concurred.

"So, until we get him tucked away and back in spirit form, you only compose during the day with somebody in the room, cool?"

"Challenging, but it makes sense." Damali ran her hand over her hair. "But here's a question. If he manifested, what if more of them are walking from spirit into flesh and back again through this rip? Like, what if all sorts of positive guides, beings, whatever, that are normally support-ive, but detached, because they've left all earthly, flesh-created weaknesses behind to ascend, and are coming to their charges—as is their mission, but when they get to them, in the flesh form, they're bugging?"

The fact that Marlene just looked at her, stunned, pushed Damali dan-gerously close to hysterics. It was too crazy to totally comprehend. As the reality fully dawned on her, Damali pressed on, her quiet voice be-coming shrill.

"Mar, think about it. Like, what if your guardian angel just happened to be some tall, dark, fine warrior that always had your back, but as he comes to you to help you out of a jam, accidentally becomes flesh, and then wigs—because all of a sudden, all of the stimuli and intense feelings of the earth plane slam that brother? Blow his mind. Make him remem-ber what human life felt like? You understand where I'm going? Hous-ton, we have a problem, 'cause all I know is, muses demand creation. Demand conception. Are jealous lovers. *Must* sire something. *Have to* connect with the artist, or the artist will practically die if they can't give birth to what the muse has planted within them. And you and I both know that there is nothing on the planet more . . . more . . . sensual, ful-filling, or completing than giving birth to a new muse-inspired thing . . . an inventor must invent, a painter must paint, a writer must write, a—"

"Girl, we gotta close that door."

Damali nodded. "Marlene, if he rolls up on Carlos . . ."

"And Carlos kills music . . ."

"That's just it, Mar. I don't think Carlos can whup this brother's ass. You should have seen him."

Again, the two women just stared at each other.

"This Neteru is bad, Mar." Damali walked away. "I love my baby, and he ain't no slouch, but . . ."

"Damn," Marlene murmured with appreciation. "You think he could take *Carlos?*"

"Yeah, like I said," Damali whispered, just shaking her head. "You know how you knew in your heart that if Shabazz went up against Kamal it would be ugly."

Marlene closed her eyes and simply nodded. "Chile . . ."

"Uh-huh. Like that, Mar."

"Damn . . ."

"That's what I keep saying," Damali said, laughing as tears came to her eyes. "Now you see why I wigged?"

"You don't have to say another word," Marlene said, placing her hand over her heart.

"The worst part of it all is, Mar, right about through here, if . . ." Damali shivered and hugged herself and looked out the stained-glass window. "I've gotta get this song outta my head. He turned me on so bad that—"

Marlene held up her hand. "Been there." She sighed and looked at Damali. "Let me repeat. I know Carlos almost got with that were demon, but you now have intimate knowledge of the urge the brother was fighting from what was then his realm. The tables have obviously turned, and the Light is going through something we don't yet understand. But like I tried to tell you, it didn't have anything to do with how much Carlos loved you. It was something real crazy-primal, and for a few, she opened his nose. Now, the shoe, literally, is on the other foot. But you're not going to be able to throw his old dirty laundry up in his face to make a logical argument. This isn't about logic; it's pure emotion. He, as a man, is not going to process the situation with the same level of accepting grace that you, as a woman, did. And before you start arguing with me about what is fair, what's right, and the new millennium, and what have you—we both know, like you know in your soul, this will *not* go over well."

"So, keep it to myself and get it out of my system while we figure out how to close the rip." Damali let her breath out hard. Grace? Marlene just didn't know. Grace was the last word she'd choose to describe how she'd handled a recent scenario along those very lines. But Marlene was right, going tit for tat about Juanita or any of Carlos's other past misdeeds versus this entity would not go over well, if she slept with it—no matter what.

Marlene looked at her hard and smiled. "Take it to your grave. This is a solo mission."

They both smiled.

"This is a porch-rocker moment, baby," Marlene said, her smile widening. "When you're an old lady, and you two are sitting out there watching the sun set, and you chuckle softly to yourself, and he asks, 'Baby, whatcha thinking about?' your response will be, 'Oh, nothing, honey. Just about how much I love you.' He don't even need to know all. But you might wanna let the old girls on the Neteru Council know, for a little help."

"Black box."

"Steel vault."

"Never happened."

"I don't know what you're talking about."

"Sho' you're right, Marlene."

A high five was exchanged and Marlene ran her finger over her lips, sealing them.

"Not even Father Pat?"

"He's a priest, and he can't give up no tapes—it's in his oath. He's the only one I can sit with to figure this out."

"Shabazz?"

"You crazy?" Marlene said. "Oh, *hell* no. Too close to home."

Damali nodded and chuckled. "Thanks, Mar."

"For what?" Marlene said with a shrug. "Nothing happened."

The bathroom door opened and startled them. Both women practically fell into the tub.

Shabazz's gaze shot from Marlene to Damali. Suspicion laced his tone. "Everything all right?"

"Of course, baby," Marlene crooned. "She's nearly packed and ready to go. I just wanted her to come back in here with me to see that there was nothing to be afraid of."

Shabazz relaxed, the melodic tone of Marlene's voice seeming to quiet his suspicions. "All right. But y'all hurry up. There's a lot of tension in the other room."

"I'm hurrying," Damali said, swallowing a smile.

"Cool," he said, his fatherly gaze roving over her, still inspecting her for damage. "It'll be good to have you home again, baby girl. Never liked you out here all by yourself alone."

CHAPTER FIVE

Damali gently closed the bedroom door within the new family compound behind her. A sense of weary resignation claimed her. Marlene was right, she had to clean up this mess, and clean it up fast—the Juanita fiasco notwithstanding. It would be a lapse and an episode to take with her to her grave. She loved Carlos. But this dangerous new situation went beyond that. Something was seriously wrong with the very fabric of the universe. She had to address that as much as she had to address her personal dilemma.

She dropped her duffel bag on the floor before the dresser and glanced around the room. They'd put her in the east wing of the house, in a plant-filled sanctuary replete with floor-to-ceiling windows that would allow maximum daylight, and had seduced her to accept her fate of temporarily living with them all again by creating the illusion that she was free. But, once again, she was anything but free.

The sad part of it all was that only when she was creating her music did the problems in her life seem to melt away. Music removed the barriers, lifted the burden of being a Neteru, and stilled her troubled mind. And if her muse had simply remained in the spirit, she could have loved him with her whole heart for all of time. That's how things were supposed to be. But, as usual, she always wound up with the complex end of the bargain.

As Damali slowly put away her clothes, she glanced around at the beautiful teak woods and ebony that Marlene had selected. Patterns from the motherland swathed every surface. Strong mojo was in here with her, she could count on Marlene for that. She smiled sadly as she glimpsed the protective ring of salt around the king-sized sleigh bed that

Marlene had discreetly laid on the floor. No doubt the windows had been anointed, too.

In the quiet of the room, she could feel the fractured nerves and team hysteria beginning to ebb and give way to returned calm. There were so many questions that demanded answers. She wondered if the being that had visited her was one of a kind, or were there more that had accidentally tripped over the invisible line between dimensions? And if every action had an equal and opposite reaction, him becoming flesh meant what in the grand scheme of karma?

It didn't take much to remember how pure inspiration had dragged her out of bed night after night like a jealous lover to answer his desire at three A.M., the bewitching hour, when she was too young to go out alone clubbing. Then as she got older, it would accost her midday, when she went on huntress night shifts, forcing her to contend with the need to create, even when she was half-asleep standing up.

She wondered if Beethoven and Mozart had been driven to near-mad obsession by a female muse that demanded their all. Did Van Gogh finally go insane and cut off his ear for an earthly love or a cosmic one, or did Leonardo DaVinci give in to the whispers of his muse, risking his life during medieval times to dare challenge the church for her?

Damali's hands lent themselves to the task of putting away clothes by rote, but her mind studied the complexities of the cosmos.

Pure inspiration was divine. It covered one with the very essence of pure love. It stopped time, made the sun come up on you from the dead of night, could keep the inspired at a task without eating or sleeping for hours on end, energized by the sheer explosive drive to complete.

Mad scientists, insane artists, crazed musicians, intense writers . . . what could make a man hang upside down on scaffolding for years painting the Sistine Chapel but a driving muse? Or what could make an architect envision the pyramids, and then be crazy enough to actually think he could build them—and do it? Or make two brothers jump into a mechanical contraption and believe they could fly—and do it?

Damali closed her eyes. Every creative person knew that this jealous lover was hard enough to deal with as raw ether . . . but flesh—incomprehensible. This thing could keep her locked in a studio for hours, had done that in the past, or had kept her sequestered in her bedroom until a song was finished. She thought of the others in the compound, how they'd go off with their muse lover and create in sublime isolation, only to return to the group haggard, worn out, dehydrated, malnourished, but deeply satisfied.

A low, knowing chuckle coated her insides as she thought of her early times with Carlos. It wasn't different at all—same thing . . . coming back to the compound all beat down, raggedy, exhausted from being at it all night, ready to drop where she stood from giving a pint of blood, but oh, so very content.

She left her duffel bag on the floor and closed the drawer, and then crossed the room to flop on the bed. Satisfied . . . that was the word . . . and her muse was suffering, hadn't been satisfied in a long time. It was all over his handsome face—need. She wondered if that, along with the rip in time, had caused him to breach the void to come to her . . . aroused, apexing, breathless, unashamed, and begging her to return to him.

Again, a light tap at her door didn't startle her, but oddly annoyed her. She already knew who it was, but was enjoying the solitude of working the puzzle out in her mind alone. She murmured, "Come in," but didn't really mean it. What she really wanted to do was sit down with this strange being and ask him about inspiration. Where did it come from, what type of light sent it? How did it focus and become manifest from one side of the dimensions to the other? Did everybody get their own muse, and were they all as fine as he?

Carlos's form appeared at her now-opened door, but a thousand distant questions still pummeled her brain, then slipped away quietly and were gone.

"I just came to check on you."

She sat up and ran her fingers through her hair. "Thanks. Listen, about earlier, I'm sorry."

"No apology necessary," he said, coming into her room and quietly shutting the door behind him. "Look, I know you don't wanna be back here any more than I do. But I was worried, baby. Out of respect, like you did for me, I didn't mention the darkening of your aura, and I'm worried that no one else picked it up, either."

"Thanks. I appreciate that. Besides, it was probably just residue left over from before finally purging out of my system. No need to get everybody all hyped." She tried to smile. "See, no fangs, no blood sweats, or anything bizarre."

"That's not the point, D. I'm still worried for a lot of reasons."

She nodded and let out a long, weary sigh. They were dancing around the real issue, the earlier fight. That was fine by her at the moment. She had no energy left for that.

"It was my fault. I freaked out, got everybody upset. So this is the result." She forced another smile and patted the side of the bed for him to sit down.

He hesitated. "You sure you want me in here?"

She just looked at him.

"Earlier, it seemed like . . . I don't know." He leaned against the wall and folded his arms.

"I'm sorry," she whispered, realizing how she must have come off. Guilt gnawed at her. She had to let the Juanita thing go if they were ever going to move forward and get beyond it. Now she had a better understanding of how crazy drama could just kick off without it really being one's intent.

Knowing that made her finally stand up and go to him to touch his face. The dejected expression in his eyes made her want to weep. "Baby, listen, I was so wrong to lay that all on you."

His wounded eyes searched hers. "I just don't know what I did wrong by coming when you had an emergency."

Again, the unspoken problem remained like a paralyzed third party in the room. He clearly knew what he'd done wrong with the other unmentionable situation; she had made herself very clear about how that had made her feel. But they'd agreed by verbal omission to squash the impasse, it seemed. The silent truce was that they'd only speak on her most recent SOS call, and nothing further. The whole thing in the alley behind the club still burrowed into his brain. But all apologies and tenderness and making up would be focused on that, and nothing more. To discuss more meant opening Pandora's box, where an emotional tide could shift, a new argument erupt, and anything could leap out of their mouths.

"If I had known coming would have pissed you off, I wouldn't have, because the last thing I wanna do, D, is make you go off . . . but that's a lie, because if I thought you were in trouble, even angry at me, I would still come to make sure you were all right—even if you didn't want me to. Figured—"

She kissed him gently to stop his words. "You didn't do anything wrong. I'm the one who's wrong." She leaned her forehead on the center of his chest, trying to find a way to explain something that had no easy explanation. "I was composing when all this went down. Something I really haven't been able to freely do in almost a year . . . and that takes a great deal of concentration, being alone, and just vibing to come up with something new. Then drama hit, and it was like everything went poof in a matter of seconds."

"Creative coitus interruptus," he said, chuckling. "Been there, and it'll make you evil as shit."

She tried to laugh, even though his statement made her cringe. "The song that was in my head was gone . . . I don't expect any of that to make any sense to you, but, trust me on it, when you're working and get interrupted like that, the frustration is beyond words."

That was as much, and the safest thing, she could tell him. She wanted to be honest with him, but there was a thin line between absolute truth and stupidity. Boy oh boy did she know that now. She cherished this man, her partner, her lover, but this part of her would probably always be a mystery to him. She could fully appreciate a black box, right through here.

His hands caressed her back and a soft kiss landed on the crown of her head. "I guess I've always been a little jealous of your time away from me to go hang out with your muse." He chuckled and deepened the kiss against her hair and fully embraced her. "It's like when you're with your muse, no one and nothing else in the world matters. But I can't deny you being with it; it's a part of you, and the music you create once you've gone off and communed with it is awesome."

She hugged him hard. His words carved at her conscience. If he only knew. "Baby," she whispered thickly. "I'm gonna leave my muse alone, okay? Maybe this whole music thing is a bad idea, long run—yeah, it paid the bills, and got us where we are now, but—"

"Are you crazy?" he said, pulling back and making her look at him. "D, from the time we met, you were singing. You would sit on my momma's sofa, scribbling in some old black-and-white-marble school notebook, coming up with the most kick-ass songs. Over the years I've watched you develop your work, seen it get deeper, more complex, sexier . . . just like you. And your performances are at the top of your game. If you stop singing, that would kill you—and if you did it because I was blowing your groove, that would kill me."

The pain in his intense brown eyes and the selfless compassion held within them made tears come to hers. There was nothing to do but love this man, hold him, and tell him without words how sorry she was for almost killing him by breaking his heart. He'd been possessed, she reminded herself of that. She knew a little of what that felt like now, too.

"No matter what happens, don't you ever forget how much I love you," she whispered thickly.

He kissed her slow and long and deep, and when he pulled away from her mouth, he crushed her against him. "I so wish that I could help you do what you do, but there isn't a musical bone in my body. I envy the other brothers in the house that can just sit down with you, pick up on a strand of your songs, add their own inspiration to it, and you all create a fusion that is so powerful . . . D, I can't even describe it. Sometimes you all are kickin' it so hard it brings sweat to my brow. So, you go on and do whatchu gotta do. I'll manage, will try to stay out of your hair while you're working, and will just enjoy being a spectator."

She almost cringed again as she closed her eyes and nodded. "Baby, listen, sometimes this thing can get out of hand—like an obsession. I'm gonna try to be more balanced, make time for us, cut it off when it's getting too overwhelming, and—"

"No, girl," he said with a sad smile, his hands running down her arms as he spoke. He chuckled and shook his head. "You get this look on your face that says, 'back off, I'm working,' and there have been days I've put my head in the studio or in your room while you were working, and you were gettin' it so good, were working a song down to the bone so hard that even I, the nonmusician, knew better than to interrupt that."

He was laughing, but she couldn't even look at him now.

"Girl, for real, about the only time when I get that kinda look on my face is when I'm with you." He nuzzled her neck and nipped it. "That's why I am soooo jealous of that damned muse of yours, you have no idea. And half the time, when I'm looking for you, it's at some wild hour in the morning when I want to roll over and get back to where we'd been, but the muse would have you—"

"Jesus, Carlos, I'm sorry baby," she said fast, breaking his hold and halfway running across the room. "I swear I didn't know it was like that. You've gotta believe me; I never ever meant to hurt you or to do anything messed up. You know it's me and you, baby, just, I . . . I, lost my damned mind. See, what had happened was—"

"Damali, baby, what's the matter?" He crossed the room and wiped at the tears streaming down her face. "Girl, I was just teasing you. I know this thing drags you out of bed at—"

"Baby, see," she said, trying not to sob. "It's really strong. It's powerful. It's not like something that—"

"I know," he said, smiling. "I'm not an artist and I wouldn't understand."

She just stared at him. Marlene's words slapped her in the back of her head. *Take it to your grave, girl. Don't break this man's heart.* "Uhm, hmm," she mumbled, nodded, looked down at the floor, and sniffed hard.

"I know, boo," he murmured. "That's cool. I get the best part, though."

She looked up at him and wrapped her arms around herself.

"Pre- and post-songwriting performances." He gave her a long, burning gaze. "So, I ain't mad."

Damali gulped. This was so out of order, there would be no way to ever make this right. Her muse had to stay on the other side of the veil until the end of time. As long as he was spirit, not a physical manifestation, and as long as she'd never seen him and only felt his presence, it was all good. But knowledge stole innocence.

"Why don't you sing the parts of the song that you remember," Carlos said in a low, sensual murmur. "I can't compose, but maybe I can help jog your memory?" His gaze raked her and sent a ripple of heat over her bare arms.

"No, no, no, that's cool; the song is gone—cold. So, you know, baby, I appreciate—"

"Then, maybe I could offer you a little inspiration for something new?"

Panic stripped the air from her lungs as she watched him close the space between them. "Tonight, we don't have to—"

A hard pull and a deep kiss stopped her words and kept her argument in her mouth. Carlos dragged his jaw up the side of her neck and sent a hot whisper into her ear.

"Remember 'In the Dark'?" he said, his voice a rumble in his chest. "Or, 'When You Call'?"

All she could do was nod with her eyes shut.

"Or, 'Remember Baby'?" he whispered, taking her down memory lane. "Those always turned me out. But 'Sweet Transition,' the way you served it in Sydney, that one makes me act ridiculous." His hands had splayed across her back and he had begun to breathe in the fragrance of her hair, allowing his voice to come out in low, hoarse jags. "You used to sing those to me in bed."

Oh, my God . . . not tonight! "See, baby, that was like over a year ago, and uh . . ."

"They'll always mean something to me, since I know what inspired them." He found the sweet spot on her neck and suckled it, and then left a damp kiss in its wake. "A year is way too long."

Her body tensed. For a second, uncertainty had her in its clutches. Could this thing that had come through the veil shape-shift? Shit!

"Baby, what's the matter?" Carlos said, lifting his head from her throat to stare into her eyes.

"Nothing," she squeaked out. "It just hit me that it had been that long, and I was like, 'Oh, wow, a whole year, damn.' That's deep."

He laughed and shook his head. "Did I tell you the other thing I love about you is you're crazy?"

She nodded, forcing herself to laugh. "I really am, honey."

"Good, then your secret's safe with me," he said, chuckling and pulling her to him again. "I'm crazy, too—for ever messing with you, woman."

As she held him and he laughed, there was nothing more she wanted to do than to banish her muse in the flesh. There was too much at stake, her man's happiness and what they had together. A temporary lapse wasn't worth all that. And Carlos had been the salt of the earth, all his mess aside. She wanted to kick herself for even going near a seduction. Carlos's tender kisses across her jaw made her want to seal away any hurt this could bring him. She wondered if Eve had gone through this yang. How in the world did she bring herself to explain some mess like this to Adam?

Then a very bizarre idea formed in her mind. What if the muse, alone, hadn't come up with everything from pure ether? "In the Dark," Carlos *owned*. The brother had branded that one into her mind and body, puhlease. Muse had to step off on that one.

Feeling more confident, she returned Carlos's kisses harder, but her mind was also working on a stopgap solution. If she composed in bed with Carlos, what would happen? If that off-the-hook muse was crazy enough to step through the rip and come into her room now, then together, she and Carlos could deal with it. At the very least, her man would know she was being stalked by a very aggressive cosmic fan, *whom she hadn't slept with,* and maybe the trust in their relationship could be salvaged.

Conversely, if the muse finally saw that he didn't have exclusive rights to her inspiration, then maybe he'd go in grace and take his ass back to where he was supposed to be.

"Wanna do something we haven't done in a long time?" she whispered, flicking her tongue along Carlos's jugular.

"Yeah . . ." he breathed out. "I'm down."

"Let me light a couple candles, the old-fashioned, slow way . . . we can slip between the sheets, and how about if I compose with you on the fly?"

She watched his lids lower and felt a slight shudder run through him. They needed to make up, repair the rift between them before anything got in the middle of their bond. So many new insights were pouring into her mind that it could barely hold them as she watched his reaction. Silently she swore she'd never travel the uncharted waters of blind, jealous rage again—made sense that one came home and sealed the fissure in a relationship after a lapse. The moment the line got crossed, the spirit registered the breach in the hull; the mind went into panic then damage-control strategy. The body became the solder to take the pressure off and seal the vessel of the relationship from incoming, rushing tides of change so it wouldn't flood with problems and tank. That kinda mess would drown the whole crew. *Lord,* she understood so much better . . . and apparently just in the nick of time.

Carlos hadn't answered her verbally, just stripped off his shirt and walked over to the bed, unfastening his jeans and kicking off his unlaced Tims. She smiled, loving him as much as the relaxed intimacy that now cloaked them. It was something to be cherished, so she took her time going around the room, lighting tallows and enjoying the anticipation that made the vibe thicken around them.

Every now and then, she glimpsed over her shoulder to catch the utter appreciation in his expression. His eyelids were heavy, but his eyes burned silver beneath them as they watched her strip away her clothes to join him under the covers. No, nothing was worth risking this.

She slid against him, her skin catching fire as it ignited his, and she leaned down to land soft caresses on his forehead and eyelids with the barest brush of her mouth. "Wounded, lover . . . I'm sorry," she crooned softly. "I should have been more careful with your love." She stopped her song to find his mouth, and then broke the kiss, sending her gentle apology into it upon a sad melody. "Wounded lover . . . forgive me. This time I'll make it up to you." Her hands stroked his hair, and glided down his shoulders to gently rake his nipples with her nails, making him close his eyes. "Wounded lover . . . I love you."

The song stopped where his deep kiss began. Her guilt ended where his touch started. Her confusion ceased where he entered her. The muse's lure was lost where her man's rhythm was found. With every ragged breath they drew, she remembered where she was supposed to be. Not even a rip in the universe could come between this, they were one.

But at three o'clock in the morning, she found herself sitting up in bed. Damali looked down at Carlos, his breathing was deep and steady, a man contented and asleep. Her mind was raging with the rest of the song they'd created. She bent and kissed him; he stirred, and reached out a lazy arm to claim her.

"Your muse calling you again?" he murmured with his eyes closed and a slight smile gracing his mouth.

"Yeah," she whispered and kissed his cheek.

"Go to him then," Carlos murmured as he yawned and snuggled deeper into the covers. "I know where to find you."

She hesitated. "I'll be downstairs in the studio, okay? Just for a little while."

"That's what you always say." He chuckled, turning over with a sated smile. He hadn't opened his eyes, and was beginning to drift off to sleep again. "I know you can't fight that call . . . and you lose track of time."

"I'll just be a little while," she said, so conflicted she'd begun to wring her hands. "We'll have breakfast together, okay? I'll make you something—"

"Damali, go 'head, baby. I ain't got nothin' for you until morning." He chuckled and stretched, not even looking at her. "I don't know how you do it."

She slipped from the bed after kissing him once more and went into the bathroom to splash water on her face. It had to be safe now. She'd made her point, made her choice. But she had to be able to finish what she'd started, had to be able to keep working with the second love of her life—music.

"Wounded Lover" demanded recording *now*. In her sleep she'd heard the rest of the song, just like she was sure she could complete the other two that had jumped into her brain earlier that night. Three cuts were screaming to get laid. Once she recorded them, all she'd have to do is let Jose hear them and he could score them. Rider's guitar would know what to do, just like Shabazz's bass and J.L.'s keyboards. . . . Mike would be on it with a second keyboard or drums, Mar would bring the bells and shakers, and they'd have a healthy jump-start to getting back into the groove.

Washing up quickly, she felt so alive she could have skipped back into the room. With guilt gone, Carlos satisfied, and her freedom no longer in question, she was energized. This drama was a fluke.

Damali quickly found a tank top and a pair of sweats and escaped the bedroom, hurrying down the hallways and a wide flight of stairs to the first-floor studio. The moment she entered the soundproof enclosure and turned on the lights, she felt like she was home. All she needed was a couple of takes, and she knew she'd nail it. Dawn would be coming through the windows in a matter of hours, and all would be right with the world.

She dashed over to the mixing board and turned on a stand mic and depressed the record buttons, not bothering to don headphones. She had this. A capella. Yeah, boyie.

Excited by the creation, she went to the mic, closed her eyes, and began "Wounded Lover." The sound of her voice filled the studio, and before long she'd improvised from the earlier melody in her head, had found notes between notes, her voice carrying raw power. Sensuality oozed from the melody that she let hover and falter, like a woman crying, begging to be understood. She sent everything into the lyrical promises, her arms outstretched, head back, feeling the music as it surged up and out of her. It was like being in church, testify. It was like being one with air, have mercy. It was electricity, pure adrenaline, as she belted out her soulful wail.

New words spun, dipped, and added to stanzas. *Yeah, wounded lover, I've missed you—would never leave you. 'Cause, you're my wounded lover. . . . I can never be the one to hurt you. Don't go, not for a little while, baby. Just listen. I can explain and make it all right again. Just . . . wounded lover, please . . . hear me.*

Perspiration made her white tank top cling to her torso. Energy-infused body heat made her sweatpants second skin. Trembling, she sang her heart out. The wail of agony she released in soprano sent shivers through her, then she dipped it to a hoarse whisper of remorse, a stuttering repetitive *baby* that ended in a crooning *ooohhh, you know I love you. Wounded lover, don't go.*

He materialized right in her arms as she finished the song, welded to her in a desperate embrace. His hard kiss captured her mouth, stole her breath, and sent prisms of new melody through her. Sound became color within her as he moved against her, shuddering. Every color was a pleasure shard between her legs that arched her back and left her limp. His kiss was filled with indecipherable words that she could feel, understood from within, but only heard once he tore his mouth from hers and found her neck.

He held the sides of her face, raining kiss after rapid kiss upon her eyelids, the bridge of her nose, her forehead, then again sought her mouth. Each time he spoke, it was with the voice of a broken man.

"Beloved, you ruin me," he gasped, his hot words touching off another orgasm within her. His caress fused to her back, his burning hands rapidly tracing down it to cover the Sankofa tattoo at the base of her spine, and the acute, erotic sensation made tears fall. "Oh, Damali, I am beyond wounded, I have been slain. Outright slaughtered."

She could barely hold on to his shoulders, the heat emanating from his skin was so intense. All reason had been wiped from her mind as she felt him climax hard in a tidal wave of pure sound, bury his face against her hair, and sob.

She stood there for a few moments, too stunned to move. This wasn't terror, this was outright horror. Her man was upstairs, an entity had released hard and was now sobbing, "I love you, don't leave me," in her arms. She'd just gotten out of bed with one man, was downstairs on the DL with another—in her family's house. She began to hyperventilate. Passing out was very possible. The fact that he hadn't actually entered her would be a moot technicality once Carlos dropped fang.

"Muse, Muse, listen to me!" she said, trying to extract herself from his warm, wonderful hold. "You have *got* to go—now!"

But he didn't budge. His nude, thick, muscular frame was pressed against her tightly. His body felt like granite had formed beneath his supple skin. His eyes searched hers, holding open desire.

"You don't understand," he said on staccato breaths. "Every time you began a song and let it die in fits and starts, you touched me . . . you did that *for hours,* all night long. When you finished, I finished, right here in your arms." His palm trembled as it cupped her cheek, his eyes never leaving hers. "I thought I would go mad from the prolonged wait . . . and you still have more brimming inside you, as do I." He captured her hand and dragged it down his torso to his pulsing shaft. "Just finish one more for me, lover."

Her eyes almost crossed when she touched him there. The look on his face was untarnished want. She understood where he was at, had been there herself. His body was so hot it felt like it had soaked up the sun. But reality and the cold light of day was an interesting mix. It brought instant sanity. She could not have Carlos come down here and find her standing in the middle of a sound studio holding a huge entity's dick.

She released him and backed up, glancing down the front of her splattered sweatpants. "Oh, shit!"

"Beloved, listen—"

"No, for real, now—"

"I wanted to fill you with all that I have. The fabric got in the way." He pulled her to him again and delivered another hard kiss. "Let me inside you, flow through you, and give you all of me as you sing."

His kiss was intoxicating, but reality was more sobering. "Please, please, please, go home, baby! This ain't the way for my man to find out!"

"Tell him, beloved. End the torment with the truth."

Damali closed her eyes. "I can't. Not yet, not now, possibly never—so you have *got* to go." She looked up at him and touched his face as tears of need shimmered in his eyes. "If you go," she murmured, trying to find a way to temporarily appease him, "I'll finish the other ballads today. But you *cannot* manifest like this on me again. Promise."

"I cannot promise what is beyond my control." He swept her mouth and released a deep sigh as he hugged her. "But pain was never my purpose, therefore, if you want me to leave you at the moment, I shall."

"Thank you," she squeaked out, and patted his shoulder. "You have got to be cool. We can't roll like this."

He nodded, closed his eyes, turned away, and then walked between the folds of time and space and was gone.

Her hand over her heart, she glanced down at the broad, wet stain on her sweatpants. If a sightline didn't bust her, the nose would. Raw sex was impossible to disguise, and her man knew that scent like a bulldog knew steak. She couldn't go back to her room. Every female in the house was probably in bed with a partner. Marlene would have a heart attack. The only person she could count on was Inez.

Dashing to the phone, she punched in Inez's cell number. It took three tries to get past her friend's voice mail, but 'Nez had a baby and always answered her phone, just in case. As soon as Damali heard her Inez's voice, she didn't bother with formalities.

" 'Nez, it's D, but don't say my name. Mike in there with you?"

"Yeah, girl, where you at, you cool?"

"No, I'm fucked up, can't explain, bring me some sweats—don't say shit to a living soul, just bring me some sweats and a garbage bag, and oh, girl, I done messed up. SOS, pull me outta here on the sneak tip, don't ask no questions, and I swear I'll owe you for life. I need a wet washcloth and some soap. Can you do that?"

"Yeah, but where you at?" Inez hissed.

"Downstairs in the studio."

Momentary silence hung on the line.

"In the house?" Inez said slowly.

"I said don't ask no questions! Mike can hear in his sleep—I hope you knocked him out good, oh, Lawd!" Damali whispered back harshly. "Come on, girl, hurry up—before Carlos wakes up!"

The call disconnected. Damali walked in a circle. The studio door opened within minutes and she almost fainted. Inez brandished the requested items, and without fanfare Damali stripped right in front of her friend and shoved her soiled pants into the bag. Tears stung her eyes. Inez's look of pure shock made Damali work faster. She wiped her neck and face off, as well as her hands and thighs, and then inspected herself while turning around like a lunatic.

"Do I look all right? I'm cool? You can't see nothing on me, can't tell nothing, right? Girl, tell me something!" Damali's frantic whisper popped and snapped in short bursts. "Okay, now, we go way back, lean in, give a good whiff, and tell me if I'm cool."

"I don't know what happened in here, and I'm half-scared to ask," Inez said slowly, taking the trash bag from Damali, "but Carlos is gonna kick your ass."

"I know," Damali wailed and closed her eyes.

CHAPTER SIX

The sun warmed Carlos's face, and he stretched and yawned, blindly feeling for Damali beside him. Then he remembered that she'd left him for her muse. He'd vowed not to come between her and her creative process, but damn.

He sat up, rubbed his face with both hands, and let his breath out hard. It would have been nice to wake up beside her, and to have another little private interlude with her before having to deal with the whole family. Glancing at the height of the sun, it wouldn't be long before the entire compound came alive, and then that level of privacy just wouldn't be there.

Thoroughly annoyed, he looked down at the tent his body made in the sheets. A wake-up salute greeted him, but his woman was gone. What was wrong in the universe when something so simple had to be this complicated?

Standing with effort, he went to the bathroom and splashed water on his face. He looked down and grimaced. He was so damned hard he couldn't even take a whiz. This was ridiculous.

Carlos stalked out of the bathroom, found his pants, and pulled them on. Why Damali always had him on a mission was beyond him. Even while he argued with himself about it, he still found himself walking through the house toward the studio. Later, maybe, after breakfast, he'd give her a piece of his mind . . . she'd promised to come back in a little while, and hadn't.

As he neared the studio, he watched her for a moment through the glass. She was singing, tears running down her beautiful face, in total rapture—how could he be angry or begrudge her ecstasy like that?

Carlos sighed, tempered his annoyance, and continued to gaze at her through the glass. It reminded him so much of how he used to pine outside her window, able to see her but not touch her . . . and the way she was moving before the mic made him need to hear her voice. He remembered how they used to press their hands to the glass, heat radiating beyond the barrier, to feel each other's vibe.

He glanced up at the lit recoding light that was on and sighed. All right. He'd wait for her to finish and just watch her.

But as she moved and her hands caressed the mic, the morning erection she'd left him to endure throbbed harder, and he knew her voice would decimate him . . . he'd be as quiet as a mouse, would just slip into the studio and stand by the exit, just so he could hear her sing . . . and before his hand fully consulted his brain, he'd opened the door.

Carlos took two paces into the room, her song was winding down, and he was sad that he'd probably missed the crescendo of it. She was so beautiful, just wailing like that. Desire flared and drew him to her like a magnet.

He walked toward her as quietly as he could, vamp stealth. Her eyes were closed, her head back, and her hands were clenched in fists. It was never his intention to interrupt her flow, but as she opened her eyes she stopped abruptly and jumped back, almost screaming.

A gold blade ripped through the nothingness, just came at him from thin air. Millisecond reflexes made him dip back and avoid the swing that was aimed at taking his head off his shoulders. He heard her scream; fire and bright white light tore through the opening, and a huge entity stepped through the flames, radiating like the sun and wearing gold armor.

His natural response was to bulk and move out of the way of another potentially lethal swing. Carlos spun, pivoted, and dropped battle-length fang.

"Never in my house!" the entity thundered. "Never when she's with me!"

Flames rippled down the edge of the blade and arced to draw a line between it and Damali.

Total confusion made Carlos hesitate for a second. It was as though he were watching events unfold in slow motion. Was it an angel, a demon? What the hell was it?

He saw Damali run toward the huge brother and shout, "No! Don't hurt him!" Was he fucking hallucinating?

"Somebody talk to me!" Carlos shouted. The entity before him stood seven-feet tall, had him by a head in height, and definitely had him by weight. Battle-length fangs glistened a warning that only his kind knew well, but it was broad goddamned daylight! He was the only one that could do that!

"Never, *ever*, come into my lair when I'm with her!" The entity growled, circling Carlos in preparation for an all-out battle lunge. Blue flames flickered at the rim of his nostrils and his eyes glowed gold-silver.

"*Your lair*, motherfucker, are you mad?" Carlos spat on the floor. He could still feel the burn mark where the entity's sword had grazed his throat.

"In here, when I'm with her, and she's finishing a song, do not *ever* interrupt her!"

The sound of the entity's voice thundered. Carlos's gaze shot between Damali and the thing that was slowly circling.

"You promised!" Damali shouted. "Stand down! Put the blade away!"

Carlos's attention fractured as it tried to hold the deadly image before him and move counterclockwise to it, and also make sense of what Damali was saying.

"When I'm with you, and we are fusing, he is *never* to interrupt that," the thing said, snarling. "That is beyond my control point, woman— know that."

"Oh, wait a fucking minute," Carlos said, the growl coming from him so low that it vibrated within his chest.

"Baby, listen," Damali said, unable to get between them. "It's not what you think, it's—"

"Tell him who I am to you!" the entity roared, leveling his blade at Damali. "He will assuredly get himself killed if you do not."

Judgment left Carlos at the same moment he left the floor. Carlos lunged, and the entity swung, missed, and he landed a hard right to its jaw. The entity landed, narrowed his gaze, and flung the blade down, and then ripped the gold armor from his chest as Carlos snatched the mic stand, broke it over his knee, and made a weapon to impale it.

"Let us do this as was once done," the entity said through a low snarl.

"Old-school, motherfucker—it's on!"

Carlos's gaze narrowed, but seeing a Neteru symbol blazing on the entity's massive chest was disorienting. Still, it was a matter of honor. Carlos flung down the sharp-edged pole. An apexing male had rolled up on his woman, had breached the compound, and had drawn on him. Instantly both were airborne and collided with a deadlock thud. His throat was being strangled by what he now knew to be the stronger male. A lot of shit had happened to him in his life, but never this.

Leveraging the heavier weight, Carlos flip-rolled the being off of him. But it landed on its feet and threw a punch that sent Carlos sprawling across the floor. Dazed, it took Carlos a second to flip himself back up and to regain floor positioning.

"Stop!" Damali yelled. "You two have to stop!"

She went for the blade; the entity drew it to him by kinetic force and flung it through the air to disappear on the other side of nothing. In the few seconds that had passed, Carlos gained a healthy respect for the strength of what he was up against. His woman's voice was screaming at fever pitch, but what she was saying was incomprehensible.

"If you hurt him, I'll never come to you again. If he dies, it's over!"

Stupefied, Carlos backed up. "Damali, what's going on?"

"Baby, you weren't supposed to find out like this, I swear!"

Carlos looked at the entity, looked at her; renewed fury sent him headlong into the entity's abdomen. The entity lost his footing from the force of the collision. Carlos swung and landed a punch that sent red blood splattering. But the returned punch knocked him across the room to slam against the wall. He was off it before the entity blinked, and the two combatants hurled against the studio glass. Pain shot through Carlos's system as his spine and head took out a section of the double-thick glass plates. The next thing he knew, he had been jettisoned outside the studio, and a lair seal as strong as the shield of Heru kept him at bay.

Rage and frustration made him bang on the golden seal to no avail. He knew how strong a master's-lair seal was, as well as the impossibility of breaking a Neteru's gold shield. The dichotomy only spiked his adrenaline higher. Everything about this entity told Carlos the interloper was from the old dark realms. Panic, fury, hurt, confusion filled him as he hollered and banged to no avail, sending his shoulder against the shield, yelling at the tops of his lungs.

Guardians' footfalls pummeled the steps like soldiers called to war. He was beyond speech. His voice was a series of roars. His woman was on the wrong side of a seal. A male vamp had her. The contender had council-level strength. It carried a Neteru blade. Came out in daylight. Arched gold-white energy. Had a Neteru tattoo, just like his. "Damali!"

This thing on the other side of the barrier was whispering to her, holding her arms, trying to talk some shit—he could see it through the glass. His woman was listening to the bullshit! She hadn't gone into battle mode, what the fuck? His ass was taller, older, wiser, and built—cut up! Dropped twelve inches of fang to his ten. Oh, hell no!

"Stand back," Mike said, "a cannon might blow the seal."

"No, my fucking woman is in there with some motherfucker she knows, and she's been with him before!" Carlos shouted. Tears fused with blood in his mouth as he pounded the impenetrable divide like a madman. Hysteria blacked out judgment. She'd left his bed to be with another man. There was a lair in the family house—for another vamp, not him? He whirled on the family, every conceivable weapon was drawn and pointed at the seal, but he didn't care. Saliva and snot slung from his nose as he roared rapid-fire questions. "How long have you known she had somebody else? How long has she been playing me, y'all! Talk to me, I'll kill this motherfucker, if it's the last thing I do! Y'all feed him, too? He family, or what the fuck?"

A sob stole his complaint, and he turned back to the seal, then charged it, only to fracture his collarbone for the effort. But when he saw the entity stroke Damali's face, lower his mouth to hers, and the Guardians look away—he lost it. Something within his fragile psyche snapped. His collarbone didn't hurt; he was going through that seal. And the instant the entity dropped focus for a split second during a good-bye kiss, Carlos was through the barrier with the team behind him.

His feet never touched the floor. The velocity of the hurdle whirled him past Damali to intersect with the entity's midsection, and they both flew backward and were gone.

Chaos imploded. Damali was walking back and forth in front of the invisible rip with her hands clutching her hair, sobbing. Unfired rounds remained in gun barrels, but everyone was yelling at once.

"We couldn't shoot it, Mar, without hitting Carlos!" Big Mike yelled.

"They moved too fast, and with D in the room," Rider said, breathing hard. "No way to get a shot off."

"Shit, oh, holy shit," Jose was yelling, walking back and forth in front of the invisible place Carlos had disappeared. "D, how could you do my boy like that, baby? In his house, the family house—girl, he ain't neva gonna be right!"

"It wasn't like that!" Damali screamed. "You of all people should know!"

"What the hell does that mean?" Juanita shouted, whirling on Damali.

"Fuck you! I am tired of your signifying ass!" Damali said, tears making her sputter. "Marlene, get that bitch outta my face. Where's my blade? I'm going in!"

"Going in where?" Shabazz shouted. "How, D? You know how to breach that void?"

"If she called him before, maybe she can call him again," Marlene said, breathing hard. "That'll open a—"

"What do you mean, called him, Marlene?" Shabazz was walking in circles. "You knew about this?"

"I—"

"No, Mar, this time you've gone too far!"

Shabazz stalked away from Marlene and Damali. Big Mike put a hand on his shoulder.

"D, listen, if you can explain to Carlos about what happened earlier this morning, maybe—"

"Shut up, Inez," Damali said, bitter sobs making her rock. "They're over there on the other side in a death struggle. There isn't time to explain!"

"Earlier this morning?" Bike Mike looked at Inez. "When you left the room, you knew what was up?"

"Baby, see," Inez said. "It was—"

"Aw, hell no!" Big Mike boomed. "You keep some serious shit like this from me, then what else you got to hide?"

"Stop it!" Damali shrieked, covering her face. What was happening to everything she knew?

"If she was in here with it earlier, and was recording, we have it on disk," J.L. said, running to the board. "They've fucked up the boards, but I can maybe pull something off there that can open a door to the other side."

"No! Don't play that!" Damali said, body-blocking J.L. "You can't. It'll make him stronger, more determined than ever to kill Carlos."

"What's on the hard drives, D?" Rider said, hocking and spitting on the floor. "There's only one thing I can think of that would take him there, and I'm praying it ain't that."

"It is," Damali wailed. "Okay? Satisfied?"

"Who is it?" Berkfield said, his voice filled with judgment. "If we have to take a body, we need to know what we're huntin'."

"He's older, stronger, and a Neteru. You're not going to be able to take him down, like that," Damali said, her voice leveling off as she wiped her face. "Carlos doesn't even have a blade on him."

Marjorie ran her fingers through her hair. "Then, honey, you're gonna have to coax him to our side with sugar. Call his name; beg him sweetly not to hurt that man. We've all been there, had somebody that we shouldn't have, and—"

"What!" Berkfield's voice imploded within the room as he crossed it to snatch his wife by the arm. Immediately Bobby and Krissy jumped between their parents.

"Don't even think about hitting her, Dad," Bobby said, his eyes filling. "You worked a lot of nights, did a lot of shit that left her all alone. You don't fucking hit her."

Krissy walked away with her hands over her face as Dan gathered Marjorie Berkfield into his arms to comfort her.

"We need to get back on mission," Dan said, his quiet authority quelling the chaos. "There'll be time to sort this all out later, once we get Carlos back, and put this other thing down. Whatever we saw, or think we saw, could have been illusion—never forget that. We don't turn on each other. We're family. We work it out. We're one."

For a moment, no one spoke. Lines had been drawn, sides taken, and nothing would ever be quite the same.

"For what it's worth," Damali said, her breaths still shaky, "I never slept with him."

Again, silence permeated the battered room and hung between everyone in it.

"I love Carlos, wouldn't do that to him, and the kiss you saw was my attempt to appease that being and send it away before anything worse happened. I was in here singing to appease it, to keep it from manifesting, but Carlos interrupted me before I finished the song, and the entity wigged."

Marjorie looked up from her hands. Her face was red, tear-streaked and her mouth quivered as she spoke. "I believe you," she said in a resolute tone, and then lifted her chin higher. "I *know* that that's possible. And while the attention was flattering, and the temptation great, I trust you when you tell us that you never did anything . . . anything *permanent*."

Marjorie's hot gaze shot around the room, landing on every male within it. "Tell me none of you have ever thought about it? Ever saw another person who simply turned your head for a moment, but then you remembered what was at risk. . . . Because maybe you were lonely, weary, unappreciated, felt like your whole life was spent giving for everyone but yourself," she said, her voice growing shrill as she leveled her charges.

Marjorie held Rider in her glare, and went to Shabazz, Big Mike, then the younger Guardians, and held her husband's eyes until he looked away. "I won't let you be hypocrites and denigrate Damali in front of me. Don't you dare make assumptions about any woman in this house!"

Marjorie stormed out of the room. Krissy went with her.

Rider nodded. "Well said, and duly noted." He sighed and holstered his weapon. "What's the bastard's name, so I can put a bullet in his head if—"

"She doesn't know," Marlene said quietly, once the storm had passed.

"C'mon, D . . . you don't even know *his name?*" Jose walked away, disgusted, leaving Juanita fuming.

"Put your guns away," Marlene said in a sad voice. "You can't kill him."

"Why not?" Shabazz snapped and looked at her hard.

"Because he's *her* muse—the muse of Damali's music."

Crash landing in the middle of a grassy knoll, hands clenched around throats, neither would relent nor drop his grip.

"You can't die on this side," the entity growled through his teeth.

"But I can enjoy strangling your ass until the end of fucking time," Carlos snarled.

The entity released Carlos and pushed him off him so hard that Carlos went sprawling across the grass. The entity stood and stared at Carlos, who was back on his feet in seconds.

"This is futile," the entity snarled. "Enough!"

"It was way fucking enough when you put your hands on my woman!"

"She was mine, first. Be clear!"

"Bullshit!" Carlos walked back and forth, trying to decide which limb to detach from the arrogant thing's body. But the fact that it was sunny outside was jacking with his mind. "When'd you meet her?"

"I am her muse; I have always been with her. You cannot compete for her in this regard!"

Stunned, Carlos stared at the thing before him. Both beings wiped the blood from their noses.

"Look around. It is daylight. This is not the dark realms."

Carlos glanced around quickly, but kept his eyes on the thing before him. The fact that it was built like a tank, and by male standards all-right looking, was really eating him up. "You got fangs, man, so you need to—"

"As do you," the entity said, glaring at him and retrieving the blade that he spied off in the distance. "Same fathers."

Carlos hurried behind the thing that had nearly stopped his heart when he'd leaned down and kissed his boo. But this new information was setting off a new wave of concerns. "You need to stop jacking with my head! My father was a Rivera, all human. And if you're trying to say some shit about my mother, the blade ain't gonna help your ass at all!"

"I cast no aspersions on your mother," the entity said, glaring at him as it picked up the blade. "Mine has suffered more public ridicule than ever deserved, therefore I do not speak ill of another man's mother—ever. We are brothers, by right, by Neteru law. All Neterus are brothers."

Carlos slightly relaxed, but not much. Having to come face to face with a slightly more robust equal was not something he was ready to deal with. It was always the thing that one had never had to contend with that presented the greatest challenges. Shabazz hadn't lied. Although, at the moment, he failed to see where any so-called growth would come from this experience.

"Aw'ight. I see the tattoo. You got da silver. Neteru moves. Blade to match it. Fine. But the crack about same fathers—"

"Dante," the entity said flatly. "He made you, that is why you still have his fangs. He made me in the Garden with Eve, which is why I still bear the family resemblance. Is your poor battered mind satisfied?"

Carlos stood very, very still. "Dante made you?"

"Correct. The old-fashioned way. Through conception, before he was made sterile for the offense and banished to rule the dark realms on Level Six by *his* father. I trust you know who *that* is?"

Carlos didn't even blink. Hell yeah, he knew who Dante's daddy was, and he remained nameless. So, if Dante made this guy . . .

"Eve gave birth to only three sons. The first one was banished. The second one killed by the first. The third went on to prosper. I know my Bible history, so stop playing with my head!" Carlos shouted, new terror increasing the volume of his voice.

"The first son was named Cain, me," the entity said in a weary tone. "Made by the first female Neteru and Dante, otherwise known as the Chairman." He looked at Carlos and smiled.

"Little brother, you and I share much in common. My name begins with the letter C, which carries the resonance of scattered energy, but is the marrying type—numerically represents three. I slayed my younger brother, Abel, whose name begins with the letter A, which carries the numerical property of one, like Adam's. Your name begins with C, and regrettably, you, too, killed your younger brother, Alejandro, although for different reasons . . . but he was your father's favorite son. We both were destined to be Neterus, but we both made several grievous choices along the way. My mission is to learn selfless sacrifice, to give the world back a harvest through, of all things, Damali's music."

"Wait, wait, wait, wait, wait!" Carlos ran his fingers through his hair. What this entity was telling him was gonna make him scalp himself.

"It is very simple. What lessons you do not master in one lifetime, you are destined to repeat in the next. I have had to incarnate many times to learn many lessons, and my final challenge was through the arts. I have not always been a muse, trust me."

"Then, after Adam, you were the second male Neteru ever made?"

The entity nodded and began walking away.

"Yo! But that don't have jack shit to do with you trying to push up on my woman!"

The entity spun and unsheathed his blade with lightning quickness and leveled it at Carlos's chest. "With her, do not test my resolve to stay in the Light."

Carlos slapped the blade away. "Likewise."

The two remained immobile, glaring at each other.

"Ultimately, it is her choice." The entity lowered his blade.

"Yeah, it is, isn't it," Carlos sneered. "And, if you know like I know, you'll stay away from her."

"That, too, is her choice."

Deafening silence bound them. Nothing but the howling wind from the hills could be heard.

"She makes it very difficult for me not to kill you," the entity finally said, his eyes blazing. "But it is not allowed."

"If you wanna go, we can go," Carlos said in a low threat. "Any time, any day. Step back to where we can dust each other, and it's on."

"You are not allowed to kill me, either."

"Says who?" Carlos spat.

The entity smiled and pointed his blade skyward. "Presents a dilemma, yes?" He chuckled. "I have the mark, as do you. The choice is simple. Disobey the Father, and we will be sent to the one that made us. Given Dante's demise, you are aware of his next of kin on Level Seven."

Carlos didn't move, but he'd heard Cain loud and clear. *That* was not an option. He could only stare at the now six-foot-five being that obviously had wisdom, discipline, and shared all his best moves. A strange feeling of sadness entered him as he began to realize that perhaps he wasn't so unique, wasn't firstborn in a line of proud men like he'd always thought. His mission was unclear now. Everything he thought he'd understood was very tenuous and this older brother had blown him away with information he didn't own.

The worst of it all was he seemed a very strong contender to turn Damali's head—and shared something with her that he couldn't begin to—music. But there was no way, in any realm, that he could bring himself to ask the question that he most needed to know. Had she gotten with Cain? If so, when, how, where, what led up to it, what would have made her go there, how could she? Did the Juanita thing really make her do something like this? Or was it that this brother's game was so righteous that, the transgression with Juanita or not, Damali had been seduced, wanted him, and went for it . . . couldn't help herself. He wasn't sure which possibility hurt more.

"I'm going home," Carlos said. Defeat laced his tone. "Where's the door?"

Cain sighed. "I don't know."

"Stop with the games," Carlos said, now beginning to feel every blow that had landed on him. "I'm out."

"There is a rip. But none of us know where it is. Here, until I safely courier you back to the other side, you are unfortunately my charge. I am, for lack of a better term, my brother's keeper. I *never* wanted that, either. However, it is what it is."

"Then how did you get back and forth to talk to my woman? What was all that shit you said about her studio being your lair, *hombre?* You need to come with stronger game than that!" Just thinking about it was making Carlos pace.

"I can only come when she calls me," the entity said in a flat, disgusted tone. He briefly closed his eyes. "No matter where I am, no matter what I am doing, the world stops and I'm on the other side."

Watching the sheer want ripple through Cain lowered Carlos's defenses. He *had* to know. "How many times she call you, man?"

The entity opened his eyes. "Calm yourself. Although it would give me great pleasure to torture you with a lie, I have learned from my past. She calls me through her music. When she composes, it summons me."

Slightly improved by the admission, Carlos tried to be cool. "Aw'ight. Then we have to wait until she does."

"The likelihood that she will be composing at all in the near future is remote!" the entity suddenly bellowed. "Why could you not allow her that? I never interfered with what she gave you in the flesh. The only thing that was mine to share with her was music. Why did you—"

"Because that's *my* woman, motherfucker, and the last I heard, muses were supposed to be spirits only, positive ones, not some guy breathing down her neck with fangs!"

"Do you think I wanted to be in the flesh? Are you insane? That carries the burdens of every earthly desire!"

The entity walked in a circle, and Carlos watched him whip himself into a new rage. He walked up to Carlos, flexing his fist.

"Young and foolish! If I could have passed this last test, I would never have had to come back!" Cain walked away, took in several deep breaths, and turned to face Carlos. "Thousands of years have passed. I've endured the gain and loss of wives, children, experienced birth, death, worry, sickness, desire. I was spirit. I was free of that! Then the earth stopped moving during a disaster of biblical proportions, a rip occurred, and for some reason I have yet to fathom, I go between spirit and flesh— but when in spirit, carry all the same intensities of the earth plane now."

Speechless, Carlos watched Cain's eyes for any sign of fraud. Rather than detecting a lie, he saw tears brim and then burn away. Either this brother was kicking the most profound truth he'd ever heard, or he had more game than him. Unable to give into the concept that anybody had more game than him, the truth could be the only culprit.

"So, up until recently, you were spirit, didn't feel things like on the earth plane?" Carlos couldn't help it; he definitely had to know.

"Pure love and pure creation is the only thing allowed to reside in the upper realms, you know that," Cain said, walking away. His tone had carried a level of shame in it that Carlos immediately honed in on.

"So, you had a pure ether love vibe happening for her and her work, up until recently?"

"Yes, why do you dwell upon it?"

Carlos jogged to catch up to Cain's slightly longer strides. "I'm just trying to understand how this place works."

"*That* is a lie," Cain said, and stopped walking. He turned to face Carlos squarely. "If you have a direct question, ask it."

They stared at each other for a moment.

"I have a lot of questions," Carlos finally admitted.

Cain sighed and waited. "It appears that you have an indefinite amount of time to ask them."

"Aw'ight then," Carlos said, hedging, but too curious to let the opportunity pass. "Like, when she was grooving to her music, before the rip, you helped her, watched over her, and was cool. Because all during her growing up years, I never saw you around."

"I was ether," Cain snarled. "My feelings were pure."

"So what made you lose your mind and try to come on my side to get a bone snatched outta your ass by me——"

Cain had grabbed Carlos by the throat so fast that he hadn't seen it coming. Cain's eyes blazed gold then went silver, his grip threatened, but didn't strangle. Carlos remained cool, standing his ground in the challenge to let Cain know he wasn't impressed. But that was getting harder to do by the moment as he truly studied the muscular bandwidth of Cain's outstretched arm.

"The rip tore me to shreds," Cain said through lowered incisors. "Her voice is like a knife. Sound became touch. She was innocent of that and didn't know. Every composition, even her laughter now, I feel as flesh. I respected your union. From our old world, she is scored at the throat as your wife—and you by her incredible bite. However, every man has his limits. A year of abstinence from her creating, because of *you* . . . a year of no communication with her, because of *you* . . . when on a summer solstice night, the eve of my solo apex, she called out low and sweet and naked in her tub, 'Muse, where are you, come back to me,' I was finished!"

He flung Carlos away from him, and Carlos landed on his feet a yard away. Carlos rubbed his throat, pissed off, but also understanding the brother's dilemma.

"I had never crossed the line, and rue the night that I did. What I thought had been insufferable, experiencing it on this side . . . I was not prepared for the intensity of the vibrations once I stepped through the rip to go to her. Now I have put her in a very delicate position of making an impossible choice—me, her music, or you."

Cain had kept his back to Carlos as he spoke, and Carlos understood that to mean this being was beyond the point of fearing an attack. Duly noted. Been there a time or two himself. Sometimes truth just fucked a man up like that, and there was no reason to go to war about it, especially when the more he heard, the better he felt about what might have possibly gone down. But there was still a question that lingered.

"You will have to ask her that," Cain said, his tone weary as he began to walk.

"I plan to, as soon as I get back."

"Then follow me, and if she ever composes again, we'll go see her."

Carlos stopped walking. "We, hell. I'm going back; your ass is staying here."

Cain looked at him. "If she calls me, know that I will go to her."

"Over my dead body." Carlos folded his arms.

"Once we cross over, my pleasure."

"You're talking out of both sides of your mouth, *hombre.* One minute you said we're not allowed to kill each other, and all this respect bullshit for Damali. Then the next minute—"

"Let us be realistic. We are both male. Both hunters. Both Neterus, and we both know that being a vampire, Council-level, does have some sufferable attributes that she does not fear, in fact, enjoys. There is one female Neteru while we are both in season. If you are honest with yourself, you also know that even you have gone to Hell to claim her."

Cain chuckled and folded his arms over his barrel chest when Carlos was rendered speechless. "I am, for better or worse, Dante's son, made by the seed of raw passion, not the mere bite. That attribute is encoded in my cells—passion. My father *ruled* the pleasure principle, just as his father is master of negotiations and the airwaves. My lineage is complex and not to be taken lightly. My undoing as the second male Neteru ever made on the planet, and your senior by many years, is her. Warring for her is not out of the realm of my sensibilities or capacity. Do *not* test me."

Haughty disdain flickered in Cain's glowing, silver gaze. "How many men have gone to war over a woman? You have sat in a throne and should well know your history. Is she not worth all of Rome, rivaling Cleopatra? Is she not the face that could launch a thousand ships to reduce Troy to rubble? Tell me, young Neteru brother, have men lost all reason before in the past and sent infantries into the desert to reclaim something more valuable than gold?"

Cain nodded with triumph when Carlos didn't immediately answer. "I am not speaking from both sides of my mouth. I am telling you the truth, as honestly as any man can. My mission is as I originally stated. However, she represents a potential change in plans. The Armageddon may be in the offing, but challenge me over her and I assure you that it will seem like a minor border dispute."

Carlos nodded but didn't verbally respond. This brother talked more shit than he did. Only problem was, he seemed like he could back it up. Carlos's mind scrambled to assess the challenge. Yeah, all right, if it was war, so be it. He could dig it; Damali would make a man lose all judgment, especially one with a little vamp in him—and this brother had serious juice in his DNA. He glanced around at the rich, fertile valley below that was teeming with entities and glasslike structures, trying to gauge how many troops the brother could raise should the shit get real crazy.

The dilemma pissed him off; he didn't have an army, except human Guardians and his boy, Yonnie, maybe Tara, and any witches Gabrielle could get as mercenaries. If other teams joined his, which was unlikely for a personal dispute of this nature, at best he could count 144,000 Guardians on Earth at any one time. Although the urge to go to battle, just outright slay this motherfucker, was as strong as his old vamp blood hunger, Damali would never go for putting good people in harm's way to start a war over her, anyhow. Plus, he didn't know what preternatural powers the beings in this realm wielded, or how many of them there were. He didn't like the odds of not knowing. A solid bluff was therefore in order.

"As Neterus, it's between me and you, not a brawl throughout the planet where civilians could get hurt. D ain't going for that, and you know it—so stop frontin'. But since we being real, even if you happen to kill me, which your ass won't, then you still lose. The Light will snuff your ass out and send you back to your daddy's people. The way I see it, you're screwed." Triumphant, Carlos folded his arms over his chest and cocked his head to the side in challenge.

"I know the resultant risks and consequences of killing you—a second younger brother—for the sake of envy. Heaven would close her doors." Cain smiled, retracting his fangs. "Given what I have honestly presented, how much wisdom do you think I have acquired?"

"Enough," Carlos begrudgingly said.

Cain nodded. "Therefore, a word of wisdom from me to you, younger brother. I will contend for her with everything at my disposal. Pure ether love converted to earthly love is a very powerful energy, laden with *many* desires. Duel. Outright battle. Gifts. Romance. Seduction. Honor. Neteru status. Good deeds. Or a Council-level war. Name your weapon."

Carlos nodded. "Bet. I can appreciate an honest man."

"Good," Cain said. "So can I. Then welcome to the Land of Nod."

CHAPTER SEVEN

The house was totally polarized: men on one side, women on the other, with clerics on a speakerphone conference call in the middle, desperately trying to bring unity and arbitrate the peace.

Marlene, Marjorie, Inez, Krissy, and—oddly—Juanita, stood with Damali in the weapons room with arms folded over their chests, glaring at the male Guardians. Juanita watched Jose so intently that it seemed like laser heat would score the air between them.

Rider sat on a chair with his head down in weary repose. Big Mike stood glaring at Inez with his arms folded, while Berkfield's eyes glittered with pure outrage as he stared at his wife. J.L. appeared torn and stood at the outer reaches of the invisible male dividing line, seeming unsure whether or not to go to Krissy or to stay with his very upset Guardian brothers.

Jose hadn't stopped pacing since they'd entered the room, his eyes on Damali, the silent anger implicit within them; this wasn't about Carlos, it was about him and her. Shabazz seemed so outraged that his locks had actually lifted off his shoulders with static electricity. But Dan's eyes held no judgment, just confused worry, like Bobby's. They seemed oddly detached and calm, like doctors who knew a serious problem existed, but refused to allow the emotional content of the concerned family to keep them from doing what they had to do. Their countenance said that they weren't taking sides, but the situation was indeed critical.

Damali honed in on the only rational vibrations wafting throughout the room, and began to deescalate her inner panic. "I need everybody to chill for a minute," she said without any apology in her tone. "I have to sense them to see if I can pick up if there's been any injury."

"You said that in plural, D," Jose said hotly. "What's with the *them* shit? The only person you need to be——"

"Jose," Damali said in a quiet but lethal tone, "if you don't chill, we can just have a real frank discussion in the weapons room that won't do any of us any good."

Juanita's gaze shot between Damali and Jose. "Well, let's just do that, then," she said in a loud voice filled with attitude.

Jose glared at Damali and walked away, leaning on the far wall. All eyes glanced at him for a moment, and then Damali, then settled on Juanita. Older male Guardians shook their heads and raked their fingers through their hair. Big Mike rubbed his jaw and let out an angry, hard breath.

"This shit don't make no sense all up in the house," Big Mike said, receiving a silent fist pound from Rider.

"Jose, you need to tell me what she's talking about!" Juanita shrieked, crossing the invisible line on the floor.

"Later," Jose muttered. "Now ain't——"

"Don't tell me now ain't——"

"Enough!" Father Patrick's voice boomed through the speakerphone. "It isn't the time," he said loudly. "What is of critical importance is what came through that rip and where it took Carlos!"

"Exactly," Damali said, walking back and forth in front of the telephone. The male response to what had happened infuriated her. It struck a defiant match within her soul that had turned into a blaze. How dare they judge her? In fact, she no longer felt guilty. Carlos had been here, semiseduced by something he'd never come across before—and the response had been directed at problem solving, not whether or not the man was right or wrong and a buncha moral junk. "You'd all better get your heads together."

Damali paced away from the phone and placed her hands palms down on the table, studying the small pyramid shape she'd created by touching her forefingers and thumbs together.

"Seems like the one who'd better get her head together is you, D," Jose spat, pushing off the wall.

Damali looked up slowly. The room had enough tension winding through it that the air practically thickened. "Be clear," she said, almost speaking to him through her teeth. "I made my decision a long time ago and have held the line—admirably." She glanced at Juanita and held her gaze until it slipped away and her adversary's body relaxed. "If you want a full disclosure in this room about *past* feelings and drama, we can do that at some future point, but not now while I'm in the middle of a divination—*you got that?*"

Stunned male eyes slid away from Damali's.

"Gentlemen, I'll say this one last time. You'd all better get your heads right and focus. This ain't about you, what you've experienced, or any bullshit going down within your individual relationships. Handle your business," Damali said flatly and drew away from the table. "Father Patrick, talk to me."

A sly smile crossed Rider's face as he pushed back in his chair. "I think you gentlemen had better stand down and let the general work."

Shabazz tilted his head from side to side, and spoke in a tight voice. "Aw'ight, Marlene, your take?"

Damali glared at him. "*I'm* doing this divination as the lead Neteru and seer on this team. My capacities outstrip hers," she said, holding respect in her eyes as she glanced at Marlene. "The baton has been passed, big brother, and you need to get with that."

Marlene nodded. "Truth, Shabazz. Has been that way since she came back from the Neteru Queen's Council. She ain't a baby anymore, and is a full-grown woman—respect that." Marlene swept up her robe and walked over to stand by Damali's side, as Marjorie also neared her.

"If Carlos had been seen with a gorgeous, female Neteru from an unknown realm and had gone through the dimension rip," Marjorie said with a narrowed glare, "would this team be wasting this much time pointing fingers and finding blame, or would we be developing a strategy with Father Patrick, Imam Asula, Monk Lin, and Rabbi Zeitloff?" When none of the men in the room responded, Marjorie folded her arms again. "I didn't think so." She kept her gaze sweeping the male Guardians. "Proceed, Damali, and tell us whatever you can pick up."

"Thank you, ladies," Damali said, again placing her hands on the table between the three stones she'd collected in Ethiopia and the one she'd gotten from Gabrielle, creating a pyramid with her fingers.

"Can you sense them at all?" Monk Lin asked in a calm tone, breaking through the charged silence in the room.

Damali breathed in deeply, closed her eyes, and let her breath out slowly through her nose. "I don't sense peril or injury. It seems as though the struggle has abated and I can feel both energies still pulsing."

She drew her hands back and then extended them in a slow sweep around her. "They're alive, not battling, but moving. That's all I can tell."

"Good," Imam Asula said through the phone. "Then perhaps we have time."

"But you don't have a name, any identifying quality?" Rabbi Zeitloff argued through the speaker. "Marks, weaponry, something that we can place in our books to use? *A name?*"

"He didn't give me a name," Damali said, frustration tearing through her brain. She closed her eyes again, and now somewhat calmer, began to replay every detail of the exchange in her mind. "Give me a second."

Silence enveloped the team and the speakerphone sat eerily quiet as Damali mentally scavenged for information. The fight with Carlos the previous morning was oddly the first thing that jumped into her head, but rather than shunt that impression aside again, she rode it, felt it, followed the course of its angry flow, hoping that it would connect the missing dots.

She could feel the old rage reenter her, making the hair at the nape of her neck bristle. In slow-moving impressions, it became vividly clear. Carlos's lapse had hurt her deeper than even she knew at the time. It definitely went beyond the thing with Juanita; him doing her fellow female Guardian was simply the last straw that had broken her back. In that regard, Carlos was right: Juanita was just the innocent victim of an all-out vamp seduction, didn't have anything to do with it, and her rage against Juanita had been misplaced, even if the girl got on her nerves. Something else within her had spiked the rage.

All logic dictated that she couldn't be angry at Juanita for carrying a torch—the girl didn't strike the match to set it ablaze, a vamp seduction had. Who could be blamed for an old, warm memory? The dark side worked with any kernel of doubt or weakness within humans. That's the game they played, and since the Chairman's demise, the game had kicked up several notches on the boards. Possessions went the same way, had to work with something that was already resident, and *that's* what had her pissed off at Carlos so badly. Not some possible fling.

As she stood silently remembering, the team's eyes on her, full awareness overtook her. Yeah, it went beyond the lapse, that's why she couldn't shake the rage. Just like Carlos had wanted absolute power and fawning lieutenants, deep down inside, which allowed him to ultimately go after

Yonnie like he had, he'd also secretly harbored the fantasy of having one last run with Juanita before getting married . . . for old time's sake, deep down inside . . . along with the power of a throne, supernatural strength and knowledge, and the ability to single-handedly blow up Hell. Carlos got that fantasy, all of it, and that's how they got to him.

Instant knowing slapped her face, and almost made her jerk her head back, the sensation was so severe. He'd never fully embraced or appreciated the gift or responsibility of being a Neteru. That was too ordinary for him. Too powerless by comparison to what he'd been before. His mind kept constantly going back to the so-called good old days of absolute power where he could cast illusion, receive VIP treatment everywhere he went, walk through walls, battle bulk, fight, regenerate missing limbs if necessary, and hit the vanishing point to blow a sister's mind with no effort. Damali balled her hands into fists; his short-sightedness made her want to scream.

The dark side had taken it to the max, albeit way beyond what Carlos had consciously wanted or intended. Although he'd never do Yonnie and Tara like that, or probably Juanita, the fact remained that if his power lust hadn't been there, with all the other dark lusts he owned, Damali knew in her soul that things wouldn't have gotten crazy. He would have been a pure Neteru, versus what he'd returned as—part human, part Neteru, part Council-level vampire. The fusion had to happen when he'd come through the heat of Hell's furnace and into the atomic-level burn of the Light.

Damali shook her head.

"You all right, baby?" Marlene asked quietly.

"Yeah," Damali said in a distant voice, not opening her eyes. "A few more minutes. I think I've got it now."

Damali ran her palms over her face, feeling the slight moistness that had crept over her brow. The last episode had cultivated a quiet, deeply personal meltdown within her and something evil had attached itself to that when she couldn't take it anymore.

From his drug-dealing days, to becoming a vampire and all the madness that went with that, to accidentally getting pregnant with him, and losing the baby—but not just losing it, but having to retrieve it and slaughter the demon thief that stole it . . . nearly losing her title for him, having to reconfigure the team to accommodate him, having to share her command of the Guardians with him, then for him to go against what the Light had told him, after being a catalyst to her loss of the Isis and having to run all over the world to get it back . . . and then him getting compromised, *again*, on *a dark throne* no less—oh, yeah, it was about so much more than Juanita. Love or not, through-the-fire devotion or not, this man had shattered her nerves.

She'd wanted a new, safe pair of arms to hold her, ones without history, ones without house consequences. An older, wiser, more disciplined soul . . . one with charisma and sensuality and music who could appreciate her gifts, his gifts, her art, and had some sexy new ways of his own, but without all the changes that Carlos Rivera had taken her through over the years.

It had been at the forefront of her mind that day like never before. As she'd driven from Malibu back to Beverly Hills the thought had almost become a mantra. She'd pleaded out loud with hot tears running down her face, "God, give me somebody I don't have to go through changes like this with anymore." She also remembered the more urgent, silent part of the prayer. "Give me a man who is comfortable in his own skin and who loves being a Neteru." She almost laughed out loud in despair as new tears wet her lashes. She hadn't named names, and wasn't specific, which was most likely why the being who showed up didn't reveal a name—*she hadn't asked for one*—even though the rest of him was made to order! Like Marlene had always told her, be careful what you wish for, 'cause ya just might get it.

Damali quietly shook her head and wrapped her arms around herself. She could suddenly hear Carlos's mirror-image-request echoing through her head with as much pain as hers had contained. "Let her know what it feels like to have everybody looking at you sideways all the time. Let her know how something could go down like it did, but not mean all what it seemed to mean. Make her know how hard it is to resist something that has you all caught up and that's stronger than you."

Two Neterus of equal power, passion, and righteous indignation, praying hard, at the same time, in polar opposite directions on the same subject? Carlos had manifested this scenario as much as she did! Damali shuddered. Surely the Light would accommodate their requests, but also let them both know it was not to be trifled with for personal nonsense. That could only mean a stern lesson was about to be taught. Her only prayer now was that her team be spared drama on this go-round, if possible.

Thankfully, when she'd lobbed the Heaven-bound request, she'd blocked any attachment she had to Jose, not wanting to put him in the middle of a potentially disastrous liaison. And even though she'd been angry as all get out with Juanita, she didn't want to go after Jose for spite—he deserved better. Frankly, Juanita did, too. But she had to be honest. Deep down, a little female vengeance had slithered through her human soul. That's what had been her weakness, and something dark had worked with what she'd given it.

Damali couldn't move as the thoughts replayed in rapidly increasing blurs of knowing. She'd wanted Carlos, just once, to walk a mile in her shoes—wanted Heaven to teach him a lesson; now she was sure that he also wanted the same thing, and also got it.

But when she'd prayed for what she did, all she'd wanted was for him to sense what it felt like when one's lover played with fire, knowing that it burned the other partner more than the one striking the match. Wanted him to see how one's lapse could cause a chain reaction of chaos and emotional fallout that everyone else had to deal with. Wanted him to be a little insecure, to count his blessings that she was his and never again dare stray under any circumstances after he got her back. *Let him twist* had been at the forefront of her mind all the way home. Damali squeezed her eyes shut tighter.

Then, she viscerally remembered wanting him to see how it felt to be the logical one holding onto the Light while *she* gave in to whatever sensory indulgence she wanted to, and allowed *him* to be the one to pull her ass out of the fire—then see how he liked that. She wanted a chance to be the irrational party for a change and to let the chips fall where they may. There was no denying how she had felt that day. Rage had strangled her reason, made her forget how spiritually powerful she was as a grown-up and a seasoned Neteru. She'd consciously wanted to hand Carlos the big broom to sweep up after she did something off the hook, then have him be the one to suck it up and move on.

Damali's hand covered her mouth. "Oh, my God," she whispered, opening her eyes to a team holding its breath. She'd definitely conjured this, called it up, and she got what she asked for. And it came to her tall, fine . . . "Okay, listen," she said, beginning to pace and rake her hair. "It's not from the dark side, but not exactly from the Light, either. That much I know."

"I have to ask this again, because I feel in my gut that we're missing a crucial element. When it talked to you," Father Patrick finally said, breaking the silence on the phone, "try to remember. Did it leave any clues?"

Damali paused and let out a frustrated breath. The team had hashed and rehashed most of what the entity said and did, her privacy edits notwithstanding. She scoured her mind for anything relevant beyond what had been told, and glared at J.L. again, forbidding him with her eyes to ever replay the recording. That was going in the fireplace as soon as the clerics got off the telephone.

"I asked him his name," she said, letting out an exasperated rush of air with the words. "He said it would make me pick up my blade again," she added, staring at the telephone and then glancing up at Marlene. "We got off the subject," she said, walking away from the speakerphone and giving the group her back, too humiliated to go into further detail. She stopped. Maybe unnecessary shame and guilt had been blotting out portions of the conversation.

Damali began very quietly as the entity's deep melodic voice flowed over her mind. "I asked him where he was from," she murmured, "and he said, 'the Land of Nod.' "

"What!" Father Patrick yelled.

All eyes went to the phone as Damali froze where she stood.

"Where's that, Father P?" Shabazz asked quickly. "A realm of Hell?"

"This is very bad," Rabbi Zeitloff shouted. "Oy!"

"It's a banishment containment center," Father Patrick said. His voice was fading in and out as though the man was moving around the room, possibly pacing away from the telephone and back to it. "It was also rumored to be Atlantis."

"Wait," Marlene said. "Let me get this straight, Father. You mean to say our girl called up something from undersea—like an old Greek or Roman god?"

"It's not underwater," Rabbi Zeitloff corrected. "That is mere rumor. To the people of the time, it may have looked like it was swept away by a tidal wave consuming the whole of it—but in more correct terms, it was like an energy tsunami. According to my late brother's work, it was enveloped and swallowed between dimensions by a significant cosmic force. This is why he was working for the government on interdimensional travel and other beings that might inhabit that dimension, when he instead stumbled upon the portals of the dark realms and vampires . . . which sadly led to his death. He was following earlier re-search done by the U.S. Navy. Do you remember, of all things, the Philadelphia Experiment?"

"Krissy, J.L." Damali said quickly, "get on the Internet and search while the rabbi talks."

They immediately dashed over to the banks of computers and began firing up the tubes as the elderly rabbi continued.

"Ironically, yes, in the end of days, Philadelphia is spoken of in the old books, and a big team confrontation happened there. But this project was an attempt by the navy during World War II, in nineteen forty-three, to make the battleship U.S.S. *Eldridge* invisible by using Einstein and Telsa's theories of bending light and matter displacement. The first time they did it, all but the hull of the battleship disappeared. The second time they ran the experiment, the ship totally disappeared in the Delaware Bay and reappeared in Norfolk, Virginia, missing some of the crew who were never found. Those who did come back with the ship claimed some of the crew spontaneously combusted, were frozen in time, vanished, what have you. Of course, the military said everyone was suffering post-battle delusions and discredited them. But my brother knew better, and had top-secret clearance to what was also known as Project Rainbow."

"There's a lot of data out here," Krissy said.

"Yeah, but only from speculative-fiction sites, and alien-watcher or conspiracy-theory sites," J.L. muttered, his eyes fastened to his tube. "Nothing with a government seal of credibility on it."

"This project is held as closely to the vest as all the Area Fifty-one alien research projects," Rabbi Zeitloff said, his tone annoyed. "They lie to the people and keep us in the dark like sheep!"

"Then, let's bust the Pentagon's files," Krissy said, her hands feverishly gliding over her keyboard. "I know I can—"

"Yo, yo, yo!" J.L. said, grabbing her wrists. "D, whatchu wanna do? This is serious shit. You breach their files, and we're gonna have to be on the move again."

"For real," Shabazz said. "You might as well open a Hell portal and not expect bats to fly out."

"Krissy, have you lost your mind?" Berkfield asked. "Sheesh, Marj, talk to your daughter!"

"All right," Damali said, letting her breath out hard again. "Last resort. We save that as a silver bullet—but good looking out, Krissy. If you've got mad skills like that, it will definitely come in handy one day."

"But not today. Shit," Rider said, standing and toppling his chair. "You kids are gonna give me a stomach ulcer. Tell her,'Bazz. Draw your weapon, aim steady at the target, but wait until you have a lock on its forehead before squeezing the trigger. You don't go shooting into cyberspace buck wild any more than you would in a tunnel to cause collateral damage."

"She was just trying to help, man," J.L. said defensively. "Stand down."

Rider's eyes got wide. He tilted his head to the side and chuckled. "Cool. Your protégé. My bad."

"Okay," Damali said, nervous energy about to make her snap. "Any of you guys on the clerical team know another way into Nod besides breaching Pentagon security to find a dimension breaker?"

"No," Father Patrick said, his tone distracted.

"Better question might be," Marlene said, going to her black bag, "what swept that realm away and why?"

"God," Father Patrick said without hesitation. "You do not breach those barriers—ever."

No one moved on the team. All eyes were on the telephone. No one even blinked, much less breathed for a few seconds.

"God?" Damali finally whispered.

"Yes," Father Patrick said in a loud, booming voice. "Him."

"Okay, okay, okay—wait!" Damali said, now circling the table like a madwoman. "If this entity came from the Land of Nod, which is in some kinda parallel dimension that ours can't see—and the scientists were using light-bending technology to try to break into it—that has to mean it's from the upper realms, right?" She didn't wait to let Father Patrick answer. "So, if this thing breached God's barrier and came out—"

"It is in serious conflict with the Most High for the offense," Father Patrick said. "Which puts you, and all of us, in a precarious position if you aid and abet it. Neither the Neteru Councils nor the Covenant can get involved in going against the law of the Most High—ever. The only way we can get involved with breaching Nod is if there is a clear and present danger to earth and it's sanctioned. We must wait for a sign."

"Whoa," Damali said defensively. "I said a prayer for it to come out, not a ritual from—"

"You said a what!" Jose was now walking in an agitated circle.

"Later we discuss it," Damali shouted. "Not now!" She returned her focus to the speakerphone. "All right, Father Pat. If this thing came out of a dimensional rip that was already there, caused by a natural disaster that was strong enough to stop time for a few seconds, make the earth wobble on its axis, and to literally shift the north and south poles by a full inch, maybe it isn't in conflict and didn't bust out of cosmic jail, so to speak, but just walked through the opening."

"We'd better hope so," Father Patrick said, his tone strained. "Do you understand the significance of this realm that sits between Heaven and Hell and mirrors our gray zone of choice on earth?"

"No. Talk to us," Damali said, leaning against the weapons table to keep from falling down.

"I can only speak from biblical references, not scientific ones," Father Patrick said slowly. "But in the Old Testament, after Cain slew Abel, God asked him, 'Where is your brother?' To which Cain flippantly replied, 'Am I my brother's keeper?' And then—"

"Oh, shit!" Damali jumped back from the table.

"What, what?" Rider said, also beginning to pace. "D, make it fast. You're compromising my bladder, kiddo."

"He said, 'This time, detriment of my soul, I *am* my brother's keeper.' And when I asked him who his brother was, he said, Carlos—and I thought it was a male Neteru thing he was referring to, and—"

"Holy moley," Rider shouted, slapping his forehead.

"Do the genealogy," Marlene said, dropping her bag on the weapons table with a thud. "On the female Neteru side, we know who sired Cain with Eve."

A few seconds of silence brought a unified response. "The Chairman."

"Lucifer's son," Father Patrick said. "Don't forget, before his fall, Lucifer was the most gorgeous of all the angels, with the most melodic voice, also known as Prince of the Airwaves, with a stronger version of every seduction skill embedded within his son, the Chairman. Dante was to be his secret weapon, but acted prematurely in the Garden. The one we try not to name has that heightened sensual capacity, which was passed down the line with everything else, containing more guile, political treachery, and power lust than is probably even known by the vampire species. The grandfather to this being is master of master vampires, and heir to the Prince of Darkness was the Duke of Darkness, Dante—

also known as the Chairman, who begat Cain. Third removed is diluted, but comparatively speaking, a fraction of dilution does not account for much, given the lineage."

Damali found Rider's toppled chair and sat down hard, panting into her hands to keep from fainting. So much tension wound around her spine that it felt like it could be pulled out from the top of her skull.

"Then girlfriend's sensory instincts obviously kicked in correct," Shabazz said, now pacing with Rider. "She put out an all-points bulletin, a psychic SOS that said she'd been visited by a Level-Seven encounter. Like I was saying back at her condo, something deep went down, blocked her from telling all. But the instant Level-Seven alert with a direct call to Jesus makes a whole lotta sense to me now." He glanced at Marlene with a slight apology in his tone. "Maybe it wasn't nobody's fault, if that's who came calling."

"No wonder baby girl wigged," Big Mike said, his body thudding against the wall like he'd been punched. He looked at Marlene. "You had to be possessed, Mar, and must be missing your mind for keeping something like that from the old heads on this team. But I can understand it now." He glanced at Inez and then lowered his gaze. "And if that's the type of energy that was rolling through the compound, guess can't nobody be mad if anybody choked on spitting out critical info."

Berkfield nodded and rubbed his palm over his scalp as he glanced at his wife and then down at the floor. "Yeah . . . sorry about jumping to conclusions. Guess we were all feeling the effects, or somethin'."

"Damali straight up called for a black-hawk-chopper extraction when it first went down, man," Jose said. He looked at Damali, trying to send an apology to her with his eyes. "If something funky was going down with her and Carlos, and she got pissed off, and maybe asked for somebody who'd understand, and this thing showed up with that much juice instead . . . hey. Could happen to anybody." He sighed hard and cast his gaze toward the speakerphone, seeming contrite but more worried than before. "But how could a prayer directed toward the Light get deflected all the way *down there?*"

"That's the conundrum of it all," Father Patrick said slowly. "I don't think it got deflected or intercepted by the darkside. They can't simply snatch a prayer like that, unless the prayer had darkness threaded within it. It's wrapped in Light. Cain is not the Antichrist. He's human, or was human, while he lived on earth. Like his grandfather, he had no problem with daylight and isn't sterile. He doesn't reside on Level Seven any more than you or I do. He killed a man, who happened to be his brother, and is serving time, but he hasn't been rendered vampire sterile, isn't the living dead or an immortal demon, and doesn't have the blood hunger. The Chairman was made sterile, with all the vampire powers and limitations of sunlight depravation, by his father, Lucifer, upon almost prematurely beginning the big war between realms through his escapades in the Garden. But Cain has sired normal human infants with no more or less proclivities for evil or violence than any other human being."

Damali closed her eyes. Her prayer was more like a rant, a dark and vengeful wish, than anything else—and the darkside snagged it. She knew that fact like she knew her name.

"Must be the solid topspin from his mother's side," Shabazz muttered, worry straining his face as he stared at Damali.

"Yes," Father Patrick said. "On the maternal side, there is Light and humanity, human genetic foundation. He is half Neteru, and half something I don't want to consider. However, it states it clearly in the New Testament, I-John: 3:12, 'Cain comes from the evil one.' Yet it also states within the biblical texts that, after Cain was discovered and God's wrath was upon him, he begged not to be banished fearing those in the Land of Nod would kill him. To which God assured him that he would not die from the hands of those in Nod due to His mark upon Cain."

"I know the story well, Father," Marlene said. "Grew up in the South, in church, but with all that was happening here, I didn't make the connection," she said quietly, looking at Damali until their eyes met. "We thought he was the muse of music, and never dreamed . . ."

"He should be gifted with music, like no other entity but the angels that guide creative expression, because, after all, his grandfather was the most beautiful voice in Heaven's choir at one time, and was the most gifted in music of all the angels before he fell," Father Patrick stated bluntly.

The elderly priest drew a shaky breath. "If Damali somehow called him, and he is who we suspect, well . . . he would be handsome beyond imagination, be so musically adept, and tuned in to her near-angelic sound vibrations—because she's a Neteru—that an instant bond could be easily established, and would also dangerously hold the very fabric of information from the Tree of Knowledge that his father breached in the

Garden when he took Eve. He's smart. Do not underestimate him at all. The only issue is as long as he's functioning as a human Neteru, then by the mark of God, he cannot be killed—or we would be going against the law. If any of us do that, then our souls would bottom out in the dark realms . . . and given our lifelong profession of demon slaying, you can imagine the penance any of us would do down there."

Damali let her head drop back and closed her eyes with a loud groan. "Oh, no . . ."

"Let me get this right, Father Pat," Rider said, sitting slowly on the edge of the weapons table. "Our girl accidentally hooks up with a mind-blowing cosmic choir director who is physically awesome by all female standards and has direct Neteru juice from the *first female* ever made on the planet. Which means," Rider pressed on when no one stopped him, "on the one hand, this guy has all the pull power-squared, of a Council-level master vampire, with all the knowledge and lovemaking skills, yada, yada, yada, of the species—directly from the Tree of Knowledge that his daddy breached, but came out in *broad daylight* and ain't sterile, and, I might add, just to keep it interesting, has a nose for female Neterus."

"When he came to me, he was apexing," Damali said quietly, cringing with her eyes still shut tightly. "Oh, my God . . ."

Rider sighed. "Well, that *does* make it interesting, kiddo, because on the other hand, from what you're telling us, Father, this guy has his good days when he's all armor and honor, from his mother's side, so holy water, silver nitrate, hallowed shells, and whatever else we've got in our arsenal won't drop him—and, again, to keep it interesting, we're not supposed to kill him because of this human Neteru DNA giving him freedom of choice to be good or bad, and the Almighty's edict in the equation. Conundrum? Father, excuse my French, but this is well beyond a damned rock and a hard place."

"Our boy, Carlos, is screwed," Big Mike said, shaking his head. He stared at Damali. "If Carlos bugs hard over in Nod, like he did when he saw you in the brother's arms, and goes vamp—sounds to me like Cain will whip his natural ass. Fang for fang, if he's Dante's boy, plus, if Carlos wins and smokes Cain, he's also screwed, and probably doesn't even know it—"

"I know," Damali said, leaning forward with her face in her hands.

"Girl, this is raggedy," Inez said, going to stand by Big Mike. "If the brother is a Neteru, too, and Carlos comes at him like that, he's been one longer, has come into his full powers over several generations, plus his momma *had* him—so even *that* wasn't diluted, D. He wasn't an *elevated* Neteru like Carlos. This guy was a natural birth. Same with being the Chairman's son . . . Cain didn't just get bitten to be made a vamp; he was made from doing the wild thing. That has got to have more kick to it, right?"

Juanita's hands went to her hips as she went to stand by Jose. "You should have been more careful, Damali. How could you put Carlos in a position like that? After all that man did for you, and the way he loves you . . ." She began to pace. "I cannot believe you!"

Damali felt herself beginning to rise out of the chair. "You don't know what goes down between me and him and I suggest you don't even go there." The urge to tell Juanita that she might remember some shit that would make her hair fall out was on the tip of Damali's tongue so hard she could taste it. Juanita's gall and audacity continued imploding in her brain, and she had to look at Jose to remember that there was more at stake than being right at the moment. But were it not for Dan jumping between them, they could have had it out in the middle of the floor.

"Plus, dude has an army," Dan said, raking his hair.

"Come again?" Damali said, snatching her focus from Juanita and looking at Dan in earnest for the first time.

"You heard Father Pat," Dan said, his blue eyes darting around the team as Damali angrily walked back to her chair and flopped down in it. "Father Pat said that Cain begged not to be killed by the inhabitants of Nod, right? You do the math. It was Adam and Eve, they had Cain and Abel, and Cain killed Abel, then later Adam and Eve had Seth after all that dust had settled. At the time Cain was pleading for amnesty, there were only three humans topside—Adam, Eve, and Cain, since Abel was dead and Seth hadn't been born yet. So who was around to off him?"

Again the room went still for a moment as Damali stared at Dan and then at the speakerphone.

"This is where old Kabbalah, the Bible, Quran, and some of the old Eastern tantra, among other philosophies, respectfully collide and agree to disagree," Father Patrick said with care.

"No disrespect, Father," Marlene said. "May I take a crack at this one to keep you and the other clerics from crossing the lines inherent within your various faith orders?"

"Please," Father Patrick said in a rush. "I can't, not sitting on a phone within the Vatican."

Marlene walked back and forth like a schoolteacher as she spoke, holding the attention of the group and the strained listeners on the phone. "If we go with the whole Atlantis construct," she said, nodding as she spoke, "that was a place of profound knowledge, an advanced civilization, also the thing of old legends, just like the Greek and Roman gods. Actually, you can find the same references in every culture across the globe. There is a belief that angels and demons mingled with humans, creating a super race with profound intelligence, surreal beauty, and supernatural powers that made mere mortals think they were gods. The angels were finally forbidden to mingle with humans like that, and had to be etheric entities that simply assisted the human race, but couldn't actively participate with, or . . . uh, cohabitate with them. The angels listened to the directive but the other side, naturally, did not."

"That's crazy, Mar," Shabazz said while nodding his agreement. "But, get back to what Dan said. Even if we buy that theory or go with the legends, then who were they gettin' busy with, if there was only Adam and Eve as the first humans? We only have an account of Eve—"

"Shabazz," Marlene said impatiently. "Yeah, if we go by the Bible only. But if you factor in myths and oral traditions of many cultures, that was the second go 'round. We're only supposed to follow that text and others like it, as those old, approved books begin our human-only history. The other info was lost and/or destroyed so people wouldn't get confused, or do what these mad scientists are trying to do—resurrect something that should be left alone."

Marlene let out a weary sigh and stopped pacing to stare at the group, but she directed her voice toward the speakerphone. "In Eden, the Tree of Knowledge was off limits because of what had happened before. Our books begin with our human lineage, not the first experiment when everything was wide open, no rules and laws laid down. Humans were made, the angels and demons regularly interacted with them, and humans had access to the Tree—so it was assumed that with knowledge, they'd govern themselves accordingly. But that's not what happened. Knowledge without wisdom got all sides messed up, and all sorts of hybrid progeny resulted. The Most High probably got weary, told them to stop, they didn't, so . . ."

"He separates that too-live crew of mixed-up entities, sticks 'em in the Land of Nod, keeps them away from his newest, pure invention, Adam and Eve, puts those two in the Garden, and says, 'Don't even go *near* that tree,'" Berkfield said, awed. "And then He starts over again?" He shook his head. "*No wonder* He was really pissed off when Dante crossed that barrier. Probably freaked, called an army up, and was ready to dust Lucifer on the spot." Berkfield's eyes went to Krissy and hardened on J.L. "His new baby girl? As a father, I can dig it—thunder and lightning bolts, flames from the sky, floods, plagues, and all." His line of vision held J.L.'s until the younger Guardian looked away. "Frankly, I'm an Old Testament kinda guy, myself."

"I'll go back to the Greeks and Romans," Marlene said calmly, deflecting a new potential storm that was brewing. "Let's take that mythology as a blueprint, just because that's all in the same region as the old biblical issues we're discussing, but think about some of their gods and goddesses." Marlene glanced around the room, receiving nods of understanding. "Pan—half goat, half boy, with a penchant for mischief and owning musical abilities. I'd bet my walking stick on what realm sired him. Medusa, with serpent hair. Centaurs and cyclops, ogres and giants. Land of the Titans. Mount Olympus, in my mind, wasn't nothing but a cliffside lair for old Zeus . . . bet his daddy was one of the old boys downtown the way he ran women."

Marlene sucked her teeth with disgust and the team's attention remained riveted on her. "But there were also some very fine goddesses, like Venus, that were good. As well as strong, honorable half-breeds like Hercules. Get the picture? I could do this in Native American, African, Asian, Slavic, Caribbean, and East Indian, pick a culture, and we could stay here all day. But the point is, these beings were given to tantrums, for all their sophistication—ultimate hedonists. They weren't about service to humankind, as is the foundation edict given to the angels, because their human side makes them, well, humanly selfish. If they've got anything else in them, it just kicks it up to the third power, making them more powerful whatever they are—good, bad, and otherwise. Not to mention they lived such long life spans that they seemed immortal. Are you following? But these temperamental, spoiled kids, who were prone to excess—"

"Made slaves of humans, demanded sacrifices and ceremonies," Krissy said. "They knew they were special, like princes and princesses of something more than human, and couldn't bend the human ego in them to actually serve anybody or anything but their lusts—and got in trouble, right?"

"Out of the mouths of babes," Marlene said, slapping her hand on the table, pleased.

"That is absolutely wild!" Marjorie said excitedly. She spun to gaze at her children, a look of glowing pride on her face as she stared at Krissy. "You see why education is so important, and why I kept telling you guys to learn world history, and geography, and science, even old literature? You *have* to know these things to function in the world. You must broaden your perspectives and—"

"*Mom,*" Bobby groaned. "Please, not now. Dad . . . tell her to stop."

"If I'm getting warm, cough twice for yes, and once for no, Father Patrick," Marlene said with a smile, "so *you* don't get in trouble for cosigning my theory."

Two loud coughs came through the speaker.

"But because they had a choice, from their human parentage, to be either good or bad and to make the most of their powers," Damali said quietly, looking at Marlene, "they weren't destroyed outright."

Marlene nodded. "Yep. I'll bet that it was initially a secluded, hard-to-get-to place on earth, given the transportation technology of that era, like an island or a mountain, something real difficult to access."

"Right," Damali said, her head bobbing as she thought out loud. "In every legend, to get to the so-called gods, a normal human had to go on some long, arduous trek to some crazy place to speak to one of them." The Oracle at Delphi jumped into her mind. Carlos had put that image into her head back in her house in Arizona, which renewed her annoyance at him. But it fit. The joint was wild, the place jumping, and every profoundly kinky vice that would make the average person squint made her shiver, just remembering what she'd seen.

"Yeah," Marlene said with a satisfied sigh. "However, these entities didn't stay put. Humans were a new, forbidden toy to these big kids. So, even though humans couldn't easily get to them, the reverse wasn't true. They came over to where they weren't supposed to be and started messing with people, sharing deep knowledge too advanced for human evolutionary development or consumption, and finally got into enough trouble by causing havoc that they got swept into the Land of Nod, or swept away in the great Atlantis wipeout," Marlene said, finishing Damali's thought.

"Well, if it's cool over there, ain't Hell and all . . . and they can do all this stuff and be whatever, why did one rip through the fabric to come here?" Jose's tone was filled with curiosity, not judgment. "I mean, for real, if there's goddesses on their side, then . . ."

"Oh, so like my girl is chopped liver?" Inez said with hands on hips.

"No, he's got a point," Damali said, standing again. "I ain't no match for Venus, let's be real. And if they can procreate, have a superior level of technology, all the stuff the scientists were after, why would they subject themselves to the human condition?"

"Probably too many chiefs," Shabazz said flatly. "Didn't Krissy say something about them making humans slaves? What fun is it to play god with nobody to worship you anymore? If they've all got da juice, hey."

Two loud coughs echoed from the speaker, followed by a round from each cleric on the line.

"So, we're not necessarily talking Armageddon here. We're talking about a basic takeover of the planet by the gods of old? You have got to be kidding me." Rider jumped down from the table as two more coughs sputtered through the speakerphone.

"All I wanna know is," Shabazz said, "how do we know which ones we can outright smoke if they pass from their dimension into ours until we close this rip? I personally ain't trying to have an angel's blood on my hands, no more than another human's."

"Sho' you right," Big Mike concurred, looking at Berkfield. "Any of us that been to war for our country already have to deal with that. But then when you put angels in the mix, me, for one, I ain't blowing up shit until I know for sure. It has to present fangs, first—feel me?"

Damali nodded. "Primary order of business is for me to figure out how to get into that dimension. It's not about calling anything through the rip until we know which entity is coming through the tear, where it hails from lineage-wise, and what its agenda is."

"I have to ask a delicate question before you go anywhere, though," Marlene said. She stared at the telephone. "If we take the team—"

A loud single cough stopped her words.

"The team can't go?" Marlene glanced at Damali.

Two coughs sounded.

"By herself isn't advisable, either, given Cain's interest in her."

Silence echoed in the room.

"All right," Marlene said calmly. "Let me ask it this way. Is there some reason why a human team cannot go with their Neteru in search of the other Neteru?"

Two coughs sounded.

"This twenty questions is kicking my ass," Berkfield said, running a palm over his bald scalp. "C'mon, Father, talk to us."

"He can't," Damali said flatly. "Nor does he know the way in."

Two coughs answered.

"If Heaven knew that this natural disaster was headed in our direction, they knew the rip would occur before the Armageddon kicked off, right?" Damali stared at the telephone.

Again, two loud coughs filled the speakerphone.

Damali began walking to help herself think. The Light always had a very good reason for anything it did or allowed. Figuring out the puzzle and adhering to what was the underlying message in the lesson was the tricky part.

"Okay, guys," Damali said, lost deep in thought. "Just like the Darkness was trying to do, the Light is concentrating, pulling in what was theirs to amp up for major battle. My guess is they're banking on mercenary soldiers from their far-flung angel corps, the ones over there in Nod that could help sway the balance and have superhuman powers, but also are grounded by a human soul and choice factor. Those that are ready in Nod have gotten themselves together and served their time well. Maybe they're supposed to cross over through the rip and really be of service to humankind in the last days."

Another excited series of loud coughs filled the phone.

"Cool," Damali said flatly as she leveled her gaze at the group and then Juanita. "So, maybe my prayer wasn't a mistake, after all? Maybe it was part of the grand cosmic design, and as a Neteru warrior, I was *supposed* to rally those troops, ya think?" Vindicated, she strode away from the telephone, now truly irritated.

"But the Light wouldn't allow the planet to be flooded by half-demons, no matter what." Marlene began walking, raked her hair, and looked out of the window. "There has to be something that's keeping the bad guys at bay. So there has to be something in a Neteru's ability to summon them through the rip. Maybe Neterus are the only ones that can do it, so we have to be careful what we summon."

Two more aggressive coughs greeted Marlene's statement. The team stared at her.

Now Damali was really confused, because an honorable Cain had come through. He spoke of humanity, of art, of the positive—while also having one thing on his mind as he apexed, like Carlos would. She knew the cosmic lesson would spank her natural butt, but had no idea it would be something like *this*. And the hardest part of it all to deal with was he'd come through more awesome than her man.

All eyes were on Damali. Silence again filled the room with tension. Yeah, she'd asked for it, but never in a million years thought something like that could be possible. Up until now, her man had been the baddest mutha on the planet . . . but she hadn't really had a chance to look around, and before all that mess had really never wanted to. Apparently Carlos got his wish, too. Something stronger than she, more alluring than anything she'd encountered, with everything that could blow her mind, had rolled up on her and weakened her resolve . . . had a little vamp in him counteracted with pure silver Neteru, too? She staved off an inappropriate shudder as the entity's image came into her mind. The man was fine. Period. No matter who his daddy was. Halfway served Carlos's ass right for even going there. But the fact remained: the not-so-fun part of his wish had also come true. She was standing before all eyes having to explain the deeply personal and very inexplicable sequence of events.

"I never called for anything negative, so Cain might actually be on our side," Damali said slowly, her gaze meeting Marlene's before going toward the window. Oddly, she was no longer worried that Carlos would die in a brawl. She sensed the entity that Carlos had rolled through the rip with had more discipline than that, given what was at stake. If Cain made the wrong choice, it stood to reason that his Neteru status would be immediately revoked, snatched, then he'd be sent into the lowest levels of the pit as a human, and with the Chairman gone . . . no.

The entity she'd just met was many things, but she didn't pick up on insanity. Why go to Hell, burn like a human, get your light stamped out and exterminated because you posed a threat from Dante's direct line to a throne versus the next Antichrist's pending rule on it, when you could do earth and stay in good stead? Level Seven had made that mistake once before by creating a premature monarch, and they wouldn't sloppily mess up like that again.

Plus, Cain had been thoroughly offended down to his core when she thought that was who he might be—she'd felt the bristle that wasn't an act. And he'd been honest in his own way, told her that if she knew his name she would jump to conclusions, which she would have. Even told her his mission, in a roundabout way, as well as his connection to Carlos. The man hadn't lied.

"Wild as this sounds," Damali said while the team quietly waited for her decisions, "he was very restrained when he first appeared, and was talking about trying to fulfill his mission of Light after reincarnating repeatedly and needing one last mission to get it right so he could ascend . . . but I was sorta making that difficult for him to keep focused."

As she spoke, the whole conversation reminded her of the way Carlos's turn had been broken to the team. She stood between them and him, forbidding a sudden execution so they could learn more, accomplish more, and they did. Damali sighed. The Light was working her overtime on this lesson. Cain had also told her if she didn't get it right the first time, the Light would repeat the lesson, harder each time, until she did. Had said he would spare her that traumatic experience if he could, but couldn't. Damali smiled a half-smile. This guy was a trip, and to be honest, she kinda liked his style. But what was the lesson?

The worry for Carlos's safety was getting further and further away in her mind. Instinctively she knew he was okay. The Light would protect him over in Nod, and would probably just kick his wayward butt with a lesson or two. The team could temporarily stand down. Not a full off-duty relax, but there was no need to panic. What was important now was finding out answers, understanding what the new mission entailed, and getting Carlos's behind back in the compound . . . why did she always have to pull him out of some mad-crazy situation?

Instant fatigue made Damali complete her instructions to the team in a weary tone. Suddenly she just needed a hot shower and to lie down. "Maybe Cain's mother's DNA is what's dominant in him, if he crossed over from my prayer—especially since he's sired normal kids in the past, regardless of his paternal link. Think about it. Strong Neteru versus strong demon, our side always wins, and the Light was all over him when he stepped through . . . Plus he was talking ascension and tried to keep his hands off me so he wouldn't get in trouble. Everything female and veteran huntress in me says if the guy was leaning vamp, trust me, you all might have walked in on a floor show." She sighed and shrugged, the exhaustion and adrenaline spikes taking their toll. "Maybe that's why Carlos isn't dead or busted up?"

The speakerphone was silent and so was the team.

"Well, the Chairman is ash, by your hand, I might add, and further down in his family tree would be unadvisable to consult, no matter how crazy you are, D. So, it's not like you can just waltz into Hell and ask his daddy or his granddad about his proclivities, to know for sure, can you?" Rider snapped sarcastically, the strain evidently wearing his nerves away.

"No," Damali said with a slow, dawning smile. "But I can go ask his mother."

CHAPTER EIGHT

C'mon, Damali. Call me. Stop playing. The refrain strummed through Carlos's brain like an incessant chant as he followed Cain, watching the thick muscles knead in the huge entity's shoulders as he walked ahead of him.

Even though he was now fairly certain that his woman hadn't totally lost her mind and slept with him, the fact that she got up out of bed and called this bastard kept Carlos's eyes glowing silver. After they'd made love? Carlos wanted to spit, but wouldn't give Cain the satisfaction of seeing just how much the whole thing was jacking with his mind.

After they'd made love? The torturous awareness began to replace his chant for her to call him. Damn . . . and he'd thought he'd put his thing down hard. Shit. Damali had called for something stronger than *that?* He knew this day would come, but had hoped it would be when he was an old man. But what did she want from him? Blood?

Fine. It was like that. Okay. So she wanted a street sample to see what else was out there on the block. All right. Just because of that thing with 'Nita—but he'd had a reason; he'd been possessed. He thought she'd finally let it go, smoke or no smoke, but it was obvious she hadn't. Cool.

Baby, call me. Aw'ight. She didn't have to go there to make her point.

Carlos rolled the tension out of his shoulders and paused. His collarbone had been broken, had snapped clean when he'd hit the barrier. But it had somehow mended on its own just like the old days, but without a feed. What was up with that?

He glanced up at the sun again, just to be sure he wasn't really in Hell. Two strange discs illuminated the sky. One that seemed to generate solar heat, and another that was a swirling opalescent fusion of oranges and yellows and pinks. Very strange. Everything around him had a slightly iridescent quality that made it look surreal. Then, suddenly, it dawned on him, with all this natural splendor surrounding them, he had seen or heard nary a creature. No birds, not even a bug. He inhaled deeply. With all the grass and flowers, no scent?

Carlos stared at Cain's rigid posture and almost snarled as they came to the edge of a cliff. The bastard had the arrogant stride of a king, head held all high and whatnot.

"I still maintain a lair at the realm's edge. You may lodge there, if you choose," Cain said with disinterest. "Or if you prefer to go into the valley and reside at my summer palace for the duration, it is your choice."

Carlos just looked at him. "Do I seem crazy to you—like I'd let you set me up in a lair up in the fucking mountains alone? You might not be able to smoke me, but one of your boys could, and my blood wouldn't be on your hands; I ain't stupid." The reference to a lair disturbed him. One near the border, one so very close to his boo . . . a place where if she tripped through the rip could be where . . . Carlos lifted his chin a little higher, fighting the curiosity of what Cain's spot looked like. "I stay with you."

"As you wish." Cain sighed and shook his head. A sly smile tugged at his mouth. "However, it is a long way down the mountainside, baby brother. If you get tired, I can always throw you over my shoulder and carry you the balance of the way. Just let me know."

Carlos's eyes narrowed.

"You'll kill yourself going down," Cain said, badly concealing a chuckle. "Look over the edge."

Carlos brushed past Cain but gave him wide berth as he passed. Just the slight bump against Cain's rock-solid frame told him the entity was getting stronger, if that was possible. He peered down the steep incline and saw clouds, then small dots of buildings and movement. Whateva. He had vamp in him and could get down unassisted.

Cain shook his head. "You have not acclimated to our vibration. Your body is still too dense. Perhaps we should wait a few hours before you enter my kingdom."

Again Carlos stared at him, gaining critical information from the brief statement. If the entity was losing density but gaining strength on this side of the rip, then that also meant that when on the other side of it, his side, he would possibly lose some power in the density transition. All right. He could work with that.

"Oh, please, you're a king, da man? Gimme a break."

"Yes," was all Cain said, and he walked toward a steep crag.

Maybe it was the flat nonplussed tone that Cain had used to answer him, but it messed with Carlos no end. *He was a king?* Damali had gone too far!

But he was forced to watch in awe as Cain slid his sword out of the heavy leather harness down his back, touched it to the rock wall, and made the illusion of natural landscape dissipate. Huge black onyx sphinxes guarded the entrance to what appeared to be a heavily columned temple. When they purred a welcome, Carlos jumped back. Cain chuckled and began walking forward. His footsteps left jeweled green energy in their wake that spread out on the carpet of what had seemed like grass to overtake it.

Carlos's attention was torn between the grass and the color waves overriding it, and the things guarding the entrance to Cain's spot. Everything here was freakin' energy? How did they eat? What did they eat? His focus split again as Cain stopped before the entrance, stroked a fawning lion's back, and it nuzzled his shoulder as the other one stood and roared a complaint to get similar attention.

"Shush," Cain said in a low, calm voice, sheathing his blade. "It is all right."

The sphinxes glowered at Carlos, nuzzled their master again, and sat back down on their pedestals with eyes forward. Cain motioned with his head for Carlos to follow him inside. But how did Cain kept those suckers fed and chilled out?

If he hadn't been a competitor, Carlos might have openly admitted that what Cain had just shown him was some smooth shit. However, any appreciation for what this brother could do would remain a very quiet secret within his weary soul. Carlos edged by the lions and kept his gaze sweeping as they entered a long, open corridor.

A gleaming, oblong, crystal-blue pool of water stretched before him in Olympic proportions, almost seeming like glass. Carlos studied it hard, and for the first time really witnessing the delicate, congruent bands of hue that made up the shimmering surface. Water wasn't water? Oh, shit, he was screwed.

Energy-generated lotus blossoms floated on the still surface, and white marble was everywhere. Carlos had to fight with himself not to reach out and touch it so that he could inspect the phenomena in detail.

From where he stood, it seemed as though pure gold was the mortar between the marble tiles. Freaking hieroglyphics with inlaid silver? And everything around him had an energy pulse. Almost gave off a tone from the slightly moving hues. The brother could hold illusion energy like that, put tone and color all in it to this degree? Dayum. Oh, hell no, his woman couldn't *ever* come over here and see this shit. If this was just a cliff-side lair, not even the main palace, then . . .

"You need some clothes," Cain said, unfastening his blade harness and casually dropping it on a white marble bench by the pool.

For the first time since they'd clashed, Carlos studied the weapon with full appreciation. *That* was real. It was held in a black, hand-tooled sheath with intricate designs of gold and silver studs that had been forced into the leather. The ornate platinum handle was crusted with diamonds, and the four blades that became one were highly polished steel, but in the center blood gutters were gold alloy with silver Neteru symbology worked along them. And the Neteru King's Council had just given him a pocketknife? No respect.

He refused to go deeper into Cain's lair as he watched him walk up a flight of twelve alabaster steps, his feet making the pale pastel colors in the masonry swirl beneath each footfall. Carlos ran his hand over the nape of his neck to keep from battle bulking again as Cain strode with unflinching authority past a massive, solid gold, twenty-four-karat four-poster bed, each post crested by a pyramid-shaped, clear quartz crystal as big as his fist.

Vivid hibiscus in vibrant color splashes, ferns and elephant grass and huge leafy jewel-green plants of energy looked like they simply grew up from the marble floor and surrounded the bed. Energy-trembling white silk linens, white-on-white satin embroidered pillows, and sheer Egyptian drapes that resonated with low, sensual harmonic tones sprawled lazily across the monument of pure decadence. Aw, man . . . tones from the colors . . . white had every rainbow color resident within it, therefore every note.

Instant insecurity rooted Carlos to the floor. Cain could probably fire up the bed like Rider could fire up his ax, pull a blossom off a nearby plant and hand it to Damali all romantic-like while composing on the fly, and make everything around them and under them do multipart harmony. *This* was the brother's studio, for real. *This* was where he probably listened to Damali's work. This put a vanishing-point move to shame—

or . . . shit, what if he could do that too, with the music vibe to go with it? Have her atomically deconstruct, tap a white-light color fusion, feel all the music, every tone to the max, and then bring her back breathless while *wurkin'*. The brother was built, even he had to admit. Plus this motherfucker could sing?

Carlos briefly closed his eyes and walked in a tight circle, and then abruptly stopped himself so he wouldn't give Cain any more satisfaction than he probably already had. No woman had ever put him in a position like this—*ever*. If his own imagination didn't kick his ass first, something told him there was a possibility that the SOB coolly getting undressed and dropping heavy armor might.

Okay, he had to keep his head tight as a matter of pride. So the man could handle his business—but he'd have to kill his ass for sure, if he ever dragged D over this threshold. Period.

He was so upset that he couldn't ignore Cain. The being turned around and casually loped toward a huge marble built-in armoire that held an ornate twelve-foot silver-edged mirror. Carlos's heart was beating harder than it needed to. If his woman ever fell by this joint . . .

Just man-up and suck it up, Carlos told himself. He wasn't no punk. Fuck it. Carlos's gaze shot around the expanse. Tall, eight-foot Egyptian pots seemed to guard each of the twelve columns that stood beside the small energy lake fronting as a pool in this brother's bedroom. Carlos swept them mentally—this was as good a place as any for a black adder to slither out. But Cain seemed so relaxed and casual it was setting Carlos's teeth on edge.

He watched Cain serve him his back, remove his body armor, and drop it to the floor like a man who'd come home from a tough day at the office. No stress, no worries, just glad to be home, and tolerating the noise his children were making. That had to be the only reason Cain was physically changing and not just willing it so—he was obviously tired. The battle on the other side of the rip had worn him out a little; Carlos clung to that, glad that something gave him the advantage.

But he wasn't sure what pissed him off more, the fact that this guy clearly wasn't worried about him—so much so that he'd left a weapon within his reach, turned his back on him, and was trying to figure out what to change into, like he wasn't even there—or the fact that he'd have to do about a thousand more push-ups a day and bench press three-fifty at the gym to *ever* be cut like that.

Carlos rubbed his hands down his face. Damali was so wrong, the girl couldn't ever get right.

Cain tossed a pair of sandals in Carlos's direction, making them whir toward him like Frisbees. Carlos caught one in each hand, and then flung them down hard. He wasn't wearing this SOB's clothes. And he definitely wasn't stepping into shoes in front of Cain that would be way too big. Truth be told, he really didn't wanna know how much bigger Cain's feet were than his at the moment, and he definitely wasn't putting on a robe that would swallow him whole—clean or not. Doing the fang comparison had been humbling enough. The man had him by two inches, which was *never* gonna sit well with him as long as he was alive.

"You cannot walk around without shoes," Cain said, giving him a quizzical look. "It is not done in the royal families." He pulled a long, elegant, gold-toned robe over his head, and began fastening the elaborate embroidered clasps with silver lion's-teeth hooks.

Of all days for him to go looking for Damali . . . no shoes on, no drawers, just a pair of pants, no shirt. Wait until he got home! Carlos stared at the shoes on the floor, willing them to be the right size. If he could just get a good vamp whirl going, he'd serve the cocky bastard across the room black Armani, a pair of leather slip-ons, and show him how it was done back in the 'hood. Matter of fact, he didn't do Old World nothing, not robes and dreadlocks, nor Egyptian braids, none of that—he did clean-shaven, precision-cut. Fuck Cain!

And, yeah, he cussed—so? If Damali wanted some romance-language shit, some corny guy carrying a blade instead of a nine, who would croon to her in what sounded like Shakespeare's era, she could have all that. It wasn't him by a long shot. And so what if he didn't sing, he'd like to see Cain's ass at a modern-day bargaining table, throwing down serious deal-making, strategy, handling business like it needed to be handled—he *had* a skill, now, she'd better act like she knows. Not to mention—

"Why are you working yourself up like this over a pair of shoes?" Cain said, seeming genuinely perplexed. "Conserve your energy."

Carlos could practically feel steam coming out of his ears. He was so angry that his throat was cracked and dry. His blood pressure was spiking so hard it felt like his pulse was pushing his eyeballs out of their sockets. He made fists with his hands. "I want *my* shoes, *my* shit, and I don't want *anything* from you," he shouted.

Cain smiled, shook his head, and went back to his closet. "Now you really *do* sound like a child."

"Are you sure?" Marlene asked, glancing around the compound's altar room.

Damali's gaze took in each of the ancestral artifacts and mementos from many lands that rested peacefully within the solemn, wood-framed room. Bright sunlight poured into it to splash the ivory walls. She took a deep breath. "Yeah. I need to talk to Queen Eve."

"Remember, Damali, that's still his mother—Neteru or not."

"I know," Damali assured her as she stepped forward, preparing to kneel.

Marlene caught her arm. "No. You *don't* know. The mother-son bond is stronger than anything you could imagine. I know Eve won't take this to the male Neteru Roundtable for a divination on her own. Not when it comes to Cain. She and Adam have been at odds for years over her son, his *stepson,* okay? I'd feel better if you went to a more neutral queen from that era, like Nefertiti. Even though her husband, Akhenaton, got elevated posthumously he holds serious advisor weight at the table—since he reintroduced monotheism into law after periods of human uncertainty on the many gods issue."

"It'll be fine, Mar," Damali said with a calm smile.

Marlene let Damali's arm go, becoming exasperated with worry as Damali knelt. Nervous and wound up like a top, Marlene paced back and forth in front of the altar, keeping her voice low and reverent. "Besides, Akhenaton had six daughters, and was always seen with his queen at his side—seven women, Damali. You know he's seen it all—all of them fine, his wife a star. Nefertiti's girls had to be the bomb and had to have everything under the sun and moon at his door coming at 'em. Why not take it there for unfiltered advice and leave Eve be, because she's conflicted. She *has* to be; she's *his mother,*" Marlene whispered though her teeth. "Her advice might be . . . oh, chile. I ain't speaking ill of one of our queens, but, remember, now, Akhenaton was the first of the monarchs to emphasize his role as a father, and with Tutankhamen as his son-in-law, you know—"

"Help me call the violet pyramid, Mar," Damali said with her eyes closed.

"All right, all right, all right," Marlene said, her tone testy as she knelt. "In and out. Keep the questions simple and—"

"Open the pyramid with me, Mar," Damali said, breathing slowly and deeply. "I know not to step on any toes. Trust me. I owe Eve, don't forget . . . she put her body on the line to direct us to the Chairman's lair. That had to be a difficult meeting. I'm sure, if Adam found out, he didn't take it well."

Marlene let her breath out hard and focused with Damali. With their eyes closed, both women turned toward each other once their palms began to tingle, creating a peaked V with their right hands, fingertips barely touching, as their left palms slowly rotated faceup to form the base of the energy structure.

Slowly but surely a violet light filled the space between their hands as their focused energy intensified. They spread their hands apart until the light radiated and remained before them on its own with them kneeling before it palms up.

"I call great Queen Eve, alone, for private counsel," Damali whispered. The light throbbed. "Enter, my child, at my permission. It is Eve."

Marlene stood and backed away with a sigh. Damali stood and walked forward into the violet light.

Marlene wrapped her arms around herself. "Tell her I said hi."

Lemurs and colorful birds made the heavy cover of trees seem restless. Damali slowly walked through the humid, heavily green-swathed terrain, her gaze sweeping as she searched for Eve. She stopped at the edge of a large pool and glanced up at the thundering falls. When the great queen surfaced from the beneath the clear water, Damali stepped back and noticed the white sheath that was warming on a rock. Eve dropped her head back, smiled at the sun, wiped the water from her face, and began to wring out her braids.

"Oh, Queen Daughter, I so love Madagascar. It reminds me of home."

Eve sighed and walked to the rock, naked and unashamed—pure, natural sensuality oozing from her as Damali handed her the soft linen fabric. She pulled it over her head, shaking lose her long hair, her face radiant with natural beauty as she patted a spot beside her for Damali to sit.

As Damali tried to decide how to begin the difficult conversation, she was so glad that her mother-seer had insisted she shower, rinse her hair with clean rosemary and sage water, and anoint herself with myrrh before coming here. Just sitting near such majestic beauty made her feel so very uninitiated to true elegance, even while wearing the light, white gauze blouse with flowing sleeves, billowing pants, and plain, flat gold sandals. She toyed with her silver ankh earring to divert nervous energy. Eve could make a plain sheath look like a million bucks.

"I am honored, daughter, that you have sought my private counsel and not Nzinga's. But why?"

"I am honored that you would have me visit you alone," Damali said, bowing her head and keeping total humility in her tone. "I mean no disrespect to Nzinga, she is warrior of warriors, huntress of huntresses, but this is a delicate matter that requires détente."

Eve chuckled. "Ah . . . and if it is about a male, why not consult Nefertiti? She is renowned for her most effective diplomacy with the other half. She bore six daughters in an attempt to offer her king a son, and did not—yet he loved her so that he remained faithful and did not seek to sire a male heir through taking other wives. She is your better counsel on that topic."

"No," Damali said, meeting Eve's merry eyes. "You were first, will always be first, and are the wisest on the council. I owe you deeply; just as the world owes you deeply for all that you put on the line for us. Thank you for that. I also thank you for guiding us to the Himalayas to find . . . a lair, before." Damali's eyes slid from Eve's with reverence, not ever wanting to mention the Chairman or hurt the elder queen with a reference to her old lover. "Therefore, I have come to you."

Eve clasped Damali's hand and swept it to her mouth to place a kiss of adoration on the back of it, accepting the compassion and respect Damali's tone held. "Tell me, child. What weighs your heart?"

"I said a prayer," Damali replied in a rush, her eyes seeking Eve's so furtively that all the merriment left Eve's eyes. The older queen squeezed Damali's hand tighter, which made Damali's grasp follow suit. "I was angry at my soul mate. He'd hurt me, had done abominable things . . . so I wanted a change, I thought. Wanted to teach him a lesson. The prayer was darkened by anger, and . . ."

Eve's eyes became wide as her free hand covered her heart. "You didn't slay him, did you?"

"No, no," Damali said quickly. "But I may have injured his spirit." Damali looked away. "In fact I'm sure of that, and I know forgiveness is a part of any relationship, but while under the influence, he took one of my Guardian sisters, and—"

Eve snatched her hand away. "He did *what?*"

Damali stared at Eve as she stood, placed her hands on her hips, and tilted her regal head to the side. "And you didn't plant your Isis in his chest?" She made a hard tsking sound with her tongue and stormed back and forth for a moment before she finally sat near Damali again. "All right. My apologies. I have just never been so galled . . . If he was under the influence, he should have never put himself in such a position to even . . ." Eve closed her eyes. "I am *the last one* who should cast aspersion," she said, opening her gorgeous brown eyes and taking in a deep breath through her nose. "This type of dissention within your home troubles me, daughter. It strikes a nerve. I detest seeing one of our queens experience such disrespect."

"Oh, thank you, Eve," Damali said on a hard exhale. "I thought it was me. That I was losing my mind for being so furious. I couldn't pull it together, and I lobbed a serious prayer."

"Oh, child, what did you ask the Most High for?" Eve closed her eyes again and kept her hand over her heart.

"I wasn't playing games of spite, I really wanted someone who would love me with his whole heart, who would be honorable, do the right thing, be strong, disciplined, courageous, and good." Damali let her voice trail off as she looked at the water. "I really meant no harm, I was hoping that it might even be a new and improved Carlos, actually, but then he manifested. Somebody else."

Eve's palm cradled her face. "Then why so blue, my child? Enjoy the gift from above."

Damali's hand covered Eve's. "I don't know that I should or if I can." Both women's eyes met.

"If you called him from a pure place in your heart, after having it so abused, why? If he manifested as all those wonderful things, and you were never married to Carlos in the Light . . . well . . ."

"He's Cain," Damali said quietly. "That's who came through."

Eve just looked at her for a moment, too stunned to even remove her hand from Damali's cheek.

"My son? My Cain? That's who came to you?"

Damali nodded and stood as Eve's hand fell away from her face. "Oh, Eve, listen, I'm so sorry . . . I wasn't trying to stir up any old hurts, or rub salt—"

"Oh, my God," Eve said, standing quickly. Tears were in her eyes as she walked in a crazed circle around Damali, half-laughing and half-crying, her hand intermittently covering her mouth. "You called for an honorable male Neteru, and the Most High sent you my boy? My baby? Oh . . ." Eve drew in a shaky breath. "They've released him? My child is coming home from Nod?"

Before Damali could respond, Eve had grabbed both of Damali's hands and pressed them to her bosom then to her lips as tears rolled down her face. "Eons. I knew he had it in him to change. I never lost hope, even while I bitterly wept the loss of his younger brother. I had lost two sons, not just the one, and my heart was shattered." She hugged Damali so tightly that Damali could barely breathe. "You have answered *my* prayers. Oh, Damali, love and light. Whatever I can do for you as your mother-in-law, just name it." She kissed Damali's cheek hard and then held her away. "Tell me, what does he look like now? Is he still tall and handsome? He is such a good man, now—I must believe that."

In that moment, Damali knew Marlene had been right. Eve was way past conflict, she had no objectivity whatsoever. So Damali dug down into her core and gave her queen a small sliver of hope, feeling that was the least she could do.

"He's tall and handsome and seems very honorable," Damali said quietly, watching silver tears now stream down Eve's beautiful cheeks. "He said, 'God bless my mother, she has endured much.'" Damali stopped speaking when Eve covered her mouth with both hands to hold back a sob. "He still bears the sword of Ausar. They didn't give it to Carlos when he was elevated to the position . . ."

"Did he come to you in pilgrimage robes or armor?" Eve asked in a quiet, strained whisper, her third eye glowing violet as she tried to see her son through Damali's eyes.

"Both," Damali said, omitting the circumstances. "First with humility, then—"

"In full battle armor to protect your honor." Eve nodded and paced away to lean on the huge, flat rock where they'd been seated. She seemed to be nearly faint with pride, holding herself up by a very slight margin.

"But, Eve," Damali hedged, not wanting to hurt her queen. "I'm not sure who sent him."

Eve snapped her head up and looked at Damali with a question and pain in her eyes. "Damali, the man has served his sentence. I *know* who his father was, and what terrible thing he did—the whole world knows that. It was my mistake, not my son's, so do not blame him for my error. But you yourself have forgiven a drug dealer, a man who drew his own brother into a dark life, a life that consumed them both, made them both vampires . . . Alejandro was slain by Carlos's own hand, too, but you were able to forgive that and love him just the same. Carlos already had a chance to be by your side, but by your own admission, he desecrated your love with your own Guardian sister! Foolish. Leave him, and move on with the more honorable man. The decision is simple."

When Damali didn't immediately answer, Eve clasped both hands together and brought them to her chest. "Please, *for me,* offer my boy a chance at redemption and happiness." She looked up to the sky. "The prophecy states that you and a male Neteru are to be one, united, and sire together the greatest Neteru ever made." Her line of vision went back to Damali's and held it. "You and my son . . . my Lord. A combination that even I dared not dream."

Nervous sweat filled Damali's palms. She'd bow at Marlene's feet, when she got home, and would go prostrate on the floor in front of her mother-seer for calling this one.

"Queen Eve," Damali said slowly. "It's not that cut-and-dried. The terrible tsunami ripped open a hole in the fabric of the universe. I don't know if Heaven sent your son, or if my call, as a Neteru, simply allowed him to be able to bypass the energy barriers to it. He seems like a wonderful guy, don't get me wrong, but you and I both know what the situation is over in Nod. If I mess up, and have accidentally called him out, and if he isn't clear about which side—"

"He is clear!" Eve shouted. "The Light wouldn't have allowed the rip or him to hone his vibrations to your voice if he were not ready!" Eve walked a hot path back and forth before the flat rock. "Do not toy with his emotions, Damali. He has been through a lot, and any indecision on your part could be the thing to send him over the edge and back to his old ways!"

"I understand, my queen," Damali said calmly, fighting the impulse to just up and run back through the violet light. "This is why we must all be sure." She kept her tone humble, her eyes on Eve, her demeanor calm but firm. "My fervent hope is that you are correct. But now that Carlos is trapped over in Nod with him—"

"Carlos went through the rip? How?" Eve stopped pacing, her eyes holding an expression like she'd been struck. "He has to leave my son alone and go back to his side! There can be no altercation while Cain is on parole."

"They already got into a fight; that's how it happened. When they collided and took a tumble, and—"

Eve leveled a finger at Damali, pointing at her so intensely that blue-violet light flickered at the tip of the digit.

"My son," Eve said in a low, lethal tone, "has been incarcerated in a realm that is devoid of sensual stimulation for years. He lived a full life on the planet as *a man,* sired children, had many wives. Then, he died. But reincarnated in Nod with full recall of *all* of those earthly sensations so that he would learn self-discipline, honor, selfless sacrifice, and you would bait him into a fight with a half-vampire, half-human male Neteru while he's *apexing!*"

Violet flames covered Damali's chest and fanned out to paralyze her before she could turn and run. "I didn't bait him, Eve, I swear. What had happened was—"

"You called *my* boy to you through song—my poor male child—who has a weakness for music, *like his father,* into *your* company, my passionate son, my virile son, the one who takes after Dante's propensity for sensual excess . . . you call him sweetly like a lover over the barrier of Nod, but *not sure* if you would yield to him . . . after *millennia* of not being with a woman in the flesh and allow another Neteru challenger to—"

"Eve, I swear to you . . ." Damali's voice trailed off as the elder queen materialized an Isis blade in her hand and leveled it at her heart.

"*My son,*" Eve said, walking closer to Damali, shaking her head with tears of rage in her eyes, "who has *pure* royal vampire strain all through him—you would allow another male with Council-level vampire lineage to make my boy produce fangs!"

Damali shut her eyes tightly as the hot edge of the Isis pressed against her windpipe. She could instantly taste the electric discharge coming off of it on the back of her tongue. "Why do they always blame the woman?" It was the only truth she could quickly tell Eve to keep Eve from cutting her throat.

Damali panted as the steel edge of the blade suddenly yanked away from her skin. Eve lifted her chin and swept away to stand by the water, her back to Damali but her blade readied. The energy field around Damali vanished, and she dropped forward on her hands and knees, coughing, and speaking to Eve in a gravelly voice.

"Queen Mother, please hear me," Damali said, standing slowly as Eve's tight grip on the extended Isis made it vibrate in her hand.

Eve glanced over her shoulder at Damali and then turned away from her as she drove the blade into the sandy shore. She continued to give Damali her back as she stared out at the water. "Speak."

"I did not call him by name," Damali said plainly, rubbing her throat. "I called for the positive attributes I described to you. That's possibly a good sign, since that's what manifested him."

Eve nodded and wrapped her arms around herself, but didn't speak or turn to look at Damali.

"I was angry, as I told you," Damali said, hoping to at least get Eve to see her point of view, even if the woman didn't agree with her decision—whatever that might finally be. "I had been traumatized by what I saw with Carlos. Even Carlos said there was some type of black smoke—"

"*Lilith,*" Eve whispered through her teeth. "Before the end of days, I will slay that bitch for this."

Gaining confidence, Damali pressed on. "It could be that Cain was released by the Hand of God or it could have been a Level-Seven diversion, if they intercepted my argument. I don't know. That's the problem. I was angry at Carlos when I lobbed the prayer . . . more like a complaint, as the case maybe. But I wasn't all the way ready to throw in the towel on our relationship. I. Am. Human," Damali said with emphasis.

"Eve, please hear me. I'm *human.* Prone to error, prone to all sorts of things, huge mistakes being one of them. But, Eve, you know me. I also have a heart, and wouldn't just jack with a brother in jail or play with his mind." Damali walked back to the rock to lean on it and stare at Eve's spine, putting a little distance between herself and the clearly devastated Neteru queen. "I'm many things, but not cruel."

Eve nodded and her breathing shuddered as though a sob so deep and profound was battling to come out. Damali almost cried for her.

"I knew it was too good to be true," Eve said quietly and swallowed hard. "But a mother can always cling to hope. I also have love for my son . . . and faith. A mother always carries this divine trinity for her child."

Damali watched Eve wipe her face with her back still turned to her and put the straightness in her spine as a queen's carriage dictated.

"You are right. I cannot blame the woman without thorough inquiry, ever." Eve took in a deep breath and let it out slowly. "I have experienced that."

"I know. That's why I brought this to you in trust, and out of respect," Damali said. "As a matter of honor, I did not go to Nefertiti, or the others, as I felt you had the right to know above all others, first."

Eve nodded, but still didn't turn. "I deeply appreciate that," she said in a quiet tone. "Your honor and discretion will never be forgotten. Forgive me for almost beheading you, but we were talking about *my son.*"

Damali rubbed her throat again, truly aware of just how close she had come to biting the dust. Whew . . . no wonder Mar was having a cow.

"Here's the thing," Damali finally said, pushing away from the rock. She needed motion to calm her nerves. "Before I can just go off with Cain, I have to legitimately resolve this thing with me and Carlos, one way or another. Then, however it goes, whomever I decide to hook up with has to also pass the Light test, because Eve, I can't even *think* about siring—"

"*That* you do not have to explain," Eve said calmly, raising one hand to stop Damali's words.

For a moment, both women fell silent.

"Eve, I didn't sleep with him, because I wasn't sure . . . and at the same time, I wasn't trying to play with him. Does that make sense? I mean, how would that be . . . I'm mad at Carlos for something foul he did, and in a fit of fury after an argument, I go hook up with some brother who ain't got nothing to do with the drama, then after me and Carlos come to terms, I dump him and go back home—or, worse, have both of 'em out in the street battling until one or both of them dies. Where's the maturity and honor in that? They deserve better; I deserve better. No Neteru or female with dignity needs to go there. Plus, it's not about all that—it's about the rip and making sure nothing untoward comes across that line. You *know* that. As this era's Neteru, all personal crises aside, I cannot let anything half-demon slip out of Nod to join with the currently weakened forces of Hell to strengthen them."

Conviction entered Damali's tone as she spoke to Eve's back and her voice trembled with emotion. "Your son is awesome, Eve. Almost made me forget any honorable intent or mission. But he also seemed like a nice guy, someone who deserved respect, someone who could be permanent, if that's where it was headed. So, I wasn't about to put him in a position like that. And, for all of Carlos's mess, he's still a good man, too, and a Neteru, so I was trying to sort it all out when they rolled up on each other. That's what happened, for real."

Damali was breathing hard as Eve turned slowly to face her. The elder queen nodded sadly and forced a serene smile.

"You did the right thing, daughter . . . he's just my firstborn boy." Eve sighed and folded her arms over her chest and shook her head. "But that you've thought all this out so clearly, I wish I had your wisdom at your age . . . and even in this disaster, that you have spoken so highly of him makes me proud. I hope he's made the right decision. Time will tell. Yet I cannot vouch for him. He's all grown up," she added, her voice so melancholy that the birds went still. "He's a man, and has been away from me so long I confess that I don't really know him anymore."

Eve paced away from the water's edge and leaned against the rock with her eyes closed, seeming lost, if not drowning, in very old thoughts. "His father never saw him after the banishment . . . that is why light perpetual shines in Nod. He could never glean information about that place, how it worked, what entities were there, or attach any relevant knowledge of it to his throne—the light blinded him, as they knew, inherently, that he would go after his son to save him from a sensory-less fate. It practically drove Dante mad to think of Cain there, but try as he might, he couldn't get to him, so he could never tell me how he was . . . and after Eden, I dared not transgress again to peek into that world."

She chuckled sadly when Damali's eyes widened with shock. "Dante never got to see our boy really grow up. I wonder if he would have admired him, and been proud, even if he went to my side?" Eve's gaze captured Damali. "When you have children of your own, you will understand. It sounds mad, but that's the thing . . . even a father who disagrees with his son's profession still holds some measure of pride if that son is the very best at what he sets out to accomplish. Tragic, all of it, the whole of it cannot be sorted out or easily explained in one sitting."

"I hope he's one of the good ones, for you, dear Queen," Damali murmured. "I'd hate to have to be the one to take your lover and your son's head . . . but if he goes dark on my watch, that's my job. I'd do him no less than I'd do Carlos, if either one of them take after Dante full-blown. You must understand that before I leave this glen, Eve. I need to get into Nod and I need your help. You were there when that realm was created."

Crystal-blue tears filled Eve's brown eyes and fell without shame.

"You see, all I remember is that head of tight curls and ringlets against my breasts. That child who stayed awake all night with a bright, inquisitive smile, and who would occasionally nick me with a hint of fang when he suckled or laughed hard. Those warm, brown, hungry, intelligent eyes that absorbed every shred of knowledge ever put before him, those same eyes that painfully looked to me to solve the problems of the newborn world . . . and that wonderful, angelic voice that would join me in a lullaby when I sang him to sleep every dawn."

Eve drew in a shaky breath and closed her eyes. "That is what a mother sees. Not the monster. Not the seductive lover. Not the man who has grievously erred and must be punished, or possibly beheaded."

"I know, Eve," Damali said, removing the formality of title between them as she walked to her queen and gave her a much-needed hug. "But you are also fair and wise and just . . . and I came to you because of all those things."

Eve hugged Damali tightly as she stroked her hair. "What I ask of you isn't fair. It is pure emotion."

"I can't commit."

"I know," Eve whispered. "Just be gentle with my boy, whatever you decide. Tell him, if you see him again, that his mother loves him, no matter what, and always will. Tell him that, even if you must behead him."

Damali swallowed hard and nodded. "That I can do."

"Freeze!"

Multiple gun hammers clicked back. Semiautomatics leveled. Men in black S.W.A.T. gear had come through the door in a Bradley, and swarmed out of it before any Guardian could take cover. Windows smashed in. A black-hawk chopper was landing on the roof, then footfalls pummeled the upper floors and stairs.

The Guardian team stood very, very still, not even glancing at each other as they kept their hands on their heads. They kept their mouths shut as nervous palms patted them down, spun their bodies around, and affixed nylon ties to their wrists.

"Problem, officer?" Rider finally said, as he was forced to kneel.

"Where's the one you call the Neteru in this cult?" a burly figure shouted, his eyes darting around the team and then toward his men. "Be careful, gentlemen. She's packing a long blade, samurai shit, and knows how to use it."

"I'm a cop," Berkfield said. "You need to start reading Miranda and explain—"

A gun butt to the side of his head stopped his words.

"This ain't local, it's federal," the lead searcher said through his black ski mask. "Homeland Security—after the Patriot Act, we don't have to tell you shit. Anybody else got any stupid questions?"

Guardians watched a team of twenty masked men peel off from the group in search of Damali, and cringed when they heard the weapons room door get kicked open.

"You see this arsenal in here!" a voice down the hallway shouted.

"Fucking Pentagon Web site up on monitors!" another shouted. "Bingo!"

"Bring it all as evidence," the leader said, motioning with his chin to dispatch more men. "Where's this Neteru chick, huh?" He leaned in toward Bobby and Dan, and yanked Dan's hair back.

"She's not here," Dan said, grimacing from the pain. "She left to go talk to somebody, okay? Now get off me!"

A gloved hand jerked Dan's hair again to make him fall. Bobby was drawing sudden breaths of rage, but knelt, unable to assist his friend.

"But we didn't do anything wrong!" Krissy shouted, trying to lift her head off the rug as she was shoved down hard and fell.

"Hey!" Berkfield shouted. "That's my daughter!"

"Don't put your hands on her!" J.L. said between his teeth while a gun barrel dug into his cheek, forcing his head to the floor.

"The kid just wants to know what charges we're up on," Shabazz said, receiving a gun butt to his stomach for the question.

When he dropped, Big Mike almost stood, but a Glock nine to the temple made him slowly go back down on his knees.

"Easy, big fella. Don't be crazy," one of the restrainers said.

Inez tried to edge toward him on her knees, her eyes sending silent daggers to the gunman who'd put a nine to Mike's temple.

"She left," Juanita shouted. "She went to go see her man's mother!"

When a gunman nodded and yanked Juanita's ponytail back, two men shoved Jose to the floor. "Hurt her again, and it's on!" Jose shouted.

"You believe this little tamale?" one guy said, forcing Juanita's head back so far she almost fell.

Multiple two-way radios sputtered with static. "All clear! She's not in the house."

"We just want to know what you want," Marjorie shrieked.

"Some people wanna have a talk with you about these experiments you're about to conduct." The lead invader laughed hard in a mocking tone. "Your asses are screwed. We picked up everything off satellite intercepts of your coded message conference call with a buncha rogue clerics—religious fanatics. So let's go see some people who are very curious about your interest in Cairo setting something off and breaking into places with a link from here . . . just some folks who wanna know about all this Egyptian theory shit you're kicking around. All right?"

CHAPTER NINE

I am due at court," Cain said in a bored voice, beginning to walk along the opposite side of the long pool to collect his blade. "If you do not get dressed, you will not be permitted to go with me."

"Well, like I told you," Carlos said, keeping up with Cain's leisurely strides, "I ain't staying here by myself."

"You have nothing to fear," Cain said, his tone weary as he fastened a low-slung gold belt and sheathed the blade against his hip.

"I'm not scared of nothin'," Carlos said, his voice beginning to escalate with frustration. "But you ain't leaving me here to be lion bait, or some other foul—"

"Then get dressed," Cain commanded. He folded his arms over his chest and waited.

"You gonna make me?" Carlos said, folding his arms to match Cain's stance.

Cain shook his head and stepped down into the pool. Carlos braced for the attack, sure that Cain was crossing the divide between them. But suddenly Cain stopped and submerged himself beneath the blue energy-filled space and was gone.

Dumbstruck, Carlos spun around, expecting Cain to suddenly materialize in a sneak attack. But soon it became apparent that he'd really gone. Growling lions tore his focus away from the strange pool and sent it ricocheting around the room in search of a weapon. But rather than two snarling sphinxes entering the chamber to attack him, a long-legged dark beauty strode toward him in a white Grecian gown.

Initially, he didn't know what to make of her, and he backed up a bit, just in case she transformed into something deadly. After where he'd been, he wasn't about to allow a pretty face or a voluptuous body make him sloppy.

"*Hola,*" she murmured, pausing at the foot of the pool to curiously stare at him.

"*Que pasa?*" Carlos said in a wary tone, looking her up and down. She was such an odd combination of contrasts that her beauty had a temporarily mesmerizing effect. Her eyes were jewel green, but her skin as smooth and dark as black coffee. Her waist-length, jet-black hair and the hue of her skin made the white fabric of her gown practically shimmer. The thin gold ropes that separated her heavy, pendulous breasts added radiance to her overall appearance. But her smile was a devastating flash of white with the merest hint that her eyeteeth were a bit longer than normal human dimensions. She had Amanthra, or something close to it, written all over her. Maybe it was the fluid way she'd moved across the marble floor without effort in a tight-fitting dress, he wasn't sure. But the fact that she knew enough about him to hail him in Spanish worried him.

"Word is out down in the valley that Cain's younger brother just tumbled into our realm. I thought I would stop by to inspect the rumor myself."

"I ain't his brother, by any stretch of the imagination, sis," Carlos said, watching her like a hawk. "So you need to state your business and be out."

She smiled, sighed, and sauntered over to a poolside bench and sat down, then reclined in leisurely repose. "Why are Neterus always so suspicious?" she murmured, but seemed totally nonplussed by his rebuff. "I see Cain left you in here all alone."

"He had something to do," Carlos said, keeping an eye on her and occasionally glancing at the door. "You his woman? That why the lions didn't rush you?"

She chuckled and shook her head. "No. Just a friend. I pose no threat. They only attack if they sense a threat or block an entry if he's in here and does not wish to be disturbed."

"What do they eat?" Carlos said, using his chin to motion toward the entrance. The fact that Cain had left him and might not return for a while began to add to his worries. All he had to do was remember his own pit bulls from the Chairman's chambers, and sooner or later the animals had to be fed. He wasn't trying to be dinner.

"What everything else in this realm consumes," she said with a sly smile. "Energy."

He looked at her with a distrustful sidelong glance. "Yeah, right. Those monsters out there eat pure vibe and don't chow down on two or three bodies a night. Gimme a break, sis, and be real."

She laughed and flopped onto her back, staring up at the ceiling. "You are just adorable."

"Come again?" Now she was seriously getting on his nerves.

She rolled over on her side and rested her head on her hand, propping herself up on one elbow. "Sweetheart, have you not noticed there is no food or water in this realm?"

Carlos stood still and then slowly stooped down to dip his fingers into the pool. A tingling sensation rippled through them into his palm and up his arm, making him draw back his hand as though he'd been burned. He knew he'd seen energy coming off of it, running through it, just like the grass, but assumed that beneath all the illusion mind games Cain was playing, there had to be something that was real.

"I don't understand," he said quietly, wishing he hadn't admitted that to some strange female, but needing to know more than his pride needed a shield at the moment. If he didn't eat, didn't drink soon, after expending all the energy he had, the blood hunger would come back.

"We absorb what we need through radiation. The second sun. We have evolved to the point that slowing down the mental and spiritual capacities for basic bodily functions is unnecessary."

Carlos walked over to a bench adjacent to her and sat down slowly. If this chick wasn't lying, that meant that in a matter of days he'd die of dehydration or starvation, and what would become of him if the blood hunger hit?

He looked at her squarely, now really needing whatever information she could give. "I noticed you had a slight fang crest—Amanthra overbite."

She nodded and sat up, holding him with her hypnotic gaze. "I am a hybrid. Is that a problem for you?" Her matter-of-fact tone carried no shame or anger, nor did her strangely pretty eyes.

"No, no problem," Carlos said, beginning to regret his offensive question. "I just wanted to be clear about who I was dealing with."

"I know all of this must be very disconcerting," she said, her eyes becoming sad. "I am no Amanthra, however." She lifted her chin a bit higher.

"Hey, listen, I'm sorry. It's just the green eyes, the slim angle of fang, too thin for vamp, not wide enough for general-purpose demon . . . I'm in a real strange place, I need to know what's up, and you walk in unannounced. I wasn't trying to signify, but you understand where I'm coming from?"

"I do. Then let us begin again. My mother was a sacrificial virgin, thrown to my father—a dragon deity," she said proudly. "But she was so gorgeous," she added with a wistful sigh, "he could not bear to roast her or simply feed off of her. I was the result. My father is a bit rash and has his bad days, but he does love his girls." She chuckled as Carlos stood slowly.

"Amanthra? I should have slapped your face." She stood and folded her graceful arms over her breasts. "I am a goddess, thank you very much. Dark realms, never. My family would never consort with that type."

For the first time in what felt like a long while, Carlos didn't know what to say. But it fit. Gorgeous East Indian human exterior. Dragon eyes, that at first glance could be easily mistaken for Amanthra. "I definitely owe you an apology, then."

Her lush mouth became friendly again as she gave him a dashing smile. "Do not worry. I do not breathe fire."

He chuckled and waved his hand before him to bid her to sit again across the pool from him. "So, you and Cain are friends. I'm sorry that I offended what has to be his prettiest buddy."

She sat with a shy smile. "Actually, he did ask me to leave court to check on you. He thought a female presence would offer you less concern, and might keep one of his male friends from having to endure an unnecessary battle."

Tension made Carlos stare at her hard. Okay, if Cain had sent some half-dragon chick in here to put a hit on him, he had no problem smoking her, too, if it came to that.

"He was worried that you would panic, start breaking things to make a weapon, and then try to hurt his pets as you left—even though you are not his captive. They do not eat meat, and are pure energy, but they do bite." She sighed. "He did not wish for you to be harmed in his home."

Feeling completely foolish, Carlos looked down at his hands. "I'm tired. I need to eat soon, or at least get something to drink, and I wanna to go home."

"Then go home," she said quietly. "Why stay, if this realm makes you so sad?"

"How?" He stared at her very, very hard.

"You are a Neteru. Do you not know how to focus your energy to go back through the rip?" She stood, covering her mouth with her hand and began to pace in an agitated line along the edge of the pool. "That is the entire debate at court as we speak. Only Cain can tune in to the Neteru frequency and hold the harmonic to cross—but he must be pulled by one anchored in flesh. This is why he rules this realm."

Carlos stood as several mental building blocks began to fall into place for him. The fact that Cain hadn't lied grated him, but that was good to know. Second issue was, Damali's call might have definitely been accidental—and, given her voice hitting high notes, if it rippled in this pool across realms, he couldn't truly blame the brother for crossing over to her. The fact that Cain also didn't lie when he said he was a Neteru and was also a king, *that* jacked with his pride, but he had to let that go for the moment. The more important questions remained: Why did these entities want to leave a relatively cool environment to cross over, and how the hell was he gonna get out of there before he starved to death?

"Listen," Carlos finally said, trying not to pace with the gorgeous hybrid who was now wringing her hands. "I haven't learned how to focus my energy on this side yet to get enough velocity going to hit that barrier, or even to see where it is."

"I know where the barrier has thinned," she said quietly, and stopped pacing to look at him. Her eyes flickered "It is not an actual rip."

"If you show a brother the door . . ."

She held up her hand. "Only if you promise to call me by name through it with you, when the time is right."

Carlos smiled. In any realm, a deal was a deal. Let the negotiations begin. "Why would you want to go to a place with chaos and disease and filth and—"

"Because," she said quietly, wrapping her arms around herself. "There is no sensual sensation in this realm."

He just stared at her.

"Just like there is no food for one to taste the succulent juice of a dripping piece of fruit . . . or for our more aggressive inhabitants to savor the salty emulsion of blood on their tongues—"

"Hold up," Carlos said, slightly offended. "No blood. I knocked the spit out of Cain and his nose bled. Don't play, or we can end this conversation right now."

"He bled?" she said, her breaths deepening. "Cain bled?"

"Uh, yeah," Carlos said slowly, watching desire make her eyes begin to more than flicker, but glow.

"We have been platonic friends for years," she said quietly, her gaze going to the massive bed at the far end of the room. "Do not toy with me. You are sure he bled?"

"Sure as I'm standing here," Carlos said, baiting her with the titillating information. "But then it suddenly dried up and vanished after we started walking deeper into the glen."

She stared at Carlos and licked her lips and put a trembling finger to her mouth. "His energy and structure normalized, then, once he returned . . . but do you still bleed?"

Carlos chuckled. "I don't know. Do I?"

Her eyes closed as her hand slid down her throat. "Do you understand that I am a being fully initiated in the tantric practices?" She opened her eyes very slowly and began to cross the pool, her gown flowing out to float along the unseen current as she stood waist deep in the middle of it.

"Do you understand that at one time I was a Council-level master, now a hybrid, with a little Neteru in me?" he said, dropping his voice to a sensuous octave. "And I am also fairly certain that I still bleed, baby. So, where's the door?"

"Come into the pool for just a little while, and I will show you."

"I never did a dragon, and don't know what y'all do. You're flesh eaters, right? Like everything charcoal roasted, so—"

She shook her head and closed her eyes, allowing the blue current to wash over her arms. Gooseflesh pebbled her flawless skin and made her nipples strain against the sheer fabric of her gown. "You can take the bite," she whispered. "As well as deliver it. And I do eat flesh, but not in the manner that would ever injure you."

"Naw, see," Carlos hedged, needing space to get the terms of the deal set before committing to anything too kinky. "Here's my problem. You and my so-called brother, Cain, are platonic friends—only because, for whatever reason here, you can't be more than that. Why start what can't be finished, right? But I think the man might have a problem if he came back home and found someone who can definitely finish what he started, in his pool, in his house, serving serious Kama Sutra . . . since you told me that's what you like . . . I do remember a lot of Eastern philosophy from my old throne days . . . but, I digress. He'll have issues if I do his very fine woman-friend in here, when he can't. Feel me?"

"He will not object. Jealousy and envy has long been banished here. It is pointless, just as attempting to possess an individual is. He will not hurt you." Her eyes searched Carlos's face, then raked down his body so harshly they almost felt like her neatly manicured nails. "Step into the pool. Just once. I will take you to the barrier and help you with my energy to cross it. Right now, you are too weak. You need to eat, rehydrate your flesh. Rest. The human form is severely strained on this side, which is why it is dangerous for all but those with Neteru in them to be here. I will help you, if you promise, once you are stronger, that you will call for me."

This woman was making too much sense. If he stayed, he'd starve. The longer he stayed, the more at risk he was to any scheme Cain had to off him. If he was the only one bleeding, and there were more like her around, who knew what flesh eaters, blood suckers, or however many other dangerous combinations existed? This was not the place to be as the only one with a pulse. Carlos stepped down into the water and watched her shudder as he neared her.

An immediate magnetic ripple disturbed the surface, eliciting a groan from her. Tingling sensations made the hair stand up on the nape of his neck and his forearms. But it was so freaky. He was waist deep in what felt like and looked like water, but at the same time, he wasn't wet. Too bizarre. Not to mention she was truly beautiful and clearly starved for touch in a way that didn't make sense. He was thinking that there oughta be a law as he came close enough to kiss her, and she quickly wrapped her arms around his neck at the same time her mouth covered his and her legs wrapped around his waist.

Her tongue nearly choked him as she devoured his mouth, and her soft lips came away with blood upon a gasp, full dragon fangs presented. Her head dropped back, jeweled tears rapidly spilled from the corners of her eyes as he held her and stroked her hair.

"What's your name?" he asked quietly, wondering why in the world a realm like this had been created. What could the purpose be to make entities this physically attractive, so seemingly honorable in temperament, but then deny them the basics?

"Zehiradangra," she murmured, pulling his earlobe into her mouth.

He chuckled against her throat. "Pronounce it, so I can call you right."

She licked her lips, and stared deeply into his eyes, holding his face between trembling palms. "You really will call me, won't you?"

"A deal is a deal," he said quietly, his hands sliding down her back to cup her bottom.

"You taste like salt," she said with a soft sigh. "It has been so long . . . skin," she said, allowing her fingertips to trace his brows and then luxuriate themselves in his hair. She kissed his eyelids. "You pronounce it, Ze-hir-ah-dan-gra," she whispered sexily into his mouth. "You won't forget me?"

"Not likely," he chuckled. "But I'm in big trouble already and this is only gonna make my domestic situation worse."

"She is jealous?" The hybrid beauty looked at him seeming confused.

Carlos nodded and smiled as he dragged his nose along her neck and watched the energy in her skin ripple. The slight caress made her thighs clench around his waist tighter in a rhythmic pulse that woke up his nature.

"If you come through the barrier, you'll have to get acclimated quick, then be on your way. My woman is a little on the crazy side, and also wields an Isis blade, *comprende?* She don't play, and has taken down more than dragons, all right?" He pulled back and stared at her to be sure she understood. "On the other side, it's real territorial, and you seem like a real cool sister, but she ain't having it. We clear?"

She nodded and touched his mouth. "Your eyes," she whispered, hers beginning to slide closed, "are beginning to turn." Her pelvis pressed against his harder. "May I?"

He hesitated. A throat strike from a dragon? "Ah . . . I don't know. What's the mix do to a brother on the other side?"

She was practically panting and he could see an opalescent sheen beginning to cover her brow. Her nails were beginning to gouge into his shoulders as she held him tighter.

"Could possibly help your flight patterns, improve navigation in the air . . . allow you to walk on mist," she whispered, "and to disappear at will." She offered him her throat. "You will not come out of this breathing fire . . . unless you want to."

While what she'd told him didn't seem all that far removed from his current skill set, still, there was the not so small matter of Damali being truly pissed off. Although he could fully explain how this was a necessary evil to get him back on the other side, lately Damali hadn't been very reasonable at all. Plus, with Cain just waiting for him to mess up, and Damali being so outdone about the whole Juanita thing . . . if he came home with a dragon bite . . . decisions, decisions. But it was not about staying here.

Before the beauty in his arms could draw another breath, Carlos leveled the sudden strike first. Her shriek almost shattered lair marble. He'd forgotten about the dragon's voice as artillery before flames. But he kept the siphon hard and strong. It was either mark her or get marked himself. He was *not* going home like that, sexy as she was. This had to be a one-way kinda thing—let her get off, then he'd go home, take a shower, and explain it all later.

Oddly, as he drew what had the consistency of blood into his mouth, and played with the tasteless substance on his tongue, he could feel himself getting stronger as she scrabbled at his back, arched, and ground her hips in a frenzied circle against him. Natural instinct kicked in; he knew what she wanted. Problem was, how to give her that and still have a valid alibi when he got home.

He pulled out of the siphon, found the front of her gown, and slit it with a fang as he held her steady with one arm around her waist. His mouth immediately covered the hardened tips of her breasts, sweeping them with his lips, as his free hand drifted along her backside to find and enter her valley.

Her response was an elongated wail of ecstasy. He almost looked up to see if Cain was crossing the floor with a long blade. Shit . . . this was not the place for a man to get caught with his pants down. He didn't care what she said about the brother being cool. As she began working on his zipper, nearly ready to rip his jeans, he made another fast decision without time to weigh the consequences.

Now it was true, he'd never mind locked with a dragon before, but there was a first time for everything, he reasoned. He pulled his hands away from her body, held the sides of her face, gripped her mind as tightly as he could, and then found her opening again as he mentally entered her.

She nearly passed out in his arms and her nails dug into his shoulders. This time when his hand slid against her mound, it was wet and not his imagination. He pushed her against the side of the pool for leverage, almost forgetting that the seduction was supposed to be phantom. There was something about a woman's voice hitting that decibel that fractured a man's reason.

When she bit him, he saw stars. Her siphon dredged a deep moan up from his diaphragm and made him blanket her against the marble poolside. He'd forgotten how good a real plunge felt. Carlos quickly glanced over his shoulder, waiting to hear the chime of a blade being unsheathed, but immediately brought his attention back to the woman writhing beneath him as he moved against her.

"As soon as we're done, you have to take me to the barrier," he said on a heavy exhale. "Your man is about two seconds from rolling in here."

"I don't care," she said, panting with her head back. "He could behead me now, and I would not care!"

Okay, somebody had to get rational. His primary question had been answered. Cain, like all men, didn't play this bullshit, no matter what their women said. That reality seriously dulled the throb in his erection. A strategic bite, a mind thrust, she released so hard she'd bitten her own tongue—he was out.

"C'mon, baby, I know you're still floating in the aftermath, but you gotta take a brother to where he can live and not die."

She pressed her face to his chest and sobbed. "I'll take you anywhere you want to go, oh, sweet Neteru."

Carlos rubbed her back, looking over his shoulder. "All right, all right, baby," he said, kissing the top of her head.

"You had not even entered me," she whispered, and began sobbing again.

"I know, I know, baby. Next time. On the other side. Let's both live so that can happen, cool?"

"You are wise," she whispered, covering his mouth with a slow deep kiss that he didn't have time for.

But he obliged, and lifted her down off his waist with care. "Okay, now, you have to pull yourself together so we can get out of here."

She nodded and wiped her glistening eyes. "But you did not have a chance to fully satisfy yourself. How could I deny you—"

"Baby, I'm cool," he said, holding her upper arms. "This time was all about you, okay? So, the door—"

"Such selfless sacrifice," she wailed, holding him around the waist. "Never in all my—"

"C'mon, girl," he said, kissing her face, her eyelids, and the bridge of her nose as the lions growled. "*Holmes* is about to walk in here—"

She jerked her head up, seeming totally paralyzed by fear for a moment. "Under the surface," she said quickly.

Carlos immediately obliged her, his heart pounding. What the hell could clear blue energy do to hide them? But he watched as Cain strode by, took off his blade, dropped it on a bench, and glanced around, perplexed. He heard Cain bellow his name, but the sound of Cain's voice was muffled. Zehiradangra squeezed her eyes shut and put one finger to her lips. As Cain walked back down the other side of the pool, she thrust Carlos's head deeper beneath the surface.

Electric-like sensations were making his hair stand up as though static was yanking it from the roots. She kept pointing down, as though trying to tell him to go further and follow the current. Girlfriend didn't have to tell him twice.

But he had to admit that he was a little messed up when she suddenly elongated, and opened a six-foot pair of silvery wings, and her entire form became a voluptuous, pastel, scale-plated water dragon. Damali was gonna kick his ass, for sure. The she-dragon glanced back with an apology in her jewel-green eyes, and slung her seashell-smooth tail toward him to hitch a quicker ride.

A hundred thoughts fought for dominance as he hung on, increased in speed, and finally dropped in a clearing surrounded by mountains. He stood quickly and watched her transform from the lithe creature into the dark, voluptuous beauty she'd been.

"I didn't want you to have to see that," she said quietly.

"It's better than what I can turn into," he said, touching her face. She was all-right people. "I thought your man wasn't jealous, though?"

She swallowed a smile. "All right, I lied."

Carlos laughed.

"Oh, he is not that bad. We used to have regular trysts before this became a prison void of sensation." She swept her arms out and let them fall with a sigh. "Then, after trying and trying until it became too excruciating to dwell upon it, we found a comfortable compromise."

"Which was?" He *had* to hear this one.

"All of us are in the same predicament. We became friends. Share each other's secrets. Use our minds to give each other joy through laughter. Share sentiment through sound, music . . . please the eye with the beauty of art." She smiled and kissed him gently. "When we get hungry for the sensual, we absorb knowledge. The unplundered original texts of the Library of Alexandria are here, the University of Timbuktu, Luxor, and Karnack, plus all the floor plans for every architectural achievement . . . we build, we learn, we . . . love from afar."

"That's terrible," Carlos whispered, really meaning it. "I'll bring you over to our side, I promise."

"He would have been angry, not because you touched my physical being, but because he and I are such old friends, and . . . in a very short time, you had touched my mind and my spirit. Do you understand?"

He didn't. Carlos admitted that by shaking his head slowly. He thought Cain was about to wig because his hands were all over her and he'd punctured her jugular.

She smiled patiently. "My friend would never deny me sensual pleasure, knowing how rare a commodity that is. That is an easily forgivable offense. The flesh is weak." She cupped Carlos's face. "But when I opened my mind to you, shared my fantasies . . . the mind lock breached his trust. That was our private sanctuary, that was something neither of us expected." She allowed her hand to fall away, and she wrapped her arms around herself as tears began to form in her eyes. She pursed her lips before speaking. "In order to let you do that, I had to trust you—something that was only his. Do you not understand, when you give someone your complete trust, you have indeed given them your heart. You have given them profound love. He felt the invasion the moment I crossed the line, and that is what brought him home."

She walked away and pointed to the edge of a cliff. "The rip is there."

Carlos glanced at it, but his eyes then returned to her sad face. "I'm sorry," he murmured, "had I known . . ."

"But I understand why you did it." She smiled as two tears streamed down her face. "You did not want to breach the way trust is conveyed in your realm. The claim to the body is offered as the ultimate trust, but fantasies, friendship, caring . . . these are elements that are freely exchanged in your world. But here, where the body is etheric, energy can fuse at will with other bodies and it is considered matter that will shift, change, and be of no consequence. But fantasies are closely guarded and cherished, as are dreams and hopes, and alliances . . . there is a matter of honor, to be sure."

Carlos rubbed his hands down his face. What she had told him was so profound he was at a loss for words. "Aw, baby . . . then why did you let me do that? I'm so damned sorry, because I've gotta leave you here, now, with a very pissed off, very strong—"

"You still do not understand, do you?"

Carlos stared at her, feeling so stupid he could have kicked himself.

"I could sense that you would not give me your body the way I needed you to," she admitted calmly, without emotion. "I was leveraging you, and I knew it." She closed her eyes. "Cain cares for me so, and felt that you were young and given to excess, so he gave you to me as a friendship gift."

"He what?" Carlos folded his arms over his chest, so indignant that he almost walked away from her.

"Hear me out," she said quietly. "He knew you wanted to go home, and has no interest in keeping you in his lair. But for all the years of friendship between us, he told me, 'Go to him, Zehira . . . let him pleasure you and then send him home. Let him give you what I cannot in this realm, for you are my dearest friend.'"

She covered her mouth and caught a sob as Carlos remained stunned and speechless. "Neither of us understood how attached you were to the young female one of your kind. It had been so long, we had forgotten the flesh bond of the earth plane . . . and I lost my perspective, needed release so badly that I betrayed my friend. I let you into my mind, did not care that you entered it, as long as you would topple me over the edge of raw sensation." She walked away, covering her face with her hands, weeping into them and sputtering as she spoke. "He was so generous, so trusting, and that I did this to him for a moment of flesh pleasure—oh, how can I face him and explain? I have dishonored him in his own lair!"

"Okay, okay," Carlos said, worry for her safety now knotting his stomach. "Is there any way you can get him to blame it on me? Like, like, tell him I mind raped you, just went in and sucked your brain out through your ear, whatever. Tell him the silver-tongued bastard he tumbled through the rip with did it out of spite because he'd flesh kissed his woman. I can't let you take this kinda weight, but I need to get back on my side to go up against him before I starve to death. I don't know . . . But baby, I can't leave you over here to get your head—"

"He will never believe that a mere unseasoned vampire–young Neteru hybrid could bend the will of a centuries' old goddess!" She walked in a mad circle. "You? A kid? Take *my* mind against my will? Oh, by the gods, be serious!"

"Damn, that hurt, sis," Carlos said, truly meaning it. He rubbed his jaw, contemplating the older woman who'd just told him something he'd never thought he'd hear a woman tell him with such unblemished honesty. It stung like a slap, but he still didn't want to leave her ass-out. "Well, still, we need a plan to keep you safe, so lemme go get enough juice to pull you through, and you lay low until we can sync up a signal so I can extract you, so he doesn't—"

"He won't kill me!" she shrieked, covering her face as her head dropped back. "He'll shun me!" Bitter sobs wracked her body. "He has the most brilliant mind in the entire kingdom! He won't touch a hair on my head." She wiped her eyes with both fists and then brought her voice to a normal decibel. "He will very simply refuse to mind lock with me ever again. I will no longer be his friend. I will be denied the silver fire within his brilliant synapses . . . his voice inside my head . . ."

"Wow . . . he's all that in the head?" Carlos asked, gazing out toward the barrier.

"You cannot even begin to fathom where centuries have allowed his mind to go," she whispered. "To be denied that . . . he might as well take off my head when I go back to him."

"Well, if it'll make you feel better," Carlos said, almost speaking to himself, "he got all up in my woman's head, too. So, where I come from, fair exchange is no robbery."

"He did what . . ."

The low, threatening timbre of the she-dragon's voice held such quiet, unmasked pain and disbelief that Carlos looked at her but backed away. It had not been his intent to start any additional drama, and the comment was only borne from his own heightening insecurity of what a mind lock with Cain might have done to Damali. He was not playing games when he'd said it.

"Yeah," Carlos admitted, too weary to cover up the truth with a lie.

"Had been coming to her for years, I understand, bringing her music, coaxing her gift . . . then finally found the rip, I suppose, and had her in his arms—in our fucking house . . . the only thing that I'm pretty sure didn't go down all the way was the flesh violation. But what do I know?"

Carlos's voice trailed off as he thought about it and remembered the erotic charge in the room. He balled up his fists at his sides as angry at himself as he was at Cain. He'd been the one to violate Damali's trust, not Cain, and her trusting, innocent heart was the most special thing about her. How many lies had he told that woman time and time again . . . ? She was right. From the drugs, to the vamp turn, to the throne elevations, to making Yonnie a lieutenant, to getting Damali pregnant at the vanishing point, to taking another tumble on Level Six, and doing Juanita on her back deck. If this older woman standing near him was right, and a soul and mind violation weighed as heavily in the higher realms as they obviously did, then he understood a little bit more now why Damali wasn't hearing shit from him.

"He gave her his music?" the she-dragon asked in a faraway voice.

Carlos closed his eyes. Mutual pain was a very deep thing. "I'll bring you over the barrier, so you can get with somebody else."

"Thank you," she whispered in a shaky voice. "But there is no one else for me but him."

Carlos looked at her, wishing he'd never disclosed Cain's mental encroachment. "I'm so sorry. You deserve better."

"As do you," she said in a quiet tone.

"I'll live. On my plane, a little fantasy never hurt anybody."

She came to him and touched his cheek, pity in her eyes. "It is better that you do not understand."

Carlos grabbed her wrist as she attempted to draw her hand away, but he didn't hold it in anger, just firm enough to make her know he needed more answers.

She looked down and hugged him, as though someone had died, and pressed two fingers to his lips. "Go home, kind lover." She nodded toward the cliff. "Your mind is too young to sort through that level of hurt. Let me show you the thinning area—"

"You know how the mind works, what is imagined is always worse than what is."

She stared at him, as though deciding. "No. It is not. Not always."

She pulled him into a gentle embrace and petted his back. "The mind has a way of creating selective, sentimental memories. It closes a wound after time, as long as that wound is not deep enough."

"She slept with him, didn't she?" Carlos found himself holding onto the beautiful creature as his breathing went shallow.

"No," she said, rubbing the pain away from his back.

Carlos let his breath out hard. "All right," he said, slowly recovering. "You were scaring me."

"I am going to go home, will address my issues with Cain, he and I will talk, and come to an understanding. If he continues to visit the young female from your world, and give her his music, then I will make decisions that must be made."

"Sho' you right, sis," Carlos said, feeling much improved. "Tell him to keep his ass home, I'll do the same. He don't mess with my woman, I won't mess with his. Everybody can be at peace. Things can go back to normal. Damali won't call him no more, I . . ." He stopped his diatribe for a moment. "I will call you, though, because you are my friend, and I promised I would. But not for spite, just to give you options you deserve to have. Even if I can't be the one to ever do you, is that fair?"

"That is more than fair," she whispered, her large jewel eyes still glittering with tears. "You are a gentle lover," she whispered. "Selfless."

"Are we friends?" he asked, pushing her mussed hair over her shoulder.

"Forever friends," she said quietly. "Tumble over the edge, and when you feel like you are moving too quickly, grab onto the bands of light before you hit the bottom of the ravine . . . they will give, a rip will open, and you will be back where you entered."

Carlos nodded. "Thanks, friend," he said quietly. "I just wish you would tell me what I'm up against in her head, so I have a fighting chance."

Maybe it was the way she covered her mouth and closed her eyes, her fingers trembling over her lush lips that made him have to know.

"You don't," she said gently. "And, because you are my friend, I am asking you not to do this to yourself, young, gentle, sweet, sweet lover, do not. Sometimes knowledge is a damaging thing, not powerful at all." She stared at him. "On this, ignorance is bliss."

Carlos swallowed hard, unshed tears suddenly in his throat for unknown reasons. "Tell me. What did he do to her? You know, now, don't you? I can see it in your eyes. You've been picking up his vibe since I slipped and told you by accident." Carlos could feel his voice about to break. "That's why he isn't coming, he knows I'm here about to roll, but also knows that he can't face you, can't stand here and accuse you without having to answer some hard questions himself. Right?"

Zehiradangra touched his cheek and walked to the edge of the cliff and stared out at the surrounding mountains, giving Carlos her back as she spoke. "He will not come here to challenge you or me, now that I know."

"What went down, Z? Just tell me, okay? Then I'm out."

"He filled a trust void within her that you had left . . . the most profound gift one can do for an injured friend. He came to her when she needed him most, a strong, admirable shoulder to lean on when her mate had betrayed her . . . and he filled her heart with hope that in time there could be another after you who could make her feel the way you once did. I envy her."

"He did all that in one or two visits?" Carlos raked his hair and began walking in an agitated circle.

She nodded without any resistance in her body as her arms dangled lifelessly by her sides. Her voice was monotone and flat, carrying the numbness of a broken spirit.

"How can he face me when he cocreated with her through her music and his, a pure fusion, with her in his arms? There is no more sensual act than cocreation, bringing forth the inner gifts bestowed from On High with another . . . more so than even physical conception. It is *pure Light.* He enlivened her body through her mind as his swept the heat of melody through it, releasing resonances not heard on your side."

Her voice faltered and she swallowed hard. "Her spirit opened to accept a trusted act of cocreation . . . her mind opened to accept his warm friendship, knowing he would not hurt her within that sublime surrender—that was not his intent."

Carlos almost wanted to weep . . . he vividly remembered when his baby girl had turned her throat to him in sublime surrender, unafraid that he would hurt her, even when he bore fangs. He'd scored her throat, nearly flatlined her pulse . . . and yet, another man with even stronger vamp DNA in him had scored her with pure sound and light, and never hurt a hair on her head. His stomach was doing cartwheels. Oh, God, help him . . . this brother was gonna pull her for sure.

Zehiradangra shuddered as Carlos neared her and held her shoulders, nestling her spine against his torso. Yet her voice remained calm, detached, as the vision poured over him in pain-filled waves.

"With those two things, she sang for him, and it ignited his flesh—and hers—and were it not for a thin remaining thread of love and respect for you . . . and, I suppose, his for me, she would have . . ." Zehiradangra jerked her head back as Carlos's fingers touched her temples and trembled. "Don't do this to yourself."

Carlos ignored her warning and allowed his palms to slowly flatten against the sides of her head. "I did this to us," he whispered. "I made her go here, so I have to know how bad it is. I'll never know peace until I understand where I went wrong or how this happened. I have to fix this."

"If you touch me and go into my mind, you will never know peace, my sweet. You cannot fix this. It is broken and already almost beyond—"

"I got this. Me and Damali go way back. I ask your permission to see."

"Cain is beyond comprehension, lover. You are not prepared . . . he is—"

"Messing with the wrong one, *me.* Crossed into *my* yard. *My* territory. He might be seasoned as shit over here, but to me, he's just a new motherfucker on *my* block, and that's *my* woman. Aw'ight?"

She nodded with a sigh and covered Carlos's hands with hers, keeping her back to him. "I will be here for you, after. You will need a friend. That I promise you."

"Cool. I can handle it, though."

But no matter how much bravado he'd put in his voice, or how much he'd told himself he could take just about anything he might see as long as this brother hadn't actually slept with Damali—the older woman was right. This was almost worse than if she'd been caught in the act.

He was not prepared to really experience the sensual exchange that had gone down. Carlos dropped his forehead to the back of Zehiradangra's neck as the impressions cut him to the bone. He almost pulled his hands away as he saw what Damali had seen on her deck, and then felt Cain's loving, healing balm sweep that all away. Melody filled him up, brought tears to his eyes, and he squeezed them shut.

The sound in his head became multicolored light, which converted instantly to waves and bands of gut-wrenching pleasure. He could feel Damali's skin heat nearly sizzle, as her fully naked form pressed against Cain's, her body arching like it had only arched for him, thunderous orgasms quaking her womb, her wet scent sending spirals of rage through him that collided with the invading male's scent as her nose dragged along his collarbone, *just like he'd shown her!* Every erogenous zone on her fired red, then went liquid-hot silver, her Sankofa climbing up her spine one vertebra at a time, her hands splayed across a massive, muscular back . . . oh Jesus, no . . . he didn't take her there!

Cain's deep breaths of sudden need ripping his gums—Carlos's own incisors lowered, his chest becoming tight with agony, his woman battling to breathe, trying to do the right thing, slipping fast, wanting to hold the line, but wondering why she should have to . . . Her voice a razor of uncut desire setting off a perfectly synced release, Cain's with hers, so intense that all Carlos saw beneath his lids for a moment was a blinding, blue-white nova.

Carlos pulled his hands away from Zehiradangra's head and drew in several shaky breaths.

"And he never even bedded her," she whispered. "Never breached your mate throat mark, out of respect—because she was not ready to accept his bite," she said, her voice becoming very far away. "Never took her to his lair, where everything is sound vibration at the cellular level . . . down to atomic structures. I remember when it was he and I and this realm had sensation . . . he was magnificent, then, in the flesh. This is what hurts me so badly," she said without turning. "He must really love her, to be so close, to want her so badly, but to force himself to back away . . . just because a small whimper within her mind begged him not to make her violate you. He could have done that very easily, in her condition. It was *his* choice not to, as well as hers. She did not have toxic silver in her veins to create a barrier, only pure endorphin rushing within her."

Zehiradangra turned to look at Carlos's stricken expression. "Cain has not been with a woman in longer than you could imagine, and was in an apex heat in the flesh density, but honored her request." She sighed, her tone sad and philosophical. "I cannot remain furious at my friend, I suppose. And yet, he offered you to me, and now I understand why . . . the man is fair. It was a gesture of repayment for the near miss and transgression."

Carlos didn't need to know any more, nor did he wait for further instructions about how to get back to the other side. His toes flexed at the edge of the cliff, tiny pebbles bit at his feet as he opened his arms, tears streaming down his face, and he just let himself fall forward.

CHAPTER TEN

The team rode for hours in blindfolded silence, huddled together like sheep in the black van that had become a temporary prison. Yanked to their feet when the vehicle finally stopped, they were shoved and pulled out into a warm climate, but couldn't tell where they were.

They could each feel a strong, angry body beside them, hurrying them along as they stumbled forward being half-pulled, half-dragged, their hands restrained in tight nylon cords behind their backs, and then the brightness beyond their blindfolds gave way to darkness, and it became cool. Instead of their footfalls landing on what had felt like asphalt, they now echoed. The Guardian team was inside a structure somewhere.

"Sit down," they were ordered, and then shoved into what felt like metal chairs. "We have a lot of questions about this terrorist cell you guys are trying to operate on U.S. soil."

No one on the team moved or spoke.

He didn't want to land here. The compound wasn't home. This place would never, ever be home for him again.

Carlos glanced around the destroyed studio with waves of nausea roiling in his stomach. Panic vibrations were everywhere. He didn't want to face the team, didn't want to see the pity in their eye or the expressions on their faces. The team had betrayed him; they knew. This was Damali's family, not his. This was her world, not his. The only real family he had left, crazy as it seemed, was an old priest and a vampire brother from his old life.

Unable to stay in the studio another moment, Carlos bolted out the door, up the stairs, and then froze. What the hell had happened in here?

A different level of panic shot through him as he bellowed out names. "Damali! Jose! Rider! Marlene! Shabazz!"

Running through room by decimated room, he looked at the destruction. The front door was splintered. Armored-vehicle tracks on the carpet? Shit! He immediately raced to the weapons room and just stood in the doorway. Computers had been ripped from their housing, glass was everywhere. Weapons gone. Furniture overturned.

Carlos began running through the house, his senses keened, trying to feel for any distinguishable tracer that could tell him where his family had been taken. Unknown human blood and sweat was in the air. He honed in on Damali, but came away with nothing.

One by one he tried to sense each team member's vibration. They were alive, but very far away. In a cell, but where? Prison, a police lockup, military base, where? They had once worked for the government, had done a job in Tibet and in L.A., so how could this be happening?

Carlos spun in a confused circle and gathered the last of his strength to propel himself home. There was no getting around it, attempts to do anything but rest for a moment, eat, drink, and regenerate the expended energy would be futile. Then he'd try again . . . would go get another soldier to work with him—Yonnie.

Damali stood in awe at a place along the Nile controlled by dams, making the massive river capitulate to being a placid lake dotted by a series of islands, which turned black or red depending on the sun's mood.

Eve had told her about the ancient tombs of the Elephantine nobles that were dug into the rocks of the Gharbi Aswan escarpment, and to use those as a landmark. Here, she'd said, was also Aga Khan's mausoleum, and an ancient Coptic monastery. A place where the ancestors kept watch over the palm groves, temple remains, and massive, old botanical gardens.

This was the beginning point. Damali peered around and became a sparrow, following Eve's directions to go toward the terminus of the valley of the Nile in Upper Nubia, where the river was no longer navigable. Her destination was Lake Nassar. Beneath it were more than twenty-three temples and sanctuaries that had been rebuilt elsewhere. Everything had been submerged, like rumored-about Atlantis.

As she sailed over the surface of the azure blue water, she could almost feel the stones speaking to her, directing her on her quest. She needed the Caduceus, the Staff of Aesclepius . . . Thoth Hermes, in order to wield enough energy to break into the Land of Nod.

She touched down on Philae Island and hopped about, tilting her head. Where was the temple of Isis and the temple of Hathor? Eve had been sure that the island that bore the forerunner name of Philadelphia would be the one.

Damali quietly and discreetly took her human form. A small rose quartz stone bit into her sandal. When she stooped to collect it, she held the fifth stone she'd received tightly in her fist. Love? But she was on a mission to keep the realms separated.

Rather than argue with the mysteries of the universe, she shoved the stone into her white gauze pants pockets. Immediately the stone warmed her leg and she closed her eyes, sensed the vibration, and once again took flight as a small bird.

Everything had been moved to the island of Ajilka in modern times. Damali saw it mentally as she whirred against the wind, excited. The pavilion of Trajan used for the complex rituals of the goddess, just as Eve had said, was there. Fourteen bell-shaped sepia-hued stone columns on one side of the temple of Hathor marked it. Damali touched down hard, anticipation making her a little clumsy and stirring up dust.

But it took a moment for her feet to move as she stared up at the monumental entrance of a temple of birth dedicated to Isis the Elder. Her palms were moist with both reverence and awe as she began to move along the wide, flat steps toward the second pylon which gave way to a colonnaded room with ten columns and a portico with twelve shrines. Damali stayed extremely still, feeling the vibrations emanating from the interior crypt and the terrace devoted to the funerary shrine of Isis.

"Oh, great Queen Mother Isis, Aset, please guide me in the right path, make my choices wise," Damali whispered.

Instantly Damali's Isis materialized on her hip, not in her hand. She could only take that as a message to be guarded, but stand down, there was no imminent danger. Damali nodded. "Thank you."

A slight flicker of light flared along the eastern wall of the portico, drawing her attention. A decree from Ptolemy V Epiphanies—same one as on the famous Rosetta stone? Damali smiled, not needing to know the decree. That wasn't the point. Epiphanies, plural, that's what the old queens were signaling. Okay, she'd go with the flow of discovery.

"But where is the staff of Thoth Hermes?"

The word *Philadelphia* echoed in her mind in response.

"I've already been to the island of Philae, and it's not there," she said in a quiet voice, her patience straining. "Please don't send me back to the States to Philly."

"Under Ptolemy II Philadelphos," an out-of-body female voice whispered.

"Begun by the king of Ethiopia, on the site of the old temple," another whispered.

"The Temple of Dakka."

"Thank you," Damali said with an exasperated sigh as she turned and hurried outside.

Small fishing boats dotted the shore with splashes of prickly bushes and dried grasses. Deep yellow sand and earth covered her feet and clung to the hem of her white pants as she found the structure. The desertlike heat, however, was mercifully tolerable because of the off-water breeze.

She gazed up at the three floors of rooms and two terraces, deciding. Simply sensing her direction, Damali slipped into the entrance and vestibule, and made her way into the dark, musty space.

Philae had given her a token of love via a rose quartz crystal. The temple of Isis promised epiphanies to come. Now all she had to do was navigate the isolated, dusty old building. The queens were deep, always answered spiritual questions in a riddle and in accordance with a cryptic numbering pattern. Three stops on this one. Damali froze. Three was the trinity, also representing man, woman, and child. Wholeness, healing. This structure had three floors. Okaaaay.

She raced up the steps and got to the top floor and counted three rooms to the right, working on a hunch. As she entered the dimly sunlit room, her eyes scanned the intricate friezes that were carved into the stone walls. Right in front of her face. A battle scene, a staff lowered over a king. The moment she neared it, the dual serpents on the scepter slid along the wall, making her jump back.

She watched the moving stone exit at the base of the wall with her hand readied on the hilt of her sword, but didn't move as two black snakes slithered along the floor, hissed at each other, struck, and then entwined in an erotic, pulsing dance. They separated so that a golden staff came between them and formed a large crystal ball at the top supported by a twined golden platform beneath it, and went still.

"Awesome," she whispered, not sure she was ready to go near the staff until the energy within it settled down. But she took a deep breath, moved toward the now all-golden instrument, and closed her fist around the smooth, round crystal globe.

Instantly, she was moving fast, everything around her blurred white, and she came to a hard stop on a grassy knoll. Majestic mountains were all around her. She glanced up at the strangely vivid blue sky that had two suns, one unnaturally iridescent, the other bearing down radiant solar heat. She scanned the horizon and slowly but surely, the mountainside wall gave way to the presence of two huge, black onyx sphinxes. Did she fall into the Valley of the Kings, or what?

Her heart beat fast, her nerves were wire taut. Even with her blade and a scepter on her, it wasn't about standing around waiting for something weird to jump off.

"Cain!" she shouted, hoping that he wouldn't materialize as something really freaky she'd have to fight.

Damali waited as she heard leisurely footfalls. She listened hard. No hoofs, okay, that was a very good sign. Two feet, not panther paws or something whack. No bat wings or the sound of leathery flight, a real positive sign. She clutched her staff tightly with one hand and her Isis handle with the other.

But her grip loosened as Cain came out of the entrance of what seemed like a temple. All he had on was a sheer swath of white linen casually tied at his hip. His broad chest was bare, his locks clasped back in a golden, scarab-studded band, his smile a serious weapon right through here.

"You came to me?" he said, his eyes appraising her without censure as he raised one knee, placed his bare foot against the onyx, and leaned against a sphinx base.

"Uh, yeah," Damali stammered, almost unable to look at him, he was so fine. "We need to talk."

"Be my guest," he said, his eyes constantly roving over her as he pushed away from the statue, gave her a slight bow, and waved her forward to enter.

Still a bit skeptical, Damali maintained her distance as she passed him. But as she did so, she could literally feel the charge of pure magnetism wafting off him. It almost knocked her down when she entered his space, and for a moment she just stood and openly gawked, unable to hide her amazement.

"This is you?" she murmured, her eyes drinking in the splendor. The pool immediately caught her attention, and she glanced at the bed, felt her face warm, and stared at the columns and ornate pottery instead.

He chuckled low and deep in a sensual, relaxed manner. "This is a part of me," he said. "Come, sit down, and we shall talk."

He bade her to sit beside him on a white alabaster bench by the pool. She did, no longer feeling quite so tense. There was no way to keep her line of vision from his.

"You have the most amazing eyes," she said, not sure where all that came from. But it was the truth.

His smile became gentle and he looked away as though her forthright statement had embarrassed him. "As do you," he finally replied. Then he chuckled self-consciously. "I thought you came here to talk?"

He'd made her laugh.

"I was all prepared to do that, and then you came through the door in a half-toga and messed me up."

They both laughed. She couldn't believe she was saying this stuff to him, especially when she was supposed to be getting hard questions answered . . . but she was actually flirting with him. Crazy!

"I was resting," he admitted with a brilliant smile. "After coming through the rip, and dealing with my wayward guest—"

"Carlos!" Was she outta her mind? She'd almost forgotten why she was over here in Nod.

Cain chuckled more deeply and sighed. "Yes. Him."

"Where is he?" she asked, now appropriately alarmed. If this brother was all chilled out after a battle and resting and cleaned up, that meant only one thing, Carlos was—

"No," Cain said calmly, taking her weapon and the staff to lay them aside in order to clasp both of her hands within his. "He went back home."

Damali removed her hands from within Cain's, and then glanced at the staff and her blade on the bench, wondering what in tarnation would allow her to let the man so easily disarm her. "How do I know that?"

"Would I lie to you, sweet one?"

She smiled. He laughed, sat back, and slung his arm over the back of the bench.

"First of all, you would not be smiling if you thought I had done harm."

Damali swallowed her smile. "All right, true."

"Secondly, you saw how we entered this space." He waited until she nodded. "We both needed to come to terms, he and I."

Now she was really nervous. "And?"

"We did what irrational males do," he said, looking at her with a sidelong, sheepish glance and a grin. "We fought until we both were battered and very tired. Then we stood in the glen hurling insults at each other, attempting to catch our breaths. Then we decided that the whole ordeal was futile, and I invited him back to my home to clean himself up, change, and rest so he could go home."

She covered her mouth and laughed. "Stop playing."

"No, sweet one. He and I were evenly matched. I was weakened from the energy distortion in your world, he from the molecular difference in mine. He had to go home, as we subsist on only energy here. There is no food or water to replenish him . . . or blood. Which is why, as much as I would enjoy your enduring company, you cannot stay for an extended visit, either."

"That is so deep," she murmured, looking at the room again with new eyes, her gaze fastened to the pool.

Cain cocked his head to the side and motioned toward the scepter with his chin. "You must have really thought we had done bodily injury to each other to come with the healing rod of Imhotep."

"I did," Damali said quietly, so glad that she'd found Cain this way. "So did your mother. We were both worried about you guys."

"My mother?" he said, his tone so tender that Damali could barely breathe. "You went to her on my behalf?"

Damali nodded. "She told me to tell you that she loves you and always has . . . always will."

Cain stood and walked down the long edge of the pool, his back to Damali. She could tell that deep emotions had propelled him from his seat, and that he was battling his composure. She hadn't meant to upset him, but had promised his mother that a message would be delivered.

His regal waist-length locks swayed gently side to side as his long, calm strides moved his body like living fluid along the reflective water's edge. "Please tell her that a thousand lifetimes can never blot the stain on my soul for breaking her heart," he said through a shaky inhale. His voice dropped an octave to soft whisper. "Tell that queen of all that is human, I love her, too."

Damali almost burst out crying, but took a deep breath instead. "I'm so sorry that I picked at an old wound, I just promised her, though, for the key into Nod, that I'd—"

Cain held up his hand, closed his eyes, as he turned to face Damali. "No apology for giving me a gift beyond compare. That you found out my name, went to such lengths to visit me with no harsh judgment in your eyes, and came to me with my mother's message on your beautiful lips . . ." He looked at the scepter in her hand. "My mother is always trying to fix what she never broke. She has sent you the spiritual teacher's rod, the healer's rod with kundalini energy tapped into the microcosm." He closed his eyes again. "Ever hopeful that I would not turn out like my father again, she sends this as a message of her hope. You did not need the staff to enter. As an in-flesh Neteru, you can enter at your focused will."

Damali looked at the staff and at Cain as he opened his eyes and pure tenderness reflected back from them. "She—"

"Is worried, by all rights," he said, lifting his chin and raking his hair. He stopped moving and stared at Damali. "Do you know how long it has been since I laid eyes on my beloved mother?"

Damali could only shake her head. His pain was so profound that it entered her pores. All she wanted to do at that moment was hug him and take it from him. How could this man be the harbinger of evil?

"I served my earth sentence as a banished man," he said quietly, no bitterness in his voice, just weary acceptance. "I lived a long time, tried to make things right by marrying many wives, living a respectable life, and caring for and loving all my earthly children. But when I died, the realms could not decide where I should go. Both had reasonable claim, so I was reincarnated here, with full memory. The boredom was nearly maddening, at first. However, I tethered my mind to learning all from every papyrus scroll in the great libraries."

"But you still have the blade of Ausar," Damali said, standing, collecting the staff, and going to him.

"Indeed," Cain replied, motioning toward it on a faraway bench. "The Roundtable of Kings wanted to see if I would bring order from chaos, would be able to even hold it—a sign that I had not gone dark."

She came close enough to him to place her hand on the center of his chest. The staff touched the floor as her palm connected with his skin.

His eyes slid closed and a slight shudder passed through him. Now she knew why Eve had sent the rod with her.

"Enough pain for a lifetime, the last one or this," Damali whispered. "I feel you are a good soul."

He covered her hand as he drew a ragged breath. "The balm . . . you would offer me a Neteru heart balm?"

"You deserve it," Damali whispered, fully embracing him in a hug. "You are a good man, son of my queen mother, of Neteru brethren, with silver in your soul. What happened before was tragic, should have never happened. But I also believe in redemption."

He held her tightly with a sob trapped in his chest, just rocking her and kissing the crown of her head. She could hear him about to speak several times, but then heard his words get choked back down his throat on a thick, mucous swallow. Yet she also knew he was too proud to allow his tears to fall. So she didn't require that he speak, or look at her, and simply allowed her balm to penetrate his heart through the patient strokes down his back.

After his inner storm passed, he held her away from him, brushed her mouth, and let go of her to walk across the room.

"You should see what I guard," he said with regal authority.

Damali watched wide-eyed as he stripped the sheath of fabric away from his body at the door of his closet, and began searching for his armor. Totally mesmerized, she had to find a bench to sit down on before she fell down.

"While here, and should you ever come due to a barrier break in the energy seals between our kingdoms, you cannot judge by parental lineage."

She wasn't sure what he was talking about. His baritone voice was running all through her, the military battle, no-nonsense tone in it making the hair on her arms rise. She almost wanted to just start some mess to see the brother pull a blade, but tucked that insane thought away and tried to listen as he mounted his golden breastplate, and put his helmet under his arm. Have mercy . . .

"Half-human, half-angel does not mean that entity is good. It may have made a choice to use the preternatural power in a negative way— just as my grandfather fell from grace. Conversely, I have a best friend, her father was a dragon . . . but she has a heart of gold. This is what makes this realm so challenging. It is a mirror image of earth, a gray zone, where choice is based upon an individual soul, not a broad category or fila. Any entity with a soul can make a choice, hence be redeemed, unlike original demons created in the nether realms."

"Then how do you know?" Damali whispered. Cain was blowing her mind with new knowledge.

"You must sense the vibrations off the entity in question. Hence, I, no more than you, am interested in having the earth prematurely flooded. There must be a very strict scrutiny for passage out to assist in the final war."

Damali nodded. This brother was pushing so many right buttons she was sure she was glowing. "Like a celestial or interdimensional passport system."

"Yes," he said, offering her his elbow as he passed.

She accepted it, but it was such an Old World gesture that she wasn't sure how to react. He brought her to the edge of the clearing at the end of the cliff, unsheathed the blade he was wearing, and used it like a pointer, lighting the sky in sparkling, golden filaments.

"I will show you the main pavilion, the broad thoroughfares, and the temples. The libraries are expansive. As are the universities. In the residential districts, each palace was the prototype for the ones later human-designed. There is a sensory space at the outreaches. The hall of whispers. This is where beings so moved will try to pierce the veil to send humanity inspiration, or nightmares, whichever their choice."

"Is that where you met me?" she asked quietly, still marveling as she looked down the building-studded landscape in the jewel-green valley below. Then she remembered the vibes coming off the alley bricks behind the club, her mind ablaze with curiosity.

"No," he said quietly. "I will tell you where, later." He smiled. "To begin that explanation will make me lose focus."

Again she felt her face warm from his words. "This is awesome though," she said, peering over the cliff. She backed up from the edge of it and glanced around. "This is all energy?" She stooped to pick a blade of grass, studying it so closely her eyes nearly crossed.

Within the cool green blade, she could see tiny whirls of energy interacting as though the atoms in the structure were visible through the translucent, iridescent-green casing. Delighted, she brought it to her ear and listened hard to the soft, humming resonance it contained.

He seemed so pleased that he rubbed his jaw and paced away from her as though needing the distance to not touch her. "I can transport you down—"

"No," she said, laughing. "I can do it."

"You can? Here?" Raw desire began to take over his brown irises. "The laws of gravity still apply, you know."

She shrugged, dropped the scepter, and unfastened her Isis, which made his eyes go straight silver. Then she became a sparrow and took off down the side of the cliff. He was waiting for her when she reached the bottom, and he held out her Isis and her scepter to her.

"You should have these as you walk," he said just above a whisper.

"Thanks," she replied, more quietly than intended. "But why do you have armor on, just to stroll through town?" *That* she needed to know.

"Because I'm with you, and you are flesh," he said calmly, his gaze sweeping the pedestrian-packed boulevard.

Spectacularly attractive beings in unique combinations from every human ethnicity nodded at him as they passed along the pristine, shimmering stone streets. She'd been many places in the world, but had never been anywhere that one could potentially eat off the glistening, clean pavements.

Some of the passersby glimpsed his sword and hers, showing a hint of fang in their smiles, but allowed them to continue onto the destination without incident. She could feel him bristle with each visually curious invasion.

"People seem to be cool, so . . ."

"I may be king, but—"

"You're what?"

He looked away and smiled and held his chin up a little higher. "I will show you where it is dangerous to be when the three moons rise. We do not have a formal night. But once the solar sun goes dark each eve, the one that bears no heat is dimmer, not reflective light. Three moons rise . . . ours, yours that can be seen through the barrier, and the one that is the lunar pulse of creation. I will also show you where there are residences to avoid."

"Y'all even have a badlands here? Deep."

"Quite, and no place for any human, much less a lady."

"What happened?"

He stopped walking as they passed a massive library flanked by huge, white marble lions. "In A.D. nineteen forty-three your calendar, foolish men on your plane, in what they called scientific pursuit, manifested a battleship into our harbor. Because of the energy distortion here, and the higher molecular frequency that only Neterus can adapt to, some of the men on the ship spontaneously combusted on impact with our atmosphere. Some got frozen in a motion stasis as their atomic structure could not make the transition from the slowed vibrations to the higher ones here. They were the lucky ones." He began walking again, but she placed her hand on his arm.

"Talk to me, Cain. This is partially why I'm here. I have to know what could happen if beings from your side come out to earth's plane."

"I was at court when it occurred." His eyes blazed with anger and pain as he spoke. "The smell of scorching human flesh hit the atmosphere and blackened it with a stench that those from the lower proclivities hadn't smelled so strongly since their time on earth. The smell of human flesh and blood created riot. Screaming human men rent the air, drawing the strongest of the dark-soul beings to the battleship first. Those with higher vibrations attempted to intervene. My parliament fractured right on the spot. Angelic-based beings tried to cover the living humans with their wings and carry them to safety, but those with equal strength and larger, leathery wingspans ripped bodies apart in midair struggles. Those humans that survived were taken to the shadow wall as my allies and I battled our way to them."

He raked his hair and looked off into the distance. "But by the time we got there, those human men had been raped and violated and passed around until their internal injuries killed them." He closed his eyes and let out a breath of frustration. "Then the ship summarily vanished with a few humans who had escaped desecration. That is when the feeding began. We sent battalions into the air, searching for remains that had been secreted away. We could not even bury the corpses. Those who burned . . . even their charred bones were fought over."

She couldn't speak as he began walking again. This time she didn't stop him, just stayed by his side in a matched stride. The horror of what he'd described put a chill down her spine, and definitely put the experiment Rabbi Zeitloff had explained into serious perspective. Cain needn't worry though. She had *no* intention of getting caught here, alone, after the three moons rose, if it was all of that. But what he'd told her also put every last piece of the puzzle in place for her. Plus, he hadn't lied to her—major points for him.

However, these beings could *not* get out. If this was what was over here all mixed up with humans and some half-angels and half-demons, then the breach had to be sealed ASAP, and any crazy military experiments had to stop. But even with all the insane information she'd just acquired, several very comforting things had also been determined in her mind. Cain was good. He was obviously supposed to have a blend of three elements—to be the mirror image of what Carlos represented on the earth side.

Cain, to her reasoning, was a strong spiritual Neteru warrior to guard the inside of the door, after serving a sentence for doing the unspeakable. This brother *knew* hard time, had been in the streets back in the day when the real biblical deal was going down, had been seasoned by experience, and knew a game when he saw one. He had to live it in order to know a demon with fangs hiding in half-human form when he saw one. Just like the Light had clearly made a younger, strong male Neteru on the outside who had similar experiences and proclivities, and who was helping to keep a lid on from the earth side of the door.

Problem was, she was *really* beginning to like this one over in Nod perhaps a little too much for her own good. She spied Cain from the corner of her eye. He was sexy, knowledgeable, and real cool. He seemed to know so much, and she wanted to spend hours picking his brain about all the things he'd seen over the years, all the aerial battles and strategy, down to the technology housed in all the libraries flanking the boulevard. He had both street smarts and ancient scroll smarts, and packaged in a body that made her wanna slap her mother-seer.

Thick vibe had settled between them as they walked along quietly side by side. The brother wanted her, but wasn't all up in her face, the time in the studio notwithstanding. He had backed off, was serving gentleman to the bone. She wouldn't hold that momentary lapse in her condo and studio against him, given an apex, anything coulda kicked off. His mom was good people, in fact, she was a queen. He exuded quiet, secure authority. Plus, by rights, when he could have just kicked Carlos's ass, he didn't. Took the high road. Now *that* she respected. Comparisons and what ifs were tumbling around in her brain so hard that she almost forgot they were walking beside each other.

Cain stretched out his arm before her to keep her from moving forward as they approached a shadowy corridor in a realm that cast no shadows. The light from above didn't reach the ground here where the small opening at the edge of the city was lined by high walls. "Draw your Isis."

Damali did, but a current of desire ran through her when she obliged. Cain hadn't told her to wait here. Hadn't said some macho bull like, "Baby, I got this, it's too dangerous for you." Instead, he'd simply put her on guard and told her to draw like an equal warrior, while nonverbally requesting that she only follow him because he'd been here before. Now that was also deep.

"The walls," he said, leveling his blade at them. "Put your hand near one."

She did, and a human face with its eyes closed and mouth opened pressed against it as though the structure were rubber: She snatched her hand back.

"Those are seekers. Humans with deep, unfulfilled desires in their subconscious, which makes them vulnerable to suggestions—good or bad. They want what is not resident in them, seek gifts that are not theirs to be had in their current incarnations, and want things from the exterior of themselves, versus what is already deep within."

Cain stared at her. "I never sought you here. You never yearned from here. Knowing in your soul that you had a gift, and you did, and wanting your gift to shine does not send you to the seeking wall, and does not draw the negative energies. That brings the Light. That brings inspiration. Not false promises in trade for the liquid sensation of mental touch at this wall."

"Damn," she whispered. "Your red-light district? This was what I saw behind the club."

"Even some good beings accidentally wind up here under the self-deluded guise that they are helping the seekers move away from the wall. When caught and embarrassed, they claim that they've told the seekers to go within, to focus on their real gifts, and to seek divine guidance." Cain scoffed. "Self-professed evangelists, who get enmeshed in the seduction of this corridor and wind up whispering more than inspirational messages of Light." He smiled. "Let us leave this foul place. But you needed to witness it for yourself. It will flood with negative energies as the moons rise."

"Where to?"

He smiled as the rejuvenating light poured over them when they exited the dank, gray corridor. "Would you like to see my palace, and where I hold court?"

She swallowed a chuckle. Once all business was handled now *he* was the one flirting. "Okay."

Damali almost laughed out loud as an occasional blue arc would creep across his armor, discharging static as they leisurely strolled down a palm-lined boulevard. Cain seemed like an excited teenager, and she could almost feel his energy quickening her pace as his anticipation built. She glimpsed his strong, proud profile from the corner of her eye. How in the world did she wind up in the company of a king, she wondered?

But as they passed a huge, glass pyramid structure that had blocked her view, she simply stopped walking and stared.

"Oh, my God . . ."

"You like it?" he asked, unable to stop beaming at her.

She shook her head and blew out a long whistle, then censured herself as the sound with vibration made him briefly close his eyes. "It's amazing," she said, recovering quickly. And it was.

A glistening white, monumental seven-columned structure sat on a slight rise with a three-block-long promenade of majestic palms before it. Above the main entrance was a carved relief of the disc of Heru, with the blade of Asuar. On one huge golden door a winged falcon was fused with a double sun, and the same symbols she'd seen on his sword inscribed into the metal. On the other was the feather of Ma'at with the forty-two laws written in the ancient language. Six white stone lions, three per side, guarded the doorway. She watched Cain snap, the lions come to life, purr and fawn at his passage as he guided her up what had to be three hundred steps, and then find their perches again to once more become stone.

With a gentle shove, the several-ton doors opened, perfectly weight-balanced. In the grand portico, they stood on a mosaic-strewn tile floor of opalescent white fused together with silver and gold mortar. She could look down what had to be a thousand steps to an azure-surfaced pool studded by indoor palms and benches that terminated with what seemed to be a parliamentary galley facing a marble podium and an ornately carved white marble judge's chair.

"Whew," she whispered. "You guys don't mess around on this side, do you? Talk about taking things to the max."

"The rest of it is behind the main court. Very similar to the smaller design that Solomon employed once he understood the architectural dynamics."

"Solomon based his temple on yours?"

"All the great architecture is based on ours," Cain said, seeming slightly offended.

She swallowed another smile and briefly thought of Carlos. If he'd seen this, then her man was definitely not all right. "Are you sure that you don't have Carlos locked away in a dungeon somewhere?" she asked, half-joking. "I know how he can be, and he might not have taken any of this well."

Cain chuckled and sighed. "Put your hands out before you. Sense for him here. Do you pick up any physical distress?"

Damali cast Cain a sidelong look and began sensing. It wasn't physical distress that concerned her.

"No," she finally said. "But I just don't see him coming here under battle bulk conditions, getting tired, chilling, and then saying see ya later. I am worried about him." She sheathed her blade and placed her hands on her hips. "Wanna tell me what really happened when you guys hit the pavement on this side of the world?"

"I really do not," Cain said with a sly grin. "But I will relent. We will save the tour of the palace for your next visit, should you honor me again." He touched her hair and allowed his hand to fall away. "I should take you back to the cliff dwelling, before I forget why you came here."

On that note, she decided it was best to keep any further questions to herself for the moment. The air had charged around them again, and she had to stay on mission.

It was all in the way he turned slowly, rolled his neck as though he was talking to himself hard inside his head, took a deep breath, and began walking. The erotic charge he left in his wake stripped the air from her lungs for a few seconds, and only then did her feet heed the command of her brain to begin moving.

"I should take you back up," he said calmly once they'd reached the base of the mountain. "You have been here a while and your energy is starting to wane. I can feel it."

That was no lie. It was getting harder to put one foot before the other, and a shape-shift right now would be difficult to pull off.

"I'd appreciate that," she said quietly, almost afraid to go near him. As the second moon rose, he was reeking raw sensuality. It wasn't that she didn't trust him; she didn't trust herself at this point.

She closed her eyes as his arms enfolded her, and felt the lift, the slight whir and pressure change, then a soft landing.

"I will take you to the ravine where the barrier is thin," he murmured, his eyes searching hers with a question. "But . . . I have questions I would like to also ask you. Will you visit for just a while longer? Please."

What could she say to that? Damali nodded against her better judgment and allowed his warm hand to cover hers as he led her inside. She noticed that he'd deposited her on a bench deeper into his cliffside palace than she'd been before, closer to the bed, and she watched him stall for time, changing into a soft white robe, losing the armor and weapon. Her Isis got discarded at her feet as she silently slid it under the bench with the staff. She waited for his return with her pulse racing. She knew she wasn't supposed to be here, like this, but . . .

"May I ask you a personal question, sweet one?" he said, sitting slowly beside her and not leaving her much room for evasion.

"I guess," she shrugged, trying to break eye contact with him. Impossible.

"What do you want for your life? How do you envision it?"

Somewhat stunned, she blinked twice and really had to make her brain work on the last question she'd expected him to ask. "I'm not sure what you mean. I have to be a vampire huntress, Neteru, whatever. That's just the way it is."

"That is not what I am asking. That is a duty. You, nor I, have any additional choice about the call that we have chosen to heed. What I have asked is, what do you want to do with the part of your life that is not already consumed by this responsibility?"

His low, sensual voice rumbled through her belly as she fought to remain centered on his question. His finger traced her temple down to the edge of her jaw, which definitely helped to make the answer fuzzy.

The truth leapt out of her mouth as she stared into his eyes and slowly took in his handsome face. "I don't know, honestly. My life is kinda crazy, and there isn't room in it for all the things I used to want."

"Examples. The past is illuminating. Did the old queens not give you the Sankofa symbol that looks over its shoulder to the past to inform its future?"

The brother was rapping so hard and calm that he was a serious contender for change. At the mention of the tattoo, her back lit with a slow heat.

"Yeah, they did. But lately I feel like I've been looking over my shoulder running from stuff, not being informed by it."

He smiled and traced her collarbone, making her nipples sting. "The huntress being hunted? That will never do."

"That's how it feels sometimes," she told him honestly, trying to keep from drowning in his eyes.

"Think of the areas in your life beyond the battles," he murmured, the pad of his thumb leisurely stroking her upper arm. "Your music. Your mate. Your home. What makes you laugh? What do you do for enjoyment when not working?"

She almost gasped as the gentle stroke transferred from her arm to the now very wet slit between her legs. "If you want me to give you a thought-filled answer, you have to stop."

He offered her a contrite smile. "My apologies. You are just so incredible that the very male part of me often gets confused in your presence." He pulled his hand away and the ache it left behind was nearly painful. "I really do want to know what is on your mind, Damali. Although it might not appear that way, I am concerned about more than your body."

Now that line, even if it was probably a line, blew her away. She swallowed hard and folded her hands in her lap to keep from touching him. And the way his voice bottomed out when he'd said her name . . . oh, man, she was in trouble!

"Uh, I don't know how much I've allowed myself to really think about what I've wanted, in all these years. Like, with the music, I didn't want to be a superstar, really. I just wanted to be up on the stage, *jammin'*, giving it, serving the people *serious* knowledge, music . . . aw, man, Cain, when I'm up on the stage, it's like, like—"

"Making love," he said on a deep exhale, his voice bottoming out again. "Sweetness, I know."

She stood up and walked around the bench to give herself some air. The passion in her outburst, and the way it had almost knocked his head back—it was time to change the subject. "I love going to the movies, rollerblading, just hanging out, grooving on people, playing cards with the fellas . . ." She stopped and came back to where she'd been sitting and flopped beside him. "But the best part is *the kids.*"

She leaned in toward him, her gaze locked with his, stone serious. "When we go to a rec center, or just out in the neighborhoods, and I see a kid really hearing me, not just mesmerized by the drama of some icon rolling through . . . ya know. Like, when one of them *gets it.* Hears me. I can *feel it.* Like, that one's got potential, no matter who their mom or dad is, no matter *what* circumstances they're living in, one of 'em got the message—*that's* what I *live* for."

He'd stopped breathing for a moment, his eyes blazed silver rimmed in gold. He nodded, stood, and paced away from her to stand behind their bench. "You are vibrationally sensitive to the human condition and want to elevate it. That is pure Light, Damali. Do not allow the battles to keep you from remembering the human condition, from being gentle with it, from returning to it regularly to recharge your spirit."

The conversation was turning them both on too much, but it was the first time anyone had ever asked her what *she* really wanted. She was drawn to finish it, didn't want to break the connection now. The philosophical exchange was opening new channels of discovery in her mind. But she also had to be careful as she listened to him labor to breathe while he kept his distance.

"That's what I want," she said in a faraway tone, her voice so melancholy that he rounded the bench, sat quickly, and held both her hands.

"I want, for the relationship part of my life, a situation that recharges my battery, and doesn't drain it."

She could feel his hands heat up and tremble so hard as they clasped hers within them that their fingers simply entwined by reflex to stop it. Her truth poured out, and flowed over their laps as she talked to their hands. Sudden tears stung her eyes for no reason at all, needing to release the tension and weariness of dealing with a high-voltage duo for so long that she couldn't remember what normal might be.

"I don't want to fight all the time," she said in a tight whisper, "or be in mad-crazy drama all the time. I want some stillness and serenity in between battles where I can create music, and work with kids. . . . I want trust, everlasting. I want to never have to walk on eggshells around egos about who's in charge . . . ya know? I want to be able to teach as well as learn—not just battle skills, but deep stuff, spiritual stuff. I want mutual respect and safe harbor for my deepest dreams. And, one day, I want to have children and not be afraid that their father is gonna go do some wild mess to put me or them in harm's way."

He slowly lowered his forehead until it touched hers. The damp sheen of perspiration on his brow had risen in shimmering, infinitesimal droplets as though his skin were leaking gold. The silver Neteru symbol on his chest had lit a neon signal beneath his sheer white robe, and had begun pulsing. Every structure in the room vibrated with slow, melodic murmurs that strummed desire through her cells. His bed was literally calling her name in a low, whispering mantra of bass lines and quiet baritone gasps. Their breaths in the small space between their clasped hands and touching foreheads created billowing warmth that spread over their chests and thighs, added a recycling heat to their faces as they both drew in and released slow, agonized breaths.

"Your spirit is sure. Your body is sure," he murmured. "But your heart is conflicted. I will not press the issue to add to heartbreak, though you cannot imagine how much I want to right now."

"I've never been with anyone else but him," she whispered.

Cain took in a breath through his mouth, cringed as though she'd stabbed him, and tilted his head. "Devastation, listen to me. Right now, you have—"

"He hurt me, Cain," she said, her eyes shut hard and her knees pressed tightly together. "This time around . . ."

"Go home. Become clear. I do not want you to do this because you are functioning from a vibration of anger or fear or anything from the lower octaves, and then blame me later. That would kill me."

She almost slid off the bench when he let her hands go, pulled his forehead away from hers, and dropped his head back with his eyes closed, beginning to hyperventilate. Her blouse and pants were sticking to her in a damp fusion with her skin. She was so turned on, it felt like she was ripening. "You sure?" She'd *never* had to ask a man that in her life.

He nodded with his eyes closed, breathing through his mouth. His voice came out on a gravelly whisper. "You are a child of the sun, as am I," he said, his sentences becoming choppy. "You are a Leo, I am a Leo, which rules the higher self, rules the will sector of the spirit."

She couldn't tell whether he was reminding himself, or trying to impart some deep information to her. But watching him try to talk, make sense, be chivalrous and not touch her, all at the same time was disorienting. His discipline was shredding hers. "That's why we're probably a perfect match."

He shook his head, now gulping air. "That is why you cannot go back and forth. He is a Scorpio, which rules the lower self—desires and lusts. You two will be at odds back and forth until the end of time."

She pressed her hand to her heart, unable to stop looking at him as she spoke. "I know. I'll go home and resolve it, either way. I don't trust him anymore."

"That is not a reason to be with me," he said, bringing his head up slowly to stare at her with solid silver irises rimmed in three layers of gold. "If you choose to be with me, let it be because you trust me. That I am your friend, above all things. That you know I will never hurt you. Understand that my honor for you is worth drawing a blade in battle. *Know* that I would protect your music as much as our children."

Hot silver tears covered his irises but did not fall. A slight hint of fang crested, which almost made her stand as his voice dropped another octave and set off a depth charge within her canal.

"*Detriment* to my *soul,* I am hunted by *you.* My pride is no more. I would share you with him, rather than to not have you at all. Me. A king. Yes. But I am so torn apart at this moment that I am compelled to tell you what I have never told another woman. I would allow him to live, rather than have you ever hate me and shun me. And if he sired with you first, I would protect what grew inside you—because it was half yours! This is why I am afraid to bed you in my own lair tonight. After that, I will be slain, and I am old enough to be aware of that consequence."

He shook his head, stood, and pointed at her. "That is why you must be clear, and there can be no back and forth on this issue. It is not fair to either of us." He pulled his arm away, placed both hands atop his head, and began walking deeper into the massive room.

Somehow she found herself on the floor, not sure if she slid off the bench, or what. Every long stride he took down the side of the pool made her want to get up and follow him. She was sweating silver; it was all over her hands as she tried to pat the puddle of moisture that had formed in the V of her throat. Her face was flushed, mouth dry, body flashing hot and cold as she watched his shoulders knead beneath fabric that should have been gone to show off his fabulous skin.

His thick ropes of dreadlocks swayed down his back like an angry lion's tail, his tight, stone-cut ass tapered into thick, marble-hard legs, and when he turned to hotly walk toward her, she fell back balancing on both hands behind her, eyes half-closed, panting.

"I've never felt like this in my life," she whispered, her gaze purely carnal as it raked its way down his torso and lingered on his groin. She had to remember to look up at his face to finish what she was trying to say, but forgot what that was as he outstretched his hand for her to stand and follow him to bed.

"Nor I, *ever,* in several thousand years."

It was now or never, and she was beyond saying no. But the fact that she was actually going to do this was almost an out-of-body experience. Forgetting that the pool wasn't water, she dipped her hand into it to splash the cool substance on her face. Last-minute clarity had been the objective. Yet it happened so fast, Cain's stooping down and yelling no, but unable to catch her wrist as it came up—the blue energy covered her eyes and forehead.

"What?" she murmured as he got down on his hands and knees, stricken, holding her to him.

"Oh, sweetness, I did not have time to remove the charged energy in this pool. No woman should ever see . . . Please forgive that it was in my home."

He hugged her so tightly as he stroked her hair that she gasped just to breathe; it wasn't passion.

"Cain . . . I don't understand what . . ." Her words slowed down as the image finally settled behind her eyes into her second-sight. Her body froze and trapped a sob that she refused to allow to break free. "He did it to me again . . ." Her head found Cain's shoulder as she absently stroked his long bundle of locks down his back. "This time it's a she-dragon?" Damali laughed, but the sound of it was discordant with the harmonic energies around her.

"And here I was trying to put the Isis in my guilt," she said, her voice becoming quieter and quieter. "Right here I was wrestling that bitch of an emotion to the ground, trying to—"

"Shush," Cain said as her hand balled into a fist at his back. "Let me take this out of your mind," he said, kissing her temple.

She shook her head no as her visions blurred with the hot moisture in her eyes. "No. I need to remember this live and in living color."

"I would not have—"

Her hard kiss crushed away his words, but to her surprise, he yanked out of her hold and held her cheek firmly, now on top of her, looking at her eye to eye.

"Not like this. Hand me the rod. You need the healing balm, not for me to add insult to your injury by fucking you. I will make love to you, but never fuck you. Now hand me the rod."

She could feel her face begin to crumble as his words and wisdom slapped her hard. It was the kindest, noblest thing any man had ever done for her, and she could no more reach for the rod than stop sobbing. She gathered up the front of Cain's robe and buried her face in it, as she felt him grip her with one arm and reach to something just out of his grasp with the other.

His calm, repetitive, shushing sounds made her cry harder as every indignity she'd experienced in dealing with Carlos and all his female side deals and shenanigans suddenly crested over the edge of her heart with bitter tears and wiped out a major portion of her respect for him. She saw it all. Cain had meant him no harm, had tried to take him to court, but, noooo . . . Carlos's pride and his side-dealing ways had him balling some dragon broad in Cain's house to get a passport home. Could he wait for her to break through—no—and why? Because *he didn't give her credit* as a Neteru to be able to quickly figure out a strategy. So doing some broad was an acceptable excuse? Not!

"I am so tired!" she shouted at Cain's chest.

"I know, sweet one. Light of my world, it will pass. Give me the pain. I will hold it."

"No," she finally said, as the fast-moving storm quickly ebbed.

She struggled to sit up and disengage their bodies, which he obliged as he laid the rod over his legs. She wiped her eyes and face and let out a cleansing breath.

"This isn't your mess. I need to go home and clean it up myself. You were right. I needed to be clear and make decisions. Being conflicted is a waste of energy. Clean break." She stood with effort and grabbed her Isis.

Cain gave her a spurious look. "Do not jeopardize your soul by goring him in vengeance, dear one."

"You keep the healing rod. I'll keep the blade when I have the conversation. If I lose my temper during the conversation—"

Cain stood so quickly that he stopped her words midsentence. His kiss crushed away her argument as his hand gently removed the Isis from her and it clattered to the floor beside them.

"Not like this," he murmured into her mouth. "Not ever like that." His tongue dueled with hers as his hands splayed instant heat against her Sankofa. "Let me take the pain."

"You can have it all . . ."

Her body hit silk sheets, blanketed by his radiant warmth. Sound fused with sensation as each fiber in the threads produced delirium-level pleasure. Lightning arced between each crystal pyramid on the four golden posts of the bed, and formed a central, blue-white globe of energy that rained down a sheet of erotic tempest that encased them. Her fingers tangled in his locks while her legs became a vise around his waist. The burn from his kiss became one with the throbbing tattoo on his chest, seizing her heart into pleasure arrhythmia as he moved against her, kissing her deeply.

The vibrations emanating from him, the perfect-pitch tonal vibrations of the bed, and everything around him, turned her gasp into a near shriek. Intoxicating scents released from the flowers and ferns, sending music into the depths of her soul with his low groans. Urgency combined with gentleness began to strip away her clothes as she arched to his touch, each caress falling upon her skin like liquid fire.

"Become my wife," he whispered, his voice ragged with desire.

She could barely breathe, let alone answer as she forced herself to open her eyes and stare into his silver-gold gaze. Her hand trembled as it cupped his cheek and touched a jaw packed with what felt like pure steel. Before she could answer, his fangs crested and he knocked her head back so hard that she literally saw stars.

Hot, steaming, desire-filled breath covered her throat where Carlos had once marked her, and her hands gripped a pair of foreign shoulders, urging the bite.

"You must answer me," Cain said, his voice faltering with need. "I cannot deliver a divorce bite to a councilman's wife without it." He licked the overly sensitive pulse point and kissed each now-visible puncture wound before poising his fangs a quarter inch wider than Carlos's at her jugular.

A divorce bite? Sudden clarity sliced at her mind. Wait . . . that wasn't from the realms of Light. Her body tensed. Cain drew away just enough to look at her and then took her mouth so hard that his fangs nearly split her lip.

"I'll replace it with pure silver and gold," he murmured harshly against her forehead, and then nuzzled her throat until she writhed under him. "Devastation . . . God as my witness, you'll never have to go home to him again!"

"Uhmmm . . ."

Lyrics filled her head, her spirit, and her very soul as a mind-altering orgasm shattered her with his kiss.

"Oh, God, I don't know—a divorce is—"

"Permanent. I don't want an affair! I want your all." Cain's tense whisper contracted her womb, spilling her wet readiness as her body flamed to another climax.

Jesus help her, she couldn't speak. The man was working on her in stereophonic sound waves of pleasure, driving ecstasy insanity to a level that made her weep. "But permanent is—"

"You are a queen . . ." he murmured into her mouth, and then swallowed her gasp. "I am a king. We both deserve the best—each other."

His kisses became more aggressive as her body began to yield again under his hold. Golden sweat dripped from his forehead to her breasts as his mouth found the V in her throat and his palms slid beneath her shoulder blades with a scorching caress.

"Damali, I can feel something just beneath the surface of your wondrous skin," he breathed out, his expression awed. "Please, do not deny me, lover; I must have your permission—you know this," he whispered, pressing hard, hot kisses to her shoulder as she arched and tried to think at the same time. "There must be complete acceptance of all that I am to you. Your body and mouth have already said yes . . . your mind is already near vapor . . . let me take you to the V-point and show you the cosmos as you have *never* dreamed of witnessing it. My angel of redemption, *just say yes* in your spirit," he moaned, now stuttering the request as he nuzzled her throat.

Cain's hands went at her skull. "Mind lock . . . while we are so close to the edge. You know how that will shatter us. Oh, Damali, what claim does that betrayer have to your soul?" Cain's words had become a frantic plea broken by a pleasure gasp. "Give me your trinity, baby. Let me take it." His head was thrown back, eyes shut tightly, the pulse in his jugular a magnet for a sudden strike.

She couldn't help herself, the bite was reflex, carnal instinct that released his voice in a thousand splinters of pure white light that bounced off the lair walls and refracted in a blinding essence behind her lids. Her black box collapsed in on itself. Only a small line of silver arc blocked him from Carlos's domain in her mind. The rumble of frustration that thundered up from Cain's groan almost melted it away.

Instantly nude, their sweat stained the sheets silver and gold, his throbbing length poised for entry just as his incisors lowered in wait for the plunge. Her head was spinning and pleasure had created a near blackout as he slid against her wet slit with hot friction, but didn't penetrate her. She could feel her spirit giving way as her hands slid up his massive back, setting off a low, aching resonance within them.

A loud gong rang out and jerked their attention toward the entrance. The unmistakable sound of both feathered and leather flight made them both sit up quickly, as Cain materialized his sword in his hand and growled.

"What is it?" Damali said, unknown terror making her heart pound. In a snap, she was clothed and the Isis was in her grasp. It was impossible to catch her breath.

"Human barrier breach!"

CHAPTER ELEVEN

The entire team watched in horror from the other side of the thick, unbreakable glass as the men who had questioned the Guardians relentlessly turned Marlene into a lab rat. On one side of the glass in a stainless-steel observation room, the team was tethered to chairs and taunted by a voice over the ceiling speaker. On the other side of the glass, Marlene struggled against restraints, but had a bit in her mouth and her hands covered in iron boxes to prevent a psychic discharge.

When the scientists had done that, the team looked at each other, a strange calm befalling them. If they knew how to neuter Marlene's powers, then these boys had obviously been investigating the paranormal, in depth, for quite some time. This was not simply Homeland Security run amuck. It was something just as bad, if not worse.

"Still don't wanna talk? Still don't know how they go through the gates?"

"We don't know what you're talking about!" Shabazz shouted. "You motherfuckers hurt her, and it's all over!"

"Well, until someone knows anything useful, we'll have to try to see if we can break the code using the one with the most psychic ability, and then work our way backward. Reverse engineering," the disembodied voice said from the lab. He lowered his surgical face mask and pressed several buttons on a control board that the Guardians couldn't fully see.

A team of white coats hovered near Marlene, watching her vital signs, computer readouts, and managing equipment that not even J.L. had ever encountered.

Marlene's strapped-down body began moving into the black mouth of a large tube that resembled CAT scan equipment. The gaping dome flickered with an eerie bluish electrical current that finally made her disappear.

"Marlene!" Shabazz's wrists bled with deep gashes from constant struggle against the restraints. Then suddenly he became still, popped the nylon, flipped a chair, broke it in one kick to create a weapon, and was summarily shot in the chest with a tranquilizer dart from across the room.

Mike was up in seconds. Pure fury and brute strength popped nylon, creating another raging bull that went down hard—but only after two darts struck his chest and thigh.

Yonnie lifted his head from Tara's throat as she slowly sat up. "Carlos is outside, and I ain't never heard an SOS like this from him."

Within seconds, both vampires had dressed and cleared Gabrielle's barriers to meet Carlos on the front steps.

"What's up, man?"

"You gotta get Gabby to work up a divination," Carlos said, his voice laced with panic. "Damali is gone. I had to regen. Couldn't get to you earlier to even send a signal. Phones are tapped; didn't wanna risk calling Gabby that way. I came as soon as I could. The team's house has been ransacked. There's a tear in a new realm we just saw—"

"We don't need Gabby for that shit, brother. Me and you can go down there and handle that shit. We'll take out—"

"They have *perpetual daylight* over there, man." Carlos began to pace. "Two suns, twenty-four/seven."

"Oh, shit, man . . . You start the big one, or what?" Now Yonnie had begun to pace. "I ain't no punk or nothin', but if you're talking warrior angels, man, I don't know."

"Naw, man. That's not where they're from."

Carlos and Yonnie stared at each other for a moment as Tara drew near to Yonnie and protectively held him.

"The only reason I'm here and asking you to get anywhere near this situation is 'cause we family," Carlos said. "I ain't trying to get you and Tara directly involved or possibly smoked, but could use a master's sensory lock to work with mine, if that's possible. I'm getting conflicting sensory data. Like, I just felt a serious panic surge on the team. I know they're in a human lockup somewhere, but that's the crazy thing. I know they ain't dead, but it's like they're in some kinda black box. I just came back from somewhere that none of our people had gotten sucked into, but now I'm feeling both Damali and another female team member over there."

"Man," Yonnie said, rubbing his chin as Tara melted closer against him for support. "If it's a divine realm with perpetual light, me and my lady can't—"

"I know, I know," Carlos said, beginning to pace again, "but that's why we need to talk to Gabby. I didn't just bust into her joint and ask her directly, because I didn't know what kinda clientele she was servicing tonight, and I ain't got time for a side battle over dumb shit. This ain't Heaven, and it ain't Hell. So I'm figuring maybe she can whip out her crystal ball and do an oracle-type thing."

Yonnie nodded. "Yeah, man, c'mon in. We family. Stay strong," he added, pounding Carlos's fist.

It took everything in Damali to keep up with Cain. Her density differential and the stress of what had just gone down was seriously slowing her up. Cain got to the ravine first, blade drawn, and backed up several hissing predators from the sky. She went to cover the ones with white feathered wings that were on the ground, body-shielding a wounded human beneath them.

"She breached our realm; we did not drag her through the barrier!" two aerial attackers said. "The human encroached. That gives us eminent domain over the carcass."

"Be gone!" Cain thundered, the gleam of his sword pushing them back.

Damali's attention ping-ponged between the half-human's hovering and diving with massive, black bat wings, and the ones on the ground covering a cowering woman. She'd seen a lot of weird combinations, but when things from the Dark Realms transformed, it was an all-body shape-shift, not this half-human, half-whatever type of creature.

Black arcs met blue arcs as the entities on the ground fended off a kinetic body snatch with deflective rays. She watched the muscle in Cain's jaw jump, his silver-gold eyes narrow, then suddenly a loud battle cry erupted from within him as he leapt, holding his blade with both hands, making a blue-white arc exit from the tip of it that blew one entity back to slam against the mountain wall, and then took off two heads with one swing.

"Do not test me!" he shouted, hitting the side of the ravine with one foot and pushing off of it to go airborne again.

Damali looked at her Isis, and kept a battle stance to protect the human she couldn't see. But, *dayum,* her Isis didn't work *like that.*

Two smoldering heads dropped at her feet and rolled around in a screaming, slow smoking circle, eyes still seeing, blinking, tongues moving. She could barely take her gaze off of the wailing heads. Even the death process was so eerily different here. And just as soon as the battle had begun, it ended. A long echoing wail followed the leathery retreat with a promise for vengeance ringing through the bright, three-moon night.

The seraphim-faced entities by her feet wept as they gently eased back and removed their wings to reveal the injured human they'd valiantly protected. A charred, smoking figure of a woman shuddered as third-degree burns covered her body. Her eyes were sealed shut as though her skin had melted and fused every feature on her face together from the heat. Her skeletal, raw hands trembled in agony as bloody hunks of flesh just hung like cooked meat from her bones and her hair had fallen away in red-ember, glowing cinders. But with her mouth sealed in raw, bubbling burns, she could only whimper and mumble as her heels dug into the rocky ground in writhing pain.

"Oh, dear God," Damali said, dropping to her knees. "The Caduceus rod—Cain, bring it to me, we're both Neterus, we can do this! Hurry, before she dies."

It materialized in his hand. "Open up her throat at the trachea. She cannot breathe, Damali. She will suffocate before we can heal her."

Damali gripped her Isis blade and rested the tip against the unrecognizable woman's throat, and then her blade fell away. Damali's rippling scream made Cain work with his hands, and he slit the woman's throat to open a hole and blew air into it, and then repeatedly pressed down on the woman's chest keeping a steady, life-sustaining rhythm.

"Do it now," he said between pants. "Hold the rod to her heart chakra. Join me." He glanced at Damali, growing impatient. "Neteru, on your mark! Begin—"

"That's my mother-seer," she whispered.

Cain glanced down, nodded to the seraphim hybrids. "Balm this Neteru while I work. She's going into shock. Guard her third eye."

"Doctor, this one has been gone for ten minutes. This is the longest we've been able to sustain the disappearance without the body bouncing back into the lab as ash. I think we should try to reverse polarity now, before we lose it entirely."

The lead scientist looked at the others in the room. "Do it."

Cain could feel his body heating, lifting, something strange and artificial pulling at his limbs, raising the rope of locks from his back as his hands grabbed the dying woman's shoulders. At one moment he was making his breaths one with hers, offering her his life force as a bridge, like his heartbeat, joining his energy with the healing power within the rod, using the conductive energy of the sacred metals, and then the next thing he knew, he was with the victim's smoldering body on a cold floor in a white and metal room with bright lights.

Masked men surrounded him, a projectile came his way, and he deflected it with a snarl and stood.

"Keep recording!" the lead scientist shouted. "One actually came through with the body and was feeding from its throat!"

"Contain it!" another voice said, making Cain spin and turn in a confused pivot.

One of the men in white slammed a panel. Cain stared down as the floor quickly separated, putting a ring around him and the injured woman, as well as the men now holding Old World crossbows made of gleaming steel. Holy water instantly flooded into the small gulley that had opened in a circle around him on the strange floor. Within the bizarre concoction he also smelled pungent garlic and wolfsbane as a steel net dropped from the ceiling with bags of the demon-barrier substances laced through it.

"Are you humans mad?" Cain swept up the injured woman and glanced at the stricken faces around the room that he vaguely remembered. "The mother-seer is dying!" He almost wept at their stupidity. Her fragile body was convulsing and her flesh was coming off in his hands.

Suddenly he realized that there were two sets of humans. This was not a cohesive group of Damali's team. Blood was in the air with her team's signature in it. Cain hesitated, not sure, his blade leveled as it materialized in his grip. They had not performed the experiment to go in search of a missing Damali.

Something stuck him in the leg, the back, the chest, his neck. Tiny bee stings from high-powered implements. His vision blurred, he could sense a vampire . . . two . . . just beyond the walls but held back by sacred objects. Bright, artificial light, and somehow he was on his knees. Men were still stinging him with the poison darts, saying to put the big bastard down hard, but not to kill him . . . who did they speak of that was a threat? Him. Absolute chaos reigned. Men in white coats screamed about another one. . . . Another what?

He could sense silver, a Neteru brother. All faces were blurry, just a tattoo let him know one of his own had entered the battle. He would not drop his blade. He would not leave the dying human female as he fell to all fours. She was his beloved's mother-seer. His words were slurring in his mouth and in his head. The carnivores in white would not befoul the mother-seer's body. He struggled to brace himself over her. He would use this last breath to pass the message telepathically. "Take the team to safety, my brother! Do not let the mother-seer die."

Two deft whirs collected the team that had been trapped behind the glass wall, the steel room around them was like a bank vault and so was the lab. Against every instinct within him, Carlos pulled Cain into the void with the others, as well as Marlene's lifeless body.

Arizona was the first thought that came to his mind, a place far enough away to make the feds have to scuffle to find them fast, but close enough for his energy to hold. He knew the terrain; it was hallowed ground. But Yonnie and Tara could cross it. If Cain was on the wrong side—his ass would fry. They had a serious core of shaman friends in the Navajo Nation, all financial bickering about the old compound, regardless. It was about quick decisions with no margin for bullshit or errors.

The landing was hard and sloppy with so much dead weight, but Yonnie and Tara couldn't help him while inside the military containment center that had been made white-hot for vamps.

"Put a stake in his chest now, while he's down," Yonnie said, looking at Carlos and then down at Cain. "Motherfucker gotta be Level Seven, sucking her guts out through a hole in her throat after torching her. Fucking flesh-eatin' bastard!" Yonnie spit.

Rider nodded, going to get a thick tree branch as Tara disintegrated everyone's nylon handcuffs and Jose snapped a low-hanging tree limb.

"We've got two big men down," Berkfield said, glancing at Shabazz's and Big Mike's limp bodies. "Tara, baby, you vamps got any way to pull the tranquilizer out without a nick, while I see what I can do for Mar? Might need 'em if those boys don't hurry up with a stake," he added, glancing over toward Cain.

"No," Tara murmured, kneeling beside Marlene. She stared at Marlene with pity glittering in her red-glowing eyes while Marlene's chest heaved and shuddered, struggling for air. "There's only one way I can extract the tranquilizer." Tara's sorrowful gaze held Berkfield's. "It will leave both men permanently damaged." She returned her attention to Marlene and gently touched the side of her throat, feeling a weak pulse. "Before her life essence goes, however, I may be able to give her life . . . but it will not be what any of you had intended."

Marj immediately dropped beside Tara on her hands and knees. "Oh, Jesus," she whispered, tears streaming down her face and causing Tara to wince and stand. "Richard, she's almost not breathing, almost doesn't have a pulse. She's so badly burned." Her gaze went to Carlos. "Don't let them turn her! Can't you heal her?"

Younger Guardians looked away. Inez's sob broke through the night and roused Big Mike to a drowsy rollover.

"Don't wake Shabazz up, yet," Rider said quietly, standing over Cain with a stake gripped between both hands. He looked at Jose. "This one and Mar. Together. She's nearly dead, already. He bit her. It's the only way."

Rider raised his stake high above his head, coordinating his timing with Jose's. Bobby wiped at his face and turned as Dan stalked away with Yonnie to avoid watching. Krissy's head went to J.L.'s chest. Juanita drew Marjorie away from the pending gore and held her. Inez dropped to her knees and hid her face in the crook of Big Mike's neck. Tara turned her back and set her sight on the moon and then shut her eyes.

Carlos nodded and found the distant tree line.

Dark entities blackened the sky. Seraphim tried to rally around her, but were outnumbered and had to pull back. A golden rod and her Isis blade stabbed and cut at slashing tails and wretched claws. She was female. She was flesh. She was meat. She knew the imperative encoded in demon DNA, Carlos had also taught her that—fuck it, feed from it, kill it. Not today!

The golden staff became a goring rod, spilling hybrid demon guts and blood as it plunged in and out and left entrails; her Isis a master decapitator, blazing, singing, filling the air with thuds of demon death. Her golden stick doubled as a nemesis blocker, wielded with everything Marlene and Shabazz had taught. Deft Capoeira ducks, fluid Aikido leverage pivots off winged bodies, the ground, the ravine wall, energy and adrenaline shooting through her system as a flip dodge, land hard, get up quick, keep moving, side to side, rock hop, crack skulls, take heads without names. "Back off!"

Energy waning, but just get to a light band, snap off the energy, add it to her own, then . . . free-falling?

She was moving so fast that air left her lungs. Impressions, her name being called within a nearly dead mind. "Marlene!"

Still fighting. Navajo shaman chants running through the ground into the soles of her feet through her sandals. She could smell vamps surrounding her. Her ears ringing with Marlene's mental wails of agony. Spinning on many bodies everywhere. Back 'em off. Oh my God, they'd killed her mother-seer! *They'd all die for that.* Mar, Cain were down, "Back the fuck up!" Blade raised, Isis ready to take another head—no problem. Mike was down, body count. Shabazz was down, oh, she would kill these beasts!

Clarity.

"Stand down," she yelled, knocking Rider out of the way. "He's clean!" Her attention pivoted. "Jose, are you crazy? Put that weapon down!"

"He bit her, D!" Carlos shouted, grabbing her by the arm and receiving a hard elbow to his ribs that backed him up.

"No, I was there on the other side with him! He performed a tracheotomy to keep her breathing when something pulled her through the rip. He wouldn't leave her body, she'd come through the veil already burned." Damali dropped her sword, not sure which injured family member to run toward first. "What happened? Get him roused, wake him up, he—"

"Your mother-seer is over there fucking dying, Damali!" Carlos shouted, pointing toward Marlene. "You got that? And you're worried about—"

"Shut up, Carlos! Wake him up! He's the superior healer. We've got three Neterus. Three serious seers. I have *the Ancient Caduceus*—do you even *know* what that is?" She shoved the healing staff forward and when Carlos didn't respond, yanked it back and went to Marlene. "No? Then stop jacking with my order and wake Cain up!"

"Her pulse is so weak, dear one . . . I don't know if even I . . ."

"Try. For me," Damali said, brushing Cain's disheveled locks away from his brow as they knelt beside Marlene with the team looking down at them.

Yonnie paced back and forth behind the ring of Guardians as Carlos paced inside the circle. Tara rubbed Rider's back as the older Guardian silently wept just staring down at Marlene and Shabazz.

"It wasn't your fault," Tara whispered gently. "You didn't know. Had to do what you had to do."

Rider nodded and swallowed hard. "Two more seconds, that's all it would have taken."

Jose was so distraught that he'd sought refuge against a tree, refusing to allow Juanita to come near him. Shabazz was on his hands and knees, his palm trembling over Marlene's forehead, unable to touch her, unable to draw away from her, huge tears dropping to the ground as he sucked in and released quaking breaths. The rest of the team formed human standing stones of numb anguish, not a dry eye in their midst.

"I will need the third Neteru's assistance," Cain said, still seeming a bit disoriented as he gazed into Damali's eyes and cupped her cheek. "This is not a demon attack that has damaged her. This is a purely physical injury, a mortal one, from the earth plane." He sighed hard. "Reversing black magic is one thing, intervening in an appointed hour of mortal death is another."

"It's not her time, though," Damali said, new tears brimming in her eyes. "It can't be."

"The poison from their darts is in my system, that with the density of this plane . . . we must make the circle of completion around your mother-seer's energies. I do not know if it will work, my love, but I will attempt anything for you, or die trying."

"Oh, shit . . ." Yonnie whispered through his teeth, rubbing his palms down his cheeks.

"I don't care what the fuck else is going on," Shabazz said, not even looking up from Marlene's disfigured face. "Suck it up, Rivera. Make the ring, and let that brother work. She's suffering, and I can't draw enough of the pain away from her to make a difference." His hands went to her temple, and then the shuddering flap of skin at her throat that wheezed in blood-wet exhales and slow inhales, but didn't touch her. "Oh, Heavenly Father, please . . ."

Yonnie and Tara hissed and turned, then bulked as a black jaguar took to a limb above Marlene, roared, but dropped to the ground and instantly transformed. The moment they saw Kamal, they normalized.

Kamal's entire body trembled as he walked a hot path back and forth behind Shabazz, unable to keep his eyes on Marlene. "Whatever I can do. If you need another seer, mon, I will go blind for her. Just tell me."

Berkfield dropped beside Shabazz, shrugging out of Marjorie's protective hold. "Man, for the love of God, let me help you. Me and you, together, with Kamal, bring the burns to us while the Neterus go in. Maybe Kamal's help can block it?"

Carlos was instantly down on his knees by Cain's side. No matter what he'd seen, no matter what was going on, the priority was to staunch the pain, make Marlene breathe, and try to keep her heart beating before hysterical Guardians went in with good intentions and killed themselves from pain-shock.

"Tell me what I've gotta do, man," Carlos said, focusing on Cain's eyes and blocking out the look of affection Damali had offered his competitor. It was beyond all that, with Marlene's life in the balance.

"Grab Damali's hand with mine," Cain ordered. His tone was that of a senior surgeon as he motioned for the correct physical, kneeling alignment. "The female Neteru at her head, each male Neteru at her side to form a pyramid—us as the platform at her heart level just beneath her lungs, and Damali siphoning life force up through the most damaged organs through her crown chakra."

Cain waited as the other Guardians quickly moved out of the way and Carlos and Damali took their positions. "The staff," he said to Damali. "Female energy, therefore, you hold it, our hands over yours. Place it on her heart chakra. Visualize the kundalini serpents coming to life. One ascending into the Fohat macrocosmic field, pure white Light, the other descending into her energy field bringing the Light from the upper realms into her being."

Cain glanced up at Carlos. "Mind lock with me, brother. See only the green bands of Light. The harmonic frequencies of healing tones. Let it radiate out of your third eye, engulf your hands, and send the gentle pulse into the conduit, the rod. Do it easy, with skill. This woman is severely injured and what we do must be delicate. Then, we wait."

Carlos nodded. Damali positioned the staff over the center of Marlene's now-quiet chest, noticing that it no longer struggled as hard as it initially did to take in or release air. Damali's grip was slicked by nervous sweat. Her mind screamed a prayer, held Marlene's mind in constant monitor, begging her not to let go or flow into the Light.

Carlos closed his eyes. Searing silver strength held his mind. His initial impulse was to fight it and pull away, but he surrendered to the invasive sensation, and tried to find the green harmonic Cain mentioned. But this was his first time ever attempting such an advanced Neteru procedure. His focus repeatedly fractured as everything that had recently happened in the frontal consciousness of Cain's mind ripped into his.

"Focus," Cain ordered through his teeth, grappling with Carlos's untrained entry. "What you are witnessing with me and Damali is of little consequence. Go deep. One mind. One path. Healing."

Total frustration made Cain open his eyes, which made the two junior Neterus stare at him. He looked at Damali. "Show him how to do it," Cain muttered, thoroughly disgusted. "If he cannot use sight, then tune his ear to the harmonic so he can do what must be done!"

Damali grasped Carlos's hands tighter as Marlene's chest went still. "Listen to me. Look into my eyes. Hear the sound in my head and follow that until the color takes over your mind. We're losing her."

Cain nodded and closed his eyes again. Damali settled down. Carlos closed his eyes but was anything but settled. In fact, so much was riding on his shoulders at this point that he wanted to stand and bolt. Not only was he shown to be the weaker Neteru in front of the entire team, his boyz—but also his woman, *in front of her near lover*, with her mother-seer's life hanging in the balance . . . and if Marlene died, it would be his fault. No one on the team would ever forgive him; just like he would never forgive himself.

The strength, this time, is in the surrender, a quiet female voice said within Carlos's mind. Oddly, it wasn't Damali's voice. He'd lost the quiet connection to her, which made him panic further. *Being the better man, sometimes, means pushing beyond one's own pain in quiet surrender. You will win if you lose. You will never win if you do not learn when to retreat.*

Zehiradangra's voice was so gentle and soothing within his mind that it made his shoulders relax. His breathing deepened as she hummed the right pitch within a sound chord that he could mentally follow and he slowly saw her jewel-green eyes filled with empathy. He watched them glow with compassion and caring and friendship until the whole of Cain's silver burning mind was threaded with the deep, resonant hue. He could feel layers of Damali's harmony wind into the mind-melody and run through his body, making him shudder, then burn his hands hot, make his clothes stick to his skin, building like slow pressure inside his chest, filling his arms with a throbbing, dull ache that demanded release through his palms.

It hurt so bad, but hurt so good, as the she-dragon's voice coaxed him each time the fleeting sensation of energy expulsion slipped back up his arms, unable to connect with the steady stream of heat pouring out of Cain and Damali's hands. His arms felt like the skin on them was splitting and opening. Zehiradangra's voice shushed him to be still, to channel it through his palms and to not let it splatter to evaporate into wasted energy within the atmosphere around him.

He was about to give up when he felt her tongue lick down his shoulder, glide over his elbow, and caress each digit on his tightly clenched fist.

Right there, she whispered, *just like it's your lover. Be one with the energy, and let it flow into the staff.*

"I don't know how," Carlos whispered out loud, feeling Cain's massive fist tighten hard enough to crush the bones in his hand. Damali's pulse beneath his palm was a distraction and his arm was now almost so laden with energy that it felt nearly impossible to keep it extended.

"Strike him," Cain murmured. "He is not that evolved."

Before Carlos could drop his arm from fatigue or process Cain's command, a blinding dragon strike scored his jugular and released the pent-up energy in waves of color throughout his system in hard, pulsing jags. His eyelids fluttered, bright flashes in every hue singed his senses. He couldn't breathe. His hand was on fire. His arm shook as the muscles within it contracted and released in spasmodic jerks. Cain pulled the brunt of the unharnessed ejection and fused it with a gold-green spiked jolt; Damali received and mellowed it, then sent it into the staff in a smooth, steady stream.

Unable to move, Carlos could mentally see the staff light up, glow golden, then become deep crimson, and then finally go burning white. The serpents opened their mouths and screamed, quickly slithering in opposite directions, leaping off the staff and catching energy rays in their mouths with their fangs to pull it down with them, connecting it as one unbroken thread of shimmer, as they instantly reunited with the searing rod. Green flames tore down the staff in a dizzying spiral and slammed into Marlene's chest. Her body arched, her throat wound sealed, her lips tore apart as a shriek pushed its way between them.

"Drop the Caduceus!" Cain shouted. "Link hands. Lower the pyramid!"

The threesome worked on reflex motor skills, quickly clasping hands, creating a wide, green-glowing pyramid between their bodies that hung midair like a translucent shield above Marlene. They lowered it with Cain's guidance to slowly sweep over the surface of Marlene's prone body from head to toe. Once the energy stopped sputtering, Cain slowly released their hands and sat back on his haunches, winded. Damali fell back on the ground with her legs sprawled, breathing hard and staring at Marlene.

Carlos fell forward on his hands and knees, panting and watching Marlene's skin begin to knit and her nose rise out of the twisted flesh of her face. Soon her eyes separated from the morass of melted, scarred skin. Her lashes reappeared, but were pure white. Then her eyebrows surfaced slowly, one hair at a time—snow white. Her charred skin slowly returned to its ebony beauty . . . but her face was so old, so wrinkled, like that of a crone. Carlos looked away.

Cain moved forward and spread his hands over Marlene's face and slowly pulled them away as her eyes opened . . . then he closed his when her irises were pure white.

"Damali," Cain whispered. "She's blind. Go into her mind." Cain wiped the sweat from his brow and whispered into Marlene's ear, but she didn't respond. "She's deaf." He stood and paced back and forth and then dropped down again beside her, watching Damali slowly move to Marlene and extend a trembling hand above her third eye.

"We must know whether or not she is brain dead. I am so sorry, dear one."

Damali closed her eyes, and placed her wet cheek on Marlene's forehead. Shuddering breaths repressed a sob as she stroked Marlene's hair.

"I love you so much, Marlene, come back whole."

A sob tore through Shabazz and put him on his feet. He walked away, deep into the brush. No Guardian followed him. Kamal put his fist to his forehead and walked away in the opposite direction with his eyes closed.

Damali continued to stroke Marlene's now all-white hair, and whispered gently. "Mom, don't die."

I have done all I have to do, you know all you need to know from me, Marlene replied in a serene voice from her mind. *I won't be alone. Christine is with me.*

"Don't you leave me, Marlene!" Damali shrieked, clasping Marlene to her breasts.

You will not be alone, child. It is time.

Bitter sobs wracked Damali as Marlene's voice became weaker and began floating. She hugged Marlene up from the ground and began rocking with her mother-seer's body in her arms. "You have to be here for my babies! You have to be here when I act crazy! You have to be here—because I cannot breathe on this planet without you . . . Marlene!" Damali's voice dissolved into hiccupping, shrill bleats.

"Let her go, D," Rider said quietly. "Baby, she's gone."

"Give me the Caduceus!" Damali shouted, glaring at Cain as he stood and slowly shook his head.

Carlos stood and stared off into the distance, eyes glistening.

Damali closed her eyes and materialized the rod in her grip when no one would hand it to her. "Now you listen to me, Marlene Stone," she said between her teeth. "I refuse to let you go because foolish men tampered with the fabric of the universe!"

She rammed the staff into the dirt, making the ground beneath Marlene's body begin to glow gold as she gently laid her down. "I call nature energy!" Damali shouted and stood, opening her arms to the dark heavens. "I call all the elements of the universe, female power to give life! Through me, I call Isis, herself! Aset, every Neteru on the Council of Queens. Eve—you owe me! Your son is beyond the barrier! I delivered your message, now hear mine! My mother-seer is my sanity! Do *not* let her die!"

Damali snatched the rose quartz crystal from her pants pocket and held it up in her fist. "Love, all the way from the original temple of Hathor, from the pavilion of Trajan in Egypt, I love her with all my heart and soul!"

Strong winds gathered. Lightning touched off dancing energy in the sky. Trees shuddered. Green grass grew around Marlene's body where it was once parched and dry. Rain fell like tears. A stunned team looked on in awed silence.

"I am woman, thus water, and water is the *essence* of life. My tears are the rain which replenishes the barren earth. I am fire—love, profound passion, the spark of conception—which gives inanimate cells motion. I am the air, which fills lungs. I am the earth, form and substance, nourishment and healing. I am pure *faith*, for I own the heart and soul of a woman. I am hope . . . because of my faith and my love. A trinity resides in my soul. My female symbol is the circle of unity. My spirit is unbroken, like the infinite circle. She will not die. Not on my watch!"

Silver tears streamed down Damali's cheeks and she stood legs wide, head back, eyes closed, arms open, begging Heaven in her mind.

Slowly, the wrinkles in Marlene's face began to recede. Her dead, white irises became warm, and living, and brown. Her hair began to grow out dark ebony from the roots as the white, dead locks became brittle and fell away. A shudder, then a cough. Damali was on her knees in seconds before Shabazz could ever reach his fallen woman. Marlene was in her arms gasping. Kamal hung back weeping. Shabazz was sobbing so hard that Big Mike had to come get him. Yonnie had silent tears running down his strained face. Younger Guardians slowly came near, too mesmerized to emote. Carlos stared down at Damali and Marlene in awe. Cain stooped and gently touched Marlene's warm, healed hand and drew his fingers back in utter amazement.

Cain finally stood and raked his hair and paced away from Carlos's side. "She is a true queen. A goddess . . . if not an angel."

Damali continued to hold Marlene as though she were a long-lost doll that had just been found. She refused to even move aside for Shabazz. She simply kept petting Marlene's hair, her face, and then would crush Marlene to her breast again. She didn't care what any of them were talking about as she and Marlene sat on the sofa, the whole team huddled into the small confines of Jose's grandfather's house.

But when Kamal came to the door, all peace in the house was shattered. Shabazz drew Sleeping Beauty with such swiftness that no one could even speak.

"Be clear!" Shabazz shouted. "While she's in the flesh, Marlene is my wife!" He cocked the gun to the side, dead aim at Kamal's forehead. "Astrally, or any other kinda way you step across the divide, you die.

Fuck a shape-shift and hand-to-hand, I'll blow your brains out. As long
as she's living with me, she made a personal *choice*! This is the last time,
I'm telling you!"

"She saved my life," Kamal snarled. "Back in Bahia, years ago, mon.
She and I were meant to be—this makes three times she almost died on
your watch!" Kamal's voice broke as tears streamed down his face. "I had
a mortal were-jag bite, and she didn't let me die. I let her leave me," he
said, slapping his chest, "to save her pain, and now this?"

"I don't give a damn!" Shabazz hollered, his finger slowly depressing
the trigger. "You're a dead man walking!"

"Don't," Damali whispered. "You kill him, 'Bazz, and your soul is lost
to this team."

"Your Neteru is correct," Cain said slowly. "I killed my brother with
the same rage, and was lost. What purpose does it serve to bring back the
love of your soul, to only be separated by the chasm of Hell? You have
won. She made a choice to be with you until her end of earth time. Let
that be enough."

Marlene stirred and sat forward slowly with Damali's help.
"Shabazz . . . don't become lost to me," she whispered. "I love you."
She glanced at Kamal. "I love you, too, but it's time to say good-bye . . .
permanently."

Kamal closed his gleaming were-jaguar eyes, unconcerned about
Shabazz's gun. He allowed his shoulders to drop and the battle bulk to
fade to normalcy. His upper and lower canines retracted as he held up his
hand. "I will always love you, Marlene," he whispered. "You will always
be my angel of mercy . . . and more importantly, always my friend. I'll
see you on the other side, when we die, and when none of this matters."

Shabazz pulled back his weapon and lowered it as Kamal turned and
loped away. "Not even in Heaven, motherfucker," Shabazz muttered and
then slammed the front door. Tears still glistened in his eyes as he
glanced around the team, looked at Marlene, and then sought the solitude of the kitchen to collect himself.

Carlos rubbed his palms down his face, gripped by the scene of two
men who had been competing for a woman's love for decades. He
glanced at Big Mike, who simply nodded and calmly walked through the
house to go to Shabazz's side for support. What the fuck was happening
to his world . . . to the team?

Damali gathered Marlene into her arms again and kissed the crown of her head, searching the faces around her for answers that weren't there.

"Since this was a hit attempt by the feds, unfriendly ones—and obviously not the guys that sent us on the mission before, and they're onto us," Dan said, his tone reverent. "We're gonna have to move underground, from now on. I put stash, IDs, weapons, all over, like Carlos had showed me. Did that after we knew who abducted Berkfield, the first time out. We've got unmarked accounts; I separated some of what we had. Swiss banks and whatnot," he said, glancing at Carlos for approval.

"Good looking out, young buck," Carlos said, nodding and glancing at Yonnie. "Never completely trust the authorities. They've got agendas, and the last one almost killed Mar."

"Sho' you right," Shabazz said, coming back into the living room from the kitchen, Big Mike bringing up the rear. Shabazz gazed down at Marlene. It was obvious how badly he wanted to hold her by the way he kept his arms wrapped around himself. But something within him seemed to know that Damali wasn't ready to release her to anyone else yet.

"We've gotta get out of the country," Berkfield said quickly, his gaze roving the room. "If they're feds, or CIA boys."

"The only place we know of that's outside the country is Bahia," J.L. said, pacing. "Regardless, that compound—"

"No!" Shabazz said. "That's out."

"Man, we can run, but we can't hide. If it's some kinda black ops groove, they have tentacles in every country. So, it's about motion, constant," Big Mike said, his voice an angry whisper. "Bahia is out, though, for obvious reasons."

"Me and J.L. can find safe harbors, wireless Internet connections, keep the signals going, encrypt them enough to make it a bitch to break, and by the time they do, we're at the next location," Krissy said, her red, tear-puffed eyes going around the room.

"Then maybe the other Guardian teams around the world will be at the ready for backup," Carlos muttered. "Any place, any time."

"Me and Tara got your backs, too. Can cast illusion, get Gabby on the crystal ball to divine before they come at you, do money transfers, IDs, shit like that to keep 'em blind topside once Krissy and J.L. find out where your next move is gonna be," Yonnie offered, staring at Carlos.

"I'll work with J.L. and Dan," Jose said. "We've gotta now figure out some mobile early warning systems that include human predators." He sighed and let his breath out hard. "I'm not sure how to do that, though, and stay to the mission of keeping everybody in the Light, since we ain't never dropped a human body, but might have to, if they're coming for us."

"Then we'd better find a way to have a private conversation with our clerical crew, 'cause all I know is, dropping a human body isn't as easy as it sounds, Jose," Berkfield warned, gaining nods of agreement from Rider and Big Mike, as well as Shabazz. "Trust me, junior, you don't want any man's blood on your hands."

Cain pushed away from the wall, speaking for the first time since they'd dealt with the near tragedy of Shabazz shooting Kamal in the small house. "This man is wise. He is correct. It is unpardonable and carries a heavy karmic debt."

Marjorie shook her head. "Avoidance. That's the best strategy. Juanita, Inez, and I are supposed to be seers, too." She glanced at the other women in the room. "Marlene can't be the only one who carries this burden for the team. She, like us, is only human. Therefore, we have to help and step up our efforts. If we can be on point, take turns, sense when a pending invasion is about to happen, then we won't have to take a human life—no matter how despicable it might be."

"Yeah," Jose said, his gaze becoming gentle as it went to Marlene. "We can leave messages for the people in our music. We can upload MP3 files on the Net through J.L. and Krissy's efforts, and go guerrilla. Those humans on our side will help hide us, those not down will have to try to decode what's in the newest release we put out there, one song at a time. No direct messages, everything in code through the music."

Cain weaved and braced his weight on the wall. All eyes turned and stared at him. "I must return."

Damali looked up at him, but didn't release Marlene who rested with her eyes closed against Damali's chest. "Are you all right?"

"My kingdom is in turmoil. My people are being slaughtered."

"What's going on, man?" Carlos said, not sure why he was suddenly so concerned.

"I can feel it," Cain whispered, "just like I can feel the earth plane's density weighing in on me. My limbs . . . the gravity is so heavy . . . the putrid vibrations of hate and violence and pain, so visceral. There is not enough Light. The night is dark. I do not like what the sensation of dark atmosphere does to me, or what it places within my mind. It is too dense." He inhaled through his mouth as though he were drowning. "Were this not hallowed ground I do not know what would become of me."

Damali gave Shabazz a look to let him know that it was all right for him to finally take up her position holding Marlene. She stood and gently slid Marlene into Shabazz's tight embrace and went to Cain.

"How do we get you back? I will go stand with you in battle until order is restored. Let me move the team into safety, then—"

"Hold up, D," Carlos said carefully. "Your primary mission is here."

If a glare could have cut, Carlos would have been feeling his throat for the slice. Fury tore through her. "I know my primary mission, brother," Damali said coolly, making the room go still. "I also know that it is not in our code as Neterus to abandon a friend." She returned her gaze to Cain. "The civil unrest, how bad do you sense it? I can—"

"No," Cain said, his breaths becoming more ragged as he spoke. "He is right. The blade of Asuar is the only thing that has kept the peace for many years. I could not in good conscience put you in harm's way, although you are more than worthy as a warrior. The hybrid beings on the side of Light are in the minority. Angels only rarely transgressed the edict not to mingle with humans . . . there are not many of those, and even some of them have gone dark. However, as you can imagine, the other side . . . the scales are unbalanced. The human breaches must stop. Each invasion creates a taunt, drives frenzy throughout Nod. Each incident wreaks unimaginable havoc."

Cain's eyes became sadder as he glanced around the team and allowed his gaze to again settle on Damali, their minds meeting with silent understanding. "Soon, I will not be able to keep them from the ravine or learning how to cross the barrier as the veil weakens. Then your plane will be overrun, Hell's weakened gates will open to join the legions with those hybrid forces. But the hybrids are impossible to delineate in their untransitioned forms, and they can conceal themselves within your human population making your people vulnerable day and night to attack. Humans could accidentally annihilate themselves, mistaking a demon-hybrid for one of their own. Karmic debt would spiral, adding to the minions of Hell's army. Therefore, I must return and guard the veil to ensure that never occurs."

"If you go back alone, then, you have to go back strong. What can I do?" Damali said nearing him, her voice tightening with worry.

"Your counsel is wise, but I do not know the answer to your question," Cain murmured, ignoring all others in the room while gazing at Damali. "I do not fully understand this earth realm now. When I walked the earth as a man, the weapons were different. The inventions were different, even while based upon our foundations of knowledge. I have read all there was up to the point that Nod was swept into the void and cloaked behind the veil. Ours was an advanced civilization, but there are new implements that leave me unknowing."

His eyes held an apology as he continued to stare at Damali for answers. "I have received impressions, from you. But that is not full knowing or comprehension of what has been witnessed. I have pondered . . . *dwelled*, on the many things your beautiful Neteru eyes have shown me. There is so much that I saw. Things . . . types of illumination, panels, poison darts . . ."

"He's talking about the lab, tranquilizer guns, all this modern technology shit . . . the computers and whatever else he's seen from Damali." Rider ran his hands down his face and let out a tension-riddled breath. "Don't get me wrong, the guy is definitely an awesome fighting machine and the wildest healer I've ever witnessed, but he's out of time. A few centuries short on what's happening or what we're up against, D. If he goes with us, it would be like putting the fastest gunslinger in the West up against a semiautomatic—yeah, he'd get a shot off before the other gunfighter could draw, but he'd probably die from the still-firing rounds of a dead man. We've gotta find a way to send him back before he takes a bullet."

Cain tore his gaze from Damali's to briefly stare at Rider. "What is this, bullet?"

Damali closed her eyes and gave Cain a hug, ignoring Carlos's instant bristle.

"I can show him, D. No problem," Carlos muttered. "A nine, hollow point—"

"If you have a legitimate grievance," Cain said, extricating himself from Damali's hold, "state it. Outside. Not where innocent women or children could be harmed, or the mother-seer will be traumatized further. Shall we?"

"No," Damali said as Carlos headed for the door. "One team. We have to get our squad to safety; Cain is weakening in this density—"

"Rest assured, my love, I am not so thoroughly depleted that I cannot crush this young, foolish—",

"Step outside, motherfucker—now," Carlos whispered. "That's the last time you call her anything but Damali in my face."

To Carlos's surprise, Damali spun on him and not Cain. Her tone was eerily calm.

"This man just saved my mother's life. This man just abandoned his entire kingdom to ensure nothing came through the veil. My mother and this whole family has been through *enough,* and we have a serious situation." She glanced at Marlene as her mother-seer weakly lifted her head. "Marlene is in recovery. We only have a few hours to act before we have to move out again."

Damali's eyes burned with an intensity that he'd only seen in the midst of sure and sudden battle. Even at the height of their arguments, he'd never quite seen her look at him the way she was looking at him now.

"Start some shit. Offend him," Damali said through her teeth, putting her body between Cain and Carlos with a blade suddenly appearing in her hand, "or call him out of his name in *my* presence, hear, and you and *I* will be the ones who step outside."

CHAPTER TWELVE

Gabrielle jerked her attention toward the door of her bedroom as black smoke slowly crept beneath it. She froze where she sat as her crystal ball shattered on the table, destroying her attempts at a divination that could help the Guardian team. Too late to summon support to save herself, she sent a quick telepathic message to her two initiates to flee and find the master vampire, Yonnie, and his wife, Tara. It was the only way.

"My, my, my," Lilith said, materializing to lean against the post of Gabrielle's bed. "You have been a very ungrateful little witch." She smiled at Gabrielle and studied her French manicure.

"Never, my lady," Gabrielle said, quickly standing to bow, and then dropped to one knee with her head down. "I stay in touch with the Guardians to always know their whereabouts, so that I can inform you."

"Ah . . ." Lilith said, her tone amused and disbelieving. "So, I am not only blind, but I am foolish."

"No, my lady," Gabrielle said as her throat began to constrict from Lilith's power. "I had a plan."

With a wave of her hand, Lilith knocked Gabrielle to the floor. "Enlighten me."

Gabrielle looked up from where she'd been sprawled, gasping as plumes of sulfur began to make her eyes water. Small Harpies slithered under the door and from beneath Lilith's long, black gown, and then began to edge toward Gabrielle with a menacing gleam in their beady little eyes.

"I'm the only one from our side now who has an earth plane, direct link to the Neteru team on many levels," Gabrielle said quickly, backing away from the angry creatures at her feet. "Jack Rider, the team's heart—Yonnie, a male master, and Tara who owes me. Even Damali trusts me, as does my family, which is now with them."

When Lilith's expression remained impassive, panic drove Gabrielle's speech to frenzied explanation. Her terrified gaze darted between Lilith and the Harpies. "I gave my nephew one of my initiates, a virgin, and I'm sending another to decimate the one who knows the Old Testament and is the team's peacekeeper, Daniel . . . I, I have a plan, Lilith. I haven't forgotten my debt, and thought it best that you know where the team is at all times, because their prayer light can oft times blind us from eavesdropping . . . but the men always come to me and my girls to tell all." Gabrielle's voice hitched as Lilith's gaze narrowed. "Sense for them— they've been here in carnal situations. I cannot lie to you, Empress of Pure Darkness."

Gabrielle watched Lilith crook her index finger toward the Harpies, and she released a breath of relief as they begrudgingly returned to the demon to hide beneath the hem of her gown.

Lilith sighed with a wry smile. "How devious. How basically treacherous. I like it. The oldest weapon in the book felling Guardians, how perfect." Lilith threw her head back and cackled with laughter. "I guess I can let you live, for now." But her gaze soon narrowed again as her fangs grew within her evil smile. "But remember this, shrewd Gabrielle. If you betray me, I will come for your sister, Marjorie, your nephew, and pretty niece. I will make Tara twist in the Sea of Perpetual Agony, once I install a new Chairman on Dante's throne. I will crush Rider's spirit and a part of yours, I presume . . . but Yonnie won't care less, once his ability to make another mate has been restored and he and I come to a wise barter. Power versus pussy . . . power *always* wins, darling. Pussy is so easily attainable, but can sometimes be powerful. Although, if you do well, I might have Yonnie make you what you've always wanted to be, a true female vampire."

Feigning awe, Gabrielle gasped. "You would do that, my lady?"

Lilith smiled. "Of course. Now, where are they?"

"Scientists took the Neteru Guardians to a holding cell, but it is surrounded by white light and holy water, as well as hallowed earth."

"Find them!" Lilith screeched. "I know the scientists took them. We lost the trail earlier this afternoon. Where are they now?"

"I've just dispatched two initiates that had not taken the dark oath yet. I saved those two for just such an occasion, so they can see past prayer barriers and report back to me." Gabrielle bowed her head in humble submission as her heart slammed against her ribs. She wiped at the sheen of perspiration on her upper lip. "This is why I kept them chaste and tethered to me, my lady. They will not fail us."

"Good. They'd better not," Lilith hissed and then folded her arms over her chest. "Do you think there's a male vampire that exists who could resist a council position? Do not be deluded into believing that Yonnie can save you if you cross me. Even the male Neteru couldn't resist the power of a throne, and Yonnie is nowhere near as strong as Rivera. So, think about it," Lilith added, and then turned to walk away. "Betray me and you'll have Hell to pay."

Gabrielle stared behind Lilith as her demonic form melted into the door and disappeared. She could only hope that her girls remembered all that she'd told them, and had sealed it in a white-hot, urgent prayer.

"Did you see the way that sonofabitch had my baby all in his arms?" Carlos walked back and forth in the woods kicking bramble out of his path as Yonnie calmly leaned against a tree.

"Yeah, man, I did," Yonnie said quietly. "Want me to smoke him?"

"No!" Carlos shouted, pointing at his own chest. "*I* want to smoke him!"

"Not a good move, but suit yourself, man," Yonnie said flatly, pushing away from the tree. "But if you know like I know, and if you go there—"

"I know," Carlos snapped, raking his hair so hard his scalp began to bleed. "D will freak."

"I think the more pressing issue is, my brother, not trying to be funny, is the fact that, uh, she seems to have already made her mind up. And, you know, you can't do nothin' with that until she comes to her right mind."

Carlos and Yonnie's eyes met. Carlos looked away.

"But why would she go there like that on me, man?" Carlos's voice was so quiet and distant that it almost echoed.

"I'm your boy. I'ma always be that. So, for me to tell you some bullshit, just because you wanna hear it, ain't what friends is supposed to do."

Carlos nodded and stared at Yonnie. "Aw'ight. Straight, no chaser."

"If I say what I gotta say, you gonna need to find a bar that's still pouring drinks with a little color. Feel me?"

"Just spit it out, man." Carlos stopped pacing and folded his arms over his chest, quietly hanging on Yonnie's every word.

Yonnie sighed and materialized a toothpick into his mouth and chewed it, thinking. "You saw that motherfucker, right? Need I say more?"

Carlos stalked away and punched a tree. The blow took out a section of the huge oak, making it groan and lean precariously. "He got into her head, man. An outright seduction!"

"That's because you left a section of it unguarded, brother. He's a man. That's what he's supposed to do—amass territory. If your boundary was weak, hey."

Carlos cocked his head to the side. "What?"

"You can get pissed off if you want, man. I ain't the one to be arguing with, though."

Carlos spit and rolled his shoulders. "Fine. What you think I didn't guard, since you out here signifying on my skills. We supposed to be tight, so tell me something."

He'd tried to stop the question, but it slammed into his mind and jumped out of his mouth so fast that he was about to slip into a hot flurry of Español. His worst fears were coming to life right in front of his eyes. His boy was standing there about to drop some heavy, hard-to-swallow science. All he had to do was think about Rider's situation or Shabazz's. He wasn't going out like that; never wanted to be standing in those old dawgs' shoes.

"You know that little thing that happened when you sat on Dante's throne for a minute?" Yonnie asked casually.

"Oh, so it's back to that—I told you I was sorry, and—"

"I'm cool," Yonnie said, his voice as smooth as silk. "Brothers can fall out, fight like dogs in the street, but once it's over, the bullshit is squashed."

Carlos let his breath out hard, but was listening to Yonnie's every word.

"Tara, although she understands what happened and forgives you, is still a little skittish around you. Hangs near me, holds onto me, just in case you flip again. She don't understand, 'cause she's female—and they *never* forget."

Yonnie leisurely strode around Carlos in a wide circle with his hands behind his back. "Mr. Councilman, open up your third eye and take a deep look inside. You ain't gotta answer to me, you gotta answer to yourself. Your woman's a seer. She see some shit with Juanita? She see some shit with, maybe, a were demon, or some other vamp? She see some new dragon tail . . . I heard the bitch's voice clear as moonlight, so—"

"Oh shit." Carlos wiped his palms down his face.

"Uh-huh . . . just like that. You left the door wide open for a new motherfucker to step into your yard, take your world, jack your throne as your woman's king, and from all accounts from where I'm standing, this bastard ain't to be trifled with. I'd fight your ass, Neteru blade swinging and all, before I went up against that Old World, gold armor and protect-the-kingdom type shit. You know who his daddy is *by seed*—not just by blood, man? You know who you fuckin' wit?"

"I know, man. You ain't making me feel better."

"That ain't my job to make you *feel better*. Shit. My job is to protect my boy's ass. To watch his back. Get his head right so he can make wise choices. Put him in a position of power, at all times. *That's* my job as your friend."

Yonnie looked at Carlos hard. "You go blow for blow with him, your ass will lose. You have to be strategic on this one . . . and I *can't believe* I'm the one having to tell *you* that shit. But I guess, under the circumstances, with it being Damali and all, your head is about ready to bust."

It was the stone-cold truth. Yonnie hadn't lied. He couldn't detach from the situation, or get distanced and rational. As much as Damali got on his nerves, this was his boo, his baby girl. . . . Carlos finally nodded and walked away toward the leaning tree, hoping it would just snap and fall on him. He was already crushed. "How'd you deal with that shit with Tara, man?"

"Waited. Bided my time."

Carlos stared at him.

"You heard me," Yonnie said, lifting his chin. "Rider had a heart lock on her, fuck a mind lock. She still loves him. I can see it in her eyes every time she's near him. Same with him. That ain't never gonna change. But something happened when . . . hey, I have to thank you, man, truth be told. You whipped my ass, almost killed me, it did something to her, don't ask me why. After that, she and I don't struggle about much anymore. And, when she goes to him, it's as an old, platonic friend who cares, but in a mellowed-out sorta way."

Yonnie sighed and smiled with satisfaction, manipulating the toothpick in his mouth with his tongue, making it do a slow somersault off his fangs and the roof of his mouth while studying his manicure. "Bottom line is," he finally said, pulling the toothpick from his lips and temporarily using it as a pointer to address Carlos. "She ain't jonesing for him no more. Not like that. When she wants *that,* she comes to me. So you might have to just let her go do this Titan and—"

"I can't even . . . man, if he takes her up in his lair again . . ."

Carlos walked in an agitated circle. "You wasn't over there, Yonnie. You should have seen his spot, man. That wasn't even his palace, just his cliff-side joint. It was worse than that shit she saw over in Sydney, which was massive, but just a retrofit of an old, abandoned forte. This brother conjured from *nothing,* okay? Pure freakin' energy, with a sound system like you wouldn't believe. Rock solid illusion. White marble and gold everywhere. Damned sphinxes and shit . . . brother, this ain't even negotiable. The bed is solid gold conductive metal, built-in sense-around-sound—total studio, you hear me? Plus, the brother's got this Olympic-sized pool right in his fucking bedroom, can you get to that? And it ain't even water! It's this mind-blowing sensory holding tank, I mean, the brother has crazy energy up in there, and sustaining it all without even breaking a sweat or feeding." Carlos shook his head. "Naw. I don't care what you say, I can't get with having D even go near—"

"Well, you gonna hafta *get with that,* because, by rights, if she does, hey." Yonnie shrugged, becoming philosophically cool and grating Carlos's nerves. "The only reason you buggin' is 'cause you were *her first,* that's your boo, I can dig it. Yeah, it's a little different pulling one *from* a situation, than having it pulled from you, and then having to get her back, but—"

"Yonnie, that's my baby . . . you don't know, man. I can't . . . brother, for real . . ."

"Listen to yourself, man. Damn!" Yonnie began walking in an agitated circle. He stopped and looked at Carlos, pointing at him. "You'd better get your head together with the quickness. What I saw out there, the brother got a mind lock that can melt steel. His ass is stronger than any master vamp I've ever seen. And you've got some unforgivable recent history with your woman. Bad combination."

"So, what I'ma do, man?" Carlos said, opening his arms and willing his voice not to falter. He folded his arms and set his jaw hard to keep Yonnie from seeing just how upset he was. "After healing Marlene, he's got the family totally compromised. He stole my family, man! The Guardians are all ready to be cool and not smoke him. I bet if he called Father Pat, he'd get all up in his head and they'd be kicking biblical convo and he'd probably be able to answer Genesis questions from first-hand experience to restore any shaky faith, and whatnot, so they'd be telling me he's cool. His mom is on *Damali's Council of Queens*, so you *know* his mom is pulling for him—I ain't got no back in the house, man. So, like I said. What? I'm supposed to just stand there, let him be all in my woman's face, do whatever, and—"

"Act like you know," Yonnie said flatly. "Right now he's holding aces, yeah. Put up a fight, and a woman like Damali will run headlong into his arms." Yonnie slapped his chest, becoming indignant. "You saw that shit yourself, brother. Right in the house. You called him out, and she drew on *you*. What about this don't you get?"

"That shit hurt me to my soul, man. Total disrespect!"

"So, where's my cool-to-the-bone smooth operator at, huh?"

Yonnie neared him and brushed invisible lint off Carlos's shoulder. He donned him in a black Armani suit and ran his palms down Carlos's lapels. "Just because you went into the Light don't mean my main man don't know how to work," Yonnie whispered. "So give her the Light, because that's what Cain is doing. Seduction by honor. Admit what you did wrong," Yonnie said quietly, circling Carlos as though he were about to levy an attack strike. "No excuses. Just fall on your sword. Let her fever for that motherfucker burn out, by letting it run its course. Be smooth. Be gentle, lova . . . Let that other bastard lose *his* cool, feel me?"

"His game is airtight, *hombre*," Carlos said quietly. "But I hear you."

"No. You *don't* hear me and your eyes are *blind*. Peep his game," Yonnie said, standing close to Carlos with his hand on his shoulder. He leaned into Carlos's throat and whispered into his ear. "The night and this plane's density fucks with him." Yonnie pulled back and chuckled as Carlos's eyes widened.

"That's right," Yonnie said, his head bobbing as he strode away from Carlos. "Over wherever he's from, he's king. All kings are arrogant. This brother is Leo to the bone—all ego. His silver burns hot, because he's got fire at his root; then put his fucking fire out, 'cause you a Scorp, bro, all water. Work with that shit. Fire burns, but can't nothing on the planet stop water from seeping into where it wants to go. Right? Seep back into, up, down, and around that stone wall she's put up, find the cracks and trickle in. Start with her dreams, man, and work your way out to the body, like he did."

"The brother's a king, aw'ight. What you talking about is theoretically sound, but in practice—"

"He used to have many wives, *comprende?* You know Damali don't play that polygamy vibe." Yonnie looked at Carlos, vindicated.

Carlos offered him a half-smile. "No lie. That ain't girlfriend by a long shot."

"Yeah. Now we're talking. But he's smart, will lock her down as wife number one, let the dust settle, then will probably try to get her to go with a King Solomon–type situation later, once she's too deep into it."

"Wife!" Carlos balled his hands into fists. "Never happen."

"Hear me out," Yonnie pressed. "That's how he's coming at her, and you. 'Cause if I remember my Old World theology, the kings back in the day didn't share and did battle over wives—over *queens,* plural, isn't that what he called her in *your face* . . . it was a sly call out, just like we do it, over female territory . . . without the unsuspecting ever knowing the strike is about to go down. He called her a goddess *and* a queen—even an angel, man, and if he's already a king, and what the Greeks used to consider a god, then he told you *to your face*—on the sly tip, mind you— that he was about to bust a move to make her his wife. He did that call out so *blatantly,* just stomped your pride in public so hard that you lost focus, man. I was stunned, standing there willing you in my mind to get up off the canvas and count my fingers, brother."

Yonnie just shook his head. "You know how this goes, holding two or three conversations at once—the one they hear, the one we mean, and the sly shit that is understood just between men. C'mon, man. Did the Light burn the basic rules of military engagement, war over a woman, out of our mind, or what?"

"Oh, shit . . ." Carlos tilted his head to the side and closed his eyes. "He played me. Right in front of the team. It got by me, man, because I was so pissed off. Nobody caught it but you."

"If the old Guardian boys wasn't all messed up and diverted to the Marlene crisis, they would have caught it, too, just like I did. But since you was all messed up, you took the bait, and lost your cool. Dug your own grave deeper every time he called her 'my love . . . my devastation,' what the fuck ever. You saw red. Lost your fucking mind. And a master without his mind right ain't worth a damn. Then he had you so tricked around that you couldn't even focus to help Marlene for a minute. I was like, oh, no, my boy ain't going out like that." Yonnie made a zipper motion over his mouth. "But it wasn't the time to speak on it. Later. When it was just me and you."

"All right, man. Talk to me," Carlos said, no more bravado in his tone. "I know this is basic, but you're right, man, when it comes to her, I can't just chill, and—"

"She's your marked territory, now own it!" Yonnie yanked his lapels to straighten them and then folded his arms. "Don't cock block, *make him share*. Let her go get some. Sample it. Get the whole curiosity thing out of her system. You be there when it's all over . . . hurt . . . confused . . . but loving her so much you can understand why she had to, but not blaming her because you know what you've done to hurt her . . . blah, blah, blah. If the king has to share, while she goes back and forth in a tizzy, that arrogant brother will definitely start demanding, will start trying to tell her what she can and cannot do . . . then, when he really messes up, her old first love is gonna seem so much better."

Yonnie chuckled and peered at Carlos from a sidelong glance. "Uhmph, uhmph, humph . . . if you play your cards right, the female mind filters away all but the sentimental, over time . . . moonlight walks on the beach, laughs until dawn up in the lair," Yonnie drew in a hissing breath. "How you used to put down your program, *hard*. Let her mentally mess up and call your name instead of his while he's wurking— since both y'all's names start with the same consonant, it'll be game over. That'll make even a normal human male wig and show his dark side. You know that."

Carlos shook his head. "Intellectually, I hear you, man. I can do all that other shit, but the sampling part—"

"I'ma tell you what your problem is," Yonnie said, cutting him off and laughing hard. "You ain't used to having to battle for no woman's affection, and that's your blind spot. It's a weak muscle."

Carlos became very still.

"Yeah, that's it," Yonnie said, chuckling. "That's why when you had a little possession up in you, you had to pull Juanita one last time, just to let yourself know that you still had her marked, if you ever wanted to go back that way again. Be real."

"Naw, man . . ."

"You can lie to me, but don't lie to yourself. Be. Real," Yonnie said, singing the words, making Carlos chuckle against his will. "When you was livin' you ain't have to fight for da chicas, *hombre*. Word was on the street that if you pulled one, her ass was lost forever. Motherfuckers shuddered and prayed you didn't breach their households. Beee reeaaal. If you marked the brunani, it was yours for life—whether you left it for twenty years and came back to it, or not. Be real."

Despite his worry, Yonnie had made him laugh. All Carlos could do was rub his jaw and shake his head, chuckling as his friend railed on, immensely lifting his mood.

"Before you was a vampire, your Scorpio ass was already a vampire, tell me I'm lying? That's why when the clerics had you on lockdown you was ready to go nuts, off da meter . . . the old boys might as well have cut off your dick and left you in the sun. Sheeit. Your sly ass had been up in so many secret locations, had tapped so much ass like a pro, and being the secretive Scorp you are, not even your own boys knew who you did—even they was looking at you out the side of their eye, with just cause."

Carlos was laughing so hard he was wiping his eyes. The release felt good, even though Yonnie was talking trash. "I ain't never breach my boys' houses, yo. I wasn't that foul."

"Uh-huh," Yonnie said, laughing with a skeptical smirk. "You had women in bed with their men, trying to remember not to call your name—biting their lips. How many divorces you cause? Then word hit the newspapers that your ass died, and you had women practically ready to slit their wrists to meet you on the other side . . . be real. You see the shrines of flowers and shit they left at your momma's doorstep? They almost needed an eighteen wheeler to haul flowers and candles to the gravesite . . . your brother Alejandro was the same way, man. The women, they was devastated." He stood up tall and opened his arms. "They ain't do me like that when I died. Talk about no respect." He walked around in a jaunty little circle giving Carlos a wide grin. "Brother, you made *the Neteru* shut down her third eye, and you *hadn't even gotten with her yet*. Puhlease. Why you trippin'?"

Yonnie pounded Carlos's fist, as they both doubled over laughing. "Then as a dead, damned vampire, you pull *the virgin Neteru* and have the Vampire Council ready to bust a nut at the table just watching you work. Be real. This is why I'm mad at your ass for wigging." Yonnie shook his head in disgust with a smile. "So how you gonna let some brother that has been *ether* all these years snatch your cool like dat, maaaan?"

"All that, regardless, he cannot sleep with my—"

"Stop," Yonnie said, sounding like an elderly professor and wagging his finger. "Take a deep breath."

Carlos's expression went stone serious. "Man, I ain't—"

"Stop. Think," Yonnie cautioned, still smiling, but his voice was firm and losing mirth. "If you let her get this out of her system, she'll come back. If you tell her she'd better not, trust me, a strong-minded woman like Damali will . . . and won't ever forgive you for being unfair as she throws mess up in your face that you did until the end of time. If you're patient, and lay . . . like a true scorpion, to sting Cain's ass to death by his own actions . . . she'll be back in your arms, and all will be well." Yonnie rolled his shoulders. "That's all I'ma say. They always come back to a good mark, if you don't fuck it up by losing your cool and gettin' all jealous."

Carlos raked his fingers through his hair again and stared at the house in the distance, giving Yonnie his back. "What would *he* ever do to seriously fuck up, man?"

"I don't know. Time will tell," Yonnie said in an amused tone. "Damn, man, you got it bad. You can't even lay for the opportunity, can you?" He shook his head in disbelief. "But, on this one, you're gonna have to. Can't rush it. Gotta bide your time."

"I know I did a lotta shit, man . . . but with this one, with Damali, I wasn't playing."

"That's why it cuts to the bone, and ain't no way to regen from a Neteru nick. Your ass is twisting, I can dig it. But that's also why you have to play this out like the best poker hand you've ever played in your life. You love her?"

"Man, what kinda question is that?" Carlos stared up at the stars and then closed his eyes. "She acted like me blowing in there with a double sweep wasn't shit. I was carrying dead weight, too—you know how hard that shit is? Required accuracy, pinpoint timing . . . like he was the only one that ever did anything for her. I even saved *his* ass, and got Marlene out of the lab with him." Carlos swallowed hard as Yonnie's hand rested on his shoulder.

"She loves you, too, man. But you hurt her bad, and gotta let her heart knit back together. That's delicate surgery, after the changes you've taken her through, and you *know that*. So be cool. Let this other brother be the place holder so she can step back, contemplate, start to see how honorable you are all over again . . . you hearing me? That's how he's seducing her—through honor."

"The thing that's fucking me up is he told me *that* shit. Straight up. Said he'd come at me with all of that."

"Like I said. He called you out. Was so confident that he could snag her, he told you to your face how he was gonna do it, and you're so messed up that you can't even step to his challenge." Yonnie shook his head and raked his fingers through his Afro. "Pitiful."

"How you step to some honor thing, man? Be serious. I don't even know where to begin. He fucking slapped my face and threw down the gauntlet, man."

"Ain't that how you got her? Think back."

They stood together, shoulder to shoulder for what seemed like a long time. Yonnie was more than a friend or a lieutenant, he was a brother. His insights were simplistic, yet profound. The quiet of the night helped to still his mind and allow memories to run through it unblocked by rage. Carlos shook his head.

"That's exactly what it was. I kept my hands off of her—even when I wanted her more than my next breath . . . and I did for her, just because . . . knew she deserved better than me. I told her without any lies what I was and what I wasn't, and she came to me with open arms." Carlos chuckled sadly and stared at his shoes. "I just loved her, man. I never seduced her. I don't even know how to."

"Well, then, you've gotta step up your game, but do it smooth, without demanding anything in return, *because you love her.* Seduce her with pure intent from that strong place inside you, man, so she can do a side-by-side comparison and think it's her choice. It is, but it's not—you follow? He's pulling her with the groundwork you laid. He just picked up the cards you left on the table and is playing your hand right back atcha. Now, if that ain't some wicked-smooth shit, I don't know what it is."

Yonnie stepped in front of Carlos to make Carlos look at him. "It was *your* hand *first*. You know her better than he does. Have you asked her what she wants from you, lately? Have you tried to give her those things? Have you updated your knowledge of who she is now?"

When Carlos didn't answer, Yonnie pressed on. "The sister I saw out there calling down the elements of the universe, who made her mother-seer get up and walk, ain't the D you knew from the old neighborhood, or that virgin Neteru who was half-scared of Hell. Shit, brother, you better step it up and respect that woman. That's why she ain't feelin' nothin' you gotta say—because did you hear what else Cain said to her? Right there in your face!"

"Naw, man, what?" Carlos rubbed the nape of his neck. He wasn't sure about anything anymore.

Yonnie sucked his teeth and spit out his toothpick. "C'mon, maaaan. He told her she was an equal warrior. You see her face just go . . . oh, wow? Every time I see you talking to her, not that it's my business, you're tellin' her what she can't do, what's too dangerous, all that type of shit. But this brother is giving her props. Letting her experiment with her power. Egging her on. Whispering to her mind, 'Baby, *yeah*, like that . . . bring it. You can do it, sweetness. Just let it flow.'" Carlos cringed but Yonnie wouldn't relent.

"Uh-huh. He's teaching her new shit to go with her new strengths, and you seem like, to her, like you're holding her back—which is insecure. Weak. A strong woman ain't gonna stay with a weak bastard, she can't. And you can't make her step down until you're ready to step up, just for the sake of ego—then, she'll hate you, in time. No, man, don't go out like that. Go learn some new Neteru shit and teach it to her, or better yet, let her teach you some shit, or at least encourage what she knows. You almost ain't got *no wall* around your territory no more, if that's what you've been doing to D."

"Oh, man . . . I didn't even realize I was going there."

"If you were, even Jose could pull her like that!" Yonnie said with a hard snap. "If you've been coming from weakness, in your soul, maaan. *I* could breach your borders. Now get to *that*."

The men stared at each other for a moment.

"Yeah, I said it, because I'm *your boy,* and your ass needs to get it together. Handle your business. Deal with this new Neteru thing and milk it, work it, figure out what you *can* do, but stop whining about whatever you lost in council. That shit's unattractive for a strong sister. Damn, man, I love you, but you're pissing me off!"

Yonnie began pacing, growing agitated as Carlos's eyes remained riveted on him.

"I haven't taught her anything in a long time . . . and, damn . . . like, I didn't know she could pull the elements like she did," Carlos murmured. "You see how she worked with that rod? I ain't even know what the Caduceus was, and—"

"Don't let that bastard get to know her better than you do." Yonnie pointed hard into Carlos's chest. "If you do something that stupid, allow something that easy to correct to happen, I will be done with you, man."

"But while all that's going down, what if she . . . like what if . . ."

"He temporarily blows her mind?"

Carlos just stared at Yonnie for a moment and then finally nodded.

"Too late, man. Her body is just a formality at this point. Blow her mind?" Yonnie spit and began walking toward the house. "He already did."

Carlos reentered the house with his gaze sweeping and every sense keened. He didn't need Yonnie's suit, his black T-shirt and leather pants worked fine. The half-hour away from the intense drama, plus a straight bitch slap of reality from his boy, was all that he needed. He didn't even bristle as he gazed around the room, saw Damali at the dining room table, conferring with Cain. He greeted the other Guardians with a nod, and stopped to appraise Marlene's condition.

"How's she doing, 'Bazz?"

Shabazz let out a slow exhale. "Way better than she was," he said quietly, stroking Marlene's hair as she reclined on the sofa and peacefully slept.

"Good," Carlos murmured, meaning it as he stooped down to gently squeeze Marlene's hand. Nonsense had almost allowed him to mess up and not be on-point for someone he really loved.

Carlos stood, receiving a quiet fist pound of thanks and acknowledgement from a weary Shabazz. He quickly scanned the room, seeing it now as a huge, living chess board. Yeah. King Cain was talking to *his* queen, Damali. First order of business was to draw the queen away from the king, so a checkmate could go down. Two huge rooks were on either side of the room, Big Mike and Rider. They had to be moved into position. Berkfield, a bishop. The other bishop, Marlene, had been Cain's score, which also felled a knight, Shabazz, with her.

All right. Jose could be a knight on his side. Maybe. Krissy and J.L . . . Bobby, Dan . . . frontline pawns, like Inez, Juanita, and Marjorie. He didn't care if it wasn't politically correct to think this way about the team; it was about extracting his woman from the dining room table where she'd been sitting in intimate, private discussion with an arrogant king. The bastard had made a tent with his fingers before his mouth in kingly fashion, leaning on his elbows in *his old chair* at the table in what used to be the family compound house! No. Not tonight.

Plus, he still had Yonnie, Tara, and Gabby . . . definitely Zehiradangra, maybe even Kamal. Hmmm . . . Later. They'd come into the game later. Right now he had to wipe out this particular board before he and Cain reset it again to battle over the best two out of three rounds.

Carlos glimpsed Cain in the dining room, new awareness filling him and making him ball his fists at his sides. If Damali was over there battling, as was Cain, and they both took heads off with blades to protect Marlene, then obviously the hybrid creatures from Cain's world could die. Maybe not in the same way as on the earth plane, but exterminating one of those bastards was possible.

Suddenly it all became so clear to Carlos. Yonnie was right. Cain had played him in such a smooth move that it almost made Carlos spit. How better to come out looking like the more honorable man than to deliver a starved and dehydrated corpse to Damali's feet, but one that was intact and had no signs of mortal combat? No doubt Damali would run a scan to get to the truth, and there'd be no lie to be found; Cain wouldn't have slaughtered her man in a battle.

That way how could Damali blame Cain for not knowing how to get through the rip to bring her dead man home, especially if she never composed again to bring him through the veil? The scientists' involvement was a fluke and probably wouldn't happen again for a while, long enough for him to starve to death. It would be fate, an accident. One of those fucked-up things that happens when two men fight over a woman.

The more Carlos thought about it, the angrier he got. Cain's plan was simple: Heal his competitor, make a fellow warrior think it was impossible to fight in Nod. Then let him die of starvation in the realm that had no human sustenance. After that, when Damali began composing heartbreak and loss songs from worrying herself sick, Cain could bring a limp body home to Damali and comfort her as she blamed herself for the death of her lover. He would let her see the vision of how the two men who wanted her had lived under a strained but peaceful truce while her man unfortunately withered away.

He knew how this would go, yeah. Damali would blame herself; Cain would tell her, "Baby, it wasn't your fault. No one wanted this. It was on Carlos, who followed me there, angel. I tried to do all I could, but I couldn't get him back to you fast enough. But I tried." Then one thing would lead to another, in the course of compassion and comfort. Her guilt would eat her alive, and so would that Song-of-Solomon, Old-Testament-touting, King-David-plotting, ruthless motherfucker. Only problem with Cain's little game was he didn't expect his adversary to get home alive and in one piece. Cain didn't know who he was dealing with—a man with nine lives who had already seen shit like this before. Okay. Now it was war, for real. Carlos smiled.

Carlos forced his attention to Krissy and J.L., refusing to give in to the pull of Cain and Damali's focus, which was now on him. "Guys, the pressure is on, but it's not fair to rest all that on your shoulders. I know you're scared to death of picking a safe house and then having something go wrong, right?"

Krissy nodded as she looked up at Carlos with wide, trusting eyes. "We don't want anybody to get hurt because we made a mistake."

J.L. pounded Carlos's fist. "Man, I don't envy you guys being the generals."

"Hey, just do your best, that's all anybody can ask. We all make mistakes." Carlos held the junior Guardians' eyes with an empathetic gaze, knowing everybody in the room, especially Damali, heard the implied admission. "Ask me how I know." He moved away from them and let out his breath hard. "You don't even have the right tools that you need."

Carlos hesitated, knowing technology was Cain's weak spot, so he focused on that, almost smiling as he felt Cain's focus hone in on him. "You're not going to be able to come up with a location until you can get some technology back up in the house." Carlos rubbed the nape of his neck and spoke to the junior Guardians in a quiet, nonjudgmental tone. "We have to figure something out so you guys can do your thing."

He could hear Damali stand, could feel the indignant bristle in her temperament as she strode toward him. He knew she was prepared for him to challenge her command or to argue over strategy. That was the last thing he was about to do.

"What do you propose?" she said, one hand on hip.

Carlos almost smiled. She was away from the table, had left Cain sitting alone. The king was exposed and vulnerable. The queen was out in the open. Cain was watching her every move like a cat watches a crack in the wall waiting for a mouse to reappear. Time to slaughter this bastard.

Rather than come back with a smart-assed quip of "Oh, now you're asking me what I think," Carlos gentled his tone. "You know how ashamed I am of my old life, baby," he said quietly, but loud enough for everyone to hear, especially Cain. He gazed into Damali's eyes and gently stroked her upper arms as though he didn't have the right to touch her any longer. "But I was thinking . . . for the safety of the team . . . to give us time to regroup, and time for your energies to restore so we can help Cain get back to the other side."

Carlos looked down at the floor. "D . . . I'm sorry. You were right. The only thing that was important in that moment was making sure Marlene was okay." He slowly dragged his attention away from the spot on the floor he'd been staring at and glanced at Shabazz and Marlene. "I've gotta give this brother his props." He let Damali go and advanced toward Cain.

Cain immediately stood, his eyes wary and angry as though ready to take a battle stance. Tension filled the room, but Damali hadn't moved from her spot on the other side of the sofa near Marlene and Shabazz.

"Peace, man," Carlos said, extending his hand.

Cain looked at it, slightly tilted his head in silent recognition of the best move, and gave Carlos a half-smile that said, "later." He gripped Carlos's forearm in an Old World warrior-to-warrior handshake, quietly crushing Carlos's arm. Carlos smiled. The SOB was getting pissed off. Cool.

"That was some serious energy realignment you did back there," Carlos said in false awe. But it really wasn't too hard to manufacture the respectful tone, adversary or not, Cain had shown him some new shit. "You know, male Neteru to male Neteru . . . maybe before you have to go back, you could school me on some things that would be valuable for the team? We've got healers, but nothing like what you did, man. And, if we're living on the run, and get in a jam . . . it could come in handy."

"Gladly," Cain said, his tone just shy of chilly. "To be of service to my Neteru's team is an honor."

Carlos refused to take the bait. He could feel the team almost bristle. Jose and Rider had nearly stood up to get ready for a free-for-all inside the house. So, instead, Carlos nodded with a wide smile and released

Cain's arm. "Thanks, man. I appreciate it." He looked back at Damali, who'd gone slack-jawed. "Baby, you, however, blew my mind."

He left Cain standing at the table and asserted his dominance in the house position as Damali's current lover. Uh-huh. Terms of endearment. Watch a brother from the barrios work.

Carlos stood before Damali and sought her embarrassed gaze, loving that she'd blushed when he told her she'd blown his mind. That wasn't a lie. She had.

"D, every day you change, learn something new . . . that's what I love about you. This last thing you did . . ." Carlos shook his head and looked at the floor as though pulling back from a moment that was too private to share with the team. *That was some of the sexiest shit I have ever seen,* he murmured to her in his mind—but left the channel open for Cain to also hear it. *I had to take a walk after it was over. Was in . . . a condition, so when the new brother said anything to you, I wasn't rational. Baby, I'm sorry. I shouldn't have acted like that.*

When her expression became warm, he reached out to touch her cheek, but didn't, just let his hand fall away to capture hers. "I am so proud of you. The Caduceus? I don't even know what that was, where it came from, how you got it, or how it works. That's awesome." He again caught her gaze. "When things settle down, will you tell me about it? I'm really trying to learn, D. Even when I go off and get all stubborn. But you got mad-skills."

She stepped in a little closer. Carlos could feel Cain's heat-seeking glance score his back. Good. *That's right, motherfucker, you don't hold check here.*

"Listen," Carlos said on a weary sigh. "You're right about us having to help him." He could feel Damali almost fall over but steady herself. Oh, hell yeah, queen nearly down—king in checkmate position. "Baby, the brother helped us, big time." Carlos lifted his chin and turned toward Cain, giving him a nod of genuine respect as a worthy adversary. The team's eyes widened enough to split. Jose actually stood up slowly.

"With honor, man," Carlos said, sending a double message.

Cain nodded, his expression stoic but his eyes nearly went silver, Carlos could feel it. Damali placed her hand in the center of Carlos's chest.

"He was just trying to help us," she said quietly.

"I know," Carlos said, pulling her into his arms for a hug while keeping Cain in his peripheral vision, in case the brother snapped. Slowly and calmly, he pressed Damali's head to his chest, and then kept a steady line of vision on Cain in a deadlocked, quiet standoff. "Damali, you're the superior healer on this team. If this brother's energy is waning, if he's unable to jettison himself back to the other side, what can I do to help? Maybe the rod with your power . . . I don't know how to help him, and we owe him, a lot."

Damali lifted her head from Carlos's chest. "Cain, what can we do to help you?"

Cain hesitated. Carlos almost laughed. Yeah, that's right, she said 'we.'

"One team," Carlos said, slyly, rubbing it in and not giving Cain a chance to respond. His adversary's throat was exposed, and now was the perfect moment for a sudden beheading.

"In fact, you know the old Neteru code," Carlos murmured, stroking Damali's hair, and bringing her focus, along with the team's, back to him. "If my brother has a realm to defend, I've got his back. I trust him, because you trust him, and your word is good enough for me." He kissed Damali's forehead with a gentle brush of his lips. "Baby, you've been leading this team in the right direction for a long time, are truthfully still the better warrior, better healer. Then raise your Isis, baby, like I told you that first battle we did together in Hell. Stand with the family. Protect them. I'll go over to Nod with Cain and help him restore order there. That's the least I can do."

Carlos looked up, his jaw set hard, determination blazing in his eyes as he made them go silver just to knock Damali's head back and then stared at Cain. "For the cause, man. I got your back. Me and you. We do this on your side, get your house in order, and we make sure, as one team, that nothin' slithers over the wall to the human side. Cool?"

"Much obliged," Cain said through his teeth.

"Good," Carlos said, nodding as he returned his gaze to Damali and let a palpable ripple of desire rock her system. "I know some people that know some people in Mexico. La Paz, which is by the ocean, gives us port access and is off the main congested city route." He allowed the information to torture Cain, knowing his adversary didn't know the new cities, towns, or sections of the world like he did. Yeah . . . this was his yard.

"La Paz?" Damali said, her hands creating a warm tingle as they rested on his arms.

"Yeah, baby. I have cash stashed, and know how to get lost within some places that even the CIA don't wanna go. These boyz got ammo out the ass, too. They'll be cool. Know I ain't in the distribution life no more, but we go way back. Mike, 'Bazz, Rider, and Berkfield would approve of the gear they can drop." He slid into the easy street patois, making Cain have to struggle to decode what he was telling Damali. "With the right amount of *dinero,* I can raise an army for you, baby . . . they'll be under your command, but you have to be comfortable, before I make the call."

"I don't see where we have a whole lotta options at the moment," Berkfield added right on cue, building and helping Carlos's cause without realizing it. "The man is making perfect sense to me, D."

"Works for me," Rider chimed in.

"True dat," Shabazz said with a weary sigh. "Here, we're sitting ducks."

"One thing we know for sure," Big Mike said, nodding, "our boy Carlos knows how to get out of a tight spot."

If it weren't for the rules of the game, Carlos would have walked over to Mike and hugged him.

"I trust his judgment to Hell and back, man," Jose said, finally sitting down again. "Rivera definitely got da moves. This way, if something goes down, Krissy and J.L. don't have to feel like they have to take the weight."

"Yeah," Berkfield said, going over to his daughter to stand by her side. "That's a lot of responsibility for a kid. I know where he's talking about, from those old maps and info from back in the day. We never tipped our hand that Rivera bled 'em out; in fact, we did it like he was trying to help them, in case we had to double back and send him in as a double agent."

"I'd feel safer going to some of Carlos's old haunts that Richard already knows and where Carlos has allegiances, than allowing the kids to surf the Net to deal with people we've never dealt with before," Marjorie said, gaining a weak nod from Marlene.

"Carlos takes care of family," Juanita said quietly. Her furtive gaze went between Carlos and then Cain, returning to Carlos. "I just wish he didn't have to go by himself . . . what if something happens to him over there in this place we don't even know about?"

He could have kissed Juanita on the spot. The damsel in distress with worry about *this team's king* going off to battle to help another sovereign, *weaker* king was practically making Cain's eyes glow.

"You know me,'Nita. I'll be all right. The main thing is Damali got this on lock, here." He had to walk the very careful line. Give Damali her props, gently rebuff Juanita, and quietly kick Cain's ass. "The brother's world is falling apart. That has implications for what's going on over here. If he's weak, he won't be able to handle his business. I have to go help him, simple as that. Friends don't leave each other ass out . . . and, if something happens over there to me, then, hey. It was my time. But you'll still have the baddest Neteru on the planet over here—Damali."

"Baby," Damali said. "I agree with Juanita. I'm worried. I don't want anything to happen to you over there. The things die differently. You'll need a blade. If anything were to go down wrong . . . if you didn't come back, I don't know what I'd do. You hear?"

Carlos smiled. Check. Fucking. Mate. "Yeah, baby, I hear you," he said, dropping his voice to a low, sensual rumble. "But we've gotta do what we've gotta do, right?" He looked down into her eyes that held worry and then kissed her slowly . . . long . . . gentle . . . and deep. The hair on the back of his neck rose as he felt Cain's incisors threaten to break through his gums. Carlos pulled out of the kiss and sent a hot message into Damali's mind. *After what I just saw you do in the yard, now this . . . my focus is getting messed up. I definitely don't want to leave you tonight. But I will. We have to help our boy . . . even though battling demons is the last thing on my mind, right through here.*

Damali nodded and put a little distance between them. He was glad that she did, because what he'd told her was the naked truth.

"All right, you two lovebirds. Break it up. Let's figure out how to get old Cain some juice to send him packing with Carlos, and figure out how to get this team to La Paz." Rider sighed and stretched his back.

"Well, let her think it over, Rider," Carlos said calmly. "It's ultimately her decision. There's been nothing but chaos, everybody's nerves are on edge, wire tight, and Damali, man, after that fantastic healing, I know she needs a moment to just be still and not have to be pressured into a decision."

Carlos almost hollered and did a Superbowl touchdown jig when she closed her eyes, nodded, and quietly whispered, "Thank you."

He casually returned his attention to Damali and then looked down at the floor. "Either way, just like that time I messed up by taking us to Gabrielle's . . . which was never my first choice, and it was wrong, I can at least get us out of the country on some old favors . . . can stretch a little *por favor,* if that's okay by you? But it's up to you. No pressure."

"I'm not still angry about that," she admitted quietly. "Hooking up with Gabrielle, and keeping the other half of our team safe . . . was probably one of the best strategic moves I've seen you make, Carlos. I'll go with La Paz as your first hunch."

Now she really had turned him on. She'd openly complimented him before the group. Had sat Cain's ass down into a chair in slow, temporary defeat. So, it was time to make a bold move and address Cain eyeball to eyeball.

Carlos nodded. "All right, but you sense the next move, okay? Your instincts are razor sharp." He meant that, but also needed to slice Cain a few more times for the affront of even trying to encroach on his household. "Just like back in Philly," he murmured, making Damali remember all the challenges they'd faced and conquered together. "You saw the flags on the parkway; you can do the location divinations with the stones we got in Africa. Go with your gut, keep a mind lock with me as I go to the other side with him, and I'll meet up with the team when I get back. I'll be all right."

He glanced at Cain. *That's right; she'll be locked with me the whole time I'm with you!*

A searing message came back at him, although Cain's peaceful, resigned expression never changed. *I will batter her mind until your weak lock gives way and crumbles to dust!*

Really? You think you can break a lover's hold—I kept a lock with her through the fires of Hell, motherfucker, while on your damned father's torture chamber wall! Harpies couldn't break it. Your punk ass can't, rest assured.

"You all right, baby?" Damali whispered.

"Yeah. I'm all right," Carlos said, catching himself and breaking the connection to Cain. "I'm just figuring out how to get him juiced enough to break the barrier again." Carlos rubbed his chin to hide the smile cresting on his face, and ran his tongue over his incisors. The bastard had almost made him drop fang.

"You know what?" Carlos said after a moment, factoring everything Yonnie had said into consideration. This had to go down smooth and it was time to take a wild risk. "You two are linked."

Damali's eyes widened. Cain offered him a half-smile. Carlos could feel the anticipation brewing within Cain. The brother thought he was going to get sloppy again, the connection having spiked blind rage. Never happen.

"You need to go to him, sit outside under the moonlight with the rod, if you're not too tired, maybe pull down some nature energy from the universe and give it to him. Just see if the healing staff can give him enough juice so he can make the journey. Over here, he can't replenish himself. I don't know if he needs to bust a grub, drink some water, or needs a blood hit, *comprende*? If he needs a blood hit . . . aw'ight. You can give it to him for the mission. You're right. He has to go back strong, has to be able to—"

"I do *not* need a blood hit," Cain practically shouted, making all eyes turn toward him.

"It's cool, man. Been there. No shame in the game. And Damali's got pure silver running through her, conductive element. Oblivion, brother. Will melt you down to the atomic level and put a velocity topspin on—"

"I said," Cain replied, slowly standing, losing all facade, "I do not need a blood hit."

"Aw'ight," Carlos said calmly. "You hungry? Inez can cook, right Mike?"

"To consume earthly food when about to journey will make me sick!"

Carlos had to chuckle as Damali swallowed a smile and Inez's hands went to her hips.

"I can cook, now, brother. What you trying to say?"

Big Mike got up and stepped between Carlos and Cain. "Baby girl can cook. So—"

"Stand down, brother," Carlos said, laughing, trying to keep the false peace. It couldn't get any better than this. Cain had offended the Guardian team? Man . . . "He's just edgy. Jonesin' in this atmosphere. You can't hold it against him." He quickly turned to Damali. "Walk your boy outside, okay, baby? Sit on the ground with him. Put the rod in the earth and summon energy for him before he loses it. I've been where he is. I can see it in his eyes. He needs to go back home after a battle lust and chill. Drain a few bottles . . . ya know."

"All right," Damali said slowly, picking up the staff. Total confusion and disbelief engulfed her face as Cain stormed out of the house with all

Guardian eyes behind him. "You sure you're okay with this? The process of exchanging energy like that is really intimate."

Carlos cupped her cheek. "I trust you, baby. It's a necessary thing. I'll stay in here with the team while you work, I'll eat, regroup to be sure I have enough energy to roll with Cain, I'll make the calls, and I'll get everything ready with Yonnie for the transport to La Paz. Don't worry. I'll make sure they put y'all in a real fly hacienda. I'm cool."

She put her hand on her hip and looked at him hard. "You sure you won't come out there and start no mess?"

Carlos opened his arms, seeming shocked. "Would I do something like that?"

CHAPTER THIRTEEN

Carlos stood on the back porch of the house savoring the victory, knowing that Yonnie would soon slide out of the shadows next to him. He didn't even turn his head as his friend sidled up to him and slapped Yonnie five without looking at him.

"*Absolutely* beautiful," Yonnie murmured with appreciation.

"Sweet," Carlos said, staring at the moon with a half-smile.

"All pro," Yonnie said with a low chuckle. "Now *who's* your daddy?"

Both men laughed and nodded, still not glancing at each other. Tara's graceful presence only caused them a mild start.

"What are you two out here scheming up now?" she asked, her arms folded and her expression containing a scowl.

"Baby, what?" Yonnie said, appearing completely innocent. "We ain't doing nothing. Why you always so suspicious?"

"Because I *know* you two," she replied, unfazed.

"C'mon now, Tara, don't be like that," Carlos said in an upbeat tone. "Me and Yonnie were just working out logistics for the road."

"Yeah, okay," she said sarcastically. "Then why do you have a sound block around the house that not even the big audio sensor can hear through?"

Yonnie looked at Carlos, and Carlos looked at Yonnie. A rapid mental connection bound them.

That you, man?

Naw, man, you throw that down?

Aw, shit.

Right.

"Tara, baby, go in the house," Yonnie said, glancing at her briefly. His tone was polite but also told her the request was nonnegotiable.

She withdrew slowly, but kept her gaze fastened on both Carlos and Yonnie. "Then . . . I'll just help with the list of items the team will need to transport and have at the ready once in La Paz."

Yonnie glimpsed Carlos, noting the way the muscle in his friend's jaw was working. "Thanks, baby."

Both men waited until Tara was out of earshot and her svelte form had disappeared into the house.

"All right," Yonnie said. "I'ma say this once. Be cool, and hold the line. He's on the defensive. Keep it that way, no matter what you hear. Otherwise, you'll undo all the ground you just gained."

Carlos didn't answer, but kept his mind sweeping the landscape and his gaze affixed to the moon.

Suddenly Yonnie and Carlos looked at each other at the same time. The bleating, feminine, SOS message pierced their minds at vamp decibel carried on a coven frequency, but the collision of female voices was unfamiliar.

Yonnie outstretched his hands, sending a black, swirling tornado away from his body as Carlos covered them both with a Neteru shield. Neither men spoke as Guardians rushed through the house, following Mike and Tara, who had both heard the dark turbine whine. Weapons were poised and Marlene was immediately covered by Shabazz. The team fell into formation taking cover and waiting to see what Yonnie's transport net had dragged in. Yells for Damali and Cain got sucked into eerie silence, confirming what both Yonnie and Carlos already knew—Cain was blocking interference.

Torn, Carlos remained steadfast. The team needed his shield, yet Damali might be in danger. He just had to pray that Cain hadn't lost his mind, even though he knew by now that Damali could battle her way out of Hell, if necessary. Everyone stood back as two hooded entities fell to their knees in the dirt before Yonnie.

"Smoke 'em," Shabazz said.

Mike lowered a shoulder cannon loaded with an RPG hallowed-earth shell. One of the hooded beings looked up, her small, frightened face nearly ashen as she stared at Mike's cannon.

"Hold your fire!" Bobby shouted.

Dodging the edge of the Neteru shield and past Big Mike's huge hand when the older Guardian attempted to flat palm his chest, the agile smaller Guardian jumped down the steps and ran toward the two women.

"Bobby, no!" Marjorie shrieked.

Berkfield was down the steps running after Bobby. "Son, no!"

Dan was on Bobby's heels, Glock raised, as the younger Guardian crossed the twenty-five-foot distance in an all-out sprint.

Before Dan could fire to cover his man, Bobby had swept up the hooded female and had her squarely behind him. "It's Jasmine! Hold your fire!"

The other crimson-hooded being lifted her head to reveal that she was human. Her eyes locked with Dan's and he slowed his dash to a jog then stood completely still.

"Gabrielle sent us," Jasmine wheezed, her gaze going to Bobby before it went to Yonnie.

Bobby stroked her long, black hair away from her face, stared into her almond-shaped eyes and kissed her hard. His fingers traced her small face, remembering every touch as a tiny flicker of blue static caressed her fragile, Asian features. "Sanctuary," he shouted back toward the team.

"Dude," J.L. said slowly, coming down the steps still armed, "we can't—"

"They stay!" Bobby shouted across the clearing.

"Robert, listen to me—"

"Stand down, Dad! Tell him, Rider!" Bobby said, breathing hard, now body-shielding Jasmine with outstretched arms, his weapon cocked.

Yonnie and Carlos just looked at each other for a moment as tension bound the team in silence.

"She was, uh . . . well, his first, at uh, Gabby's," Rider said, his expression strained to the limit as Marjorie covered her mouth. "The timing is bad, but since when did that stop our team, huh?" He looked at Yonnie. "If Gabrielle sent her, and I can vouch for the fact that she's an initiate of hers . . . she's clean." Rider peered around. "Aw, c'mon, guys . . . if they're initiates, they haven't taken a dark oath yet."

"What about the other one?" Mike said, only lowering his shoulder cannon by a hair.

"She's everything Christine promised," Dan murmured, walking toward the young woman who cowered on the ground.

"What?" Marlene croaked through a strangled whisper.

"Oh . . . man . . ." Carlos dropped his shield. "Everybody hold your fire."

"When did my daughter come to you, Daniel?" Tears brimmed and fell as Marlene pushed her way to the back porch rail.

Dan looked up at Marlene from where he stooped beside the hooded young woman. But his attention soon left Marlene as a pair of wide, stricken gray eyes met his. He pushed the crimson hood back from the girl's face and a profusion of shoulder-length, auburn curls spilled forward, partially covering her creamy tea-and-milk complexion. "What. . . . is your name?" Dan whispered in awe.

Rider slapped his forehead. "Oh, for the love of Pete! Not now, son."

"When," Marlene repeated, "did Christine come to you, Daniel?"

"In the mansion compound," Dan said quietly, his eyes never leaving the gray ones that held him for ransom. "She told me she would come bearing a message . . . God, you're gorgeous."

Marlene shook her head and leaned against Shabazz.

"And she told me you would be mine," the young woman whispered, drawing Dan closer.

"You stay," Dan said quietly. "Sanctuary granted."

"Coven vibration, man," Yonnie said through his teeth. "You need to back up off that, brother, until we're sure what we're dealing with."

"Jesus wept and I know why," Big Mike said, shaking his head and finally lowering the cannon.

Dan helped the young woman up. "She stays—or I'm out, with Bobby. Period. Fuck it. End of discussion. A team angel sent her! For me, that's enough of a passport." He and Bobby stood shoulder to shoulder in front of the two hooded women.

"My daughter is an angel?" Marlene's eyes searched Dan's.

"Yeah," Dan said flatly. "In my mind, she just earned her wings."

"Shit . . ." Jose said. "Can't do nothing with that. I guess they stay, huh?"

"The message?" Yonnie shouted, losing patience.

"Que pasa?" Carlos yelled, opening his arms with a frown. "You don't roll up on a Guardian compound under these circumstances unless you bringing serious word or knowledge. We can't carry dead weight, especially not right through here. So, what's up?"

"I'm Heather," the girl behind Dan said. "Jasmine and I are the last ones left at Gabrielle's. She said not to speak to you unless the space was sealed with a prayer."

"Mar, you up for it?" Carlos said, issuing an apology with his eyes toward Yonnie and Tara.

Marlene nodded as the two vampires walked away and the team drew near the porch. Once Marlene had murmured Ashe, Heather held Dan's hand, kissed him quickly, and began speaking a mile a minute in broken Scottish brogue.

"I'm 'alf Scot, Druid, my mother is of Stonehenge. Me Da' is from Gambia, West Africa, and is one of the last keepers of the Wasu Stone Circles. I work with stone energy, and Gabrielle was to give me citizenship here in exchange." Heather dropped Dan's hand as her eyes filled and her gaze went to Jasmine. "She's able to draw pictures to life . . . learned in the Philippines, and escaped horrors to be safe with Ms. Gabrielle."

Heather looked up at Marlene and then Marjorie. "We have to bond with your daughter—she's got the wiccan gift, too." Her wide-eyed gaze went to Bobby. "He's almost full wizard and needs the Stonehenge magic. But there's so much trouble . . ."

Marjorie was down the steps before anyone could stop her. "My sister, what's happened? My son's a wizard, my daughter . . . I can't even say it—talk to me!"

"Lilith came," Heather said quickly, the tears now spilling down her cheeks. "Gabby told us that one day she would come, and she felt it in her bones. She wanted us all safe, and began sending all her girls away for safety, one by one, and we were the only ones who could be shielded with a prayer." Heather looked away. "We hadn't taken the oath, or a man, and—"

"That's bullshit, if ever I heard it, and you'd better come up with a story stronger than that," Berkfield said, crossing his arms. "This old cop ain't stupid. Both these chicks have been working in a brothel, and ain't none of them kids—what are you, hon, twenty-three, twenty-four, and this one—"

"It's true, Dad," Bobby said, meeting his father's glare. "And do not ask me how I know." He held Jasmine's hand tightly and immediately flung two wicker chairs off the porch from where he stood, yards away. "Convinced now?" He turned back to Jasmine and hugged her, ignoring the stunned team. "She brought that out of me, and she stays."

Krissy covered her mouth. "Oh, my God, Bobby . . . you can do that now, too?" She laughed and looked at J.L. "I thought I was the only one in the family!"

J.L. looked down at his shoes. "I thought we'd be letting your folks know about it under different circumstances, Kris . . . timing, in front of the team." He looked at her quickly and then at Berkfield's revolver. "When your dad didn't have a gun . . ."

"Can we get back on point?" Carlos said, giving Berkfield a glare to stand down. "What's the deal with Lilith?" His gaze roved the emotionally spent team and he cut Dan a look to get his hands out of the redhead's hair.

"She's gonna install a new Chairman and start rebuilding Level Six. That's what Gabrielle told me to get to you in exchange for sanctuary. She's worried about Master Yonnie and his wife, Tara. That's all she knows, but Lilith is temporarily running the Vampire Council, and she said anyone who has that in them could be tempted into a throne."

"Tara isn't his wife," Rider said, and then hocked and spat over the porch rail.

"Now you believe 'em?" Dan said, holding Carlos's line of vision. "Isn't that enough to give them sanctuary?"

"Yeah," Carlos said. "Open the lines. I need to go talk to my boy."

So much of what Heather had said made sense that Carlos slowly descended the steps and placed his hands on Heather's skull to sense for fraud. None was there. He had to shake his head to keep his focus burrowing into her mind as the sexual charge flitting between her and Dan practically arced in his palms.

Carlos drew his hands back. The newbie was a keeper—it was either that or put a bullet in Dan's skull. The woman also wasn't lying about never having a man. But he'd take bets that Dan might try to rectify that tonight. Carlos nodded with a resigned sigh; Gabrielle's topspin, plus Christine's spiritual intervention had definitely led her to them, as the old tracer from her days as Raven was unmistakable. Just looking into Jasmine's eyes and feeling the vibe wafting off Bobby, he didn't even need a security check. Both women had clearance.

"Y'all go into the house and get these newbies weapons. I need a word with Yonnie and Tara." Carlos let his breath out hard. Just what he wanted; the cosmos had a perverse sense of humor. Two scared newbies and Damali temporarily out of her mind.

"I'm going with you," Rider said calmly as Carlos crossed the yard.

Carlos didn't have the energy to even argue, and when Yonnie and Tara met them, he sent the full message of what they'd learned telepathically, to keep it from Lilith. Yonnie nodded and then wiped his brow.

"If it goes there," Yonnie said quietly, "you be the one to dust me."

"Naw," Carlos said. "It ain't gonna go that far. I went to council and came back holding. Could use a good man on the inside. Remember, as long as there's hope, there's a fighting chance."

"I don't know if I can resist temptation like that, bro," Yonnie whispered, his gaze going to Tara and then, oddly, to Rider. "Keep her behind whatever barriers you've got, if I take a throne. Can't say what would happen."

"You can resist," Tara said, going to him and touching his face, but then pulling back as she saw Rider's reaction. "I'd asked you for a human, and you—"

"What?" Rider whispered, stunned.

"He didn't, though," Tara said quietly. "Don't ask me the circumstances."

Rider began walking away. "I guess this really is good-bye, then."

"Hold it, hold it," Carlos said. "This is important info. Need a seasoned sharpshooter on this, man, just in case it gets wild."

Rider stopped but didn't turn around. Yonnie looked away, as nervous sweat formed on his brow. Tara closed her eyes and neared Carlos.

"Give us all some hope," she whispered.

"For real, man," Yonnie said just above a murmur as he stared at Carlos. "You know what that level can do. If I go there, I ain't got a fighting chance at Light conversion . . . at least she will, unless I get back to her first." He turned away. "After an elevation like that, I know I will— and she *will* come to me."

Tara turned away, holding her head high.

"I'll wait for you with her, then," Rider said between his teeth as he spun to face Yonnie. "Hollow points locked and loaded."

Yonnie simply nodded. "Take your best shot. But she'll take the bullet first for me as my wife. Ask Carlos to school you on what a wife in the Dark Realms will do." He stepped closer to Rider who had a weapon leveled. "Rivera—that's the only motherfucker I'd take a bullet for. Him and me ride or die."

"All right, y'all," Carlos said, finding himself once again trapped between alliances and loved ones. "It hasn't happened yet, we got time, and I'd feel an elevation if it happens to my boy. Rider, keep your aim on anything tagging along with Tara or Yonnie that ain't right, since you got da nose for sulfur and can shoot dead aim blind—but my boy ain't the target, so listen up."

Waiting until all eyes were on him, Carlos shot the telepathic message first to Yonnie, then Tara, and then forced it into Rider's head: *The thing of most importance is that Lilith is in the mix again. That's critical info. If she's down at Level Six, we know how to feed her bogus vamp leads for a while, especially if Gabby sent us two operatives to work with that Lilith thinks she can trust. But if she's rebuilding council, no doubt she's also laying for those beings in Nod to flood out of the breach.*

Carlos looked at the group hard before resuming his message. *Think about it. One nick that isn't lethal and she's got daywalkers with super powers. The prime directive is to get Cain back on his side of the veil with the rip sealed before Lilith can find a way to open it further. The way I see it, the clock is ticking like a motherfucker.*

Cain was standing by a tree deep in the brush by the time she caught up to him. Just by his rigid posture she could tell he was furious. He heard her approaching, she knew it was impossible for him not to, but he kept his back to her. Damali sighed.

"Carlos was only trying to help," she said quietly.

"You defend him after what he has done to you?" Cain turned and stared at her with fire in his eyes.

She didn't give a damn, and was sure he wasn't expecting to see her arms folded over her chest. "That's *our* business," Damali said, glaring at him. "What went down privately within our relationship has nothing to do with you." She let out her breath hard and dropped her hands to her hips. "Now, listen. The man trusted me to come out here to do an energy exchange in good faith, so—"

"Spare me the lesson on chivalry," Cain bellowed. "He's playing games!"

"And you're not?" Damali said, cocking her head to the side.

Cain folded his arms and gave her his back again. "I most assuredly am not, and take offense at the suggestion." His voice had come out as a low, disgusted mutter.

Damali shook her head and smiled. "You all are both posturing, and you *both* know it."

Cain turned around, seeming genuinely shocked.

"Queen? Goddess? Angel? In front of my man? What were you trying to do, start a war in the yard?" Damali closed her eyes and ruffled the locks up from her shoulders to allow the night breeze to cool her neck. "And Carlos hasn't called me 'baby' so many times in one sentence since I don't know when."

She thought about the kiss Carlos had given her in front of the team, too. Showmanship, but she'd gone with it. Cain was wrong for verbally overstepping his bounds on family property. They were both wrong as rain, but Carlos deserved to at least have his dignity salvaged in front of the team. He'd only kissed her in front of everybody like that once, when he'd breached the compound for the first time. The sweet memory flowed over her and almost made her chuckle. Carlos Rivera was a trip. Men. She looked at Cain hard. Another trip on two legs. "Y'all both need to stop."

"I'm sorry if I offended you by stating what is my truth."

Aw Lawd . . . Damali sat down hard on the ground Indian-style and laid the golden staff across her lap. "Cain," she said on a weary exhale. "It's late. You have to go home. We need to do this transfer to get you back through the rip. After everything that's happened, and with the team on the run, I can't deal with this."

"I am sorry that I have become such an energy drain to you."

She rolled her eyes but forced patience into her tone. The last thing she needed on her hands was an entity with an attitude. "Listen," she said, as delicately as possible. "What you showed me back there was nothing short of phenomenal. I owe you. I care about you. I want you safe and your world secured. Everybody's nerves are on edge, and this atmosphere is dangerous for you."

Her statement seemed to bring him around slowly and to take some of the sting out of the rebuff. He pushed himself away from the tree, came to her slowly, sat before her, crossing his legs like a huge yogi, and stared at her with less hurt fury in his eyes.

"I am sorry," he repeated quietly, seeming a bit embarrassed for his outburst. "It is this density. The night . . . all the new wonders. This world is so vastly different than I imagined."

He tilted his head, offering her a quizzical look. "In my pool, I would receive impressions from you about phenomena that I did not understand. But as I sit on this earth, and have touched nature, my mind is being bombarded by sensations and knowledge that makes me unsteady. Do you follow?"

She didn't quite understand and nodded just to mollify him. But as he stared at her there was something very different about his eyes that drew her to their liquid silver fire.

"Your irises," she whispered, watching the silver and gold in them shimmer, but in a translucent way. Just under the metallic hue she could see fast-moving blurs of information careening by as though one long streaming video that stopped for a second each time he blinked. Maps of the world, La Paz's grid. Computers. Laboratories. The space shuttle.

Cain massaged his temples but kept his now unblinking gaze on her. "Damali," he whispered like an excited child. "Men have walked on the moon. Have taken flying battleships there? What are the half-human half . . . I do not know? They are in white coverings."

She smiled, feeling a warm sense of comfort in sharing with him. "Yep. Those are astronauts, humans with suits to help them breathe. Here's how we record music. Movies. Videos. Uhmmm . . . oh, clubs. Airplanes. Yachts . . . Here's New York. L.A. Philly."

He laughed as she opened her mind, and she could literally feel him pulling not only from her but from everything else around them. At one point the information siphon became so intense, she winced.

"Slow down, slow down," she said, laughing. "You'll give us both an aneurysm."

"This is unbelievable," he whispered and sighed. "Normal humans can see cells with machines and do the surgeries that once only the master healers could do? Incredible."

He reached for her hands and she gently placed them within his palms as he stared into her eyes. But his gaze was distant, as though his focus went right through her in order to watch the newness of the world. She enjoyed how utter fascination etched across his handsome face.

"The weapons are terrible," he murmured, his eyes momentarily growing sad. "Horrific. But many great advancements, yet these are also misused. So many dichotomies. Why do they not respect the delicate balance of the elements? That which is natural? This black smoke . . . oh, the dark, oily waters . . ." He made a face.

"You'll have to ask someone way wiser than me," she said, chuckling and loving his awe as he took it all in with pure innocence. It felt so good and so right to share with this kind, handsome entity that meant her no harm. His affection was misguided, but . . . as entities went, in her mind, he was good people.

Finally she felt him slowing down and he took a deep breath as though coming up from under water, winded.

"That was a lot for one sitting," she said with an easy smile. "I'm gonna miss you. Like you once told me, you tickle me."

He smiled and squeezed her hands. "Thank you, sweet one. This is the best gift anyone has ever given me."

They sat that way for what seemed to be a long time, although only a few minutes had passed.

"Do you feel ready to try the transfer?" she asked, not wanting to rush him, but also not wanting to tap dance on Carlos's unusual restraint.

He nodded reluctantly. "If I must."

"Aw, don't sound like that. You said it yourself, you have to go back."

He shrugged and then set his jaw hard. "Yes. That is imperative and the right thing to do. I just abhor withdrawing from you."

Damali swallowed a smile as his expression became forlorn. "It is the right thing to do."

"I do not suppose you would visit me from time to time . . . just to update our conversations?"

She couldn't keep the shy smile off her face as she looked down at his wonderfully graceful hands and shook her head no.

"I have missed my opportunity, then."

She glanced up at him and his eyes had normalized.

"The conundrum will always be a puzzle to keep my mind occupied." He smiled at her, his gaze seeming to imprint her into his memory inch by inch.

She arched an eyebrow, silently asking for clarity.

"What would have happened if I had allowed myself to flow with the very deep impulse I had . . . by the pool . . . or in my bed?"

Damali swallowed hard, no smile on her face, as the hot memory flashed back with all the heat the scenario contained. "We wouldn't have gotten to Marlene in time. All things work for the greater good."

"Wise. Yes. You are becoming an oracle."

They both chuckled to break the tension.

"But I shall have your energy in my lonely space . . . your voice, a whisper echoing off the pool's surface and in my sheets. Your vibrations . . . every detail within it, down to your sweat, held within my sanctuary."

"You should cleanse your space so that—"

"What, and chase you from my bedroom?" he said with a slight smile, shaking his head slowly. "Never again."

She was flattered beyond his imagination, but still . . . it was time for him to go. "Okay. Before this gets thick again between us, and we kick up any more drama, let's do the transfer. You've got a kingdom to put in order. I've got a team to get to safe haven."

"Spoken like a true queen." His voice was less than enthusiastic, but he closed his eyes, began meditative breathing, and relented.

"Thank you," Damali said quietly, beginning to go into the Light trance with him. But it was odd. Nothing was happening. No energy was flitting from her hands to his.

They both opened their eyes at the same time. Only problem was, his had gone silver again.

"I don't know what's wrong."

He looked off into the distance. "I cannot concentrate. My stomach . . ."

"Your stomach?"

He closed his eyes and shuddered, and then dropped her hands. "There is a burning . . ."

Damali covered her mouth as his fangs crested and his hands began to tremble. "Blood hunger . . ."

"No. Impossible. I have never had to deal with that abomination." He gathered his arms around himself and began to slowly rock back and forth. "This is just . . . The cramping will stop. I have expended too much energy during the battle within my realm. Then in the place called laboratory. Then while we healed your mother-seer. It is only fatigue. My muscles—" He stopped as a mild convulsion seized him for a moment and made him begin to pant.

Damali watched beads of clear sweat begin to dampen his brow. She dug the rod into the ground, hoping to get it to charge from natural sources, but with her own energy so low, it didn't. It was like working with a dead battery.

"Cain, no offense, but, I think in this density, at night, after all you've been through, you might have a slight problem that up until now, over on the other side—"

"You are so beautiful," he rasped, now gazing at her like she was both dinner as well as a conquest.

Damali stood in one lithe jump; he matched her.

"You need to eat. I'm gonna ask Yonnie or Tara to drop a deer for you, brother. All right? Maybe—"

He'd pulled her to him so hard and fast that their bellies collided, temporarily knocking the wind out of her. In one shuddering sweep, he dragged his nose from her collarbone up to her throat and inhaled so sharply that the sound set off butterflies in her stomach.

"I don't want a deer, I want you," he said in a harsh whisper against her neck.

She tried to extricate herself from his iron hold, but couldn't. Oddly, she wasn't afraid; it was just a bad situation to be in with her man several hundred yards away. It also wasn't about setting off a brawl by freaking out and calling Carlos.

"You may have never experienced this on the earth plane, but you've got a little vamp in you, and y'all get like this after a battle. You have to let me go," she said calmly as he nuzzled her neck. "I'll get you fed, and . . . okay, you have to stop," she added, trying to stave off the heat he produced by his hold. "This is beyond tacky. I don't do tacky, okay? Lemme go."

"After a battle . . . devastation, I've never felt it like this. You torment me. I remember . . . in my lair. By the pool. In my arms in bed . . . I can actually *feel it*. The look on your face . . . your scent," he whispered through mating-bite-length fangs as he dragged his nose back down her neck, turning her knees to jelly. "When your valley flooded, the scent is still—"

"All right, all right, see, now, this is gonna really get us in trouble, big time. My team is inside, my whole household will be in a possible uproar—no. Marlene needs her rest, and this will definitely upset her. Chill. I'll get you the deer; you feed, and come down. Okay?"

"One nick," he whispered, his breaths so ragged that he could barely stammer out the words. "He even agreed. He knew I was turning, transitioning . . . and offered you. He knew, just as you know, a deer will not stop this burn in one as old or as strong as me. It will be days before I normalize. Agony, only wetted by the taste of a fawn. This is why he agreed. Rather this and my swift departure, than having to endure my stay with you between us for another night."

"I think that was a theoretical bluff," Damali said, trying to peek over Cain's shoulder to see if Carlos was anywhere around. It made sense, but still. Permission to receive a nick was crazy, and she was fairly sure that Carlos wasn't really down for *all that*. However, what she did know for sure was Carlos wanted this guy gone fast, and he of all people would know what an energy-exhausted, post-battle vamp would need to give him enough of a hit to bring him down and send him packing. Okaaay . . . She glanced over her shoulder back toward the house.

But just turning her head had exposed her throat more than intended, and the slight pivot had sent a shudder through Cain that quickly ignited one within her. The look on Cain's face was paralyzing. But something was also happening to the night. It seemed suddenly darker, denser in a way that she couldn't define. She had to get him out of the earth zone and back over to Nod!

"I have never broken a vein with a woman in my arms," he rasped against her throat. "*Ever* . . . and I can smell the blood within you, sweet tinged by silver." He pushed her hand down his abdomen until her palm made contact with his erection. "Your pulse is here, too."

"Cain, you have to feed fast before you lose it," Damali said, panic making her stand on tiptoes to peer over his shoulder for signs of Carlos. When he battle bulked and held her tighter, her throat went dry. "But not my jugular. My man will wig!"

"Then not where he first marked you," Cain finally whispered, becoming positively unhinged as she turned in his arms and he found the other side of her neck to nuzzle aggressively. "Respect for another man's province, but he should not have thrown a bluff so sweet in a starving man's direction."

She didn't know if it was Cain's complete understanding of a Neteru's capacity to burn out a vamp's insides from an unsanctioned siphon, or if it was because he still maintained a level of honorable control, but under any other circumstances, she knew she should have been dinner by now. She was about to flat palm him to back him up when his hands slid down her sides, caressed the now-writhing Sankofa on her spine, and made her crazy. Her fist found his hair and she jerked his head back to make him stop, gain some mental distance, and look at her.

"One nick," she said firmly, no nonsense in her tone. "Not where I was first marked. You take a short siphon, enough to temporarily stop the burn, get your energy balanced, and get your head together. Then we work quickly to get you zapped back to Nod."

"As you so desire," he whispered so hotly she almost closed her eyes.

His granite hold on her relaxed to a sizzling, erotic caress. She could see his eyes almost cross as his lids slowly closed and she released his hair with a trembling hand. The moment she let go of his locks, he found the permitted side of her throat. His attention to the now-oversensitive skin made her whole body dampen with both fear and anticipation.

She'd never let another one of them do this . . . this was wild . . . it was sorta exciting, very strange, she had to relax, not keep waiting for Carlos to go ballistic . . . damn this Neteru vamp entity was all that . . . her mind was reeling as he took his time and found her sweet spot.

A wet, glistening enamel fang slid up her throat, sending so much pleasure into her skin she could feel the vein constrict and rise on its own. She braced for the sudden strike, but instead felt the slow, agonizingly sensual depression on her neck that caused pure delirium. Her heart skipped three beats, her spine practically liquefied beneath his steady hold.

The soft siphon dredged tingling, moving, vibrating sound up through every cell. She could hear her own pulse thudding in her ears then become a low bass line of insistent rhythm. His gentle suckle released ribbons of color beneath her fluttering lids that chimed like tiny bells. His hands worked against her back as though his palms were smooth, hot stones massaging profound sensations through her spinal fluids until it wet her mind and wrapped around it in a silvery glow of near orgasmic pressure. Intense pleasure parted her thighs for him to stand more tightly between them. Even through her clothes she could feel his deep phantom entry all the way to the hilt. Her voice expired on a long, quiet gasp. "Oh . . . my . . . God . . ."

He pulled out of the bite with a blinding shudder that left her wanting. He didn't even have blood on his lips as he kissed her deeply and then groaned into her mouth at such a low rumbling decibel that she came.

"Devastation, do you want me to stop?" he whispered, his eyes searching hers for permission to take her all the way. "Come to me, in my house, and I will show you so much more that your body can do." His deep, sensual voice stole her reason, filleted it, and sent subsonic waves that contracted her womb with each word. "He is a young amateur. You have not even begun to enter your full glory as a queen. Let *a king* provide you with that insight. Cross with me."

She hesitated, panting, while his fingers gently depressed their way up each vertebra of her back, hitting chakra points like pebbles skipping still water, setting off a hard climax with each touch. What did he ask her? For the first time in her life, she wasn't really sure of anything. "Uh . . ."

He lowered his head and kissed the place where he'd bitten her, making her fingernails dig into his shoulders. She could still feel him inside her, moving against her like a slow, thunderous tide although he remained physically still. Her whole body was vibrating, tears stained her cheeks. Guilt lacerated her, but he felt *so good*. She couldn't lift her head, or get her mind to cooperate to make her mouth speak. She'd thought all bites were the same . . . delivered by a sudden strike, but knowledge was a dangerous thing. All seduction bites *were not* created equal. Oh, shit, this brother was awesome. She was definitely the slain, not the slayer tonight. She was feining for a hit worse than he was, which was so out of order that it scared her.

She looked at his gorgeous, glistening fangs that caught moonlight, and tried without success to understand what had just happened. A slow dissolve of her old reality began to settle into her mind like a thin mist of sudden questions. Why had she felt so guilty? Why was this wrong? Why was it all right for Carlos to fully experience the world, but not her? Why was he allowed to still have close contact with female friends who had been more than friends, but not her? Why had developing the full range of her gifts or herself been so adamantly opposed? What gave a double standard the right to exist? Why did she feel like a gate had been closed around her, up until now?

Damali's gaze sought Cain's for answers that she knew he didn't own. The answers were within her, where her choice resided, but she couldn't go there at the moment—not messed up like this. She tore her eyes from his, looked back at the house through half-shut lids, and then up into his mesmerizing silver-gold eyes again and practically melted as his hot gaze focused on her cleavage.

"Decide, before I go in again. I will not be able to stop," he whispered. "I am also human."

CHAPTER FOURTEEN

"Hold the line, man," Yonnie said, matching Carlos's desperate moves to get around him. "This is why I hung back and even let Tara go in the house with Rider after our little meeting—one team, right? You da man, you cool. You told him he could nick her to get his energy right so he could jet."

"He fucking bit her," Carlos said, shaking his head, eyes wild, walking back and forth on the porch. Then he stood still and looked at Yonnie, incredulous. "He bit her. *In the throat.* And she *let* him." Carlos's voice was a whisper of numb disbelief.

"Well, yeah, man. That's generally how it's done, right?" Yonnie raked his hair but kept his stance readied for Carlos to bolt.

"In the wrist . . . yeah, maybe," Carlos said, his stunned gaze set on the horizon.

"He's a king, man. He ain't going for the wrist," Yonnie said, trying in vain to make what he was saying sound logical. "It's cool. That don't mean nothing."

Carlos brought his gaze down slowly from the moon and held Yonnie's. "I'm done."

Yonnie began pacing. "You ain't done, man. Be serious."

Carlos shook his head slowly, turned, and headed for the screen door, leaving Yonnie to stare behind him. Damali's desire-filled whisper carved sections of his heart into slivers. "No, man," he said quietly. "I'm done."

The way she'd breathed, "Oh . . . my . . . God . . ." followed him into the house and repeatedly planted her Isis squarely in the middle of his chest.

She walked up the front steps in a daze, dragging the golden staff behind her. When she opened the door, the team looked up. No one said a word for a moment.

"You okay, kiddo?" Rider finally asked. "We, uh, got some newbies—incoming while you were sending Cain back, and uh . . . you okay, D?"

Damali just nodded, and then glanced around the room to find Carlos. His vibration was coming from the kitchen, but she didn't move toward it.

"The energy transfer work?" Shabazz asked carefully, visually and tactically scanning her.

Damali shook her head. "Where's the rest of the team?" Damali asked in a monotone voice.

"Krissy, Juanita, and Marj went into one of the bedrooms to stay with Marlene while she gets some rest." J.L. glanced around. "Bobby and Dan are on point in the back rooms in deep discussions . . . well, uh, that's the thing—Gabby sent us two new females, Heather and Jasmine and—"

Too spent to even cope, Damali just help up her hand. "Where's Yonnie and Tara? We all have to move out."

"Yonnie's got the windows from the roof, just to be sure nothing bothers Marlene while she tries to rest and while Mike is working out the weapons list in the shed with Berkfield, trying to gather up whatever they can salvage from before," J.L. said, sheepishly glancing toward the door then over to Shabazz.

"Good," Damali said, too weary to say more. Fine by her. No more drama.

"I gotta say this," Berkfield said, coming into the house from the back. His gaze held Damali and then the others in the room. "She don't look so okay. Where's Cain?"

"Outside meditating," Damali finally murmured without elaborating. It was a struggle to use her voice for more than one-word statements.

"Okaaaay," Rider said, worry adding tension lines to his brow. "So, if the exchange didn't work, and he can't propel himself back through the rip, where does that leave us?"

"Yeah, D," Jose said, adding to the bombardment of questions. "Is he coming with us or what? I don't think we can just leave him here, but him going with us is a little shaky as a plan." He stared at her hard. "You okay, D? For real."

"I don't like him," Inez said, serving much attitude with her comment. "I for one think you need to leave his ass here, but who am I?" She sucked her teeth and rolled her eyes. "I'm just your girl. What do I know?"

Big Mike nodded, coming into the living room and dropping and ax with an armload of wooden stakes on the coffee table. "I don't like how you looking, D."

"You do seem a bit pale, honey," Marjorie said, entering the fray from the hall and trying to keep the peace, but clearly concerned.

"You sure you ain't nicked, kid?" Berkfield said, beginning to stand to go inspect Damali.

"She tried to do the energy transfer on limited reserves," Tara said quietly, parting her form from a shadow in the room and going to Damali's side to stop Berkfield's advance. "But after all that she'd already expended to bring her mother-seer back, she's simply tapped out. You are simply witnessing severe disappointment and nothing more. Her defenses are lowered, and she's completely exhausted. Just tapped out."

Tara's hand landed on Damali's shoulder as both women's eyes met. "Don't forget, she also traveled far to acquire the Caduceus, then entered Cain's world in search of Carlos, and then battled hard to survive over in Cain's land and return home. She may be a Neteru, but she is also only human."

Damali's gaze transferred a silent thanks, which Tara's accepted. She noted that Tara had also spoken loudly enough to be heard in the kitchen. A double thank you was definitely in her eyes. Tara had her back.

"All right, then cool," Rider finally said, pushing himself away from the wall. "Ten minutes, we saddle up?"

Damali nodded, calmly left the group, and walked toward an empty bedroom with Tara quietly gliding behind her. No words were necessary. Both women knew that a private moment to confer was in order. A woman-to-woman soul purge was required before the whole team was swept via vamp transport to La Paz.

"Can you please sound seal the room," Damali asked, looking at Tara and willing tears not to fall.

Tara nodded and complied.

"What is *happening* to me?" Damali whispered.

Tara gazed at her intensely, slowly touched her throat, and quickly drew her hand away as though burned. "I have been here. This is deep, white *hot*, raw, and *very* new. There is no cure."

"There has to be. I'm not making sense."

"Yes, you are," Tara said quietly. "That's what's frightening you."

"I think Carlos heard me," Damali said, not ready to address Tara's evenly delivered wisdom.

Tara calmly nodded. Damali closed her eyes.

"And?" Tara said with a bite to her tone.

"And? What do you mean, *and*?" Damali's gaze shot toward the door, fighting against the bubbling hysteria within her. "One of 'em is sitting out in the woods horny and pouting, the other one is in the kitchen fuming and ready to flip, and—"

"Let. Them. Twist." Tara folded her arms, her words succinct and sharp enough to draw blood. "Do not be held hostage in the male power-play game. Right now, what's between your legs is for ransom, along with your mind. Your heart will be collateral damage in the fall-out. Pull yourself together. That's what's draining your energy. You're stronger than *both* of them and don't even know it. I saw it with my own eyes when you healed Marlene. That's why I'm shaking my head."

Tara's forthright assessment splashed her face with much-appreciated cold water. Damali couldn't immediately reply. The charge stung, but also strengthened her, and snapped her right out of Cain's daze.

"So what that Carlos heard you? Haven't you heard or seen things that have nearly stopped your heart?"

Damali folded her arms over her chest. "No lie."

Tara tilted her head. "I am going to tell you something I swore I would never disclose . . . because he's your brother."

Damali braced herself. As the words had come out of Tara's mouth, the part about telling her something she'd vowed not to ever disclose had caused a mild heart seize—not being sure if Tara was about to launch into another Carlos misadventure or something else. She was selfishly glad that it was something else, this time.

"I am old, you are not," Tara said flatly. "I've wasted *years* in this predicament. My hope is that you don't." Her pretty brown eyes held a strange combination of deeply wounded rage, yet mellow understanding. "Rider was my first. I loved him with my all. Parts of me still do. Each time he was with another woman, each occurrence had plausible excuses . . . reasons . . . layers of circumstances that were always supposedly beyond his control." She let her breath out hard. "The man has done the world for me. There has never been a doubt that he loves me, or that I love him. That is not the issue."

Tara paced across the room and held on to the dresser as though it might offer her immoveable support. "But he and I were connected, just like you and Carlos are. Like you, I have heightened sensory perception. My ears are tuned to the night. My nose is able to pick up the nuance of any tracer. My eyes can see far beyond the normal human range. So the blond hairs ground into, and woven within the fabric at his shoulder, I saw. The residue of perfume and other things I shudder to mention, I smelled—even after he showered . . . the heart-shattering sound of his . . . voice." Tara turned away. "Or hers echoing behind it in the distance, I heard."

"Oh, Tara," Damali whispered, not sure if she should go to her, or bolt out of the room to kick Rider's ass. She stared at the vacant mirror that Tara stood before, watching the eerie confluence of the woman's body in front of her without a reflection.

"These are the things that carve out a woman's heart, rob her of respect," Tara said, pointing at Damali without turning. "There *is no excuse,* after the first incidence. Not from Rider, or your young, hot, impulsive lover, or this new but seasoned king who speaks to you in sensual decibels and never uses foul language. Hold the line and refuse to be swayed by their antics."

After the few moments she seemed to need to collect herself, Tara turned and spoke through her teeth. "The commitment is what gets violated, as well as your heart in the process." She stared at Damali hard. "You don't owe *either* of the men competing for your commitment *anything,* until *they* are ready to give to you what *you* have given . . . total . . . complete . . . unwavering resolve. Carlos *never* had to compete for your affection—let him *work* for it, after all the heartbreak that man has made you endure."

Damali rubbed her chin and glanced at the door. This information coming from a female vampire was a bizarre contrast, but sound. Truth was truth, whatever the source. But she was still unsure, not wanting to get caught up in Tara's reality, which had a slightly different set of circumstances than hers.

"Then what do you suggest?" Damali finally asked, fatigued from thinking about all of the variables too hard. "Since it seems Cain will be with us for a few and Carlos ain't going nowhere until he does, what can I do to keep the peace and get a little breathing room just to get my head together and figure out what I want?"

"Do what a man would do," Tara spat. "In every other aspect of your life, you are clear, but in this?" She began to pace as though holy water had been sprayed in the room. "Outside, during the healing, you heard the she-dragon's voice, correct?"

"Yeah, I did," Damali admitted, renewed fury beginning to crest, "but I had to let that ride, had to focus, Marlene was more important."

"*Exactly.*" Tara stopped moving about the room and stared at her, red beginning to flicker in her eyes. "A man would say, 'I haven't made up my mind,' and would keep both aggressively competing females at bay, doing whatever he chose with either of them until he was sure— because he hadn't fully committed. Men are also quick to tell a woman, 'But you knew that going in, baby,' like that matters, like that makes it all okay, like that stops your heart from being broken—even when you know, how do you keep your emotions from closing the distance the male created? If you sleep with them and your heart is involved, you're wide open."

Damali nodded, suddenly feeling too vulnerable to respond.

"If a man were in your shoes, my Neteru girlfriend," Tara added with a sad smile, "he'd eventually pick one or the other when *he* finally decided, or maybe find an entirely different woman without history altogether—but he damned sure wouldn't allow himself to be backed into a corner by childish games, or allow his focus on his primary mission, his job, whatever, to be fractured by tail. Ask me how I've learned this?" She folded her arms. "What do they always say?"

"'Later,'" Damali snapped. "'Baby, I've gotta focus on what I'm trying to do.'"

"*Exactly.* And it has to be later, or you, as a female, can step. And they do not freak out if that's ultimately what you do—why?" Tara asked with a tight smile. "Because in their minds, the universe is bountiful."

"Girl . . ."

"They cry in their beer for a few, and then become philosophical, recover, and move on." Tara shook her head and gazed at the door. "Right now, they are holding you hostage. In the middle you stand with an entire team's safety on your shoulders, weighed down, literally, by the fate of the world, and they are pulling you in opposite directions, trying to run the ultimate seduction."

"You *know* whaaaat . . ." Damali sucked her teeth and let her hands fall to her hips.

Tara snapped her fingers and pointed hard at the closed bedroom door. "Tell that arrogant king of old to take a cold shower! Tell that foolish young prince in the kitchen to back off, keep his dick in his pants, and get out of your face until he can respect your job. And if either one of them moves on you and arouses you too much by his sensual floor display of seduction, do him."

"Kill him?" Damali rubbed her palms down her face. "A little drastic, Tara, but I feel you."

"No," Tara chuckled. "*Do* him."

"Ooohhh . . ." Damali said, laughing and feeling a lot better. "But, girl, uh . . . what do I tell the other one?"

"What did they tell you? Do them both, if you're concerned about equity and fairness."

Both women stared at each other and then laughed softly, but very hard.

"Are you married to either of them?" Tara asked with a sly smile.

"Nope," Damali replied, with a mischievous grin.

"Are you engaged to either of them?" Tara prodded.

"Nope," Damali said, her smile broadening. "Well . . . maybe, kinda sorta to Carlos, but—"

"Have they been good boys?" Tara arched an eyebrow.

"Not."

"So, if Carlos steps to you, look him dead in the eye and tell him the truth. 'I heard all your shit. It broke my heart. This new brother turned me on, and I'm only human.' "

Damali paced away from her. "Whew. Just like that?"

"You carry the sharpest blade on the planet, darlin', and I take it you know how to back someone up off of you with a direct slice. You'd better learn to use your tongue that way, too. Gore them if they pressure you."

"Oh, shit, girl, you're lethal."

Tara shrugged. "Deadly when provoked." She smiled a wicked smile. "Tell that other panting bastard in the woods that he's been no angel.

You're flesh and blood, and aren't an angel, either. Make sure he understands, just like his male mind has probably told several entities in Nod, 'Baby, you knew what this was going in.' "

"Chile . . ."

"No, you'd better hear me. I know you're saying, 'Oh, but he hasn't been with anyone and is so lonely.' Right?"

"Yeah, I kinda feel bad, and he's—"

"He's male. There are female entities over there. Get real. As wise and sexy and passionate as he is, he has not been celibate for centuries, trust me. Yonnie ran the same game on me, but ultimately pacified himself at Gabrielle's establishment until I made up my mind. He didn't die because he didn't get any from me. Cain will live. Puhlease. So will Carlos."

Damali stared at Tara for a moment, truly dumbfounded. "But he said . . ."

"All right," Tara replied, her tone impatient. "So he hasn't had a woman in the flesh in a while, but I'd dare say that he's learned how to fine tune his mental capacities to a point whereby he has a string of quivering, etheric concubines that are so-called *friends*. I hate to break it to you, sis, but you're just new—and that's what is blowing his mind. New *always* does that for a man."

"Oh, shit," Damali whispered. "He played me!"

"No. You played yourself. That's different," Tara said coolly, now studying her nails. "He told you what you wanted to hear. You decided to believe him without thorough investigation. You were highly flattered. He seemed lost, trapped, intense, hot, in need of salvation, and came at you during a moment when you were worn down and emotionally exhausted by Carlos's drama, and therefore vulnerable. *Old game.* Executed very professionally."

"How could I be so—"

"Don't be too hard on yourself and definitely don't beat yourself up. Happens to the best of us, and that's what they bank on." Tara's tone grew peevish, as though revisiting her old hurts as she spoke. "You're *not* stupid, just green, and that's not a crime. It's an understandable oversight for a loving, honest, trusting woman to make. If Cain came seeking me, Yonnie would just have to get over it."

Tara looked up and Damali burst out laughing.

"Girl, you wouldn't!"

Tara scoffed. "Like Hell."

They both laughed, now unconcerned about the volume of their mirth. Let 'em twist.

"You only become totally committed once they've become totally committed," Tara said calmly, holding Damali's gaze. "Once they cease playing games, you cease playing the field. The universe is very large. You are very young and very eligible and extremely attractive. You have fabulous gifts and an awesome career. Are you ready for babies and ready to hang up your blade?"

"No," Damali said without hesitation.

"Why do you think they keep trying to get you pregnant?"

For a moment, Damali couldn't answer. "First it was daywalkers, then—"

"Yeah, yeah, yeah," Tara said with a wave of her hand, dismissing Damali's answer. "They want what you sire just as much as having you on permanent lockdown, your focus always on them and what they're doing, which keeps you under control."

"What?"

Tara smiled, vindicated. "No different than a mate bite in my world, new life in yours is pure Light that links and binds *forever.*"

"That is too wild, Tara," Damali said, now pacing. "Like a territory marker? Oh, girl . . ."

"The core issue is," Tara continued calmly, "once that happens, a woman's career changes, because her focus changes—I don't care what they tell you, ask your mother-seer or Marjorie. *The woman* takes the weight."

Tara paused to allow her words to implode with impact. "The man—married or not, is still relatively free, more or less; the woman is not, if she has children. We are conditioned to marry to have children or to simply have children—but the procreation imperative is real. So take your time deciding, and only do it when *you're* ready to take the weight. Always be prepared to do that, because at any given time, you might have to do that solo. Don't go into that marriage or relationship equation blinded by love, promises, and passion, then on a gorgeous moonlit night, slip up and ooops. Vampire or not, if it's male, you must be at the ready to take the weight—that's why *the choice* must always be yours, and you *never* surrender control of that. Guard it like your blade, girl."

"I don't even know what to say to you, Tara," Damali admitted. "The queens were telling me this, Marlene . . . but up until now, it wasn't sinking in—because I was in love! Oh, shit, I'm so mad . . . so pissed off, I can't believe—"

"Well, believe it, because it's innate, in female DNA, something at the cellular level that seeks peace and harmony. I may not be a mother, but from my observation, the female's focus becomes the one thing in the world that she values more than anything else, her child. She will try to home to that biological father, no matter how crazy he is, how ridiculous he behaves, or how off the wall his family may be, she'll give it a good try before walking away. During the interim, while she figures it all out, *he has control.* She will suffer many indignities, just to keep the unit intact. Reasonable women have nearly lost their minds trying to do that while the baby's daddy did whatever."

Tara shuddered. "The only thing that makes me feel better is you used the past tense, 'was,' when you referred to being in love."

"I did?" Damali said quietly. "Damn . . . I did, didn't I?"

Tara nodded slowly. "Yeah, because now your head is getting twisted back on straight. But think about this, how many women have had their bright star of potential prematurely eclipsed because of this sort of crap? It's not that having children is a bad thing; in fact, it's one of the most profound gifts that I'm bitterly sorry that I can't share in. So, I'm *not* blaming the children," she added in a huff. "But with this gift comes responsibility, so *nobody* but the one who has the responsibility for dealing with it should be in your face rushing your choice. Got it? How many years have talented women wasted embroiled in domestic struggles, rather than focusing on their gifts or even their children?"

"That's why the queens took my blade . . ." Damali stood gaping at Tara with her hand slowly going to her mouth. "The whole blade ordeal was really them sending me a double message. The blade represented all of that. Wow . . ."

"Doesn't your Isis cut both ways? The blade was simply an example, a harsh one, a metaphor, but not as hard as the real lesson they were trying to teach. Don't all relationships have a double-edged blade to them—passion that cuts so good but also cuts so badly and deeply when misused?"

Tara tucked a stray wisp of her hair behind her ear. "Damali, I've had *years* to ponder these things, and the moment you ran it down to us ladies in this very house, I knew *exactly* what the old girls were trying to tell ya. But for the same reasons Marlene and Marj wouldn't just spit it out, I kept my mouth shut, too. Some lessons are so personal they can only be learned from experience. If we would have tried to tell you, you would have told us that Carlos wasn't like that, blah, blah, blah, so we zipped our lips. So, yeah, I would have slapped your face to get you to wake up and taken your Isis, too, were I on the Queens Council, to save you from yourself, if I could," Tara said, her tone firm. "At twenty-one, had I known what I know now . . . Rider wouldn't have had to merely worry about Yonnie. Believe that." Tara chuckled. "Before you slaughtered them all, there were several very eligible masters available."

Both women laughed again hard.

"The mission first; this yang later." Damali shook her head. "Basic."

"And . . . if you happen to experience a lapse along the way," Tara said with a grin, "your answer will be?"

"Aw . . . Baaaby . . . C'mon, now . . . don't be like that. I'm *only* human."

"Good," Tara said, coming to Damali to hug her. "Now sit your butt down on this bed and let me tell you what is *really* going on."

Damali sat slowly. Tara flopped beside her.

"I'm a wreck," Tara said flatly. She covered her ears and squeezed her eyes shut. "Put me in a prayer seal so I can speak."

Damali murmured a quick prayer, and touched Tara's arm when she was done. Tara wiped the sweat away from her brow.

"See," Tara said weakly. "It's getting worse. Even I can't deal with a prayer seal for long. I'm out of this room in a moment."

"What happened?"

"While you were getting the best siphon of your life, Gabby sent us two initiates. One is a virgin, slated for Dan, one was with Bobby, and the two young bucks went ga-ga and added them to the team."

Damali was on her feet. "What? Carlos did it while—"

"Relax. They check out, and come with powers. The problem is Lilith is reconstituting the Vampire Council." Tara looked down at her hands and her voice became quiet. "She'll make Yonnie an offer he can't refuse . . . and if she does, I don't know if I can pull away from him." She glanced up at Damali and cupped her cheek. "That's why, while I'm still able to help you and can be in your corner, I'm saying all these things to you." Her hand fell away and her sad gaze drifted toward the door. "I love you, Damali. But you know what a councilman's wife must do, right?"

Damali held both of Tara's hands and then brought them to her lips. "I know. You have to ensure his power is never challenged."

Tara closed her eyes. "I will also have to feed properly to do that . . . as will he." She shuddered. "In all these years, I was able to avoid it, and I held out hope that one night, we'd be free."

"Don't give up—not yet. Not now. Just—"

"Damali . . . your heart is as big as Rider's. If Yonnie descends, you have to let me go. I will feed that first night, and it won't be deer." Tara's fingers traced the side of Damali's face and she pushed a lock behind her ear. "The other night, I felt Lilith's rise. I could feel new energy hit the throne level of Level Six, and . . ."

Tara's words trailed off as she stood and walked across the room. "It was female energy, Level Seven that slammed a throne. The energy went to me, first, as she pulled at the dark filaments in Carlos's line." She looked at Damali, who was now sitting, and held her gaze with solid red eyes glowing. "I was out of my skull with need for a body, and begged him, sobbing at V-point to bring me one. That's when I knew something was wrong and so much stronger than me."

Damali got up from the bed slowly and went to Tara to embrace her. "I love you," was all she could say as her heart crumbled into a hundred pieces.

"Make it quick, is all I ask. I have no idea where my soul will bottom out." Tara's cool embrace rubbed pain into Damali's spine as she laid her head on Damali's shoulder. "I don't know where Yonnie's will go, and mercy be unto him if he bottoms out in the were-demon realms. Carlos will have to make it a surgical strike."

"I can't think of you as anything else but a member of this team," Damali whispered with her eyes closed.

"The Light sent you two new female initiates from Gabrielle's and they will replace—"

"No," Damali said quickly, holding Tara's arms and looking at her hard. "They may add to the family, but will never take your places." She dropped her hold on Tara and began pacing. "I so owe that bitch, Lilith . . . if she comes for either of you, I swear . . ."

"She's coming," Tara said, her tone weary and resigned. "Soon, there will be new master vampires, a new Chairman . . . the night is darker, denser."

Damali nodded, hating that Tara was right.

"Those in the Land of Nod cannot escape," Tara said in a fatigued voice. "They have access to daylight. They don't have to be fatally nicked in order to turn. This is why, all this man drama notwithstanding, I'm trying to shake the primary focus back into your mind. Lilith's games are clouding your judgment, and everyone else's . . . even mine. But while she's weak and gathering her forces, that's her strategy. Let the teams implode on themselves."

For a moment, both women just stared at each other.

"It's so perfect," Damali whispered. "Bring out the forsaken in Nod through the rip while we're all confused and battling ourselves, even the Neteru Queen's Council is in chaos over Cain . . . with Eve's sentiments involved. Then we won't know, readily, which hybrid was nicked, is a daywalker, or what, or which one to smoke—until it's too late, and until the Vamp Council seats are loaded, and there're so many vamps populating the planet that it'll be like roaches infested the joint."

Tara simply nodded and touched Damali's shoulder as she passed. "Take care of Rider for me," she said quietly. "I owe Gabrielle dearly . . . for her healing love of him, but when he found out that Yonnie marked me as his wife and almost brought me a human, part of that man's soul died." Tara's sad gaze held Damali's as tears brimmed. "He can't even go to Gab anymore, not while Lilith is stalking her. Despite all he's done and all I've said . . . I love him that much to want him to know peace."

Damali watched Tara slip out of the bedroom without a sound, knowing in her heart that all the bitter words Tara had shared had only been a cold shield to keep Tara from quietly bleeding to death from the love hemorrhage. Damali closed her eyes and wrapped her arms around her waist. How did a woman love a man so much that she'd rather him be in another woman's arms, than suffer? It was a profound lesson that a sister from beyond the grave had just taught her.

ℭ CHAPTER FIFTEEN

Carlos stood quietly alone considering the dawn. The crystal-blue waters of Los Islotes, right off La Paz, seemed so serene, something his spirit needed right now. The cruise ships sat idle in the distance, buoyed by gentle waves. Gentle, just like he'd tried to be with Damali's heart. The pulse of the environment was that, gentle, and he'd hoped she'd feel it here on the Baja peninsula.

But Damali had missed the irony of his choosing La Paz, which simply translated meant, the peace. He was trying to tell her that by the destination. Didn't she care that he was trying to pick up the lost thread of what had once been their very private connection to weave it into the torn fabric of their relationship, mending it back together?

There was nothing Yonnie could say to him about this. Be cool? What was that, when it came to her? Another man had bitten her right in the throat . . . her soft, beautiful, Neteru throat that was only his, until now. It didn't even occur to her that he'd picked this place just for her, because of its name, what it represented, and because it reminded him so of the blue Caribbean she thrived in . . . near a beach with a white blanket of sand, thundering waves, where she'd given him back a heartbeat. Then she practically took that away, stopped his heart with a gentle gasp for another man. Waves . . . Yes, waves of hurt now represented the beaches.

There were no words. He'd experienced being a dead man walking, but never like this. Pain constricted his chest until he could barely breathe, but the torturous part of it was he'd live.

Carlos kept his back to the sprawling, beachside hacienda and shut down his sensory sweep of the new, makeshift compound. He didn't want to even consider where Damali was, what room she might be in, or have to face Cain's smug mental expression. It was bad enough that he'd had to look at him as he'd returned to the family compound, slightly winded from the seduction feed.

The sensations ran through Carlos's body again and he quickly jettisoned them from his mind. But the haunting images pried their way back in until he could hear the kitchen conference explanations, logical ones, but infuriating, plain as day.

Yeah, right, they were too exhausted to do the transfer. Oh, sure, if Cain ate regular food he'd be hanging around for days until it digested and replenished his body. Now he had to still have Cain in his space until he fully rested after the feed? Yeah, right, only Damali's blood had enough silver in it to recharge his battery. Bullshit that venison wouldn't have worked. *Kiss his ass* that Cain had to take a hit from her throat and not her wrist. What about putting it in containers, saving it in cold storage, refrigerators, in packs—like he'd had to endure? Then the SOB had laughed at the suggestion? Now back on his old stomping grounds in La Paz, he'd see about *all of that.*

Carlos let the water lap at his boots. And yet there was no denying he still loved her. He was ready to go down on his hands and knees to get her back, if it would make things right. Sad reality was, it wouldn't. What good was being a free man when he didn't want to be free?

Damali was freedom personified . . . the freedom to laugh, love with his whole heart, wake up every morning with a reason to live. She was indeed the elements . . . the air that allowed him to breathe, the earth that grounded his wild side, the fire that burned him up day and night, and the cool water that chilled him out. *Mercy, woman, don't you know I care?* Without her, he was pure, raw ether uncontained, an unrealized, free-floating radical, nothing to anchor him, no way to feel this gift of new life. She was his wife, no matter what they said, no less than Marlene was Shabazz's or Marjorie was Berkfield's . . . Damali was his. Period. He didn't need to wait for Father Pat for that. But if she didn't think so, what did it all matter?

Carlos swallowed hard and kept his gaze on the sea's horizon as rose-orange dawn kissed it. If this was what heartbreak felt like, never again. She'd brought the Light into his life like the dawn and had now incarcerated him in perpetual night. Why? For a few indiscretions that meant absolutely nothing? He couldn't wrap his mind around it. Didn't she know, she was *the one?* There was no emotion in any of that. Carlos closed his eyes. But Damali was all emotion . . . so if she gave her throat, there was something more than the physical involved. Trust, caring, friendship, loyalty, probably love . . . Carlos shuddered. When did that happen? *God, give me an answer, please! Send a sign . . . anything . . .*

He opened his eyes and clasped his hands behind his back, remembering a friend who had spared him ultimate humiliation in front of Damali and the whole family. Another friend behind bars, someone who wanted and deserved freedom, had helped him twice in his most panicked hour. With his world in shambles, the least he could do was honor the promise to a friend.

Her name came to his mind, and pushed past his lips in a soft whisper. "Zehiradangra . . . thank you. Baby, if you can hear me, I'll set you free. Lock in."

Slowly, he could feel a gentle presence enter his mind, and then in small waves of tingling sensations become embodied next to him.

"Oh," she exclaimed quietly, her hands covering her heart as she glanced at him and then the beach. "You didn't forget your vow. You called!"

Carlos nodded and gave her a hug. "Yeah . . . and you don't know how much I appreciated your helping me heal." He stroked her hair absently, staring at the sea. "Marlene is like a mother to us all; if she would have died, a part of me would have, too, and it would have killed Damali. Shabazz would have died of heart failure on the spot. The rest of the team would have never been the same. What you did meant more to me than helping me bust out of Nod. Giving you your walking papers is the least I can do."

She squeezed him tightly and then released him. "My dear friend, I said that I would help you, and you have been a man of your word. That is so rare." She paused, kissed him quickly, and stared at him. "I love being your friend, thank you for being mine," she whispered, brushing his mouth and drawing away. "She's angry about my biting you, isn't she? I can feel it."

Carlos looked at the gorgeous creature for a moment, but there was no reason to keep up the ruse. He nodded. "Yeah."

"Oh," she murmured, her jewel-green eyes becoming genuinely sad. "Then, I have to give her a gift . . . an exchange. I must let her know I meant no harm."

"Naw, that won't be necessary," Carlos said with a weary sigh.

"Yes it is," Zehiradangra said, smiling widely as her gaze went to the waves. "Don't let her stay angry." She clapped her hands excitedly. "A pearl. That is it—"

"No, Damali doesn't need—"

"Oh, yes, Carlos. What goddess can resist? Pearls are mystical. Teardrops of the moon, thought to be the passage of angels through the clouds . . . I insist. It is your mystical birthstone, too."

He chuckled. "I'm a Scorp. Topaz is my stone."

She wagged her finger playfully. "No, no, no. That is your zodiac stone. Your mystical birthstone, oh man of deep passionate waters, is the pearl . . . In my culture, it is your Ayurvedic birthstone. It is the oldest known organic gemstone worn by brides, a symbol of purity and innocence—which she is. Do not allow Cain to make her his wife. He has had many; you have had none but her. This is unfair and unbalanced. She must know that you two are linked through your mystical birthstone to her innocence. This will be my gift to quietly tell her, I meant no harm. Let me do this, *please?*"

She didn't wait for him to answer as she walked toward the water, beginning to skip like a child as she approached it. She bent down and touched the sand, feeling the grains of it as the water's attention tickled her feet. She stood, spun around, and laughed. "Carlos, it is so different from Cain's pool! I had forgotten how alive and how vast the sea is . . . oh . . . I shall find something magnificent for her, do not worry!"

She ran into the waves and splashed about. Carlos watched her from a faraway place in his mind. He remembered Damali's communion with the surf at night in St. Lucia, how she laughed and splashed as though seeing waves for the first time.

A deep sadness weighed on his soul. A creature as lovely and good hearted as Zehiradangra had been captured and kept in a large fish tank devoid of full sensation? Cruel. He now better understood why Cain had water everywhere in his palaces . . . it was for her. He would have offered her no less, if that was all he could do. It was also clear to him now that she was Cain's main woman. He knew it like he knew his name as he watched her dance with the rolling tide, sliding in and out of it, and then finally transforming into the elongated, pearl-scaled beauty that could no longer resist the pull of the sea.

That's where she belonged, a free spirit open to the seas of the world.

Laughing, alive, ignited by nature. Mystical, wondrous, unbridled, no boundaries. Cain could capture all the sensations he wanted within his still, artificial tanks, but he couldn't give this odd beauty what she needed . . . room to stretch her wings and fly.

"Fly away, baby," Carlos whispered. "Find the roof of the world, the depths of the sea, and never look back."

There was no resistance in him as he watched her gleaming body form rising and falling flashes of dawn-lit scales, each hump surfacing to quickly submerge in a sea serpent dance. *Dance with the waves . . . forever, my friend.*

"Are you mad?" A deep male voice thundered, almost knocking Carlos down.

Cain instantly appeared by his side. Nonplussed, the territorial outrage made a half-smile tug at Carlos's mouth.

"Fair exchange is no robbery, *my brutha.*"

Cain glared at him and then the sea. "Zehiradangra, I forbid you to go any farther!" Cain paced a hot path back and forth along the water's edge, and then he spun on Carlos when her body disappeared under the blue-green surface. "You young, stupid fool," Cain spat.

"Hey, like you told me," Carlos said with a casual shrug, "if you can't keep your woman contained . . ."

"Call her back," Cain demanded.

Carlos chuckled and spit on the sand. "Fuck you. No."

"You have made her something that will be hunted on this plane! She was my closest friend and did not deserve to have her heart shattered to the point where she will not heed my warnings. I would have brought her experiences and touch through the veil, that she might not languish."

"Does Damali know that?" Carlos asked, studying his nails.

Cain raked his hair and walked back and forth between the water and Carlos. "Her heart is filled with compassion. In time, she would come to understand that—"

"You don't know my baby at all. Damali doesn't share or do sloppy seconds."

"There is nothing sloppy about a creature as exquisite as Zehiradangra!"

"Yeah, well, lemme ask you this," Carlos said, thoroughly enjoying Cain's agitated state. "Would you be able to deal if Damali decided to keep dealing with me, while with you? Because, the way I see it, when you're with Damali, I could hang out with Z . . . then, hey, when uh, you have to go put in some time with Z, you know, a brother could back off and go home, get up with Damali, chill. . . . We can work it out, man. We cool—since you already *bit* her."

Cain made a tent with his fingers in front of his mouth as though summoning calm. "That would not pose a problem for me," he said, forcing smugness into his tone. "If she felt compelled by pity to occasionally resurrect an old, sentimental visit, I would honor that."

Carlos refused to allow Cain to best him on the beach, so he scavenged his mind for anything to make Cain drop fangs and start the rumble. "I appreciate that . . . maybe she'd come see me, sing to me like old times, and I could accept the loss a little better with her sweet voice making the bullshit medicine go down my throat a little easier. Yeah."

Cain bristled and his eyes had begun to flicker.

"Yeah, I thought so," Carlos muttered, vindicated. Every muscle within him was keened, waiting for the battle to begin, but instead, Cain's attention snapped toward the sea.

"Call her back," he whispered, his tone so gentle that Carlos stepped back to avoid a potentially sudden lunge.

"I told you, no, man. If she's yours, and you got her on lock like you think you do, then—"

"You are so *foolish* and *so young*," Cain said, his eyes holding the sea. "Zehira, please, I beg you, come to me!"

Carlos folded his arms and shook his head in triumph. Damn, and he'd been all worried about Damali? For what? Not even twenty-four hours in the damned sun and this bastard was already—

"She does not know the densities of this plane! Her body has not had time to adjust or strengthen to match it!" Cain shouted, panic in his eyes.

"And how is that my problem?" Carlos said, glaring at Cain, waiting for him to make a false move.

"She's a sea dragon!" Cain bellowed, his arm extended as he pointed toward the water. "Her kind once plundered wooden Viking ships, Roman ships, Greek vessels made of *wood!* That is why humans put false dragons on their mastheads and tried to ward off a feeding attack by making the dragons think another dragon had already claimed it! She is new to flesh, hungry, in a quest for sensations denied. Call her back. She is headed for suicide, a *steel* cruise ship, the hull impenetrable to organic flesh matter. She will snap her neck. The turbines will grind her up into bits!"

Carlos raced to the water and went in waist deep. Cain didn't have to tell him twice, as he began shouting. "Zehiradangra!"

Damali soaped the natural sea sponge until it burst with lather, and then made soft swirls on Marlene's arms and shoulders. Every so often she'd kiss Marlene's temple as her mother-seer reclined in the huge, old-fashioned claw-footed tub. White adobe walls, mud-sculpted so finely that the designs seemed like lace, created a safe haven, a sanctuary for healing.

Pretty yellow curtains blew away from the window on a balmy sea breeze, the surf a distant rhythm of peace. Only the sound of the bath being disturbed filled the room around them. Terra-cotta tiles, with blue and yellow and white flowers were underfoot, helping to generate an echo each time the water was gently poured over an almost lost body that was badly in need of tender nursing. Damali devoted herself to the task as though making oblations at the shrine of Isis.

"You don't have to baby me," Marlene said weakly.

"Yes, I do," Damali whispered, collecting warm bath water into a small porcelain cup and allowing it to chase away the suds. "How many times did you do this for me when I was all hurt up?"

Marlene smiled. "That was what I was supposed to do."

"Loving you back, ain't that what I'm supposed to do?" Damali said, fighting against the tears and then smiling. "Why are you always so stubborn?"

"Because my children make me that way," Marlene said, smiling through the tears.

"I know we do," Damali sighed, beginning to softly soap Marlene's locks. "So, close your eyes and let me be the mom this morning . . . even if I can never, ever fill your shoes."

"That's 'cause my feet are too big, chile. Not because you can't hold your own," Marlene murmured with a self-conscious chuckle, closing her eyes as tears fell. "That was some mighty powerful juju you did out there for this old broad. Couldn't have done it better myself."

"Who you think taught me?" Damali whispered, kissing the soapy crown of Marlene's head and then pouring cleansing rosemary water over it, careful to keep soap out of Marlene's eyes.

"Ah . . . well . . . but some of the new things you're learning, even I couldn't teach."

"You gave me the foundation. Without it, anything new wouldn't have a leg to stand on."

"You always answered me word for word, child. Umph."

They both chuckled softly as Damali finished rinsing Marlene's hair.

"So, what are you gonna do?" Marlene asked with a smile, keeping her eyes closed as Damali soaped her hair again.

"Marlene, the last thing I'm worried about is any of that. *You* are my primary focus, as is this family. From this point forward."

"You're a Neteru, not a nun. The family is a big burden, one you don't have to take on all by yourself. Me and Marj can hold up a couple of those sides of the pyramid. Chile, you've gotta distribute the weight or it'll crush you. The family's too big now for you to be trying to carry it all alone on your back."

"You've been holding up this pyramid all by yourself for years, Mar. It's time for you to rest, and let—"

Marlene opened her eyes and stared back at Damali with a gentle but firm gaze, stopping her words. "*That* would kill me, to see you retreat from life and happiness, if nothing else would."

When Damali sucked in a shuddering breath trying to be strong, Marlene's wet hand sought Damali's cheek and she cupped it. Damali immediately kissed the center of it.

"We're not supposed to leave all this on our children, honey. The generation that goes before is supposed to pave the way through the bushes so the ones following behind don't have such a tough road ahead of them. Why would I leave sticks and stones and boulders in your path to trip on, when I love you like I do, sweetie? I'ma help you and be your mother until the day I close my eyes, and move every stone I'm strong enough to lift out of your way, *no matter what*. You can't stop me. It's in my blood, my cells, my mother DNA." Marlene sighed as two new tears rolled down Damali's cheeks.

"That's right, child. You go on and cry. Let it out."

"I thought I'd lost you," Damali whispered, sniffing, unable to lift the sponge so much pain had suddenly wrapped around her chest. She squeezed the sponge, forcing white lather between her clenched fingers. "If . . . Lord, Marlene . . ."

"I know, baby. Hurts my soul how many times my suga-girl-child gotta go to Hell and back, even if it is her job. My heart leaps right into the pit with you every time. Know that, darlin'. You ain't never alone. Mar and the angels are right there with you."

Marlene nodded and traced a tear on Damali's cheek until it plopped into the white bathtub water. "Yeah, you're grown, but you still have a lotta life left to live. Advice is probably hitting you from all sides by now, I'm sure. Now, your heart is heavy, I'm still living, so state your bizness. This don't bother me—talking. Seeing my grown girl child all twisted up, *that* bothers me. So, whatchu gonna do about these crazy men?" Marlene smiled, which brought out a sad smile on Damali's face with it.

"I don't know," Damali whispered.

"You still love him?"

Damali stared into the suds. "Yeah."

"This new one. You know him? Really know him?"

Damali shook her head and began rinsing out the sponge.

"Seems to me, you and Carlos go way back."

"We do," Damali said, twisting the sponge. "But things change . . . he did a lotta stuff, Mar."

Marlene nodded and took the sponge from her hands. "Every relationship is different. Every man is different. All advice aside from your girlfriends and bystanders, you follow your heart. Just remember, keep true to that. Never kill anything that you want to get up and live one day. Don't injure or cripple it, either. If you all argue, and draw blades, which is bound to happen from time to time, make sure you cut with a practice, blunt edge . . . something dull, so he can get back up and recover without bleeding." Marlene stared at her hard. "Don't use the Isis in your mouth to do that. Hear? I don't care what anybody else told you." Marlene continued to stare at her without blinking. "Other situations are tainted by bitterness. That ain't a part of your soul, so don't let it slither in there, no matter how good a friend the advisor is. It doesn't mean the counsel wasn't well-meant, or the person evil, just that the method was flawed."

Damali went still. "Your third eye, Mar . . . how is it?"

"Sore, but still a laser, and can see nonsense around corners, through shadows, and written all over your face. Don't need it. This is age and wisdom, not magic or telepathy. I know my child. That's all I have to see to know what I'm talking about."

Marlene drew herself up to stand with a grunt, and Damali helped her and got a towel. She wrapped Marlene in it as she stepped out of the tub and hugged her, drying her, petting appreciation into her as she wiped water from her fragile body.

"I just wanted to let him know how it felt."

Marlene sighed and twisted water out of her hair over the tub. "Oh, baby . . . I think he knows. Now it's a matter of damage control."

"But what about . . ." Damali let her words trail off as she helped Marlene to sit so she could begin to apply healing creams to her skin.

"You dance," Marlene said simply.

"Dance?" Damali chuckled.

"Yep. You dance, you investigate, you take your time to decide. You learn, you cry, you laugh, you sample—I ain't telling you what you should do with your body, you're grown. Lord knows," Marlene chuckled, "I sampled. Uhmph, uhmph, uhmph, did I sample in my day."

They both laughed.

"You find out what you need to know, then if you want to, you come on home," Marlene murmured. "Just know that if you take the risk, home as you knew it might not still be there. So you ask yourself, are you ready to put it all on red? Whatever you do, you're gonna still be mine. Whatever you do, you're gonna still have options. I just don't want to see you do whatever you do, brazen, tacky, spiteful, or mean. Even if you switch dance partners, there's a way to do it respectfully."

Marlene made Damali look up by finding her chin with the soft pad of her index finger. "That's not for them, honey. That's for you. So you can sleep at night without any negative karma adding to the weight of your world. That's not weak, that's quiet, serene, regal, goddess strength. Understand? *Always be a queen,* even while quietly sampling . . . with discretion."

Damali covered Marlene's hand with her own and allowed her eyes to slide shut as she sat at Marlene's withered feet on the tile floor. Slowly her head went to Marlene's lap, in tribute, in homage for the wisdom that had been imparted. Quiet tears added to the white bathwater that had absorbed into Marlene's towel. Older, gentle female hands stroked weariness and confusion from her mind without magic.

"There is no one on the Neteru Council who compares to you, Queen Mother," Damali whispered. "Thank you."

The sound of Carlos's hysterical voice oddly fused with Cain's belting out a foreign name made Damali leave Marlene and Shabazz's side.

"I have to go," Damali said quickly.

Shabazz stood up fast from the wicker bedroom chair, but glanced at Marlene, who remained relaxed in bed.

"I'll be all right. This is where you should be, not down on the beach," Damali said, trying to keep her voice even and calm.

Shabazz nodded once Marlene had nodded.

Damali exited quickly, shut the door quietly, and then tore from the room, her bare footfalls echoing against the Spanish tiles. White walls, terra-cotta, brilliant yellows within the massive hacienda became one blur as she headed for the beach. Sleepy teammates opened bedroom doors, but she held up her hand, saying nothing, just signaling for them to stand down. This was personal.

Two male backs stood on the shore with outstretched arms, voices pleading toward something in the distance. They turned in unified slow motion, both holding an apology in their eyes.

"She'll die," Cain whispered. "I have to go get her."

Carlos was already waist deep in the surf. "D, it's not what you think. She doesn't deserve to go out like that!"

Damali watched, remaining very still as Cain closed his eyes, balled up his fists, and an orb of strobe light entered it. The muscles within his massive shoulders contracted, and rippled down his forearm as he drew it back and then hurled the light in his fist.

Awe claimed her as the orb went out from him, becoming a tiny speck, then he snatched the air, and a blue-white energy line appeared between the faraway orb and his palms. Instantly, he wound it around his fist several times, and turned to Carlos.

"Grab the line and hold her, she's strong," Cain ordered, yanking on the beam of light.

To Damali's utter fascination, a huge, pearl-scaled serpent leapt from the waters, twisted like a snared marlin, its pinkish iridescence gleaming in the bright rays of the orange dawn. Her attention immediately went to Carlos, who was holding the line with both hands, being dragged deeper into the sea, his feet digging into wet sand as Cain went farther out, planted his feet, and grabbed a section of the light line and pulled hard. Then both men fell as the line snapped.

"I did not feed properly! I cannot sustain her weight in this infernal atmosphere," Cain shouted, his hot glare on Carlos as they both jumped up sputtering. "She no longer trusts me. If she dies, it is on your head!"

Damali ran to the water's edge. "Who is she? If I can—"

Before she could get the statement out, Cain winced, his head jerking to the side, and then his shoulders slumped. Both she and Carlos watched in horror as he backed away from the water and wrapped his arms around himself.

She'd never seen an expression as stricken as Cain looked at her, silver tears forming in his eyes, and then his gaze left hers for the water.

Cain sucked in a huge, trembling breath and stepped backward until he was on the dry sand, just shaking his head. Carlos was still in the water as Cain dropped to his knees, opened his arms, and a slow, gentle vibration exited his body.

Carlos stumbled to the beach and went to Damali's side, she only yards from Cain. Then slowly a limp, battered dragon filled Cain's arms, weighing them down as he stroked its head and buried his face against its still chest.

"Why did you not listen . . . I was still your friend." Cain's soft sob became muffled against the creature's breast. His wide shoulders shook as he tried to lift her heavy body from the sand.

"Aw . . . shit, man . . . I'm sorry," Carlos said quietly, tears now filling his eyes as he left Damali's side to squat down. "Maybe we can feed her . . . get her over to Nod to regen. Man, she's good people, I never—"

"Do not speak to me," Cain whispered between his teeth, his gaze deadly, as Carlos slowly withdrew. "Do you know how many years she has been *my friend?* Do you understand how hard I tried to *always* keep her safe and unharmed? I *know* she is good. I *know* her gentle heart. I *know* her inquisitive mind." He looked down at the creature in his arms and kissed her forehead. "I know."

A pearl rolled out of the dragon's mouth and stopped at Damali's feet. She and Carlos stared at it.

"Pick it up," Cain whispered, nuzzling the fallen creature. "A gift from the sea from Zehiradangra. An exchange for her invasion of what she believed to be yours. A dragon's apology, Damali. Accept it, she meant no harm." Cain looked up at Carlos. "Your seduction did this to her. You could have had her without her death on your hands. I am going home to bury her as she should be in Nod."

Damali grasped the pearl and held it tightly in her fist, dropping to her knees beside Cain. "The Caduceus. Take it with you. See if once she's ether, maybe? Try," she urged in a desperate whisper. "Just like Marlene. I showed you. Hurry before she's not been breathing too long." She materialized the golden staff in her unclenched fist and held it out for Cain to accept.

Cain nodded, gently lowered the she-dragon to the sand, and stood over the lifeless serpent body, a leg on either side of the huge beast. He quietly accepted the staff, his eyes holding Damali's, lingering for a moment, and then he drove the golden, healing rod into the sand near the fallen. "If it works, I will hold this gift as a debt to you in my soul for a lifetime, Damali. I will return it to you with everything else that I own."

She nodded, wiped her face, and stepped back as a blue-white brilliance made her and Carlos squint. She watched Cain grab the edges of nothingness, fold it around him, the staff, and the dragon at his feet like a cloak, and disappear.

For a long while she and Carlos said nothing as they stared out toward the sea trying to comprehend all that they'd seen. But the moment she heard him draw a breath to speak, she spun on him.

"Don't even say it," she said in a low, threatening tone. From some unknown place within her, a master switch got flipped, the slow, steady whine of turbine rage began to spiral within her, gaining velocity until it made her limbs tremble with repressed fury—she knew any moment, she was likely to blow. *Don't let him take me there, Jesus, I'm not responsible. Not today.*

"It wasn't supposed to go down like this," Carlos replied solemnly, merely shaking his head as he glanced at her and then at the seashell-strewn shore.

Damali opened her fist and almost wept as she stared at the strange, pinkish-white, iridescent pearl in her palm. "What did you *do* . . ." she said so quietly that he looked at her and became nearly paralyzed, "to make this woman feel like she had to *fucking die,* Carlos, to go after an apology gift like this?" She shook her head and closed her hand over the pearl, not sure if she should keep it out of respect for the sacrifice it contained, or just pitch it back into the turquoise blue sea.

"Damali, it's not what you think, and I feel more awful about it than you'll ever know. She was good people, D. She wasn't just some stray . . . it all happened when I was trying to get out of Nod. I wasn't—"

"You played with her mind and broke her heart, Carlos. That's what had to—"

"Naw, that's not it, not what happened," he said quickly, trying to defend himself as he raked his hair, unable to withstand her gaze. "She was his main woman and—"

"No," Damali said coolly. "She was *his friend.* She was no less friend to him than Tara is to you. They weren't *lovers,* but yes, he loved her dearly. She was family to him. Did you see the look on that man's face?"

"D, wake up! That was his main woman in Nod, that's why the brother was so broken up. Aw'ight. I feel like shit about what happened to her, but if we gonna talk facts, let's put it *all* out on the table."

"Yeah, let's do that," Damali said, her tone brittle enough to snap. Her voice had escalated to a level she hadn't intended, but so help her, if Carlos Rivera told her another lie . . . "Because I'll tell you what happened. The short version, since I'm not blind. You finally do some foul shit that I just can't live with. So then I decide that maybe it's time for me to go see what else is out here in the world, because I don't have to take this crap from you—so you get all jealous, jacked up, start sweating me, and have a problem when some other man, an honorable one, I might add, steps to me—and then you get mad because I don't back him up as hard as you think I should. Yeah, I said it," she added, her head now bobbing with her words as her arms slowly folded. "So you run that old 'fair exchange is no robbery' vamp bullshit, and pull this girl, a dragon no less, and do her in the man's house, then put her in harm's way for spite, just to let him know you still got it like that, and—"

"You are so off base, Damali, it ain't even funny!" He walked away from her and spun on her, pointing when she dashed behind him in fury. "You got a helluva nerve, anyway. In the throat! In earshot of me and the family? What was that shit, D? Are you crazy? I've never—"

"What! You never *what?* Oh, puhlease, I know you ain't going there!" She held up her hand. "We're done. Period. End of story. Ain't nobody ever died because I slept with 'em. I don't have a string of suicidal men pearl diving for me, okaaay! What I need is somebody older, stable, not crazy, not off da hook, not—"

"You think *that* motherfucker is stable and *I'm* not? Are *you* crazy?"

Carlos shouted back, sputtering, his blood pressure spiking so hard and fast it made his ears ring and his face burn hot. "Does *he* know that *you're* the one who took off his old man's head? Do *you* realize who *his* family is on his *daddy's* side, girl? You—"

"Who are *you* calling a girl?"

Before he could speak, she'd slapped the taste out of his mouth. Before he could turn his head back to look at her, she'd unsheathed her verbal blade and was going for more blood.

"How many bitches, Carlos?" She shrieked. "How many? What variety? What did you make out there in the street that I don't know about?" She was screaming so hard, her voice became hoarse. Spit was flying with every word. Internal fury imploded, became flashpoint mist, zigzagged through her gray matter at maximum velocity, arced over rational synapses, slammed a mental wall, burned up her windpipe and vocal cords, cracked a heart valve and blew. "How many? Tell me! When does it end? The Light didn't fry the bullshit out of you, did it?"

The presence of Guardians gathering at the front of the hacienda didn't matter. The train wreck was unraveling before their eyes in slow motion, but she didn't have the emergency breaks to stop herself. The box cars just kept piling up, skidding, sparking along twisted logic tracks.

"The last time I had to go through this with you, Carlos, it was a Guardian that I now have to live with! Before that, it was something on four legs in the Amazon! Damned vampire hoes up in the clubs—who knows where you and Yonnie go? Probably to lay some snake booty up at Gabrielle's! I don't trust your ass as far as I can throw you! No, cancel that, I can throw your ass farther than I trust you!"

She wasn't rational as she screamed, but didn't care. Too much sly Scorpio water had gone under her bridge to hold it back. She could feel rage bubbling, practically turning to steam within her so quickly she feared she might evaporate.

"Now a fucking dragon bit you," she railed, leaning forward so far that she almost fell as she fussed, fists raised. "So you think I'ma let you drop fang on me before your sneaky ass gets tested, huh? Girl. Girl? Oh, I got your girl right here in my fist—you no good, lying, pussy-chasing, Neteru-frontin' vampire bastard!"

He backed away from her, sniffing up the blood that tried to ooze out of his nose after the hard blow she'd landed and licked his split lip, his eyes pure silver rage. "Hit me again, hear? I'm tired of that shit, D. Least I ain't fall in love with nobody . . . what was that? Huh?"

"That's the best you can say to me? That's *all* you have to say? Yeah, and I'ma tell you why, because I ain't *doooo nuthin'* like you did!" She opened her arms, screamed, stomped her feet on the sand, and began walking in a circle. "Father God, help me, stay my hand, oh Lord, I'll kill him!"

"I don't have to explain nothing, D! You're the one who needs to tell me what's going on! I ain't have my shit all up in the family house, ain't get busted—"

"What, *whaaat?* Wait, wait, wait a damned minute," she said, singing it out, waving one hand with the pearl clutched in the other as evidence. "Oh, *whose* house didn't you have *what* in? Oh, you didn't get caught wrong, dead busted, up in *nobody's* house? Right? Come again?"

"No, see, see, uh uh, you going backward into the past, D! We talking about today, right here, right now, the bite—explain that to me!" he shouted, slapping the center of his chest hard. "Me. Your *husband!* The man who loves you. Tell *me* how in the *hell* some man who's supposed to be energy-depleted can do what we just saw Cain do on the beach and go home at will—unless his ass got a little more than a sip. Tell *me*— the man who walked through Hellfire for you and back—what? No words? Now you ain't got no comeback? No explanation, right? I ain't crazy, ain't blind! What the fuck went on out there in the woods, Damali?"

"Oh, you want an explanation, I got your explanation," she said in an unnaturally calm voice. Rage within her mind had gone so far over the top that she was standing outside her own body, speaking, witnessing some other crazed woman eviscerate some guy she used to know—she was going for his scrotum this time, so help her God. It was like watching a stage play.

Damali stared at the man before her. Carlos was nearly snorting fire as he waited for her to say something. Then she thought of the she-dragon's bite and almost blacked out from the fury spike.

"Unlike you," she said, seething, her words so loaded they quaked as they slipped between her teeth, "my explanation is sound, not a buncha rhetoric mixed up with a pack of lies."

"Den say whatchu gotta say, woman," Carlos replied through a silver glare, his arms wide, his expression arrogant, as he leaned forward and his voice took a falsely calm, sarcastic dip. "You're right, you ain't no little girl no more—you all woman now, so be a woman and say whatchugotta say. You grown, sho' you right. So don't be all dramatic, stalling for theatrical impact—spit it out, since you gonna tell me something about how that bite went down and make me understand the unthinkable."

"*That,*" Damali said coolly, her eyes narrowed, her tone slow and dangerous, "was *a woman,* making *new* choices, because she finally got tired of drama and dumb shit and she decided to let your ass twist."

Her statement had come out so evenly and so cold that for a moment he froze then slowly lowered his arms.

"*That* thing out there that happened, the unthinkable—as you call it—was what happened when *this* woman finally got to see that your ass ain't the baddest mutha in the valley, ain't got the smoothest game or fang entry, and now knows that there's somebody else out there who can obviously whip the power better than you—you've seen him work. *The brother's got skillz, baby.* And honor to go along with it. He knows how and when to put his hands on a woman, has patience, discipline, and doesn't have to tag everything that gets in *his face.* So when he brings something down, he brings it down *righteous.* Doesn't cuss . . . is smooth. Can be a female's friend without doing her, but if he wants to be more than a friend, saying no is a hard word to dredge out of a woman's vocabulary. Okay. Is that enough of an explanation for you? Did I mention he can sing? You've seen his spot; is there something else you need me to clarify? 'Cause if there is, lemme know."

She sucked her teeth and straightened her back. "Sorry, my bad, baby, I couldn't help myself 'cause I'm only human. So, when I got out there, hey. It didn't mean nothin', though. Don't dwell on it. You know I love you."

She waited patiently for him to say something else to her. Yeah, bring it. But to her surprise, Carlos's shoulders relaxed, the silver left his eyes and tears filled them instead, but they didn't fall. He just straightened his posture, nodded, and walked away.

Uh, oh . . . She knew there was this invisible line that the old girls had all told her about, but until this very moment, she wasn't sure where it was. She had no map, but now that she was here, she was inadvertently standing in the middle of the land of "never say certain things to your man."

Older married female Guardians had warned her not to go there; but her female vamp friend had said check it out, and she did—thought it might be a day trip, not a place of no return. Both sets of advisors had been right in their own way . . . but this strangely quiet, eerily serene place bordered on the perimeter of "never throw it in his face," another man's prowess.

She now saw with her own eyes that the river that flowed through it was the river of "you can't take it back, girl, once it's been said." Hell's Sea of Perpetual Agony was a wading pool compared to that muddy river, or maybe just a tributary that fed it. She wasn't sure which as she watched Carlos drowning in it. He went down without breathing, each cement-weighted step a thud as he walked toward the hacienda and saw that the family had witnessed it all. That's when he submerged and lowered his head.

Oh, Lord, this place where she'd tripped to was a bountiful terrain, with trees of knowledge, weeping willows, that dropped the fruit of "girl he's cut to the bone—are you crazy," at your feet. The road back was blocked by boulders, heavy words, pride, wounded ego, the air supercharged by scorching glares and deep hurt. No extraction team possible, once there you were on your own. Steep mountains surrounded this very surreal frontier: Mt. Say You're Sorry Before It's Too Late, Mt. He Ain't Neva Gonna Be the Same, Mt. Why'd You Go There . . . while female buzzards circled crushed male bones in the valley . . . his. Damali cringed.

Oh, shit . . . This no-man's zone didn't have atmosphere, no air for a woman's lungs, not if she was still in love but just angry. This was no place to be stranded if you still cared. She struggled to inhale slow breaths and began to feel weightless. Heaven help her, she'd gone too far.

This place was a very small speck in the cosmos, but loaded by mines that could nova and terminate a once-fertile world. Damned if she didn't tap dance over all it. Big border breach. Oh, shit . . . mortal wound. Okay, okay, okay . . . yeah, he'd had it coming, but why did she feel so awful once he'd dropped his blade in total defeat? Her heart pounded as her mind hollered after him: *Fight your way out of it, baby, you know how we do! This one just got a little rough, I was pissed off, that's all.*

The sweet taste of verbal victory was bitter and the TKO hollow, just as Marlene had promised. Damali briefly closed her eyes and sheathed her sharpest blade behind her pursed lips.

"All right," she finally shouted at Carlos's retreating back as he loped toward the house. Why did she suddenly want to cry? "My bad. Maybe

I went too far, but you have, too, and you have no right to be getting an attitude about anything I do, after all you've done!"

He didn't turn around. Didn't hold up his hand to stop her words, like old times or old fights. Didn't defend himself or hesitate or stop plodding toward the house. Her legs almost functioned on autopilot from her heart, but her pride kept overriding the bleating command to go to him and apologize on her knees. During the seconds of internal battle, while her wounded ego replayed all that he'd done wrong, her heart cancelled out each offense. But the contest was relentless, his wrongs leapt up, her rights stood to meet the challenge, his offenses versus hers dueled for dominance in her mind. Yet it was a draw. Still this wasn't a practice bout with dull blades, or a sparring match with head gear and mouthpieces. This time somebody got hurt.

Damali watched in quiet panic as Carlos quietly slipped into the house to bleed to death alone.

Stricken team Guardians stood on verandas. Marlene hung her head and closed the shutters to her window. Shabazz solemnly went back into the house. Rider sat down heavily on the steps like he'd been punched. Berkfield and Big Mike simultaneously ran slow palms over their bald scalps. The youngbloods shook their heads and disappeared without a word. Jose just looked at her as though his throat had been cut. Female teammates stood in shock, seeming unsure whether or not they should go toward her or let the mortally wounded rest in peace. The two new females quietly retreated as though they'd seen it all before and were ashamed to witness it here. Juanita's eyes held silent horror as she turned like a zombie, passed Jose without looking at him, and numbly walked back into the house. Sudden knowledge. The family would never be the same.

Marjorie stood like a statue, her wide eyes brimming, her hands twisting the bottom of her blouse. The cornerstones of the family had shifted out of place and crumbled. The entire pyramid was in jeopardy of fatal collapse. There was no mortar left between any of the bricks. The Caduceus was in Nod, but there were bodies all over the beach here that needed healing . . . yet she was no healer, she'd been fire, raw fury, a tongue tempest. Carlos had been no healer, he'd been a raging ocean, a nonrespecter of the fragile flora and fauna of emotions within the delicate ecosystem of the house.

How could they close a rip in the fabric of the universe, when they couldn't even close what had begun as a series of small tears until it became an energy-diffusing gulf that just sucked everyone in the household through it into a void? She didn't even know where to begin.

Damali took a walk down to the water line and simply stared at the sea.

@ CHAPTER SIXTEEN

La Paz was a beacon. Fight or flight hormone rocketed through him. He had to get off the island. Get back to the mainland. He had to get away from the house. Space. Distance. Anywhere but here. The small colonial town of La Paz had his name on it. He'd wade into the human pool of two hundred and sixty thousand people and disappear for a while. The City of Pearls.

Carlos headed straight for his room to grab his gear. His mind was so besieged that he couldn't materialize anything but a normal, physical escape. That's when he heard it, the distinctive click of a Glock nine hammer going back. A woman's wails—Juanita!

He skidded into the living room. Guardians had made a semicircle around her as she kept her shuddering body pressed against the fireplace mantle, a nine to her temple and her eyes closed. He stood helplessly watching as Jose's voice crooned to her in a steady, pleading tone.

" 'Nita, baby, listen," Jose said in a calm voice singed with hysteria. "I don't care what happened. I didn't see anything. I'm not blaming you. Let's talk about it. Just put the gun down, sweetheart. Do that for me, all right?"

Juanita released a piteous wail as her arm shook, sweat covering her body. Her eyes snapped open, tears streaming down her face. "But I'll know, forever," she whispered. "I can't live with that."

"Tell her something, man," Jose said through his teeth, his furious gaze briefly going to Carlos, and then becoming gentle when it went back to Juanita.

Sunlight danced off the gleaming silver. Carlos's line of vision sought it, then found Juanita's eyes. "I am so sorry, 'Nita. Please put the gun down."

Suddenly Juanita yanked the gun away from her head and trained it dead aim on Carlos, holding the weapon with both hands, just like Rider had shown her. "You bastard," she whispered. "I, of all people, didn't deserve that."

"No, you didn't," Carlos said calmly. "Of all the people in the world, you didn't deserve any of it."

Her arms shook as she lowered the gun. But as Jose took a step forward, she instantly returned the nine to her temple. "That's all I wanted to hear," she said quietly.

"Baby, listen," Jose said, slowly going to his knees. "I love you. There isn't anything else in the world that's important." Huge tears rose in his eyes. "Do you love me?"

She nodded as a fresh torrent raced down her face. "That's why . . . I don't deserve you," she said thickly, her hand shaking as she fingered the trigger. "You've been through so much. I betrayed you. You're such a good man. The whole family . . . I—"

"You'll kill me," Jose said quickly. "Pull the trigger, and you'll kill me. I swear to you I'll die without you."

The team held its breath as Juanita slowly pulled the gun back and lowered the weapon. Bitter sobs rang out through the house as she dissolved into a puddle of humanity on the floor. Jose went to her on his hands and knees, pried the weapon from her grip, put the safety on it, and slid it to Rider, and then gathered her into his arms to rock her as she wept.

Transfixed, every muscle in Carlos's body had been temporarily paralyzed by what he'd just witnessed. Profound agony; profound forgiveness. What had he done when he hadn't been in his right mind?

His younger Guardian brother had just shown him life-saving magic. Jose had demonstrated selfless healing, a power stronger than any he'd witnessed to date. Love that went beyond pride . . . a stronger contender had taken Jose's woman, yet he'd still possessed a quiet dignity that didn't fear the public humiliation, could care less what others thought or said. It wasn't about them, it was about salvaging what he had, saving a soul, repairing a broken spirit, letting the past rest, forgiving the weaknesses of the flesh, putting balm on a tortured mind, mending a shattered heart, and bringing all of it back into the Light with love. That was strength.

But the destroyed woman Jose rocked had also shown him something very deep in those sweat-tense moments. Emotional pain from being betrayed, the way that ripped through a woman's soul, shredded it, courier delivered it right to Hell's doorstep, then tipped it over the edge of the abyss and let it plummet with a mind, a beautiful body, and a gentle heart and spirit. Life, and all the generations of potential it contained, could have splattered against the stone fireplace wall just like that. From bullshit.

The huge living room was too small. He couldn't breathe. All eyes slowly turned to him. He knew the attack was coming, the emotional lunge eminent.

"That was your brother, man," Shabazz said quietly. His expression had gone to a serene place beyond rage to contain total disbelief. "Now I understand why Damali did what she did."

Accusation glittered in all eyes. He was out. They didn't understand shit.

"How could you?" Marjorie whispered, her eyes holding so much hurt that it scored his mind and opened it.

"How could I?" Carlos shouted as the faces around him became blurry. Something fragile within him frayed and snapped. It happened so fast that it burned past his internal filter.

Everything that had happened to him ripped to the forefront of his mind. The angels' commands. His accidental fall into the Chairman's throne . . . and oh, did he let them see the transformation in living color. A shriek pierced his ears. He didn't know if it was Krissy's or Inez's, but he didn't care. They wanted to know why he would have done anything to get out of Nod. They wanted to know why he'd die, first, before ever being incarcerated in a foreign realm again? They wanted to know why he feared being weak and at the mercy of another more powerful entity?

He gave them Hell on the silver platter of his mind. His mind spit out the horrid slurry it contained. The Chairman's torture wall, the burning sun. Every entity on every level that he'd seen when he'd tripped into the pit. Then he let them see his prayers on the Arizona plains in Damali's backyard. Let them feel the battle to get something so terrifying out of his system and the white-knuckle-producing fear of knowing that he was a virus, an agent of destruction, a carrier of demonic possession, a disease he feared more than cancer.

He didn't care that their bodies had sunk to the floor. He didn't care that the team was breathing hard, panting through the fantastic images that not even their worst nightmares could have produced. He didn't care that Bobby vomited, or that Rider was clutching his chest. Fuck it, they wanted to know. Fuck it, they'd already judged him. Fuck it, they could walk a mile in his shoes!

"That's what happened!" Carlos shouted, his gaze a laser on each Guardian in the room. "No, it wasn't her fault. Yes, it was wrong and fucked up. Am I sorry, oh . . . you have no idea."

Glassy-eyed stares met him. But the only person who had not dropped to the floor was Marlene. She stood straight, not a tear in her eyes. Her arms were folded over her chest, and her voice was scary calm.

"Now that you have blown our minds and stolen our peace forever," she quietly said, "we have a better understanding of what went down."

Carlos nodded. "Good. Then we're clear."

Marlene nodded. "Clarity works both ways, darlin'. Let me show you something, all right?"

"No," Carlos said. "I don't need to see—"

"Oh, *yes* you do," Marlene said, her voice so slow, so deadly that he instantly raised a shield to his mind.

"Lock with me," she whispered. "Just me and you, one-on-one."

Carlos shook his head no. He'd never been afraid of any human in his life, but as he looked at Marlene, something told him she was about to mentally kick his ass. As soon as the thought crossed his mind, she smiled a tight, angry smile of knowing.

"Drop that fucking mental shield," she said, sweeping toward him at a velocity he didn't know she owned.

It freaked him out so badly that he actually raised the golden shield of Heru to keep her back, and to his complete horror, a purple arc deflected it. Marlene drew his energy into her palm and sent it crashing to the floor. Guardians started, but didn't get up off the floor. Everyone seemed rooted where they sat.

"I have had *enough*," Marlene said, never raising her voice. "This family is on the brink of collapse. A house divided can never stand, and we must stand united against the unimaginable, or all will be lost. What would have been our purpose?" She cocked her head to the side and folded her arms again. "Generations are to be built on your Neteru shoulders. The family is the *cornerstone* of communities yet to come.

Decimate that because of lusts and passions and rages and foolishness, and there is no family—*no foundation,* therefore, no future."

She got up in his face, unafraid. There was something in her eyes so old, so wise, that the strength of ancestral knowledge wafted from her in molten energy bands to surround him.

"So, today, you *are* going to mind lock with me, or we'll fight all over this hacienda until I tackle your young, stupid ass to the floor, sit on your chest, and force-feed the knowledge to you!" She walked away from him and stood across the room like a Western gunfighter. "Open your mind. Don't make me go in there by force."

The challenge bristled within Carlos. Fucking Harpies hadn't been able to go into his mind by force, and Marlene wasn't gonna stand there and threaten him, not today! Not after all the drama he'd been through.

"You can try, but I'd advise you to back off. You've seen what's in there, and that was just a peek."

"I don't want what's in your brain," she replied coolly, "I'm gonna give you what's in mine."

Carlos set his jaw hard and looked out the window toward the vacant beach. "There ain't nothing you can tell me, Mar, that I don't already know."

"How did I break your shield, then?"

Now she had his attention.

"Because what I've got can go through any substance in the universe."

Carlos just stared at her. Now he really wasn't letting Marlene get all up in his head. Uh-uh. He folded his arms. "I said, back off."

"I told your ass no, boy. Come here!"

"What?" he said, so indignant that he almost couldn't get the words out. "I ain't no boy."

Marlene shook her head. Shabazz stood up.

"Mar. Don't do it," Shabazz said. "You're tired, baby, and he doesn't know how—"

"'Bazz," she said quickly. "I got this. Don't step in between me and this kid. I'ma spank his ass today, so help me. It's bigger than him and Damali. The rest of my family got put at risk. He has to get this lesson down, now, once and for all!" Her voice escalated as she began pacing. "I will not tolerate dissention in the house to this degree! I'm not having it! I'm not going to have my family splinter and fall apart while he learns!

Enough, 'Bazz. Sit down." She spun on Carlos. "I'ma ask you one last time."

Carlos had backed up to a far wall. The fact that Marlene was slightly scaring him made him worry. He didn't want to be in a position to have to fight her. If she got hurt, then they'd really never forgive him. "Mar, I'm warning you—"

"Don't make me snatch you across this room. I said, come *here*." Her eyes blazed with righteous indignation.

The sight of her challenge with the threat embedded in it did something crazy to him. She'd called him a boy in front of onlookers. What was left of his pride had already flattened on the beach. He just couldn't take it anymore. Not another indignity. He battle bulked, dropped fang, and glared at her, feeling the hot scorch of silver enter his irises. "I said *no*. What part of that didn't you hear, Marlene?"

"That's it!" A violet current ejected from her outstretched hand and seized Carlos's chest. "*Nothing* I feed, nothing I hold to my heart, nothing I care for and let into my home to be with my daughter will ever threaten me or this family! Ever!"

Jose was up with a gun in his hand, but to Carlos's surprise, Marlene slapped it away with an arc, yet could still hold him.

"This is between him and me," Marlene said coolly. "Nary a Guardian move, hear! I'm not afraid of him, never was."

Carlos battled Marlene's hold, trying to send a silver arc through it to break it, but her hold was too strong. "Lemme go, Mar!" he shouted, twisting in her violet light and trying to get it off of him.

But Marlene's eyes remained steady. "You wanna blow me away? Do it. You wanna punch me or knock me down? Do it. Want to rip out my throat? You already tore out my heart, so do it. I can take it. Hit me with your best shot."

Fury and frustration collided within him as he grappled with this old woman's superior mental hold. She'd found the black box, hit the invisible seam of it with what felt like a crowbar and was lifting it.

"Get off me, Mar!" he screamed. "Get out of my head!"

Marlene didn't speak as his conscience began to slowly leak out of the black box in his mind. It oozed onto the floor of his psyche like sepia-hued blood. Suddenly he was on his knees sobbing, and she'd pissed him off so badly that he hurled an energy ball at her, but to his surprise she caught it and cast it away.

"Put that down, boy," she said softly, "and come to me without a fight."

The tone of her voice lifted the lid off the box and everything came out, just poured it all on the floor until he was mentally standing in it waist deep.

"Stop, Mar," he begged, sobbing harder than he ever had in his life. He could feel her warm body come down to kneel beside him. A pair of aging arms surrounded him, even as he tried to shrug them away. Healing hands petted his back. A gentle rock made more liquid sludge pour out of the black box. He was drowning, couldn't breathe. Marlene breathed for him.

"I didn't mean to hurt anybody," he said into a strong, bony shoulder.

"I know, baby," Marlene whispered. "Get all the poison out. Give it to me, I know what to do with it, but I'ma hafta show you what it feels like to carry it on the other side."

Emotional pain so severe stabbed his conscience until he wailed.

"That's what she's feeling," Marlene whispered. "Because that's how much she loves you." Marlene allowed everything that Damali had been through to pass from her heart into his.

"Oh, God, stop, Mar."

Marlene just shook her head. "You know how much that girl loves you, baby? You know how conflicted she is? You know what she felt each time you did some man-crazy drama and twisted her heart into knots? Feel it. Embrace it. Know it, up close and personal."

His fist went to his chest. His heart stopped beating and seized, and then restarted. He turned and vomited, but Marlene didn't move or let him go as his body slumped.

"She carried your baby . . . feel her womb contract and ignite with life. Feel that joy and the fear—the cold sweat of it," Marlene whispered through her teeth. "Now feel it clawed out of her, and her heart along with it."

"Oh, shit, oh shit . . . Marlene, for the love of God . . ." His sobs had turned to hiccupping wails.

"Yes," Marlene said calmly. "For the love of God."

He sobbed so hard and long that other Guardians stood and came to circle the twosome on the floor. He could feel fangs in his mouth, yet Marlene still held him.

"That's enough, Marlene," Shabazz said in a tender voice. "Let the boy go before he has a nervous breakdown."

"No," Marlene whispered. "I'm taking him to the rock."

"Mar, darlin', please listen to Shabazz," Rider said, going down on his knees beside her. "Can't no man endure going to the rock like that. C'mon, baby, I know you're angry . . ."

Marlene kept her eyes tightly shut. "Rider, back off, before I take you there too, for Tara. There's not a man in this room that I can't take here, so you go find a place of peace and rest while I work—but *do not* interrupt me again. We clear?"

Rider stood quickly and paced away to the wall. Berkfield backed up, glanced at his wife, and lowered his gaze. Big Mike began to walk in a circle as Carlos's wails escalated to the point where it made him cry. Jose squeezed his eyes shut and clung to Juanita. Dan, J.L., and Bobby were leaning on furniture, the walls, anything that would hold them up while they sucked in hard breaths. But the women in the group remained steadfast, standing in a ring around Marlene as she worked.

"Bring it all up, Marlene," Inez whispered. "I remember my girl . . . how she loved him when we was kids."

"Uhmmm, hmmm . . ." Marlene muttered and then sent a whisper into Carlos's ear. "When she held out hope that you would leave the streets."

His head dropped back as a new wave of nausea claimed him.

Juanita had left Jose's arms and moved forward on her hands and knees. "When she had to leave you, and I took her place," she said quietly. "She was devastated."

"For every woman you burned. Every heart you played with. Every hope you dashed. Every man you left feeling some type of way, because his woman was marked by you, feel it," Marlene whispered harshly against his temple. "A woman's mind is not a playground, Carlos, whether you love her or not. Her body is not a jungle gym . . . her heart not a roller-coaster to take on spiking highs and plunging lows. Noooo . . . baby, you gonna get this straight today. You took Damali and Juanita on the tilt-a-wheel, honey. Let's go there now."

A new wave of sobs invisibly split Carlos's chest wide open, carving at the soft tissue from the inside out. "I know . . ." he choked. "I know."

"The look on her face," Marjorie whispered, her eyes distant as the vision entered her mind. "When you came back from the ashes . . ."

"Don't tell me, don't tell me," Carlos pleaded, but Krissy was now touching his shoulder.

"The way she would look at you every time you entered the room . . . oh, Carlos, she loves you so much. Why would you think otherwise?"

"I don't know . . ." he wailed, finding Marlene's shoulder to bury his face into it.

"Now do you understand what's at stake? What's at risk? What you were about to throw away?"

He fervently nodded against the older woman's shoulder, so completely exhausted all he could do was breathe.

"Do you understand," Marlene said, "how your actions, no matter how justified you think they were, still hurt her . . . still sent her to a place no lover should go?"

Again, all he did was fervently nod.

"She could forgive your transgressions. But what continually ate at her until it broke her down was that you wouldn't take part ownership, wouldn't validate how *she felt.* You could only see your side of it, how *you felt.* But in all these changes you've gone through, *she* was the injured party. *She* was the one holding the line while you learned and bumped your head against life. But you never acknowledged her sacrifice to regally hold the line on behalf of something greater than her—your relationship, and *you never* called her a queen—which is what *she is! That* was the crux of it. She instinctively knew that the whole was greater than the sum of the parts . . . old mathematics, ancient wisdom of synergy. Women invented it. It comes from beyond Kemet. We gave it to them."

A sheen of sweat had formed on Marlene's brow, but she wouldn't relent or release Carlos from her tight grip as she spoke slowly, with purpose and definition in every word. "It's not that she couldn't forgive what happened several times for various reasons, but your acknowledgment that she had a right to *feel* the way she did about it never came from a true place of contrition within your soul—*and she felt that, too.*"

Marlene's warm hands continued to pet his back, rubbing the purification salt of truth into the freshly opened wound, making him wince with every stroke across his sweat-drenched shirt. "*That* is how another man got into your household, baby. It wasn't because of anything she hurled at you on the beach."

When new sobs overtook him, Marlene's voice became gentler, but also more firm. "If your fortification was strong . . . you could be blind, crippled, poverty stricken, disease ridden, and no knight in shining armor could have ever breached your barriers. *He* didn't seduce her, *you* abandoned her heart. *He* didn't pull her, *you* pushed her away. *He* didn't have more power, *you* relinquished yours. It is just that simple, honey."

"Marlene, I didn't know . . . I didn't understand," Carlos whispered harshly, unable to even lift his head. His body went limp against hers. His size normalized and his fangs retracted. All the energy within him felt like it had spilled out onto the terra-cotta stone floor.

"*That's* how a woman's mind works," Marlene murmured, now stroking his hair. "And she would have had your babies, fangs and all. Would have raised her Isis against any encroachment of disrespect to your kingdom. And would have died fighting to protect your dignity, your ego, and your honor . . . but you didn't *validate* how *she felt*—*you* did that. Not Cain. He didn't pull her away because he was the better man. He's strong, yes, but no man can go up against a pure love like that and win. That's a wall of pure white Light. That's how I was able to cast aside your shield—with pure love . . . because I love you like a mother, Carlos. Ain't no shield for that. I want you two kids to work it out. Heal this family. Get yourselves together. Stop hurting each other and therefore hurting the rest of us. You muddied the waters, not just by your actions, but by what you didn't validate within her. That's where the first, critical brick fell away from the wall . . . the tower began to lean, and then you both kept chipping at it until it came down. Now you've gotta rebuild from the rubble, brick by heavy brick." She sighed. "It didn't have to be all of this."

He could hear his mother's words, his grandmother's entreaties, could see every pair of hurt female eyes looking at him. His brothers' women, wishing their men weren't in the drug life. Mothers from the neighborhood standing over caskets so bereft that no more tears would fall. Mothers with young sons sending prayers up to God on their knees to spare theirs from the same fate. Women pacing the floors at night waiting on some errant male that was connected to his energy to return home. Damali's worried eyes, that time she'd come to his club, decimated him. Moreover he could feel the vastness of their multiple feminine disappointment, their broken spirits, their unrequited hopes . . . the magnitude of it nearly sprawled him out on the floor.

"How do I make it right?" Carlos whispered. There was no resistance, no game, no fraud, or false pride left within him. He'd been taken to the rock so hard and body slammed against it that the Chairman's wall now seemed like it had been made of foam rubber.

Marlene gently held him back and wiped his face with her hands. Love seeped from her palms as he stared down at the floor, too ashamed to meet her tender gaze.

"Baby, look at me," she murmured.

He shook his head. "I can't."

She lifted his chin with an easy, slow placement of her palm beneath his chin until their gazes locked. "You are a good man. Just young. This lesson you just learned in fifteen agonizing minutes, some men take thirty years to get. Some never learn it at all. You're blessed, even if you don't feel like it at the moment." Marlene sighed and smoothed his disheveled hair. "This was a hard gift, but I had to give it to you." She smiled. "You saved my life, so it was my debt to save yours. Like you always say, fair exchange is no robbery, Carlos."

He smiled weakly and closed his eyes, too fatigued to reply.

"Do you understand that I did this from a place in my heart that is held especially for you?" Her tender gaze made him open his weary eyes and stare at her. Marlene nodded. "That's right. I've claimed you as one of my own, baby. That's why I called you 'boy.' Not because you aren't a man. But because you're mine. Hear?"

He nodded and looked down as new tears streamed down his face. "I'm sorry, Mom."

"I know you are," she whispered. "That's why I'm willing to go through all of this with you."

"How did you get so wise?" he asked, his voice raw and thick. He wiped his nose with the back of his hand and stared at her.

"Because I've had the privilege to lie under the wings of angels," she said, closing her eyes as the group simply looked at her. A serene expression came over Marlene's tired face, adding a surreal glow to it that was lit from an inner, unknown source. "I crossed over, too," she murmured without opening her eyes. "My body was burning. I was in so much pain that I couldn't even scream, then this magnificently caring being dropped over me and shielded me from predators. He sent healing white Light of pure love into the very marrow of my bones. The pain receded, even as someone slit my throat. He didn't know me from a can of paint, but he loved me, cared that I survived, and hoped if I died I'd go out in the white light of blissful surrender."

Tears rolled down Marlene's cheeks as she spoke. She stood with effort and clasped her arms about herself. "He made me see the wrongs

I've done, too. Made me purge my secrets, rethink my actions, feel the effects they had on others. I had to face my own shit for the pain to stop." She glanced down at Carlos and offered him her hand to help him stand. "I'm not perfect. None of us in this room are. We don't judge you, because you're right, we've never taken a walk in your shoes. But now that you know how we feel, that should temper your behavior from this point forward. This gift that was given to me, I pass it to you." She glanced at Shabazz. "I owe you a serious apology. But we'll talk about that later, privately."

Shabazz nodded and swallowed hard. "You got all that over in Nod?"

"Yeah," she whispered.

Carlos's gaze sought the window, hoping he'd see Damali down at the beach. "I just wish I could fix this, Marlene. I don't even know where to begin."

She came to him and gently cradled his face with both palms. For some unknown reason, every time that she touched him, new tears fell. It was as though her hands contained a siphon, finding deeply hidden reservoirs of unspent emotion tucked away in wells he was unaware of until now.

"First, let me tell you . . . I know my daughter. She loves you."

"After all I've done, she has a right not to, and I can't blame her."

"She has a right to, but her heart made a choice not to follow that advice." Marlene offered him a tender smile and kissed his third eye in the center of his forehead. "Open that up. She still loves you." Marlene pressed her forefinger where her lips had swept. "May I go in and tell you something?"

Carlos gave Marlene a half-smile. "Do I have a choice?"

She chuckled and shook her head no.

"I didn't think so," he said, yielding to her.

Marlene hugged him and rested her head on his shoulder. *You are her king. There will never be another one that can ever take your throne. Another man might sit in it, but you own it. She stands behind you, before you, beside you . . . as a queen, she moves, her role shifts, depending on the circumstances to guard the kingdom—which is what you two build together. If she ever stands before you, it is not because she doesn't respect you, it's because duty calls. You must understand that. When she stands by your side, it is because she is your equal partner. When she stands behind you, it is not because she's to be your submissive mate; she is choosing to stand aside because it is your time to reign. You must learn to be what you are, a king. Your queen has been waiting for you to accept the responsibility*

*with dignity . . . because she'd tired and wants to stand down for a while . . .
all you have to do is be ready to stand up—without taking her dignity in the
process.*

But, Marlene, there's no denying he's better—

Hush, boy, and listen to your mother, hear what this old woman's got to say.

Carlos nodded and relaxed again.

*You've been bitten by another, now she's been bitten by another. That was a
breach of flesh. It is done. Inconsequential, given all you two have endured as
one. But Cain never entered her royal chamber—not what's between her legs, I
can't speak to that. That's simply her court. Yes, there were thieves in the castle.
Regrettable, but not—*

Marlene petted his back when he bristled. "Shush," she whispered.
"Hear me out, baby, what I'ma tell you is profound."

She waited until Carlos settled against her again, even though his hug
was tense. *Her royal chamber where her deepest secrets are held, the blueprints to
an empire, the keys to all that matters, is her heart. You are in there. He couldn't
pry that open with a crowbar. She held her Isis high, stood before it, and fought
him off valiantly. She didn't even allow him to nick her throat over the first bite
you gave her . . . think, man, think.*

Carlos pulled back and looked at Marlene, his hug slowly easing to a
gentle embrace as he quieted his spirit and laid his cheek against the
crown of her head. *Oh, Mar . . .*

*Yeah, baby, now you listen to old Marlene. She reserved an ounce of hope that
her king's cavalry would come. You're her kin. I keep trying to tell you. She's
standing at the door, guarding her heart, exhausted, bone weary, nearly defeated,
but would rather die than allow another to take your throne . . . and she's weeping down at the beach, spent. She knows she went too far with her words, I know
my child, if I don't know nothing else . . . but her king, you, her lover, her friend
accused her of treason, and she lost her mind, drew on you, because all she could
think of was how loyal she'd been. Go to her, after you contemplate all that I've
told you. Take back your throne, majestic child of mine . . . filled with potential,
and start you a world. Never look back.*

Carlos nodded and slowly withdrew from Marlene's embrace.

She patted his cheek and folded her arms. "Now, was that so bad?"

"No," he said quietly, his gaze slipping beyond the window. "Thank
you."

"I want you to do something for me," Marlene said, bringing Carlos's
attention back to her.

"Yeah, Mar. Anything." His gaze searched hers. After this, Marlene Stone had his utmost respect and loyalty.

"I want you to use that exquisitely analytical mind of yours to work out a puzzle for me."

Somewhat taken aback, for a moment he could only stare at her. The other Guardians did, too.

"All right," he said slowly, not sure where she was headed.

"Let me say this straight. I don't like him. Too smooth. Something's shaky."

Nervous chuckles passed around the team, and a half-smile tugged at Carlos's face.

"Like I said, Mar. Anything."

She walked to the window, leaned on the sill, and gave them all her back to watch as she spoke. "Number one," she said, her voice no longer mellow. There was battle strategy in it. "I want you to step past the pain and insecurity, Carlos, and dissect everything that older, smoother Neteru male showed you how to do."

Her words stung, and he didn't immediately answer. She turned and looked at him hard, like a mother sending her child out to fight a bigger kid in the neighborhood to squash the bullying once and for all.

"You listen to me, Carlos Rivera. You have the best mind that I have ever sensed on the planet. That guy is older, so suck his brain dry. I want you to go back over everything you saw him do, and *master it*. You got that? Learn from your enemy. That is your charge. You saw him heal in a new way, use the Caduceus. You saw him materialize raw ether. Saw whatever, but learn it. Don't let him beat you because you don't feel like you measure up. You're a Neteru, too. Both have a little vamp in your DNA. He's a king, but dammit, you're one, too, and this is *your* yard!" She walked a hot path between the window and him.

As Marlene railed he could feel new vertebrae being added to his spine, making him taller, making his head lift higher. Sho', she was right.

"That's right, man," Shabazz said, pointing at him. "You learn quick. He developed his shit over several thousand years, but on this side of the rip, you got him. You just have to sidestep the rage."

Big Mike pounded Shabazz's fist. "That's a slick bastard. Shit, you one, too. Sooo . . . feel me?"

"Right," Rider said, nodding and coming to Carlos to shake his hand. "Listen, young buck, he ain't coming into this family without a fight."

"One team," J.L. said.

"One cause," Dan echoed.

"You family, he ain't," Jose said with a nod. "Peace."

"Peace," Carlos murmured. "And many apologies."

"I don't even know whatchu talking about, man," Jose said.

Both Carlos and Jose nodded.

"I done tol' y'all I ain't like him," Inez said, her hands on her hips. "If I have to feed him, I'll poison his ass first. And, if he gets in my girl's face, I'll work on her mind and talk about him like a dawg until she screams, hear? Oh, I know how to break 'em up, if it goes there, puh-lease." Inez sucked her teeth and made everyone laugh.

The release that went through the room was so torrid that one by one, people sat down to rest not only weary bodies, but spirits.

"Carlos, we're not supposed to be in it to this degree," Marjorie said, her soothing, motherly tone breaking through the mirth, but also adding to it. "But we moms know how to mount a campaign to . . . sort of . . . derail things, if we must. You're our favorite . . . sooo . . ."

"My mother can derail *anything*," Bobby said, laughing and giving her a hug.

"My aunt Gabby ain't no slouch, either," Krissy offered. "If you need an extra ace up your sleeve . . . uh, we know some people who know some people, like Shabazz always says, right, Mom?"

Heather and Jasmine shared a glance.

"With me and Jasmine and Krissy on it, we could probably make him have all sorts of problems," Heather said with a shrug. "Warts . . . lesions?"

Jasmine smiled. "I could draw him very, very small." She winked and then covered her mouth to laugh behind her hand.

"Not allowed, ladies," Rider said, raising an eyebrow with a smirk. "That's cold. I'm gonna have to talk to Gabby, and you two are gonna have to do a round with the Covenant before we turn you loose on anybody. Sheesh!"

"Okay, Rider, maybe not warts, but I could zap him," Krissy said, glancing at her mother. "What? He'd never know it was me."

"Well, maybe just a bee sting zap . . . aimed just so," Marjorie said, pointing low on her body.

"Aw, Lawd," Marlene said, chuckling. "The Berkfield girls are ready to work juju for you, son, and put roots on Damali for ya, so you'd better handle your bizness."

"I got this," Carlos said, chuckling. "Aw'ight, aw'ight, nobody do nothing crazy. I've done enough of that myself."

Juanita's quiet move to the sofa made everyone go still. She looked up, her face red and puffy. But her eyes glittered with a level of strength that no one had ever seen. "All this was supposed to happen," she said in soft, faraway voice. "Sometimes you have to burn down a whole house to get to one rat." She looked at Carlos tenderly. "You aren't that rat. Cain is."

All eyes were on Juanita as she twisted her hands in her lap and kept her gaze lowered. "It's not Yonnie that Lilith is gonna put on the Chairman's old throne . . . it's Cain." She peered up at Carlos. "I felt it as I was ready to die. I had some of the other Carlos inside my head—that's who hurt me, not you."

Marlene and Marjorie were at Juanita's side in an instant, each holding one of her hands. Jose was at her back, both hands on her shoulders, his forehead resting on the crown of her head with his eyes closed. Carlos went to her and knelt to be eye level with her.

"Oh, my God, Juanita," Carlos whispered. "I'm so—"

"I saw it," Juanita said quietly. Her voice was so peaceful and so far away that it almost echoed. "Padre Lopez held my hand. He said not to let Cain learn more about the advances and weapons on this side." She glanced at Carlos and then Jose. "He's not supposed to learn this realm."

The rest of the team gathered near her as she stared at Carlos. Suddenly her body convulsed, sending panic through the group as her eyes rolled back in her head, showing only the whites. Carlos was on his feet as the two seers held her tightly. Jose began to rock her against him in horror.

"She's burning up," Jose said, rushing around the couch to better hold her. "Do something!"

"Don't touch her," Marlene said. "She's in a trance. I got her." Marlene moved around and waved to stand Carlos closer. "Let her pull from you."

"I was the only one on this team who had ever slept with you before you went vamp," Juanita said in garbled voice. "I was the one who knew your weak spots . . . your entire family, from mother, to grandmother, to brothers. They couldn't get to Damali, but they got to me to break this family down. I was the weak link, and when they thought I was about to commit suicide that darkness went down to the last place they'd had you—my essence linked with yours on the throne of Dante. For a split second, I saw it. Cain doesn't even know he's being manipulated. Lilith must have a Neteru with Dante's line in him to appease her husband. Without that, she cannot appease the Beast. I'm female, she's female, Damali is female; Lilith's fear of her husband is also resonating from that throne. She cannot fail."

"Mar, she's going over the edge," Jose said, terror gripping his every word as Juanita's voice became more gravelly. "She's not an experienced seer, and she's going in too deep! Pull her out!"

"Pull her out, Mar," Carlos warned. "Fuck a Level Seven extraction—we'll figure out another way, but shut 'Nita down before something happens to her."

Marlene just shook her head. "Let her work, this is what we do. It's scary . . . talk, 'Nita. What does the Beast want?"

"Lilith has worked on this family night and day . . . worked on Damali to get her to break the walls of Nod. To break you, Carlos. If Cain sits on Dante's throne, he'll be the only ruling-level vampire, other than you, that has ever tasted Damali's blood . . . in the woods at the old house, they worked on them both, drove you insane . . . will break Eve's heart . . . will fracture the Neteru Queen Council . . . will come for your old line . . . Yonnie, Tara, Jose . . . will release the forsaken. The Beast is waiting for this to occur. They think all have been positioned for the fall . . . but they didn't know how much I loved you all, my family, more than heartbreak. They didn't know the priest angel held my hand . . . or was in the line to know, to remember."

Just as suddenly as the trance began, Juanita lurched forward, shaking, sweating, and threw up a black mass of tadpole-like creatures, then slumped against Marlene, panting. "That's all I got," she said through heaving breaths. "Did I do okay, Mar?"

"Douse it, Mike!" Marlene said quickly, scattering Guardians to bring whatever purifiers they had in their arsenals. "Get my black bag—baby, it's gonna be all right, you did good, real good, for a first vision out."

Guardians bombed the black slurry on the floor with every salt, holy water, anointing oil, and garlic concoction they could find. Marlene rummaged in her black bag as Shabazz held it open, and extracted crystallized frankincense to hurl at the dark puddle, her lips moving in a fervent murmur. Hands clasped, prayers filled the air, and they watched the abomination sizzle and burn away in a sulfur plume, then disappear.

"All this time . . ." Carlos stood staring at the floor, remembering exactly where the dark fluid filled with black, maggoty parasites came from. He almost vomited himself as he turned away, disgusted. And that it had been deep within Juanita from the breach shamed him to no end.

"It wasn't you, bro," Shabazz said, shaking his head. "Now all this shit makes sense . . . from the contagion on—from Philly, really, they've been jacking with us from Level Seven, sending bullshit our way day and night. Damn!" He looked at Carlos and walked over to him to land a hand on his shoulder. "You all broken up and emotional, me, Damali all out of sorts, Kamal flipping, this scene in here, think about it, my brother, even vamps tripping, Rider, no one was exempt in the house . . . everybody was all fucked around, man . . . it wasn't just you."

"Cain's gotta stay in Nod," Carlos said, his tone serious and even. "Not just for personal reasons, the brother is being set up. His queen mother's spirit will die of heartbreak, if Lilith pulls this off . . . then Adam will turn over the Roundtable and wig. This is *way* bigger than some bastard in Damali's face."

"Yeah, but like you say, Carlos—knowledge is power." Marlene's arms enfolded Juanita as she smoothed her hair back. Marlene looked up at Jose and then Carlos. "Didn't I tell you, love conquers all? They were banking on jealousy, team dissent, but our girl Juanita here came through like a champ—forgiving Carlos, loving him and this family hard, and loving Jose harder . . . enough to wanna live. Plus, they never banked on a young cleric they'd killed, one still connected as a brother to this team, still bound by love to three souls: Juanita, Carlos, and Jose. Have mercy! Bless this chile; her spirit followed the thin white line up and out of the darkness holding information in her."

Marlene closed her eyes, crooning to Juanita to calm her. "Bet the bastards never counted on that, though, and now we've got their asses."

℮ CHAPTER SEVENTEEN

Without really being conscious of where she was going, her legs had taken her to a rock-hewn corner of the beach, far away from the hacienda to sit alone under the bright rays of morning sun. Her heart was so heavy that she was sure it had stopped beating. Guilt kept her chest tight, and squeezed the air from her lungs, forcing her to make an effort to inhale.

Damali straddled a small puddle of clear water and stared down into it. Seashells glistened in the shallow tide pool. Tiny crabs moved about. Grains of sand floated and resettled as a gentle breeze intermittently wafted over the water. She lowered the troublesome pearl into it and watched it drift to the bottom.

It sat there like a nickel-sized pink-white jewel, absorbing the sun rays. Maybe some lucky, poverty-stricken person would find it and be able to hock it. She'd never seen a pearl that large and knew the pinkish color had to come from the she-dragon's essence added to a natural pearl. As she'd walked with it, the gem had warmed in her hand and then gone cool. She knew in that moment the last flicker of life had been extinguished within the bizarre creature on the other side.

But as much as she'd wanted to hold on to rage within her about what had happened with her man, she felt nothing but love from the pearl, and oddly felt sorry for the crazy, mixed-up dragon. There was no anger, no animosity, no negative charge coming from the pearl it had left. All she felt radiating from it was a free spirit, one with no malice of intent. The bite had been pure pleasure. There was no encroachment ever designed into it.

Damali picked the pearl back up and placed it in her palm, staring at it with new eyes. "Who were you?" she whispered.

Her gaze went to the sea. If it had dragon essence on it, no human needed to have it—who knew what it carried? She was about to stand to pitch the pearl to a much larger place that it deserved to get lost in when it began to glow. Damali slowly lowered it back into the water to wash it off, and to make sure that her eyes weren't just playing tricks on her. The sun was bright, she was weary, and all this madness had undoubtedly messed up her mind.

"A dragon's gift," a light, disembodied female voice whispered on the breeze, yet it was also coming from inside the underwater pearl at the same time.

Damali looked around, sensing, and then looked down at the now-white-glowing pearl, and talked directly to it as she kept her palm submerged. "Why did you give this to me?"

"Because you needed to know," the pearl quietly replied, each word causing a slight strobe beneath the clear water.

"Yeah, well, I know you bit him, but I ain't mad—"

"Good. Because I gave him something, too."

Damali frowned. "I'll pitch your little pink ass—"

"Wait," it whispered. "I gave him insight."

Damali could feel herself about to get angry again, but something about what this dragon pearl said made her need to hear more.

"I was Cain's lover for years," it murmured. "The Neteru needed my insight."

Damali stared at the stone. Oh, shit . . . Carlos had been right. Information she'd gleaned from her journey to Ethiopia and at the Neteru Council of Queens began to refresh in her mind and then slam it. The inscription at the Isis Temple in Egypt almost made her stand up. An epiphany. The queens had forecasted one was coming. "Okay," Damali whispered more reverently, "talk to me."

"He needed to learn how to heal," it whispered quickly, harshly, but with a loving vibration emanating from it. "How to throw energy. To do all that Cain knows how to do. It is resident within him, takes time to perfect, but he does not have the benefit of time. My bite was a peace offering, actually, to you. I taught him, so you could receive that gift as well."

Although Damali didn't like the sound of it, and it had the ring of dragon double-talk, she was more curious than wary. "All right, then. Say, if I were to go with that theory. I haven't witnessed—"

"He is afraid," the pearl whispered. "He is insecure."

"Carlos insecure? Puhlease," Damali scoffed. "He musta really blew your mind when—"

"No," the pearl argued, becoming a darker shade of pink as though agitated. "I felt it running all through him. Cain inspired that. Something else darker did, too."

"Deep." Damali just peered at the pearl and brought it up out of the water. But then it went still until she submerged it again.

"Thank you. I need the pools of natural waters to work."

Damali chuckled in awe. "Wow. So, you're like a minioracle. A cosmic iPod that just downloaded dragon essence, huh? Too freaky."

"All the best oracles use them," it murmured. "I am the newest and last made. I am rare. Do not cast me away. You will need me."

"Whoa . . ."

"Cain is not who you think."

Damali stopped smiling. "Who is he?"

"Dante's son. He is aware that you have slain his father. He means you no direct harm, in fact, you have helped his cause. He is infatuated with you, truly he is, but will wreak havoc on your world."

Damali almost stood up again.

"His seduction skills are unsurpassed. He has seduced you. His mother; an able queen. He had seduced Carlos to believe that he cannot match him. He has seduced your family into turmoil, so that you cannot stand united as one. The houses of the Covenant are embroiled in dissension over his reappearance. This is why they cannot come together to aid you this time. His is the ultimate seduction. There is also something he wants from another female I dare not name."

"Oh, shit."

"You must guard yourself. He can now cross the barrier at will. He will build an empire. You will be essential, as his goal is to sire with your superior Light energy. You mesmerize him, your energy is so strong. He demands the best. Your lineage is important. I do not know if he has chosen to rule the Light or dark side, but he is positioning you to be the conduit for his heirs, nonetheless."

"How? How can he cross? That can't happen!"

"All he needed was one sip from another Neteru, a strong female to balance his dominant male energy. You gave him the protoplasm. I felt it as you ran on the beach. I began sealing my essence into the pearl as I made my choice in a way that he would not immediately perceive. I knew he would leave my gift in your hands to further drive a wedge between you and your mate. He is so wise. It almost worked."

"Oh, my God!"

"Yes. He has sought you since Dante's throne has been abandoned. He is also a Neteru. He has finally adjusted to your atmosphere. He has absorbed full knowledge of your new world and can raise a nearly unstoppable army. He has disdain for the weakness of humans, he hates that part of himself . . . he blames that weakness for his once-uncontrolled jealousy, the reason he slew his brother, Abel . . . he blames it for his incarceration, and desires to eradicate raw emotion devoid of logic. He truly believes that our beings are superior and deserve to rule the realm of sensation—earth."

"I'll butcher him first."

"Do not be angry, just well advised."

"Now I have to ask if you're crazy," Damali said flatly.

The pearl giggled, but the soft voice emanating from it remained serene and unfazed. "This is coming from a very pure place of conviction within his soul. We have debated this over many wondrous, pleasure-swept nights in his pool. My position has always been that all things of the earth should be free. I am a free spirit, I am a dragon . . . this is at my core. I am nature energy, wild and uncontained and undisciplined. This is why I could never be his vessel for children; I was not acceptable in his mind. But a very hidden part of him is drawn to that nature of unpredictability. He adores that in you—you are his greatest challenge."

"Oh, if he likes 'em crazy, I'll show him craaazy, okay?" If Damali didn't have to keep her hand in the water, she would have stood and begun pacing.

The pearl laughed low, and deep, and sensually, its melodic voice rising to the surface of the water with tiny bubbles. "When he could not suppress his urges any longer, he always sought me as his favorite release. You've replaced that now, in his mind . . . you are wild, uncontained, but have a measure of discipline that I did not. He tested that, and your Neteru will and prowess simply slaughtered him. I felt it nearly strangling him as I expired. He is in rapture with you—he gets to have the wildness, but within a disciplined queen that will bear regal heirs. Your lineage and bloodlines suit his fancy. Still, he feels that humans, in general, are undisciplined, are not worthy, are—"

"What!" Damali shrieked so upset she could barely keep the pearl beneath the shallow water. "He's nuts!"

"Perhaps. But he has had millennia to perfect battle tactics. He has unsurpassed discipline to be patient to wait for the right move. His mother felt his essential vibrations from your visit, and he was able to enter her heart just from that . . . you carried him to her, she has no resistance against him . . . she unearthed the Caduceus for him—which only an etheric Neteru queen can do, which you gave to him to help me out of pure compassion . . . another seduction. My young queen, he is also drawn to the pure Light in your heart. He feeds off energy, the purer the better. It is his aphrodisiac. He practically levitates when it enters his system. Then, with your silvery blood, he is now . . . oh, my, at the point of no return. I do not believe I have ever seen him this way."

Damali felt like she'd been punched in the stomach. "Pearl . . ."

"He could not have wrested the Caduceus from you, it had to be willingly given. Just as he could not take your body . . . but he did not want it with the tainted energy of hurt and spite resonating in it . . . that would have reduced his vibrations, therefore reduced his pleasure. He knows you are capable of pure, unrefined ecstasy, and that is what he wanted from you. He needed your trinity for a larger plan that he would never divulge to me, but I could feel his mind working the strategy daily."

Damali groaned and closed her eyes. "Tell me about the Caduceus." She couldn't even think about how close she'd come to just giving this schizophrenic entity her body.

"Although created by Imhotep, he did so with the healing energies of Mother Nature, thus it contains female power, conferred queen to queen. Cain had to manipulate circumstances so that you would give it with your blessings attached to it, or the rod would go dead. He knew that. I was a pawn, even though we were friends . . . lovers . . . he could sense Carlos would panic and act prematurely while in Nod, he knew my weakness for pleasure, and put us in a volatile position. He knew that I had to be seriously injured in order to get you to part with the staff . . . just as he knew Carlos would be estranged from you for his actions . . . I love how Cain's ambitious but twisted mind works. He is brilliant."

"But you were *his lover*—for *how long?*" Damali shouted, nearly faint.

"You were *his friend,* and he let you snap your neck to get the Caduceus? And you're not mad?" She was incredulous. "You're all right with that?"

"Those sentimental facts were not as important as his overall goal. Why remain angry? I have enjoyed his pleasure for years. I am free. His actions impact his karma, not mine. So, why harbor resentments that only lower one's vibration?"

Again, she could only stare at the pearl in her palm. This sister who'd encased the essence of her spirit in it was so cosmically cool and philosophical that it was bugging her out. "Girl . . . *what* is your *name?*"

"Zehiradangra," the pearl replied happily. "Oh, Damali . . . Your heart is so good. I love your energy. Do not let him break it, or your heart. He will use the Caduceus to heal his mortally wounded in battles so they may repeatedly rise when felled. If he has his way, your Neteru Council of Queens will be divided on this issue, Eve and your complicity in this disaster . . . which will separate you from your power source of Aset, Isis . . . then he will not be stopped."

"He set his own mom up?" Damali just stared at the pearl, her hand trembling. "Oh, yeah, this is *definitely* Dante's son."

"I knew his intent the moment I felt his presence on the beach. That is why I would not go to him. That is why I would not return to the honest one, Carlos, when he called after me. If Cain got me back and trapped me, I would have been remanded to his pool of exquisite sensation again . . . or maybe banished from it. I do not know. Either way, I could not bear the limitations of the pool after a dip in the ocean. Nor could I fathom being totally denied it. The dilemma seemed hopeless."

"You weren't going to eat the people on the ship?" Damali whispered, hot tears now wetting her lashes.

"No. I would *never* do that . . . I was simply curious. That is in my nature, as a dragon. I have never seen ships such as these. If I died, I wanted to die in the sea."

"It was suicide. You popped his energy bands . . . aw, girl . . . if you had only told us, you could have hooked up with our team."

"I did not pop Cain's bands. He let them go as I panicked, knowing I would run headlong from him. At that moment, I did not know that you would trust me. But I was sure that the younger Neteru would not be understood, and this would cause you pain. In the chaos, Cain would have had time to siphon the truth of my gift to you from me, and then he would have been angered by my betrayal of his plan. I did not know how far he would go to punish me, if he learned that I would not stand with him. I have seen him in battles. His valiance knows no bounds— just as his rage knows none. He is the son of Dante, after all, and you do know who sired Dante, of that I'm sure. It is all for the best. I could not risk being captured and forced to go back after I felt the change within Cain. This plane, and a blood feeding, did something to him that I did not like. He frightened me."

"Okay," Damali said quickly, a new level of panic cresting within her. "How do I beat this guy? Get him secured on the other side?"

"You must find a way to seal him in Nod. In ether, he is an honorable king. In the flesh, he is something dark that frightens me. Although I don't like what his grandfather's wife did to him on the earth plane, I do love him, but he has a sickness."

"Lilith! She—"

"Oh, please, Damali, do not say her name around me. I am a sensory creature, vibration driven . . . after what I felt, I could not be with him again. I was moving too swiftly to stop . . . my neck . . . I am in a better place now."

"But it was suicide. What level of Hell—"

"No. I willingly gave my life for a family headed by two Neterus. That elevates." The dragon giggled, humming. "One day, there may be a baby?"

"Oh," Damali whispered.

"I received my desire," the dragon's spirit said brightly. "I'm *free!* I am in an ocean so vast and so beautiful, you can never conceive it until you come here . . . which will hopefully not be for a very long time. Live well. Keep me close with the other stones. I will not abandon you. I am the sixth of the seven you will need. Be gentle with Carlos's heart—do not stay angry with him for also being wild, uncontained, passionate energy. I so enjoyed him. He makes me smile." The pearl flickered. "Be also gentle with Cain, in Nod . . . *he is wonderful.*"

"Don't go out," Damali said, her tone urgent. "How do I keep him in Nod, or close the rip, or whatever?"

"You know how. You already have. Deplete his energy. You know this method."

"I don't know anything!" Damali said, nearly screaming at the pearl. "I do know that I've gotta get to my queens, drop this science on them, gotta protect the family—make sure they're battle-station ready, gotta make contact with Father Pat to be sure the Covenant knows what we're up against beyond their theories, gotta talk to Carlos and get his head right. . . . Girl, come on, I don't have time for riddles. How do I get Cain to temporarily stay in Nod and not bring an army over the barrier, and get the Caduceus back from him?"

The pearl flickered once more and then went still. "Thoroughly seduce him."

The SOS to Queen Aset fired in Damali's mind so quickly that she didn't even need the long process of divination, stones, or anything else. She was on her feet, looked out to the ocean, and hollered, "Queen Aset! Private counsel, stat!"

Instantly the violet pyramid opened before her. She didn't have to walk into the Light; it practically yanked her through it. When she landed on the other side, she was in the regal queen's private chambers. Lazy white lions grumbled but didn't get up as Aset moved toward Damali with panic in her eyes.

"Queen Daughter. The level of distress in your tone . . . explain."

Breathless, Damali stood before Aset, opened her palm, and produced the pearl. "Great Queen Mother, I have news so crazy that I don't know what to do. An army is about to be raised against humanity! But they aren't exactly vampires, per se . . . I don't know what they are, but they come from Nod. Cain might have even hooked up with Lilith, or something wild like that to take Dante's throne."

Aset looked at her with alarm in her eyes, and then down at the pearl. "You were given a *dragon's pearl* as your sixth stone?" She carefully lifted it from Damali's hand and studied it for authenticity. Her exotic Kemetian gaze returned to Damali slowly. "Do you know how *rare* this oracle tool is?" Aset gaped and pushed it around in her palm. "*This,* with the others, gets set in platinum and silver, my darling. When you receive the seventh stone, the necklace becomes your amulet."

Had her great queen gone mad? What the hell was jewelry at a time like this? Truthfully, she'd no idea how rare a dragon's pearl was, nor was she really all that interested in fine gems. The point was the information that it spewed.

"That's what told me everything, Great Queen," Damali said, tempering her tone.

Aset nodded and placed the pearl back into Damali's fist. "I am aware of that which you speak. It is a delicate matter, however, one that requires the most skilled levels of detent."

The queen swept over to a long, alabaster bench and bid Damali to sit down with a slight pat of her hand on the seat beside her. For a moment, Damali didn't move. The great queen would allow *her* to sit next to her? On a bench. Like they were girls?

Aset smiled warmly, sensing Damali's awe. Her gorgeous dark eyes held tender excitement as though she were about to burst with pride. Yet, even caught off guard and clearly relaxing in her sanctuary, this royal beauty exuded such dignity that her simple gesture of offering a seat was hard for Damali to fathom.

She stood there immobilized, staring at Aset's flowing, sheer gold gown that practically made her flawless ebony skin shimmer. The entire bedchamber was laden with gold. The huge Egyptian white marble columns terminated in the fine metal. Gold friezes in ancient hieroglyphics littered the walls, a gold vanity, and a luxurious chaise lounge.

Damali's gaze took a quick sweep of Aset's haven; even the bed was made of the substance, replete with lush silks, glistening sheer drapes, and a profusion of pillows made from fabrics of the same hue. Oddly, for an instant, it reminded her of Cain's lair . . . especially the veritable garden of palm plants and the placid, still pool. But this bath had a silver surface, much like that of a looking glass. Damali glimpsed into it as she began walking, cringed and stopped.

She was sandy, dirty, had been in battle, had argued, and hadn't taken a shower since she'd gone to Eve. Her entire white-pants-and-blouse ensemble was ripped, stained, and ragged. How could she even stand in front of Aset, much less sit beside her great queen?

"Daughter, please, dispense with formalities. Come sit and tell me all."

Damali went to Aset and complied, talking a mile a minute. After a half-hour of breathless monologue told in a series of stop-start non-sequiturs, Damali inhaled and wrapped her arms about herself.

"So, that's what happened." Damali felt like she would jump out of her skin as she waited for the great queen to respond.

"I see," Aset said calmly and stood.

Damali stared behind her. I see? What did that mean?

"We must call in Nefertiti and Nzinga on this matter," Aset replied, answering Damali's thoughts without even needing to do a mind lock.

"You were right to call me privately, and not the council at large, as my dear sister Queen Eve cannot be impartial on this grave matter."

Damali audibly released her breath. Total relief almost made her keel over. Aset wasn't angry, but was going to work on the problem. Thank you, God.

The great queen became still and pressed both of her palms together before her heart, elbows bent so that her forearms were perfectly horizontal to her breasts. She murmured something quietly that Damali couldn't hear, and within moments her palms glowed violet, then Nefertiti calmly strode into the room from the veranda, trailing a long, sheer silver gown. Nzinga followed her wearing a long copper-hued robe. Each queen bowed slightly and then peered at Aset with great concern.

"We have a situation, Queen Sisters," Aset replied, and then simply placed one hand on each of their shoulders until their eyes widened.

Nefertiti swept away from Aset with her hand pressed against her stomach and looked at Damali. "Dear, dear daughter, we shall rectify this."

"I say make quick work of it," Nzinga replied, her gaze filled with blazing fury. She materialized a battle-ax into her hand. "Go in, grab the Caduceus, and then cut his balls off for even attempting to rob you. Then there's no issue of his siring anything."

Damali was on her feet.

"Patience," Aset said, shaking her head. "Nzinga, this must be delicate. We would not want to breed dissention at the Neteru Queens' Council. I have asked you here to provide battle tactics once Damali leaves Nod, but Nefertiti is here to help her with an entry strategy and diplomatic exit. If we play this right, we can allow Lucifer to stomp Lilith's worthless carcass into a black puddle without creating a problem for our eldest Neteru council members."

Nzinga made the battle-ax disappear. "Although I defer to your rank as our sovereign, let me be clear when I state that I am not concerned about the level of dissention at our table over this particular issue. Eve knows her son is crazy."

Aset laughed. "As do we all. However, what the dragon's pearl suggests is wise."

Damali watched pure awe spread across Nefertiti's and Nzinga's faces.

"She has acquired a *dragon's pearl*?" Nzinga murmured. Then she laughed and shook her head. "My protégé has come into her own!"

"Yes!" Nefertiti exclaimed, going to Damali and hugging her hard, despite her ragged condition. Nefertiti held her back with tears in her eyes. "Oh, my, my, my . . . the lessons I have for you. We must begin, immediately. Clean her up. Get her into the silver pool. Stand back, Nzinga, and watch me work."

Damali was so stunned that she wasn't sure what protocols were in force any longer. Nefertiti had stripped her of her ragged clothes and had practically pushed her into Aset's bath.

"Call Sheba's handmaidens," Nefertiti said excitedly to Nzinga. "Ask her to bring me the seven swaths—"

"You are not going there," Nzinga said, laughing as Aset sat down heavily on a bench.

"Isn't that drastic?" Aset asked, her voice strained.

"Girl, I was married to Akhenaton for years," Nefertiti said, unfazed. "I gave him six *daughters*," she added with a sly wink, "and he didn't mind. Not to mention, one of my princesses actually pulled Tut—need I say more?" She clucked her tongue and returned her attention to Damali. "Believe me; I *know* what I'm doing."

Pure curiosity flowed over Damali as Nefertiti's hands worked. Her skin felt like it was actually drinking in the silver waters as Nefertiti's graceful ministrations cleaned the grime off.

"Dear Queen, with all due respect," Damali said, embarrassed, her gaze going first to Nefertiti and then the others. "I should be washing *your* feet, you shouldn't be—"

"Shush," Nefertiti murmured. "I had daughters. They are grown and in spirit now, and this reminds me so much of the old days. Let me tend to you. Yes, we had servants, but the most private time when I needed to truly educate my girls was when we'd have moments like this. Allow me?"

Damali's heart filled with an emotion she couldn't describe. The older queens had taken her in. Yes, she'd been a Neteru all her life, but more like an accidental bystander with her nose pressed to the mysterious glass of their leadership. This, however, was admission to the real inner circle, something very different, very special and she recognized the profound gift. Damali nodded. It was an invitation to participate as a full member.

"I am honored to learn from the great Nefertiti, as I am also beyond words and humbled by the knowledge of Nzinga's battle tactics." She looked at each queen with reverence and allowed her gaze to settle on Aset. "And I am in awe and wonder that I was so graciously accepted into Aset's private sanctuary. Thank you."

"Each of us has a specialty," Aset said, seeming quietly pleased. "Nzinga is renowned for her war strategies, our Amazon sister for her courage, Eve for her skills in détente, I excel in law, our Aztec sister in magic, Joan is bound by unwavering faith and visions, our Asian sister for her medicines." She smiled and offered Nefertiti an arched brow with a nod of respect. "My dear sister queen who attends you . . . there is no better one on the council to teach you about men. Let her work."

Damali couldn't keep the wild-eyed expression from flashing across her face as the older queens burst out laughing.

"Yeah, she does, little sister," Nzinga said, plopping down on the bench beside Aset. "I stand down."

"Thank you," Nefertiti replied, lifting her chin. She gazed down at Damali. "Feel your skin."

Damali allowed her palm to glide over her damp forearm. "Wow . . . what did you do?" she murmured.

"The waters of the Nile infused with essence of Hathor," Nefertiti coolly replied. She leaned into Damali, took a deep inhale. "Oh, yes, he will not be able to resist."

"What!" Damali pulled back, stunned as the queens erupted in laughter again.

"If your goal is to seduce him, then let us do this the old-fashioned way."

Damali blinked, opened her mouth, but nothing came out for a second. "I, I, I'm supposed to kill him, right?"

"Yes," Nefertiti murmured, her voice low and sensual. "*Kill*. Him."

"I don't understand, then," Damali said quickly, almost wanting to bolt from the bath. "I—"

"Spell it out," Nzinga said with a sly smile. "Hey, I wouldn't have picked this up, either. Me, I'm blades and arrows, okaaay? This finer art is way past my specialty."

Damali bobbed her head and offered Nzinga a glance containing quiet thanks.

"Draw out of the bath, darling," Nefertiti said, opening a large Turkish towel for Damali to wrap herself in. "I want her shaved as clean as a newborn," Nefertiti commanded, clapping her hands twice and making two young initiates appear.

"Oh . . . wait . . . dear Queen . . . uh, talk to me, okay?" Damali tightened the towel around her as two beautiful brown-skinned teenage girls approached wearing big smiles, bright white gowns, and their hair wrapped up in crisp white cotton. She peered at the golden trays they carried bearing exotic, shimmering bottles in every hue. Each crystal vial seemed to contain lotions and potions foreign to Damali, but she immediately recognized a straight-edged razor, then panicked.

Nefertiti sighed. "Don't they teach you young queens *anything* today?" She shook her head with disgust, waved the girls to sit on the floor at Damali's feet, and made Damali sit on the rim of the tub next to her. "My goodness!"

"Dear Queen," Damali said, her voice becoming shaky as she saw the resolve in Nefertiti's eyes. "I'm supposed to do what, exactly, in this process of killing him?"

A broad smile spread across Nefertiti's face. "I want you to go in there," she said in a calm, breathy murmur. "I want you to so distract him and so deplete his energy that he will hand you the Caduceus without bloodshed or struggle . . . and when he attempts to follow you across the barrier, we can tie him up, siphon the rest of his flesh protoplasm, and send him back. After which, he will not have enough energy all on his own to be able to cross at will."

Again, words failed Damali as she stared at Nefertiti.

"Meanwhile," Aset said coolly, "I will confer with Ausar about lending us a shield or two." She stood and began to pace. "That will be a delicate conversation. You know how the old kings are . . . even when our counsel is wise, they must debate it into infinity until they think it was their idea. They always object to us assisting in their affairs, even though they regularly require our wisdom. And, given this issue is about one of their own, a male Neteru, I don't know."

Nefertiti smiled. "Then, take it to the pillow, dear sister."

Aset smiled a half-smile. "As I said, my discussion would be a delicate one."

"Oh, brother," Nzinga sighed. "You married queens have to go through such loops over the basics that it frays my nerves." She stretched out on the bench to watch everything from a distant vantage point. "Just tell Ausar he's violated the rule of no two male Neterus being on the planet at the same time, and the one in Nod is empire building."

"Empire building isn't exactly considered an offense from their perspective," Nefertiti said, still smiling. "You know how the kings of old view that. They've all done it. War, from their perspective, is often a necessary byproduct of being in the right. They may only slap his wrists until they are clear he is truly offending their codes. Thus, Aset could be in negotiations for months arguing the merits of having the superior Neteru rule humanity . . . they could vote either way, and avoiding war at all costs is not even in their DNA."

"Yes," Aset replied, finding the chaise lounge to recline on. "We have this debate regularly. He feels that sometimes it's necessary for the right cause, whereas you know our Queens' Council abhors war as an option. Too many innocent lives . . . especially women and children get caught in the middle of male-created disputes. Even if Cain is talking about dominating humanity with a super race of hybrid entities, with the shape that humanity is presently in, as long as his forces are not strictly demons and have a soul, my *dear husband* might think Cain's plan has a rational basis." Aset let out her breath hard in frustration.

"But, by law," Nzinga argued, "Ausar has to give up a shield of Heru so she can place the shield over the breach from the earth plane side to strengthen where the veil is thin. Once placed, we can obscure it to human sight. He already has a young male Neteru in training that, in time, we hope, comes to his right mind. Nevertheless, he cannot allow two brethren Neterus to battle, nor can he allow one to kill the other over a woman. Open and shut case." She peered at Aset with a firm gaze. "So, what's the problem? Why all the delicate talks? Just tell him what time it is."

"She must be delicate, dear Nzinga, because if she goes the legal petition route that could take months before he'd be forced to relent by law. Although you are correct, we don't have time. My way is more efficient," Nefertiti crooned. "Let Aset take it to the pillow . . . let her explain that there is word in the valley that Lilith could be behind this—if told in the right tone, no evidence of this potential threat need be debated. Since we only have dragon hearsay about Cain allegedly being positioned to take Dante's old throne . . . You know how stubborn they can be, and how easy it is to become embroiled in a test of wills that only devolves into rhetoric."

"The indisputable fact is this, Nzinga: We need the Caduceus back under very quiet circumstances. It was taken by guile, thus will be quickly and efficiently returned by the same method. You are well aware if Adam *ever* found out that Eve assisted in it being delivered to her son, there would be strife on the councils for eons." Aset let her breath out hard. "Therefore, it must be in our possession to not only heal the world in the end of days and to raise felled Guardians in the coming wars, but it is the only tool we may have able to divine which entities that spill over from Nod have gone light or dark. It divines the heart chakras."

Nzinga let out a grunt. "All right, Aset. You take it to the mattress, but get the shield."

Aset nodded with a smile and winked at Nefertiti. Damali's gaze had been riveted on the short-lived dispute. *Damn . . . if Aset had to negotiate with her man . . .*

"We all do, darling," Nefertiti cooed. "That is why, since you clearly have one that you're not willing to let go of, a bullheaded one, I might add . . . it is time to teach you some new strategies that will help make your life easier to reign as a true queen. The fewer disputes, the smoother and more quickly your law gets put into effect. Understand, young one? It is about outcome, not methodology. Be liquid fire."

Damali let out a long whistle, unable to stop herself. The old girls were deep. Had she only known. "But not to throw a monkey wrench into the operation—because I'm down to stop Cain's crazy scheme. But, uh, see, this is gonna cause serious problems, now that you mentioned Carlos. I think it's only right of me to put it all out on the table. If, see, dear Queen, if I uh, actually *do* Cain, uh, there's gonna be everlasting repercussions. The bite, alone, created static like you can't imagine."

"First of all," Nefertiti murmured with a smile after a weary sigh. "You *never* tell them everything, even when provoked." She cocked an eyebrow and stared at Damali with big, beautiful eyes. Firelight danced within them as she spoke, her easy, melodic voice pouring over Damali like warm water. "Second of all, never lie—tactfully *evade*."

The older queen stood and began counting off the lessons with her graceful fingers as the two young girls and the other queens sat rapt. "Third of all, to seduce a man doesn't require sleeping with him. His most erogenous zone, especially for an arrogant male like Cain appears to be, is his *ego*. I'm going to show you how to stroke it . . . suck it, torture it until he's in tears," Nefertiti whispered. "Caress it. Nip it. Lick it," she said, releasing her breath in staccato bursts. "Fondle it. Tease it until it spills over into your hands. Then, you ask a small favor to be pleased in return. Am I clear? Always allow him to ego-orgasm first . . . and multiple times, at that."

"Whew," Damali said, raking her freshly shampooed locks. She just shook her head. "You bad, Queen. If I can pull this off, it'll go down in the history books, because I've never been all that . . . I mean, seriously."

"Yes, you have," Nefertiti said, coming to Damali to cup her face. "You just did it naturally, and weren't aware of what you were doing. Now we are going to shape all that raw skill into a very deadly weapon." Nefertiti glanced at the tub. "I want her feet done, they should feel like butter. I want her hands done, all body hair, except what's on her head, removed. Essence of Hathor, from crown to toe."

The two young girls scrambled to meet Nefertiti's command, helping Damali to sit at the edge of the large pool so they could work while Nefertiti spoke.

"But, Queen," Damali said, not wanting to anger Nefertiti, but still not fully understanding where this invisible seduction line was drawn. Yeah, she'd flirted and whatnot, but this seemed way more involved. "Okay. I'm going in there all dolled up, and I sit there and tell him all this great stuff he wants to hear. He's just gonna hand me the Caduceus? I've been with him. When this brother pushes up on you, there's no telling him, 'Oh, I changed my mind,' ya know? How am I gonna get in and out of there without actually doing him, so that I don't have to lie to Carlos about it? Both of them are energy sensors, they can pick up a lie a mile away."

Nefertiti smiled, materialized a small throne before the pool, and sat gazing at Damali with a sightline on her sister queens. "You will cross the barrier with the truth, dear one. You'll tell him how much you two need to talk, that is true. That you couldn't wait to see him again, also true. That you know no one like him, also true. He is a king and he has . . . how do you say, *blown your mind*—that is not a lie. Also tell him that you and Carlos had a huge fight over him, *his bite,* the dragon and her demise, classic truth—he'll feel that down to his soul . . . and say that after you received her pearl and felt the energy from it, you *had* to finally come to him . . . you just couldn't help yourself. Where is the lie?"

"Dayum . . ." Damali whispered, unable to censor herself as the raw awe flowed out of her mouth.

"Now," Nefertiti said, not the least bit offended by the outburst, "you will go to him, *breathlessly,* and tell him that since he left you, your mind cannot rest and that he has something that you want so badly you almost *cannot* speak. Hesitate, look away, then rake his body and murmur, 'Cain . . . I cannot forget your staff. Since I felt it come alive, I have been . . .' Then allow your words to deliciously trail off. That is true," she continued, when Damali bristled. "You want the Caduceus, correct?"

Damali burst out laughing with the other queens as the young girls who were working on her feet giggled.

"Ya know what?" Nzinga said, shaking her head. "You, my sister, are deadly. I take back all former reservations. She gonna slay him going in there like that."

"It's all tone, inflection, the use of your eyes, and well-timed breaths," Nefertiti said proudly. "It is a dance of emotion. It works like a song. You must begin with purpose, crest, dip, move . . . flow, each approach adding more urgency, but his ego strokes are the refrain."

"Wow," Damali said, "I'm listening, *hard.* You are definitely awesome."

Nefertiti dropped her voice to a low, seductive whisper. "Let him make assumptions by the way you appear at his door. If you go in with a suit of armor, he will expect a battle. If you go in, your hair swept up, adorned in a crown of wrapped gold . . . your naked, perfumed, satin-smooth body draped with only seven sheer silks of chakra hue . . . your feet bare, no weapon in your hand—your eyes rimmed in Egyptian kohl as your weapon . . . your mouth sweetened by mango as a drug . . . the essence of Hathor trailing like a steel net . . . and your fluid, graceful movements a sign of surrender, believe me, Damali, he will not be in the mood to fight."

Aset chuckled and covered her mouth. "He'll die of heart failure. Nefertiti, go easy, we aren't supposed to actually kill him, just contain him."

"He will never be able to admit this to Ausar," Nefertiti said coolly. "This level of devastation cannot, by ego, be spoken of between men." She arched a perfectly waxed eyebrow and returned her attention to Damali. "Now. Do not be afraid to go near him. Touch is essential. Your warmth and skin are his handcuffs. He prides himself on his discipline, and his ability to seduce you . . . that is what makes him vulnerable. Allow him to think that he already has."

"Yeah, but," Damali said, feeling a little unsure. "Even as crazy as he is, this brother ain't no joke in that department."

"Good," Nefertiti said quickly. "If he's adept and handsome, that will make it easier for you, not more difficult, darling. Then your responses won't be fraudulent, which any seasoned male can detect. Relax, allow him to taste your mouth, caress your skin, and unpin your hair to let his fingers luxuriate in it. Let him see your skin pebble from his attention. Let him know by the way you press against him and breathe out his name that he has aroused you. When we began this lesson, I said not to lie."

"Okay, but stop right there. When I get home," Damali said, now talking with her hands, "Carlos—"

"Only needs to know the truth," Nefertiti said, folding her arms with a smile. "That you had a very treacherous, very delicate negotiation to handle in order to get back the Caduceus."

Nefertiti unfolded her arms, leaned forward, and closed her eyes, sending her voice into a frenzied panic. "It was frightening. Your heart was in your mouth the entire time. Sweat broke out on your brow, your hands had white knuckles." Nefertiti winked at Damali again as she excitedly mimicked the script Damali was to follow.

Nefertiti began waving her arms about. "With your graceful palm over your heart, you tell him you almost didn't know what to do. Cain nearly attacked you—you had to think fast on your feet and get out of there before it was too late! Oh! Tears were in your eyes, it was so . . ." Nefertiti settled back into her throne and allowed her voice to lower to a calm whisper as her hands found the armrests, "And then let your words *trail off.*"

Nzinga stood, walked in a circle, and sat back down again. "She's the master, Damali. Listen to every word this queen has to say!"

Damali only shook her head as the young girls worked on her feet.

"You never, ever, *ever* tell your man about some of the feminine wiles required to negotiate a deal," Nefertiti said, wagging a finger at Damali. "His ego remaining intact is *paramount* to being able to work around him, through him, over him, at will. Ten years from now, the story remains the same, etched into *granite.* If they ever learn that you pulled this on them, poof, the magic is gone. Even Cain needs to think this was all an accident. You got so thoroughly aroused, lost your head, became conflicted, and had to leave because you were so overwrought. *Neva* let 'em see you work."

"Queen . . ." Damali whispered, "you are da bomb."

For a moment the entire chamber went still. There was so much respect for the science Nefertiti was dropping that not even Aset flinched.

"You are going to dance for this man," Nefertiti said with quiet authority. She held up her hand when Damali began to protest. "The seven veils."

"Oh, my God . . . I can't. Queen—"

"You can, and *you will*, because he is from the Old World!" Nefertiti exclaimed, slapping a flat palm on the throne armrest. "He is particularly sensitive to music. You will begin swaying as you keep your physical distance from him. You will walk around his sensory pool, your eyelids heavy, your breathing stilted, and then you will look up with an expression that will devastate him, and you will admit that a song, just for him, is torturing your mind. Pick one that you did, indeed, compose for him earlier—that way, the statement is still not a lie. Then sing it, right there in his bedchamber for him, undulate to the sound of your voice as it echoes off his marble walls, and shred a veil at each stanza, until he's *vibrating*."

The suggestion was so hot that Damali wiped her brow.

"I want him to *feel* this from across the room," Nefertiti said, raising her voice. "I want him to crave it!"

"Okay, okay, okay, I can sing, do a stage performance, I guess. Only thing is, once all the veils are gone . . ."

Nefertiti let her breath out hard in clear exasperation. "You'll cut out his heart when he sees the tattoo."

Damali stood, almost toppling the two girls who were working on her. "What tattoo?"

Aset's mouth opened and closed. Nzinga raked her hair and stared at the floor.

"She's gone over the top," Nzinga said, chuckling.

"Queen?" Damali squeaked.

"It's only temporary silver, comes off with solvent. Never worry."

Damali stared at Nefertiti until the older queen smiled and stood.

"You need props for this theatrical event." Nefertiti sighed. "Now, I caution you to never do this permanently, even if married . . . things sometimes don't work out—and if your king dies, and Heaven forbid you should remarry, well, it could be an unnecessary obstacle . . . but you will need to wear it for this excursion. The fate of the world and the

Caduceus is too valuable to trifle with variables." She placed her hands on her hips and stared at Damali hard. "This, my dear, is the blade. Cut him dead."

Damali sat down slowly before she fell down.

"In your palms, also anointed with the oil of Hathor, will be his male Neteru tattoo. His is *kuntinkantan*: four linked circles with a fifth one in the center overlapping all. It means humility is required, and you are sending a quiet message that you are willing to be that for him. Everywhere your palms land will ignite the one on his chest, send pleasure through his meridians, and blow him away." Nefertiti stopped pacing and stood behind the throne, leaning on it. "Oil of Hathor is rare and much more concentrated than the essence you've been bathing in. It has the effect on the skin to produce the sensation of . . . fertile planting. That is what that wondrous goddess rules, yes?"

Nefertiti pushed away from the throne with a mischievous chuckle. "Use it sparingly. There's not a male Neteru I know of that can deal with it, except in moderation." She clapped her hands. "Now. Here's where things become delicate and up to your discretion."

Damali was almost limp with relief, once she learned the tattoo was only going on her hands. That she could deal with. But when Nefertiti lowered her eyes and chuckled hard, she knew she was in trouble.

"On your cleanly shaven mound, and the insides of your thighs, with a hint of Neteru ripening that we keep bottled for the older kings, since he does have a bit of significant vampire in him . . ."

"Wait, y'all keep ripening Neteru in vials like Viagra?" Damali closed her eyes.

"Much better and more natural a substance, and when a few drops are applied to your—"

"No, no, no, no, no," Damali said as the older queens laughed. The young girls at her feet looked away and covered their mouths, too shocked to even giggle.

"Here's how you play that one," Nefertiti said confidently. "Advanced training, since we have so little time. At some point, this man is going to snatch you into his arms. That's a given. When he collides with your skin, grab his hair at the nape of his neck and pull hard to expose his throat like you're about to strike it. His eyes will roll into the back of his skull. The oil of Hathor will dissolve into his skin, as his own tattoo sends him into mild pleasure shock." She took off a tiny, golden scarab ring from her pinky and slipped it onto Damali's. "Strike him. Bite him as hard as you can. You know where this goes. It's been soaking in oil of Hathor *for weeks.*"

Damali stared down at the ring and up at Nefertiti, unable to form words. Nefertiti shrugged and nodded.

"It the only way, darling . . . if you don't want him to enter you and need him to ejaculate so hard that he sees stars." She glided away and sat down again, leaving stunned expressions to stare after her. "But don't let him do that right away. The moment he crests, catch the orb of building energy at the base of his spine in your palm, blow on it, hold it, use your freeze technique to stop it with a cool breath. . . . I'll show you the technique once you get dressed. However, just hold him back until he's stuttering, begging, sobbing, then heat it up and run it up his back. All right, darling? Rim his sphincter until he hollers and then plunge the ring. Simultaneously capture his mind with your silvery Neteru visions and let him momentarily believe he's inside you. Move with him. Lick his tattoo, since he's so much taller than you and it's right over his heart chakra . . . I may even add in a mystical falcon feather for you to work with." Nefertiti placed a finger over her lips as her gaze became distant while she decided.

"Ultimately," Nefertiti said with a satisfied sigh, "I want you to take him to *creation point,* the opposite direction of vanishing point. Bring him to supernova, cell splitting, galaxy annihilating, light fractals that only reconstruct when and how *you say so.* When you're done, I want that man on his hands and knees, too weak to breach the barrier, but willing to crawl over it with his last ounce of energy, like an addict, to get to you. On the other side, you thrust the Caduceus in the ground, supposedly to revive him as he apologizes profusely for his lack of control and you siphon the last of what he's got from him. Your gentle embrace and tender words telling him that it's all right are to wrap around him like a silver vine. Bondage. Tie him up. Then jettison him back, for you fear your lover is coming to attack him . . . of course he would, and you don't want two Neteru males to kill each other—truth. Cain will surrender without protest to your gentle shove through the rip, because he'll be in no position to deal with a battle-bulked, irrational male who is beyond outrage."

The regal queen laughed so hard she covered her mouth for a moment before composing herself again. "Open the ring, douse the tattoos, and be totally undone when Carlos finds you—which, by that point, I'm sure you adequately will be. Then never, *ever,* again, bring up Carlos's transgressions . . . and allow him to benefit from the battle with Cain. To the victor goes the spoils. Such is the rule of war. All men understand the concept. Harmony will be restored. All dignity preserved. Cain knows how this works, and his ego will allow him to take comfort in the fact that you simply had no other choice or you'd die at Carlos's hands." Nefertiti laughed harder. "That, too, is probably not a lie."

Aset stood and paced with Nzinga. "Nefertiti, remind me to confer with you about oil of Hathor before I go into negotiations with Ausar for his shields."

Nzinga chuckled. "Gives a whole new meaning to going to war." She patted away the dampness that had risen to her cleavage, picked up a bottle from one of the trays, then simply held it up to the light, shaking her head.

"Prepare her to my specifications," Nefertiti commanded the initiates with no nonsense in her tone.

"I just have one question," Damali said, not bothering to disguise her hysteria. "Can you block this from Carlos until the end of time . . . especially if it goes down badly?"

Nefertiti winked. "That's a given."

He'd looked everywhere for her, but no Damali. Carlos sat down on the beach and simply stared at the water. Based on her state of mind when they'd parted, she could be anywhere. He couldn't blame her as he kept sensing for her life force. He didn't perceive she was in danger, but it was clear from her lack of response that she wasn't ready to be found.

Marlene had ripped open his mind, made him see and feel things that he hadn't fully realized before. Juanita had gone so far into the Darkness and had held so much of it inside her for so long on his behalf that it scared him.

Carlos pitched a seashell into the waves. Damali had been right. A good dragon had died unnecessarily. He'd also hurt so many people that several lifetimes couldn't make it all up.

When he went to her this time, he vowed it would be with humility, a listening ear, and patience beyond compare. If she would just hear him out and let him beg her forgiveness . . . he'd go down on his hands and knees. No matter what she'd done, or where she'd been, he wouldn't ask. Didn't have the right to, after all the changes he'd taken her through. Now he knew that, too.

Until she came home, he'd guard their almost shattered family. Until she came home, he'd keep a light on in the window at the house. From this point forward, he would treat her like the queen she was . . . if she would only come home before it got dark, and anything else crazy kicked off.

Damali stood before Aset, Nzinga, and Nefertiti awaiting their response. The queens hadn't allowed her to look in the mirror until Nefertiti gave the nod.

The queens smiled. Nefertiti closed her eyes.

"I approve," Nefertiti murmured, and then gently turned Damali to look at herself.

The transformation was so startling that for several moments Damali could only stare. A pair of dark, sultry, Egyptian eyes stared back at her from the mirror. A fine gold dust made her skin shimmer in the waning sunlight. Oil of Hathor glistened on her lips as though they were wet.

Her hair had been twisted up into a high crown wrapped in silver-and-gold serpent clasps. Her throat was bare and her breasts only covered by a drape of three sheer silken scarves knotted at one shoulder which allowed her nipples to peek through. The loose knot slung low at her hip precariously held four more delicate scarves, and each time she moved they glided over her satin-sheen body to expose her thighs. A hint of the silvery tattoo on her mound was almost invisible beneath the fabric, and the intricate patterns inside her palms glowed.

They had affixed long strands of golden Kemetian coins to her ears that gently chimed as she approached the mirror. The large diamond in her navel caught prisms of light and almost stole her breath.

"The diamond is your seventh stone, a conductor of knowledge, of compressed organic matter, stored energy that you can release at will . . . and a way to directly call to us," Aset whispered. "Diamonds are always a girl's best friend."

"Wow . . ." Damali murmured. "I've never looked like this, even on stage."

"Natural beauty," Nefertiti replied with quiet satisfaction and pride. "Less is more."

"You think you can pull it off without incident?" Nzinga teased, cocking her head to the side.

"Look at her," Aset fussed. "Is this not a queen worthy of pyramid inscription?"

"The question is," Nefertiti murmured, her sultry, burning gaze holding Damali. "How do you feel?"

Damali continued to stare into the mirror with the queens behind her, pondering the question. "Nervous," she admitted. "A little scared. A little devious."

"Good," Nefertiti whispered. "That will put butterflies in your womb." She gently kissed Damali's cheek. "What else?"

"I don't know," Damali said, suddenly feeling too exposed.

"How about sexy?" Nefertiti crooned, now taking a position fully behind Damali and softly clasping her shoulders. "How about sensual . . . unstoppable . . . powerful . . . in control?"

Damali looked down, unable to continue to stare in the mirror. "I've only felt like that with one man in my life, because I love him," she admitted quietly. "I don't want to feel like that with Cain."

To Damali's surprise, Nefertiti nodded. She'd expected the older queen to be annoyed that after all her hard work, she was still unsure of the mission. Instead, a tender smile crept over Nefertiti's beautiful face as tears rose in her eyes.

"Then you are ready," Nefertiti said calmly. "You love him, so you will not sire for another tonight."

Damali turned and just stared at Nefertiti.

Nefertiti nodded. "It is so easy to be swept away by one's own powerful magic. Love is a ground wire. Never release that. But do know the effect you have on other men. Now . . . take a deep breath."

Damali complied as tears almost spilled over her eyes.

"No, no, no," Nefertiti said quickly, blowing the tears from Damali's eyes to keep them from spilling. "You will ruin your makeup . . . but I've left some for Cain to believe he put them there."

Damali chuckled and sniffed. "You are so bad."

"Uhmmm, hmmm," Nefertiti crooned. "I want you to think of it this way. Your man's dignity has been abused at the hands of another man. His territory encroached, your kingdom nearly destroyed by devious means. What would Carlos do under those circumstances? Would he not cross the border to rectify the offense?' Nefertiti said, answering her own question.

"Definitely," Damali said, standing taller.

"Would he not use every weapon in his arsenal, including ruse, to best his opponent?"

Damali smiled. "Every time."

Nefertiti nodded. "For this mission, what I have given you is the preferred weapon of choice. Now," she said on a deep inhale, "do you feel powerful, sexy, unstoppable, in control, and righteously justified in slaughtering your opponent?"

Damali chuckle a little harder. "Queen, you have a serious way of flipping the script."

"But you did not answer my question." Nefertiti waited. "It is imperative that your mind is focused, you have no trepidation, other than the quiet nervous tension that all warriors feel when a significant negotiation is pending. Do not carry guilt over that barrier, or any insecurity."

"All right," Damali said, holding her shoulders back. "I feel sexy, unbeatable, in control, and I'm ready."

Nefertiti arched an eyebrow and placed a long slender finger over her lips for a second. "There's something else you need to be feeling to make this authentic." She motioned for the tray of potions, as Damali and the other queens looked on confused. "I'm going to place a drop of something sweet on your tongue, darling, to relax you. It is not fitting to go in there with your fists balled up at your sides the way they are now, your shoulders set to take a blow, and ready to reach for your Isis." Nefertiti shook her head with a smile as she removed the stopper from a small, ruby-crusted vial.

Damali opened her mouth and allowed the warm droplet to hit her tongue without questioning the elder queen. As her eyes slid shut and reopened half-mast, Nefertiti sighed.

"Now, darling, how do you feel?"

Damali's fists unclenched slowly, her shoulders relaxed, her spine became fluid, and every pulse point lit. Her breaths were so shallow she was becoming dizzy. "What's in that stuff?"

"How do you feel?"

Curious gazes passed between the other queens.

Damali looked at Nefertiti. "Horny."

CHAPTER EIGHTEEN

Carlos sat on the deserted beach, his intense gaze focused on the stars in the sky. *Where did she go?* The darker it had gotten, and the later it had become, the more his resolve to just wait for Damali to return ebbed away. He really didn't want to know the answer to the question of where she'd been, but at the same time, he did.

Initially it had been easy to lie to himself, to tell himself that she'd just secreted herself away to get some head space. Then he'd nursed the concept that perhaps she'd been abducted and was in some type of danger. That, he told himself, was the valiant reason he needed to go on a search-and-definitely-destroy mission to find her, even though his gut never registered any pending threat. But with the surf pounding before him, a sound and motion too reminiscent of what might really be going on, it was hard to shield his mind from the probable—she was with Cain.

Complete knowledge was a terrible thing; half-knowing a brutal horror. Fuse that with a true understanding of just how hurt and angry his woman had a right to be, and the recipe created devastation. Carlos closed his eyes, remembering all he'd forgotten.

"I never had anybody to show me the way," he admitted in a whisper, hoping Damali would hear him. The fact that she wasn't responding to a mind lock increased his sense of quiet panic.

It was the truth, the rawest version of it, and he hoped she'd key in on the honesty of the vibration in his whisper and simply come home. There hadn't been any male role models for him, dead or alive. Every male had shown him violence, power lust, how to hustle, game, but no one other than Father Pat had given him anything to really teach him how to run a household like Marlene expected of him. Plus, he reasoned, Father Pat was a priest—and that definitely wasn't him. So how was he supposed to fix this, rebuild?

"D," he said softly, just putting the quiet truth out on the evening breeze for her to catch, "I never had any guides, not like you did. No real Neteru team just for me . . . no male version of your rites of passage. They left me hanging. I had to figure it out on my own and made a lot of mistakes. I'm so sorry, baby."

He drew a ragged breath and kept his line of vision on the stars. "The old kings . . . they made me and left me, D. I was free-falling." He chuckled sadly. "They gave me the tattoo on my throat to seal the turn wound, gave me another one as birth control, told me not to mess up and not to make no babies, and then threw me back on the old block— no instructions, no serious insight, just basically said 'Be a man,' and rolled." Carlos sighed. "I know this ain't making no sense to you, and I'm not making excuses for any way that I hurt you or the family . . . but . . . Damali, with all my heart and soul, what I wouldn't give to have had the lessons that might have avoided all of that."

His peripheral vision caught a glimpse of gold in the corner of his eye and he immediately stood and turned toward it, anticipation rushing through him. The splinter of radiance on the beach quickly became a twelve-foot-long golden obelisk the width of a door, and he held his breath as he waited for Damali to walk through it. But the entity that came out of the light made him instantly bulk and snarl. It was male.

"Where is she?" Carlos demanded, not caring at this point that his cool game was in shambles. He wanted his woman back. Period.

The entity gave him a weary sigh, and leaned against the frame of the lit door. Carlos studied him with a razor scan. The illumination around him made it impossible to immediately make out a face, so Carlos assessed what he could see and prepared to lunge. Six-six or seven in height. Dark ebony skin. Braided goatee. Shoulder-length locks. Square jaw set hard and possibly containing significant fang length. But the brother was cool . . . all relaxed and unarmed. Had the nerve to be sipping a drink from a crystal glass. Feet bare. Gold linen robe tied at the waist by a sash. Hadn't battle bulked, but was so muscular he didn't have to.

Damn . . . he'd put his heart out there on the beach for Damali, had bled all over the sand, and she now disrespected him so much that she'd let Cain answer the call and come to the door? Had actually let his competitor get up out of bed with her to calmly tell him what? There was nothing to say. He didn't want to see this brother's smug victory expression.

Carlos turned and began walking back toward the house. Respect for Marlene was the only reason he'd let the family know that he was leaving for good, but he was out.

"Knowledge is power, but without wisdom it is sheer stupidity," the entity said in a low, mellow rumble behind Carlos.

Carlos kept walking. Fight him? About what? The battle was won. Even if he killed the bastard, at this point there'd be little satisfaction in that. Damali was gone. Had taken to another man's bed. If Cain became the new Chairman, he and the team would deal with that when it happened.

Mild heat entered Carlos's back, slowing his retreat.

"I would advise you to drop the energy line," Carlos whispered, his voice low and lethal. "Don't think about fucking with me right through here."

Carlos waited as the energy receded and resumed walking.

"You finally asked for my help, and I'm going to give you that—if you can get past your ignorance."

Again, Carlos stopped walking, tilted his head to the side, and felt new sinew growing around each disc in his back. He would slaughter this SOB.

He turned slowly as the entity pushed off the lit frame.

"Me and you over a drink, man to man," it said, changing into a loosely constructed ivory linen suit and brown, slip-on alligator shoes. Seeming distracted, he looked back at the door, slammed it shut with a wave of his hand, and then let his breath out hard. "Your timing, young brother, is trying my patience. But I do suppose this conversation is long overdue."

The aggressor folded his arms and waited. Carlos simply stared. This was the brother with the hooked blade that had marked him. One of Cain's boys, or what?

"Hardly," the entity said. "I am Ausar, an archon of the King's Roundtable." He smiled a half-smile. "And you just interrupted a very delicate negotiation. So, let us have a very brief discussion tonight, brother."

Still unsure, Carlos hesitated, but also normalized. Pure curiosity made him stare, trying to sense for game.

Ausar raked his locks at the crown of his head and glanced back to where the obelisk had disappeared on the beach. "Man, name your bar, or wherever you feel safe to hold this conversation. But do so with haste."

"How do I know who—"

Ausar pointed to his Adam's apple which owned the symbol of authority. "Remember this?"

"I remember that you cut the bullshit out of me, and—"

"We had to work quickly as you were being pulled from the pit. That was for your own good, and I numbed it until it healed. Your problem is what, exactly?"

Carlos folded his arms and sent his angry gaze toward the surf. He was not about to admit just how wigged out he'd been by the action, and the numbing process had almost made him lose his mind thinking the worst. Rather than rehash that, he deflected the route of the conversation. "How I know you ain't helping him? He has your blade; all I got was a damned pocket—"

"Jealousy has no place in a king's psyche. It will make you weak," Ausar rumbled. He let his breath out hard again. "I knew this was going to take longer than anticipated. I told her that, but she would not relent once you said her queen daughter's name with pure Light." He walked toward Carlos. "Do you know how gorgeous Aset is?"

Ausar chuckled when a slight, peevish smile came out of hiding on Carlos's face. "Have you any idea how *convincing* a queen of her age can be when she wants something? You do not have to worry about which side I am on at the moment." He paused to allow the import of what he was stating to sink into Carlos's mind. "Young brother, I do not feel like arguing, battling, or anything else. You called for answers; I am here to deliver those. Speak. Fast."

Carlos relaxed, but was too embarrassed to immediately open a dialogue with this older male. This was not what a man was supposed to call in reinforcements about. "I know this little bar over in La Paz, on the main—"

"Let us find one closer," Ausar said, and instantly they were sitting at the rail in an establishment Carlos had never seen.

Ausar stood and rounded the bar and sat across from Carlos. "Name your poison," he said, seeming perturbed.

Carlos shot his gaze around the private enclave to get his bearings.

The bar was thick-etched crystal seemingly held up by pure white mist, the stools solid gold, the walls shimmering and covered with silver hieroglyphics that told a very long story. "Remy. Neat."

Ausar nodded and complied, materializing two rocks glasses in his hand, shoving one toward Carlos. "Women are very complex," he said, taking a sip of his drink, wincing, and setting down his glass. "A mystery of the universe."

Carlos nodded and took a sip of his drink. "Tell me about it."

"My wife brought your case to me in chambers," Ausar said with a wry grin. "I knew the moment she walked into the room trailing essence of Hathor that she was working me, but as you get older, you'll learn to let them do that . . . the benefits are astounding." Ausar took a healthy swig of his drink and studied the color of it in the light. "You young brothers do not know the subtle art of losing the battle to win the war. Sometimes when she is clearly in the right, I pose challenges that I have already decided in her favor, just to allow her to work *hard* to change my mind."

"Glad that something I did has some benefits." Carlos couldn't help but smile as he took another sip of his drink and watched the older Neteru, growing less suspicious.

"Yeah," Ausar said, and then presented his fist for Carlos to pound. "But then you called me, and she said so sweetly, 'Ausar . . . go to him, my darling. Talk to him. He needs you. Just as we need your shields. He is your newest made.' My response?" Ausar said with a chuckle as he took a generous sip from his rocks glass. " 'Tomorrow, my weakness. Can it not wait until the morning?' But she would not hear of it and could not relax." He set down his glass with precision. "So. We talk."

Carlos chuckled. "Damn, man, I'm sorry . . . uh, what can I say?"

"I did not catch all of the prayer . . . I admit to being distracted. But you wanted to know how to fix things, I take it, from what portions I heard of your plea." Ausar absently stroked the braid on his chin. "Basic. Realign her chakras. I do not know why you called me for this?"

When Carlos just stared at him with his drink midair, Ausar held his head in his hands.

"Oh, man . . ." Ausar sighed. "The vampire experience and the relapse to a dark throne have indeed blocked some of your knowing. All right. Now I understand her concerns. Remind me, before I go, to tap you into the Akashic Records so you can get true knowledge from the Book of Tehuti. Damn, brother I need to school you hard."

Carlos set his drink down carefully. "Am I still messed up or something, man? Like—"

"No. Just a little slower to adapt to wisdom contained within your Light knowledge base."

"Like a learning disability?" Incredulous, Carlos stood and began to pace.

"Something like that, but I can rectify your unknowing. Sit and let us talk." Ausar waited until Carlos had calmed down enough to take a stool again. "Remember, you did not eagerly and willingly accept this new transition."

"Yeah, I know, man, but—"

"An unwilling spirit. That was the first blockage to true understanding," Ausar said, cutting him off. "Then you did not have the humility to ask the Roundtable of Kings directly for assistance. Therefore, until you were ready to ask for guidance, none would be offered. That is how it is."

"All right," Carlos said. "I'm asking, because knowledge is power, and I definitely gotta get my house in order."

"Good," Ausar said with a wide smile, his regal posture tall as he sat across from Carlos. "Then let me explain. Vampires have knowledge, but the wisdom aspect comes from the Light. The dark side, thus, uses power in heinous ways—no wisdom. You know of chakra alignment from your old experiences and have worked with this energy to imprint her only to you. But you did it from the wrong base."

The visible question in Carlos's eyes made Ausar laugh in a deep, resounding thunder. The tone wasn't malicious, just thoroughly amused.

"Young brother, you began at her base chakra, the one that glows red, the one that rules reproduction . . . the one between her legs." Ausar shook his head as Carlos lowered his gaze and took a sip of his drink. "Foolish. That only binds as long as you are there to keep it glowing."

"Yeah, so I've learned," Carlos muttered.

"You should have stared at her crown chakra, the one that opens to divine insight. Then, my brother, you work your way down to her inner vision of you—her third eye . . . then down to her throat chakra—"

"Naw, man, I worked *da throat,* okay?"

Ausar shook his head. "Her throat *chakra.* Her *voice.*"

"Like I said," Carlos muttered, "I—"

"Never *heard* a thing the woman was saying to you."

Both men stared at each other.

"I have no doubt you could open her voice to glass-shattering decibels," Ausar said, pushing away from the bar to fold his arms. "You are one of us—a male Neteru," he said, sounding so indignant that it made Carlos sit up taller and nod. "There is no question of this capacity. We would have been ashamed otherwise."

"That's what *I'm saying*," Carlos said, pounding Ausar's fist.

"But," Ausar replied calmly, his tone low and controlled, "did you capture her voice, the things she has told you over the years, understand it, and hold the important energy of it such that you could articulate it back to her?"

Again, Carlos couldn't answer the charge and the older male simply nodded.

"Her link to divine inspiration and insight comes through her voice, what she says . . . and if you truly hear what she says, you enter her heart chakra—the bridge. You guard that bridge with your life, not what's between her legs. Because once you have the bridge won, my brother, you have her mind, her dreams, her voice always speaking well of you, defending you to the world . . . then you have conquered any gall that may erupt in the fifth chakra . . . did you feed her and work on her stomach?"

"Feed her?" Carlos pushed back and folded his arms over his chest. "I fed her as a vamp, I took her to dinner, I—"

"Did you feed her with spiritual food?"

Carlos stared at Ausar, unblinking.

"You have *never* taken that woman to dinner, then."

All façade crumbled as Carlos leaned forward eagerly trying to learn. "Aw'ight, aw'ight, like . . . I don't—"

Ausar closed his eyes and ran his palms down his face, annoyed. "No wonder Cain walked into your home and plundered it!" Ausar spoke with his head hung back. "Brother, brother, brother . . . did you feed her truth and honesty . . . a genuine appreciation for her gifts? Did you drizzle her mouth with the succulent fruit of a lover's pride in everything new that she learned, every achievement, every single win that she won all by herself?"

Ausar lifted his head and stared at Carlos when he looked away. "The woman was starving, brother. Just as in your old vampiric incarnation, your job as her man is to *feed* her!"

The statement was so basic and profound that Carlos was on his feet again, pacing. This time Ausar was up and following suit behind the bar, raking his locks.

"I cannot believe that you let a woman of this magnitude practically starve to death in your care because you resented her gifts. Now I *am* ashamed," Ausar said, shaking his head. He pointed at Carlos's back. "Have you ever made her dinner?"

"Yeah, man, plenty of times I brought in whatever she wanted to the lair, and—"

"No," Ausar said in a rumble so low that it made Carlos turn and face him. "Without magic. Without powers. Have you ever taken the time to bring her whatever her favorite fruit is to your bed, and feed her while you told her of your pride for her . . . ever allow pineapple and mango juice to dribble down her chin as you looked into her eyes and told her, 'Baby, I am so proud of you'? Something so simple, something that required you to work with your hands to uncover the sweet meat inside the fruit you were preparing for her, while she watched your hands pare the skin away. Have you?" Before Carlos could speak, Ausar shouted, "Read the Song of Solomon, then! It is in the Holy Book! You call yourself her husband?"

Ausar snatched off his suit jacket and flung it to the floor. Carlos stood very still, thoroughly expecting the old king to mop the bar with him.

"That is how you bind her forever at the primal chakra! Once you have slowly conquered each zone, one through six, the seventh one is a given!"

Pure humiliation held Carlos rooted where he stood.

"It is obvious to me now that you worked your way through her system from the bottom up. Primal first, fed her not, stoked her gall, broke her heart, ignored her voice, bludgeoned her third eye with things no woman should ever see, and made her lose faith in you at the divine level! Are you mad? Did you think you could lay enough rod between her legs to rectify that? I should just leave your young, stupid ass here in this bar and go home to my queen! The only thing keeping me here is the fact that I cannot go home to her failed!"

"Man . . . I didn't know all that going in," Carlos said, unable to look Ausar in the eyes.

"She is a child of *Light*," Ausar grumbled and finally sat, pouring them both another drink. "You can only temporarily hold her like that.

So let us repair the damage," he said begrudgingly, clinking Carlos's glass as he came back to the bar, accepted it, and sat with a thud.

"Maybe she is better off with Cain, if I did all that to her." Carlos stared into his drink. It was bad enough what Marlene had shown him, now to really understand it in male Neteru terms, all he could do was hang his head.

"Oh, brother . . ." Ausar said, tossing back his drink hard. "Don't give up the battle so quickly."

"Now I know why you were about to cut off my shit," Carlos muttered.

"Why would I do that to another man?" Ausar said. "Especially when it was done to me."

Again, both men's eyes met.

Ausar nodded. "Set, also known as Satan, desecrated my body after I fell in battle. Aset, my heart, searched for every limb torn apart, bound me back together, and literally prayed me back to life."

Carlos nodded fervently. "Yeah, man. That's love, for real."

"As you know from the Akashic records, she was a virgin. I never got the chance to be with her before I died."

Carlos raked his hair. "Been there."

Ausar smiled. "So have I, so why would I not assist a younger man walking down the same road?"

"But you were always, you know, in the Light. I wasn't."

Ausar scoffed. "I was focused upon battle, war, empire building. Let us just say that I had my wilder days, too. I was no saint." He chuckled sadly and tossed his drink down hard. "However, you recall, there was one thing she could never find."

Carlos looked toward the door and then down at the brown liquid in his glass. That level of honesty between men made him uneasy. Ausar was no joke, had come raw clean, even as a king with pride, and what he'd said was almost too much information. "Man . . . I don't how you lived after that."

"I could live with it because she made a replacement, an obelisk of granite, healed me with the Caduceus so I could feel it and so could she, and all is very well in my world. Had my son after that—Heru. What I can I say?"

Carlos chuckled and pounded Ausar's fist. "Sheeit . . . I guess all *is* right in your world, maaan . . . granite. Damn." He laughed hard, needing the tension release. "Every major monument in the world has a replica—scary."

"I am not boasting or attempting to instill insecurity in my brother regarding who has a stronger staff. No. It is just you and me here speaking as men. The point of this information being," Ausar said, still chuckling as he sipped more of his drink, "that I had not already bedded her when tragedy struck. But I had all but the seventh chakra conquered."

"Now that's deep," Carlos murmured with genuine reverence.

"Do not be so hard on yourself. You did, too—before you undid your own good work."

Carlos stared at Ausar. "But you said—"

"Hear me out," Ausar said gently. "Young brother, you were *magnificent*. With no guidance or training or mentoring you had inspired her most divine hope by showing her your vast potential." Ausar motioned to his crown chakra. "Then you opened her third eye to allow her to see the selfless sacrifice you were willing to make just for her . . . you stood valiantly before all—just for her."

When Carlos looked away Ausar landed a firm grip on his shoulder.

"Then you told her how right she had been, how much you loved her, and meant every word of it." He extracted his hand from Carlos's shoulder and touched his throat. "Then you pierced her heart so much that she shared her heartbeat with you to give you one. You gave her a reason to be galled at even Heaven for not giving you a second chance," he added quietly. "And you fed her hope . . . until she could not resist, which allowed a virgin Neteru to sleep with you, in whatever manifestation you were in, until she wept. That, my brother, was awesome." Ausar chuckled. "You undoubtedly have skills . . . just need to remember them."

"But what do I do now that I've messed up and reversed all of that?" Carlos's gaze sought understanding as he stared into Ausar's wise eyes. Yonnie had said the same thing, in so many words—everybody couldn't be wrong, as the saying went. Yeah, this older hombre was definitely a friend.

"If she transgresses, you must forgive her." Ausar sat back and folded his arms. "Each of us has one wife . . . me, Adam, Akhenaton, the entire brotherhood of archons. But none has suffered more than Adam, and yet he was able to forgive."

Carlos nodded, although what Ausar said wasn't something he wanted to hear.

"Think of it," Ausar said flatly. "Who knows what was going on between them when a youthful mistake created a child within his woman's womb, one that ultimately killed *his* firstborn. Yet they repaired the rift and went on to sire another together, one that became the foundation for generations after him. They got over it."

"Yeah," Carlos said, still unconvinced he could do it, "but Eve was the only woman on the planet at the time. So after awhile, I would guess Adam would just have to suck it up and deal or become a monk."

Ausar laughed and tipped his glass to Carlos, making him stare at him. "True. You have a valid point. However, if this is the only woman in your heart, one that has tethered every one of your chakras to her, is there any other female on the planet that you desire?" He waited as Carlos's gaze slid from his. "Is it not as though Damali *is* the only woman in the world for you? I fail to see the difference in your dilemmas."

"Philosophically speaking," Carlos muttered, becoming tense again. "But, if she's rhetorically my wife, whatever happened to love, honor, and obey?" Carlos threw his drink back hard.

"Ahhhh . . ." Ausar said, refilling Carlos's glass. "Misinterpretation through many translations in the texts, the word *obey*."

"So I've gathered," Carlos said, too disgusted to say more.

"No. You do not understand." Ausar let out a patient breath. "If you love her and cherish her, she will love you and honor you, if you forsake all others, she will listen to what you have to say with respect—but I do not know any woman who just blindly follows the lead of a man who has left her with questions." He sighed. "In fact, they never *obey*." Ausar chuckled. "It is a matter of *trust*. If she trusts you to truly have your mind on the right path, and her best interests always at heart, and trusts you . . . even if you make decisions that give her pause, she will confer with you about it first—and if your response is logical, she will go with your strategy. Following your lead is a form of obedience, but I have problems with the interpretation of the word. The semantics are wrong, loaded."

"But I'm always debating—"

"That's your problem," Ausar said, his smile knowing. "Do you debate with your male comrades, or hash it out, discuss many options, and then come to a mutually agreeable plan of action?"

Carlos couldn't answer him, but held his gaze, thinking of the way he and Yonnie rolled, how he and his brothers used to roll, and even the way the male Guardians in the house brainstormed solutions. "Deep."

"Very. Does your queen not deserve the same level of respect, if not more, since she is more heavily invested in your welfare than your friends?"

"I never thought about it that way, truth be told." Carlos sipped his drink carefully. "But females have a different approach to things, sometimes their methods aren't as decisive a strike. You know what I mean? Sometimes—"

"A man has to go to war," Ausar said plainly. "Yes. This is true. But it is the method and reason."

"How do you know when you're right?" Carlos stared at him unblinking.

"When I was desecrated and came back, for me the transgression called for nothing short of war."

"I can dig it," Carlos said, sitting up taller and pounding Ausar's fist again hard.

"I had bloodlust in my eyes. Pure silver rimmed in gold. I was after that bastard like a locust plague, and would not be denied."

"Sho' you right!" Carlos nodded and folded his arms.

"But I heard her out."

Both men stared at each other.

"I had just died, and she had just brought me back." Ausar waited until Carlos unfolded his arms and sought his drink. "She was frightened for my safety, wanted me to just love her . . . and I did. *Then,* once she saw how deep the scar to *my spirit* had been, she mounted up with me in strategy as my primary general. My gem of the cosmos was ruthless in her plotting. She was out for blood against that which had so injured her king. She cared not that she could be harmed, so much so that she inspired fear for her safety in me."

"Whoa . . . I've seen Damali get like that."

Ausar nodded. "A strong household cannot be defeated. Trust is the cornerstone of the marital alliance, which generates respect—the obey part, if we should call it that. But she will follow your lead, if you set the right example. Nothing can come between man and wife once they have aligned against outside forces. Not even children can split that asunder, hence how Adam regained control of his home."

Carlos just shook his head and sipped the rest of his drink. "That brother was the one."

"Yes," Ausar said flatly. "But he did not do it by force. Rule your home, my brother, but you must set the tone from a righteous place and stellar behavior as head of household. To try to take control otherwise is not only foolish and impossible, but devolves into internal power struggles that fracture the fortress at the seams. Anything can get in, then— demon or mere mortal. Take brutal command, and you are not a king, but a dictator. And we know from history that dictators always inspire rebellions, coups, assassinations. Martial law is then required. Resources become strained. Conversely, magnanimous, generous kings inspire loyalty, love, near worship, and an entire nation—your household—will be ready to go to war to protect their sovereign's rule. Basic principles of a long-term leadership, son."

"You droppin' science, *man,* that's so profound I don't know what to say."

"Any man can be redeemed if his heart and spirit is right," Ausar said, raising his glass. "King David set up his *best friend* to be killed in order to take his woman, had an illegitimate heir, and totally shattered the foundation of a nation—not just his household. Remember!" Ausar said, his voice rising with conviction. "He brought plagues to *a nation*—do not whine about the temporary virus you carried into your household. Be a man and correct it. But seeing his error, he went into deep, complete contrition and begged mercy, made amends, and then went on to rule an empire that began generations of glory. He is only one recent example; though I could begin at Adam and take you forward throughout history . . . but I do need to get back to my queen. The hour draws long."

Ausar stood and looked at the door. "You have shown her that you are valiant in battle and can protect the fortress of humanity. You have demonstrated your ability to provide. You have excelled, physically, as her lover, and thus have shown her all the *exterior* things that a man can show any woman. *That* is the issue. The cornerstone to putting your household aright. You have shown her what could be given to any woman . . . what have you shown her that is only hers to keep?"

"I—"

"You would serve and protect any female on the planet. That is in your nature, as a male Neteru. In fact, your job is to protect humanity, period."

"That's what I've been trying to do, man—"

"If there was an incoming threat to your compound," Ausar pressed on, undaunted, "you would body-shield any female in the house, and any weaker male. Honorable. But that is not an attribute of you given to her alone—nor should that one be. You have provided safe haven for all, would feed, clothe, and shelter all. Honorable. But not that's not hers alone, nor should it be. You have given others your friendship, loyalty, and trust, as you should." Ausar's gaze went silver around the edges of gold. "Your excellence as a lover, she *knows* has not been hers alone—recently." He folded his arms over his broad chest. "Therefore, what can you give her that no others can share?"

"The alignment?" Carlos's gaze furtively sought Ausar's wisdom, while feeling so totally foolish for not knowing the answer.

"Yes. Words, loving whispers, mean nothing to a woman after time and again they are not backed up by granite actions. Trust is the mortar between each brick that fell in your home until the relationship crumbled. Before every major action that could jeopardize your home, your co-unit of sanctuary, you owed your queen the respect to discuss it with her, and she would have returned the favor . . . if she thought you would listen and not discard her wisdom out of hand just because you are male, and thus believe yourself to always be inherently right." Ausar shook his head. "She is not your lapdog to obey your every command with her tail wagging for you. If your ego requires that, I suggest a puppy that you can train. Never your woman—especially not a queen."

Carlos raked his hair and stood.

"This is why the original archons had only *one* wife. Later the younger kings thought they could improve upon Adam's model because so many men had died in battles that it was expedient to bring more women into their households for safe haven, presenting damnable temptations, and they sought a logical way to be able to replenish the sons that war had wiped out—so they invented polygamy . . . much to their chagrin."

Ausar closed his eyes. "Problems that you cannot begin to fathom erupted thereafter. The only way to bring peace into homes was to close off the voices of their wives, deny their higher minds, and to ignore the damage to their hearts, leaving gall and malnourished spirits in their wake with foolish laws that made a woman's every attempt to elevate

herself an offense. Half the population of spiritual warriors, wasted behind the silent walls of blind obedience."

Outrage made Ausar's aura become cloudy and dark as shards of silver
swept through it while he attempted to regain his composure. Carlos remained mute, knowing that was probably the best thing to do until the
older king chilled out again.

"Thus, on the earth plane," Ausar railed in a booming voice, "in many
regions, the only connection between man and wife was the one you attempted to rule your queen by and failed. Some of our brothers have
completely lost their original vision and have even taken pleasure from
their flower by actions more drastic than the mere marking I gave you."

Ausar held Carlos in a hot, glowing gaze. "Imagine being so confused
that you would take away the delicate bud of pleasure from the lotus between your wife's legs with a knife. Insanity. But the tragedy remains
that even if you have not stooped to physical female circumcision, as the
man she loves in her soul, you can *still* cut away her pleasure with harsh
words, hurtful actions, lies, deceit, mistrust, until she feels *nothing* that
would allow her valley to flood and become fertile for you. This is serious, man."

"Oh, shit . . ."

Ausar smiled. "*Now* you understand. It is old law that a man can only
take a second wife and beyond if he can give *each* wife the *same* level of
attention, creature comfort, and alignment." He laughed softly. "One
wife is more than enough to handle for me, even with granite between
my legs. If they think it is all right because their wives have been brain-
washed to believe it is acceptable to do otherwise, and all laws have been
conveniently levied against her stolen voice, then they are only lying to
themselves. This is why said kings have been excellent providers,
materially—but they could never align with each wife to the core as I
have advised you is best."

"No doubt," Carlos said, blowing his breath out hard in agreement,
imagining more than one Damali on his hands. If he'd just understood
all this before and had the gifts Cain possessed . . . plus the wisdom of
dealing with more than one wife before, too, he might have done things
very differently.

"I did not give you my sword, before, because you were not ready."

"Clearly," Carlos said, no argument or offense in his tone.

"Since you know that you weren't and have accepted this fact means that you are." Ausar smiled.

"Cain got that, and the one thing that meant the most to me. He was the better man, so, hey, and I fucked up." Carlos looked out the door. "Thanks, man. You should go home, I guess."

"Until you were ready, I could not give you that blade. I knew you had to relapse at least one more time; your spirit was headed in that direction. But I also needed to watch how you handled your recovery. Very well done, under the circumstances of no guidance."

"Yeah, well, thanks . . . but little good did coming back from the ashes do me, given the situation now."

"The blade can only be passed to a living Neteru."

Carlos shrugged, and still kept his gaze fastened to the door. "After a throat nick and a siphon, the brother is all flesh. So . . ."

"He has a very good copy."

Carlos jerked his attention over his shoulder to now stare at Ausar.

"He needed it to keep his household in Nod in order. I provided him that out of respect for the brotherhood, and to also see what he would do with his opportunity." Ausar leisurely brought his hands up over his head and drew them forward, a glistening blade in his palms.

"His is silver-coated steel with gold inlays. Mine is titanium with silver, platinum, and gold alloy. Each blood gutter along the four blades that come to one is marked and etched for the instant demon burn." He tossed the blade to Carlos with pride, and Carlos caught it with one deft grab. "Feel the weight."

Carlos gaped at the fine weapon as he turned it from side to side. The handle was studded with diamonds, but with rings of chakra-colored precious stones that allowed his hand a perfect fit. "It's light as a feather."

"Ma'at worthy. Test it on the bar," Ausar said with a sly smile. "Eight inches of pure cosmic crystal."

Carlos bulked for the challenge. Ausar shook his head, staying the premature swing.

"You don't need that extra muscle to get the job done—like making love, do it smooth," the older king said calmly. "Finesse the cut, find your point and focus, one stroke, and go through the barrier with authority."

Carlos normalized, rolled his shoulders and stared at the thick bar, and swung. A high-pitched chime rent the air. The blade went through the structure like a hot knife through butter, and seconds later both halves of the cut crystal slowly fell away from each other with a thunderous boom to the floor.

"Whoo, *man,* she's sweet," Carlos said, marveling at the weapon. Then with a sigh, he handed it back to Ausar handle first. "You could definitely take any head with that, even the Devil's, brother."

"The universe didn't take anything away from you that was yours, young brother. Every obstacle was helping you build the strength of character and spirit, since your body was already built. You would not have been able to wield my blade to go through the crystal otherwise. The bones in your arm would have shattered instead. If you use the lessons correctly, you can be king in your household and build an empire in the Light."

"She don't want kids," Carlos said, staring at the halved bar on the floor. "Not from me."

"Not yet," Ausar said with a gentle voice. "Repair first, and then build. But this time, build on bedrock, not sand like the beach I found you on, and where I will return you."

Again both men stared at each other.

"When she's ready, her symbol will glow gold." Ausar smiled. "Yours will, too, trust me . . . you'll know, brother, and there will not be a thing you can do about it when it hits you like that. You will sweat gold, not silver, and will practically find yourself in another dimension."

Both men laughed.

"So," Ausar said, studying the blade, "I'll hold on to this for you until you really need it. First, you must repair the damage at home—even I do not have the power to rectify that."

"I appreciate all this, man, especially your steppin' away from your queen to school a brother. . . . I don't know if I would have been able to do that . . . like, you mighta seen me in the morning, feel me," Carlos said, chuckling sadly.

Ausar smiled and sheathed his blade. "I do *feel you,* as you say, but when you have sons . . . you will step away, especially if your queen has tears in her eyes for them. But it was not easy, I assure you—do not let it happen again."

Carlos laughed and raked his hair. "Say no more, I hear you. But I swear to you, man, even though I'm learning all this science, and appreciate it . . . there's still a part of me that wants to kick that motherfucker's ass soooo *bad,* I can't even tell you how much—since we're being honest."

"You do not have to explain, because we are both men."

They stared at each other.

"I have been waiting a very, very long time to do that, myself."

Carlos didn't blink. "I thought Cain was—"

"The bane of my brother, Adam's, existence." Ausar paced. "And he had the mark . . . so we all had to let it rest. *However, if he transgresses once,* and you hold your line, *nothing* would give me greater pleasure than to confer my sword upon you."

They held each other with steely respect in their silver glowing eyes.

"Set your household aright, young brother. Do *not* allow him to take your woman."

"Done!" A sense of complete outrage nearly made Carlos drop fang.

"Let 'em drop," Ausar roared. "If I had them, mine would, too! I am glad that you still have that capacity—you will need to match this challenger at every skill level, at every turn, at every potential advantage. That is why the Light allowed you to keep them!"

"They knew—"

"The All knows *all!*"

Stunned, Carlos didn't reply, but watched rage on his behalf throttle the wise king brother before him.

"If Cain disintegrates your household against her will, I shall mount up Hannibal with Akhenaton and we will ride winged stallions into Nod so quickly to slaughter that half-demon bastard with you, if he . . ." Ausar began to pace as Carlos's fangs dropped to battle length. "Noooo . . . I do not care what Aset says about Eve's sensibilities on this issue." He stopped and wiped his hands down his face, unsuccessfully attempting to garner control. "Adam cannot be involved in this, but me? Oh, my brother, my brother, my brother, you just do not know. Learn from what he has shown you; quickly gather it into your arsenal."

Although totally ready for a posse assault, the thing that most shocked Carlos was the fact that the kings, plural, had his back. *Now this was squad.*

"Do you know how long it has been since I have been to war?" Ausar asked, slowly unsheathing his blade and gazing at it with unvarnished affection. "Do you know how badly we have wanted to go into Nod and just be done with it? How many warriors we could resurrect from all our armies of old, simply by sowing the dragon's teeth?" He shuddered and put the blade away and stared at Carlos. "When the gates of Hell opened briefly, I thought Aset might have to chain me to the wall, the temptation to call to arms was so great."

"Next time, man," Carlos said, breathing hard from the sudden testosterone rush. He extended his fist for Ausar to pound, but Ausar grabbed his forearm in a warrior's handshake and brought him into a hard embrace.

"Get her back the old-fashioned way," Ausar said and let him go without breaking eye contact. "Handle your affairs so that we do not have to step in and do so, thereby creating havoc within each one of our palaces, or defying a direct command from On High. But should he come for her, or you, violating *her* choice . . ." Ausar shook his head. "We go to war."

"We go to war," Carlos repeated. "Thanks for having my back."

"We cover your back, your front, and your flank," Ausar rumbled. "But the ultimate choice remains hers."

CHAPTER NINETEEN

Damali stood at the tingling border of violet pyramid light. A gentle shove from her queens sent her into its brilliant glare. She called out to Cain three times as her form dissolved into radiant energy. It was imperative that he met her, knew that she was on her way. He had to prepare a safe haven for their exchange and not be embroiled in the civil war. She had done courageous before, even crazy . . . but this was definitely insane.

Her feet met white marble floor. He stood waiting, clad in ivory muslin, his eyes soaking in her gaze. For a moment, they said nothing.

"You came to me," he finally whispered from the other side of the pool.

"I was worried," she murmured. "I couldn't get you out of my mind."

She watched his Adam's apple move within his throat as he swallowed hard and fought to breathe. But beyond raw desire there was a deep melancholy that kept his irises natural brown. She could feel waves of intense sadness practically strangling him as she stood momentarily paralyzed, not sure what to do. Compassion leaked from her pores without effort. For all his insanity, Cain was still not a being she wanted to destroy.

"Tell me what happened," she said quietly, fighting the urge to go to him.

He shook his head and looked off toward the far entrance. "I cannot even speak upon it."

She waited, didn't move, just allowed her soothing presence to bring his eyes back to hers. "Cain . . . what happened?"

To her surprise he didn't come toward her. Instead, he went to a bench across the pool and sat down. He stared into the water, his shoulders slumped, hands clasped and dangling between his knees as he leaned his forearms on his thighs.

"The Caduceus didn't work," he said flatly. "It must be in contact with living organic matter. The earth. What is ground here is not that."

"The dragon," Damali whispered and closed her eyes.

"Zehiradangra," he corrected. "She was a friend of many, many years . . . and she would not come to me, even in spirit."

"Oh, Cain . . . where's the Caduceus? Maybe I could take it on the other side and recharge it?" she hedged, hating the ruse as it left her mouth.

He absently motioned toward the huge closet near his bed. "Over there. In Nod, it is useless metal. It does not come alive with Imhotep's energies unless connected with female nature energy, that which can reconstruct flesh."

Damali hesitated. Timing was critical. She knew he and the dragon were lovers, but he'd betrayed Zehiradangra. Yet, in his own odd way, he did love her. The whole affair was so twisted. But part of what he'd said sent a chard of defiance through her. She could also detect that in his mourning for the dragon, an unhealthy part of it included the fact that he couldn't come to terms with her flight from him. His commands didn't stop her. That was as much of the issue as Zehiradangra's death.

"Maybe she's in a better place now," Damali finally said in a gentle tone.

The one thing she and the queens hadn't factored in was a variable like this. What could she do for a man in acute mourning? The lovemaking would need to be tender, careful, healing, soul repairing . . . not energy depleting, back arching—if he asked her to stay the whole night, oh shit!

"I could not even properly carry out burial rites for her," he said thickly, two large shimmering tears rising in his deep brown eyes.

She almost went to him just from the pain in his voice. Zehiradangra had become her secret friend, too. Damali hugged herself. "Why not?"

"She was bloodied flesh in my arms." The tears Cain had been holding back fell. "I stood over her body, refusing to let them take her like carrion. But I had used up so much energy . . ." He stood. "I had to make a decision. In my brief absence total chaos reigned." His gaze returned to hers and absorbed all the compassion it exuded. He lifted his chin. "I made a trade."

Damali didn't speak for a moment. "You did what you had to do."

He nodded. "Twelve days of peace, for her body. The normal twelve days of funeral rites, a truce. During those twelve days, peace talks and new boundaries will be discussed and established. I have only twelve days to weave this delicate, fragile world back together, when twelve years would not be enough to mourn a friendship like that."

"But in those twelve days, there will be peace," Damali said in a quiet, firm voice, holding his beaten gaze without fraud. "You did the right thing." She began to walk toward him. "Her spirit is in the higher realm ether. If she was your friend, she had to have a good heart. She would have willingly sacrificed her discarded flesh to give you, her dear friend, a moment's peace . . . of that I'm sure."

He swallowed hard again as they remained only several feet apart. His gaze was so tender that she almost had to look away.

"That you would care enough to even discuss her, when she was the beginning of the end of your world with your former lover . . . I do not have the vocabulary for the emotions you inspire, Damali."

"She was your friend," she said, her voice a soft whisper. "You cared for her deeply. I can see it in your eyes."

She stopped herself before she said too much. She had to remember that being with him for a variety of reasons wasn't an option. He seemed so beaten, and so already depleted that there was no need to torture this already tortured soul. Her mission had changed. Her goal was simple. Ask him as a friend for the Caduceus, quietly seal him within his embattled realm, and go home. So she told him the only truth that she could.

"I never want to hurt you, Cain. You are a complex being. I don't claim to understand you fully. But I know that you are a king . . . out of time. Rule here, and rule well, my friend."

Although sleeping with him was not in her plans, nor was allowing him to overrun the earth with a battalion of hybrids to reinstitute slavery for the lesser gods, and perish the thought of him becoming the new Chairman, her arms still ached to hold him and rub his back, and let him weep for the twisted confluence of events that had turned out so very wrong. What if it was mostly Lilith and not him, Damali wondered as she watched Cain's inner turmoil from afar. So much devastation laid in Lilith's wake that it wasn't out of the question.

"And you are indeed a queen," he said quietly after a moment. "Thank you for being my friend."

He might as well have just stabbed her. Guilt had already plunged hilt deep into her spleen.

"And, you, for being mine." She nodded and backed away from him, needing distance and she sought it on the other side of the pool. "You taught me a lot," she said in a strong voice. "Showed me what was important. Helped me make critical decisions. Showed me the hard choices that come from true leadership. I couldn't have learned those lessons any other way."

She wasn't playing with his mind or jacking with his libido. This was fact. And given what she had to do to keep his world from spilling over into hers, she wanted to say it straight, loud and plain, so whatever happened after this conversation, he'd know it wasn't from malicious intent. It was simply a queen checkmating a king's imperialistic desires—but it was not a friend betraying a friend, as bizarre as the circumstances were.

"I will raze modern Cairo to the ground," he said, his eyes beginning to burn silver for her. "Wipe away the filth, and the crime, and the poverty, and build the Valley of the Queens in your name, Damali. Hatshepsut's temples will seem like hovels compared to the monuments of pink granite I will raise for you, my dearest of all friends."

He closed his eyes. She was horrified. Her honesty and the compliment it contained had inadvertently begun the dance.

"I will restore the majesty of Luxor, the colossi of Memnon . . . revitalize the old city of Memphis . . . Giza is in ruins, humans have desecrated the complexes of Khufu, Kafre, and Menkaure, but I will rebuild them all." His right fist pounded his palm as he gazed at her with determined ambition. "Your palaces will be filled with cypress . . . gardens within gardens. I will bring you rare, mystical amber from the city of Punt. You deserve no less than the best. Damali, when I'm done, it will be a new world."

"Cain," she said, her tone gentle but very steady. "While I am flattered beyond words that you would do all that for me—don't. *Promise me.* I know the modern world is a cesspool . . . but you cannot raze cities, cleanse humanity by just killing off those that offend, or enslave those you believe to be the ignorant masses. I'm out there every day fighting against that with everything I've got. This is *not* the Old Testament era, honey . . . you have to chill."

He looked at her, stunned for a moment, but then his expression mellowed to a tender, patronizing smile. "My love, do not trouble your mind over the harsh realities that come with progress. Your feminine compassion will not allow you to countenance it, nor will you ever be able to understand it. Shield your mind from such turmoil. Remain here, so that you bear no witness to what must be done. Know that I have already taken my petition to Ausar. It is under consideration as we speak. I do this not only for you, but for *us,* the future . . . and to ready the planet with only the *best* warriors—only the most evolved beings—for when it is time for Hell's gates to open. The purge is eminent. Our fortification will be strong thereafter. The streets already lined with gold when the Armageddon begins. This is what a male Neteru must do. It is what is required of kings."

"Oh, my God . . ." She began to pace on the other side of the pool. Every plan in her head evaporated. If Ausar had this proposal on the table and was considering it . . . oh, shit! What if Aset couldn't get the shield? What if the Neteru kings of old looked over the edge of their Roundtable, saw the horrendous condition that humanity had fallen into, and had given Cain the green light? Lilith might not even be a factor, if Cain could rule with his hybrids—why would he need her dead ass? He still had the sword! New panic arced a current down Damali's spine. And he wanted her to stay here, while he swept the planet clean of foul humans? Not.

"Listen to me, baby," Damali said, her voice beginning to strain. "You've been through a lot. Got a lot on your head and shoulders right now. This is not the time to make snap decisions. Think about it, uh . . . weigh all the options, uhmm, really see some of the cool things going on with people—they're not all so bad, ya know. And, uh—"

"If they are not living up to the laws of the old books, they are gone," he said quietly, his voice dipping to a sensual low. "If they are not intelligent, are weak of spirit and faith . . . they are gone. In the last days, we do not have time for them to learn. They have already had millennia to do so. Love, do not worry, I have had plenty of time to ponder these issues."

His gaze raked her. "But that you came *to me,* out of concern for my well-being and safety, and offered such compassion . . . that you would beg me not to battle and stay here where I could not be harmed." He briefly closed his eyes, and when he opened them they were pure silver-gold. "I would be honored to die for you."

"I don't want you to die," Damali stammered. "I just don't want you to—"

"My queen, with you waiting for me, I will not lose."

Damali just stared at him. Nefertiti had not told her what to do in a situation like this. All her life she'd been worried about whatever slithered over Hell's doorstop. Now the tables had turned and she was facing one of her own. What was she supposed to do with a gallant, deranged, zealot being, who had a soul, so she couldn't just smoke him, who was really good at heart, just twisted, was a friend of sorts, so she couldn't betray him to the bone . . . but she couldn't let him get out of Nod to wreak havoc on the planet, yet hated to lock him over here, and hated that he was all jacked up and in love, and she *had a man?*

"Sing for me," he whispered.

She almost blurted out, *"What?"*

"You are so torn with worry for me, that I can feel it literally ripple across the pool." He breathed in deeply and exhaled slowly. "Devastation, do not worry about the human cities . . . you have already razed me to the ground."

Now what was she supposed to do with *that?* If she went *there,* they wouldn't be friends when it was all over. If she went *there,* Carlos would have a fucking heart attack.

If she went *there,* she would have a fucking heart attack, because this man, clearly, was not playing tonight. Okay. What to do, what to do . . . do him, or *do him?*

He shook his head as his eyes stripped her. "I cannot believe you have lost your voice for me," he said in a tense whisper. "It's caught in your throat. I can feel it from where I stand."

She nodded weakly, as his gaze made each thin layer of silk she was wearing feel like a brand. This was not how the mission was supposed to go. As his slow visual unveiling went down her belly, the diamond in her navel began to radiate sudden heat throughout her womb.

"You wore essence of Hathor for me?"

She swallowed hard as he stopped breathing when he spied a glint of silver beneath the sheer wisp of scarves that made her skirt.

"Tell me that is not what I think it is . . ."

Damali nodded and opened her palms for him to see. "I went to the queens of my council, and told them about you . . . and they gave me these for you." Her voice had dropped an octave on its own. She wasn't playing, just couldn't help it while looking at the expression on his face. He shut his eyes and quickly turned his head as though she'd slapped him. "The Creator has blessed me." Then he slowly opened them and began walking toward her. "And they advanced your ripening for me?"

His voice held such quiet awe that she wasn't sure if she'd heard him, but there was no doubt about it, she could read the look on his face. If her voice would give her some wiggle room, now was the time to find it.

"Let me sing for you," she said, moving along the edge of the water in the opposite direction from him. "At least let me do that for you." She glanced around quickly to see what was available for another diversion. There was none. "And I wore these," she said, lifting a scarf with two fingers, "so I could dance for you."

He stopped. Incredulous. "You would even do the seven veils for me?"

"Yeah. If you want me to," she said quickly, anxiety spiking through her.

He shook his head, his murmur tense. "At this point, you don't have to. Just sing to me in my arms." A hint of fang crested. "Just the fact that you would . . ."

"But the acoustics are better over here," she nearly shrieked, dashing over to the shallow side of the pool.

He chuckled low in his throat. "No, they're *way* better in bed."

She could have kicked herself. She sounded like a complete bubblehead! Aw Lawd, Nefertiti didn't give her an antidote for this! Without much room for evasion, she fled down the wide pool steps and went into the sensation tank. He simply folded his arms and looked at her, seeming both amused and even more turned on.

Her skirts were floating in the strange, tingly energy that looked like water but wasn't wet. She glanced up at him and he seemed to be thoroughly enjoying the effect. Okay, the pool was working. She'd do the floor show from here. She'd do whatever was necessary to buy some time. She began belting out the first song that came into her head. "Wounded Lover," yeah, that would work, it sent an apology for what was about to go down. Even though it was new, *this* one she knew by heart. She'd actually composed it for Carlos, and shit, after this morning, and definitely after tonight, he'd need to hear that, too.

But something was very wrong. As she kept singing, Cain's rapt expression of desire had begun to dissolve into something she wasn't sure of. When he battle bulked, she froze for a second, took two steps back, and leapt out, putting the pool between them.

"How could you! In my house! When you know I am ready to put the world at your feet!"

"Yo, yo, yo," Damali said quickly, "I don't know what you're—"

"Look at your hands!" he thundered.

She glanced down at her palms quickly, her eyes wide, and started backing up. "I don't know how that happened, baby."

"Because you had him on your mind! His energy is in my pool and betrayed you! You sing to me—a lover's song, *in my pool,* composed and created for *another man,* and put your desire for him in it so strong that it literally changes your tattoo for him? Are you mad? You bear *his* tattoo in *my* house?"

When Cain headed for his closet, she headed for the door. She didn't need to be a telepath to know the man was going for his blade. She wasn't waiting around for old biblical justice, served king style, either. An eye for an eye, sheeeit . . . Off with the head of an adulterous bride, aw hell no, she was a sistah from 'round the way.

Her bare feet slapped the floor; the room was a blur. She could hear marble explode as the closet door left its hinges. But at least that meant the closet was open. She kept running, pushing herself to go faster, while she reached her hand back as the velocity of headwinds stung her cheeks. The Caduceus filled her grip. Two angry sphinxes stood and snarled.

"And you would rob from me, too!" a furious male voice bellowed behind her.

It was snap reflex. The Caduceus gripped tightly, something stronger and faster and bigger than she was on her ass. Two huge lion-bodied statues had dismounted for an attack. She went airborne, dragon style. It was the first image that popped into her head.

Her body nearly collided with the roof of the entrance as it elongated, picked up every color of the scarves she wore in its scales, and spiraled high past the sphinxes. She opened massive pearl-colored wings and set her sights on the three moons, clutching the Caduceus to her chest. She didn't know where she was going but she was out!

But as sure as the moons were her guidepost, she heard frenzied leather flapping coming her way. Darkness was covering the moons. She looked back to Cain's lair, and watched in horror as he hurled an energy ball toward her.

Her body jerked to a midair halt and she had to strain to stay airborne. Something tight and burning had wrapped around her waist. She didn't need to look down to know what it was. He'd lassoed her! A combination of fury and outrage made her redouble her efforts as he pulled. It was a test of wills and endurance. Defiance magnified the adrenaline spike. No man was gonna pull her out of the sky once she took flight! No arrogant king or whatever he was! She was definitely angry enough to breathe fire, but the image she'd pulled was Zehiradangra's placid, water dragon, love child vibe.

Damali screamed a battle cry as she dragged Cain several hundred yards. He held on to the line as though she were a huge dragon kite. The friction from his planted stance drew sparks from the pure energy ground as he began to move forward against his will. She didn't care; he had to let her go. But oddly, she refused to take him over the edge of the ravine. She was angry, but not murderously so.

Regardless of the test of wills between she and Cain, the moon was blackening as several thousand leather-winged predators covered it.

"Come to me!" he shouted.

"Not with a blade in your hand!" What, did he think she was stupid?

"The blade was for them, I *knew* you would run if I chastised you!"

Damali hesitated and stopped pulling away so hard. "Then let me go! I'll come to you on my own volition—pull me, and we'll both—"

"All right, all right!" He dropped the line.

Immediately the restriction left her with a gasp. But there was an even bigger problem than Cain. Nobody had to tell her. She was adrenaline spiked, they'd just eaten a dragon, she was trailing oil of Hathor, pseudo ripening, and to them she probably seemed like airborne sushi.

Smaller feather-winged entities were headed her way, too, as though ready to make a last suicidal stand. Cain looked so exhausted he was leaning on his sword for support.

"Tell them to get back," she hollered. "Your side will get slaughtered! You stay here and restore order!"

"No! Not without you! Until the last entity stands! Come home to me and I will defend your honor!"

Was he nuts? He was clearly energy depleted, could barely lift his blade. Whatever siphon he'd gotten from her had already been used.

He'd burned it all up restoring order when civil unrest broke out over the first dragon. She wasn't crazy. It was as plain as day. Grief had stripped him. The pool had sapped him. The tug-of-war had drained him. And her emotional drama had sucked him dry. It wasn't about being yard scraps for pride. She wasn't trying to let an old warrior save her; she would save herself and his ass in the process.

Frustration claimed her as she turned away from Cain and yelled the command to the feather bearers and followed it with a Neteru battle cry. "Go back! I'm going home!" They could either listen to their insane king or take an order from a queen who was making total sense. "Retreat!"

"Never surrender!" Cain yelled, dropping to one knee from exhaustion. "I will come for you in victory one day, my queen!"

Yeah, whatever—but not tonight. She watched Cain's forces pull back as hundreds of advanced forces of heavily armored, leather-winged hybrid soldiers careened over the edge of the ravine behind her. Thousands were behind them, the strongest had made it to the front line. They were taking the bait. The rip was right there. She could see the sky lighting up with golden shields dotting the horizon. *There were multiple rips?* Oh, man . . . which exit wasn't blocked?

Tumbling in a high-speed nosedive toward a thin barrier of light, she closed her eyes, said a prayer, and hollered Nzinga's name.

He'd walked for miles after talking with Ausar, just like he had after the whole blowout at the hacienda. Right through here, he needed a peaceful place, far away from the house, far away from the maddening tourist vibe. The moon had been up for hours, but Damali hadn't come home. What Ausar had told him was wise, but if Damali didn't come back, what was the point?

Carlos looked up to Heaven, wondering why God hadn't answered his prayers. But he knew in his heart the answer was simple; this time, he'd gone too far. The older king had told him, just like Marlene and Yonnie had.

Sometimes a man's luck just ran out, and all his bullshit finally came back to bite him in the ass. Carlos stood facing the ocean simply listening to the waves roll in and out. Some things hadn't changed since the beginning of time, like the tide, it rolled in, and rolled out. It was time for him to be out.

"All I asked for was a sign," he said quietly, pitching the last seashell in his fist.

He looked up and stood still.

A spiraling, sparking stream of light shot across the sky. The shooting star held his attention as the dense, gray clouds seemed to brighten, go golden like a shield of Heru had been raised, then went instantly black and disappeared. But the star kept moving . . . or was it a comet?

Carlos keened his eyes on the phenomena in awe. It looked like a whirring rainbow lit by lightning or something. All right, what did this sign mean? He should have asked for the answer to go with the mesmerizing spectacle that seemed to be moving closer and closer . . .

Oh, shit . . . it was headed his way!

He dodged what he thought was a fireball, hit the beach, covered his head, and waited for the explosion. Instead he heard laughter.

"Oh, my God, Carlos!" a very familiar female voice shouted.

He was on his feet in seconds looking at a beautiful, disheveled woman who'd come out of the sky in a blaze of sparks, half-naked, wearing scarves, hair all wild, eyes gorgeous but crazed, and walking in a circle clutching the Caduceus.

"Whooo!" she exclaimed. "The drag coefficient on this golden rod ain't no joke, brother!"

"Damali?"

"Yeah, baby, lemme tell you what happened! It was wild!"

CHAPTER TWENTY

It was the most elaborate of dances, just like the old queens had shown her. The fantastic story she told on the beach had a foundation of pure truth, enhanced by exotic, graceful pivots and turns. Evasion was not done with malice, but from a solid place of love within her soul. None of what she told him was illusion as she peeled away onion-thin layers of his hurt, allowing each veil to flow over his ego and drop to the sand while she exposed herself to him bit by bit.

There was a family to maintain, crazy scientists still on their trail, men of knowledge without wisdom who had almost blown up the world. There were so many things out there that still went bump in the night. An almost-lover was still in another realm eating his heart out . . . but all of those problems could wait for another night to be resolved.

In all this mayhem that would probably never cease, she'd learned on this adventure that to fall on one's sword was not an act of weakness or surrender, but sometimes the most courageous thing one could do. She'd learned how to pull back, retreat, and live to fight another day—something she'd never fully understood until now. She also understood from firsthand experience how her man had gotten himself into precarious situations, and would forever suspend judgment after all she'd been through. She'd definitely learned the power of an apology meant in earnest, and where the invisible border of the Land of Going Too Far was. In all these important lessons that were crucial for the development of a true queen, she'd figured out how to pace herself and prioritize.

Right now, the man sitting on the beach with her was that . . . a dear, sweet priority, who deserved time, attention, healing, and more. A good man who'd backed himself into an ego corner, had lashed out, and gotten hurt, but now needed her, his woman, to open the secret door to salvage his pride. So she danced a flowing dance, explaining all but not everything. She let his mind fill in the blanks during every delicate pause and breath.

"Now does that make sense?" she said gently, still talking with her hands as they sat side by side.

Carlos nodded, but kept his gaze on the sand. "I thought you weren't coming back," he admitted quietly. "After all the mess I've done, I couldn't blame you."

"I wasn't going nowhere," she said, hoping that he'd look up and see the truth in her eyes. "I had to be the one to go get the Caduceus . . . it has healing powers that only work from a woman's hands. Eve gave it to me, so it holds my charge, and I have to be the one to give it back to the queens for safekeeping."

"That why they called you for the meeting?" He'd asked the question while digging a small hole in the sand with a shell.

She paused, evaded, but would not lie to him. "They wanted me to learn some lessons."

"Guess we both got taken to school today, huh?"

She smiled when he looked up at her. But his eyes seemed so sad as he considered her disheveled condition and went back to digging in the sand.

"Like I said, I can't say nothing to you about what probably went down . . . or whatever you had to do to get him to give up the staff." Carlos shrugged absently and pitched away the shell. "I ain't mad; I don't have a right to be."

Damali looked over her revealing outfit and sighed. "They sent me in there with theater," she admitted. "Thought it best if I went in unarmed, and appealed to his Old World sense of what a woman was supposed to be, instead of going head to head with him as a warrior."

Carlos nodded, the muscle pulsing in his jaw. "I know. I understand why you had to be the one to do that, and why I couldn't. It's cool."

"They wanted me to catch him off guard," she said quietly, "but not kill him." She let her breath out hard. "They also didn't want me to kill you . . . and I told them that if I went too far, it would."

He looked up at her with a very quiet, unspoken yet urgent question shimmering in his brown irises. Then he looked at her hands. "Did they give you those?" he whispered, staring at his tattoo in her palms.

Damali turned her palms up for him to inspect. "I wanted to go in there very clear about what I would and would not do." She could almost feel the silent one-ton weight lift from his shoulders. "He was very disappointed that I had only come for the Caduceus. But he'll have to get over it."

She watched Carlos swallow a smile as his quietly pleased gaze sought the sea. "I'm sorry that I allowed him to nick me in the throat," she said. "That was wrong."

Carlos lifted his chin, pride putting tension in his shoulders again. "Like I said, it was cool."

"No, it wasn't," she said softly. "But for the record, it didn't leave a mark."

He gave her a sidelong glance. "Hey, we don't have to talk about it. It's squashed."

She began digging in the sand between her feet with a small shell. Ahhh . . . Nefertiti was so wise, the queen's bath so mystical. . . . "I want you to lean in, open your vamp radar, and inspect my throat."

"That ain't necessary, D, after all we've been through and everything you told me. It's enough for me that you know what this asshole was trying to do against humanity, so—"

"Do it for me," she said softly. "So I can sleep at night knowing you know, even if you don't care. Thinking that you still don't trust me, even if you do, will worry me beyond the grave. It's a woman thing . . . can you do that for me, baby?"

Carlos gave her a slight scowl. "Only because Mar showed me how y'all's minds work am I gonna do this, Damali. But not because I needed to—it's because you needed me to. Okay?"

She simply nodded. "I know. It's not for you, it's for me."

"'Cause, if in the back of your mind, you really wanna be with this guy, not that I can blame you, after all the stuff you said this morning about what he was, and what I wasn't—which was the truth . . . hey. I messed up. You have a right. So, you know. I'm cool."

"What I said on the beach this morning," she murmured, "was coming from a fit of pure fury. I can't take it back, because once said, it's been heard. But I can tell you I was dead wrong to ever compare you to another man. That won't ever happen again, especially when there's no comparison." She let out a sigh, but it wasn't theater. Truth was what had expelled it from her lungs. "I can also tell you that when I went before the queens, I challenged even their plan . . . because I knew who was the better man. They made Eve excuse herself from the discussion because the things I had to say and learn, no mother should ever hear about her son."

She paused as Carlos looked up at her, this time his eyes were filled with quiet pride.

"The better man," she continued, holding his gaze in an unbreakable lock, "he was with my family at the hacienda, not power tripping over in Nod. And I asked those old girls, tell me, what can I do to make it right? They told me to go get the Caduceus and heal my household before I tried to tackle healing the world." She waited as more resistance left him. "Now will you inspect the bite . . . and I want you to tell me what you see."

Reluctantly, Carlos took her jaw between his forefinger and thumb and turned her head to the side. He almost cringed, half-afraid to see a huge signature left there by Cain's virile strike, but had to move closer when he couldn't detect a thing at all. Ausar had been so wise.

"There's no mark," Carlos said quietly, getting closer to make sure his eyes hadn't lied.

"No," she said calmly. "He ain't all that. It was a feed. That's it. At least for me."

"But . . ." Carlos's words trailed off as he turned her head the other way and knelt before her.

"That's your side, where I got my first mark. Do you think he could pattern over that?"

Her words stilled him as her hands covered his. The warmth they contained and the love they exuded made him lower his forehead to rest against hers. He released his breath in a slow stream of relief. Oh, yeah, he'd rebuild from the ground up, from her crown chakra down. Never again. Everything the older king had said was the truth, and his ears tuned to Damali's voice to hear it for the first time.

"You marked me as your wife," she whispered. "Yeah, he tried, but he didn't have that much juice . . . and my soul wasn't willing, neither was my body. He came up out of that bite without even blood on his lips. I wasn't giving him anything, but what I wanted to . . . and I'd never give him your throne. I've only got one king."

He looked down at his queen who seemed like a shimmering, gold-dust-covered pixie. Hair wild, golden bands twisted through where it had once been swept up into a regal crown. Ripped and ragged scarves precariously covered her body, and yet a diamond still sat in her navel. She had one earring missing. Her feet were bare. But even half-naked in another man's lair, she had held the line just for him.

His senses swept over her butter soft skin . . . skin that now seemed more satiny than it had ever felt before. Cain hadn't even held her or kissed her when she'd gone in after the rod. And yet, by rights, she could have if she'd wanted to—he would have never known . . . the profound gift that she'd given him was that she hadn't wanted another man's touch, *hallelujah.*

That truth rippled through him like clean baptismal water as he held her face and leaned his head against her third eye. The awareness that she'd silently opened her inner vision to him to let him see that truth, washed away so much hurt he almost wept. She didn't care that he couldn't release his old double-standard, that it mattered to him that she hadn't crossed the line. She let him feel it, know that she knew he still held it. But there was no bitterness within her, just a quiet acceptance of his character flaw.

With that knowledge of her gentle acceptance came power. He would *never* cross the line to break her heart again. What could he do with this off-the-hook woman but love her? She was such a gift, and he'd almost thrown it away. His hands trembled as he held her face as though it were made of fragile glass.

"Let me heal my wounded lover tonight," she whispered, rubbing her palms over his hands until they burned. "Let me show you some things that the old queens taught me . . . just for you, my king."

Carlos closed his eyes, almost unable to bear the sensations her voice produced as it murmured the truth. It bound his heart to hers, just as Ausar promised it would, removed all worry from his gizzard, and fed him with confidence. In six levels' deep, he was supposed to be aligning her chakras to his tonight, but for the life of him, he was in silver bondage to hers. The last pulsing one she owned outright.

She gently withdrew from him and pushed him to rest back on his elbows. Then she stood without effort and picked up the Caduceus. "I can probably only do this once. I was saving this just to heal you. After it goes back to the queens, I don't know."

Damali smiled and gazed at him tenderly. "I love you, baby." He didn't need to know that some of Nefertiti's techniques would be with her forever, or that they were taught in an avatar seduction class. He didn't need to burden his mind trying to figure out what was taught by the queens, or how much of their private business she'd told them, or they'd learned, or even worry that what she was about to do was taught in part by his competitor.

While truthfully it was a combination of all of the above and she'd learned a few more things being out in the world, the important fact was she was saving that knowledge for him.

Tears filled her eyes as she looked at him, realizing just how much she loved him, and how close she'd come to losing such a gift. That was why he never needed to question the new things she was about to show him . . . things he hadn't taught her . . . and then attribute all that exquisite knowledge to another man. Cain didn't own it, *she did.* What he really didn't need to know was the mystical Caduceus also contained the magic of male ego placebo. She thrust it into the sand and let it form a gentle golden light beneath him.

"I love you," she whispered again. "Trust me and relax."

"I love you, too."

Warmth penetrated his Light-encircled body as he watched Damali move a few feet away. She had danced for him before, but her sultry Egyptian eyes had never held such serene authority. Moon and surf was her backdrop. This woman was in control. The steady sound of the waves lapping the shoreline was like distant instruments as she began to sing. She'd sung to him before, too, but never like this. Midnight-blue heavens framed her while she moved and swayed as though water itself, dropping a scarf at each stanza until it was hard for him to breathe.

A small golden scarab ring that he'd never seen her wear caught his eye as her hands passed her beautiful face. For a fleeting moment he wondered if it had been a gift from Cain, then banished the thought with complete trust. It had to be an amulet, he knew his baby better than that. But she also wore a new scent . . . something *incredible* that he'd never smelled on her. The hint of her signature ripening was threaded all through it and wafted toward him as she danced.

He'd been so upset, he hadn't really processed it all before . . . and Cain hadn't been able to take her when she was wearing *that?*

Soon where she had been or what she might have done peeled away from him with each dropped veil. Whatever she was doing was healing more than his soul or mending his heart. She'd put the shield of Heru around his ego and given him an erection made of steel. When she dropped the last scarf and he saw her tattoo, it no longer mattered.

"You went in there like that for me . . ."

"*This* is all yours," she whispered. "Take your clothes off or they'll probably burn after I'm done."

He gladly complied, but when he started to stand to go to her, she shook her head, wagged her finger at him slowly, and kept her expression stone serious.

"Don't move."

He didn't know what to make of her command, but had surrendered a few minutes ago when he'd spied his symbol on her clean-shaven mound. So he simply watched her come to him in her own sweet time in a sexy saunter forward. She dropped to her knees and then crawled toward him on the beach, her supple spine dipping beneath the moon as her gaze held his.

"I am going to apologize on my hands and knees for ever taking you where I took you," she whispered, nuzzling his neck.

In reflex his hand reached to touch her, but she gently shoved his hand back down.

"I said not to move, didn't I?"

Her voice was a warm wash against the Neteru symbol on his throat. If this was how female Neterus negotiated . . . oh, yeah, any night, any day, he'd confer with his queen. He could only close his eyes as her tongue found the beginning of the mark and traced it, producing a shudder. But there was something about her mouth, the new heat it contained that seemed to draw every pulse point within him to one agonized place on his skin.

"Oh . . . Jesus . . ."

Her delicate palm had found the center of his chest, and it felt as though the tattoo within it had connected to the one she suckled at his neck. The dual sensation caused mild delirium and made his scrotum contract. He had to touch her, but she refused to allow it. As her palm gently circled his nipples, his head dropped back and he began breathing through his mouth. When her hand slid down his torso, he almost sat up.

What kind of magic did she own? What had she dredged from the Caduceus, he wondered, but didn't care. If he had known that it held such erotic healing power, he would have gone to Nod to get it for her himself.

His mouth hungered to taste hers so badly only a whimper escaped his lips. Instead of answering his unintelligible plea, she kissed his chest and pulled one of his nipples between her teeth. That's when his back hit the sand. His tattoo burned so hot he thought it might bleed. She had a flattened palm gently rotating against one side of his chest while her mouth nipped the other. His stomach was in knots; his hips lifted needing to move. He had to get inside her or die.

Then she stole all the atmosphere around him with one slow kiss that dissolved him. Before the moan could even come up from his diaphragm, she ran her hand down his stomach in a hot, lingering sweep and held him tight, pulled back gently from the kiss, found his throat mark, and bit him as she squeezed hard.

He lost it. Fangs lowered. He couldn't take it anymore. But she held him in her grip, gave him a look that spoke volumes, and swept her mouth across his stomach until new tears filled his eyes.

"Let me work," she murmured, and ignored his outburst, unfazed.

The moment her mouth touched him and drew him in, he cried out. There was something so different about it, the siphon so damned hot. It felt like a double plunge, like she was working his throat at the same time and flatlining him with pleasure until he had sand beneath his nails. The sensation was causing cold panic sweat. Silver gold rushes. He was right there. She had him at the point of two seconds past too late, and he couldn't even stutter that fact.

Then she held his sac like she never had, cradled it in her palm in a slow, agonizing, but gentle pull. The tattoo in the cup of her hand burned pleasure all through it, and made his seed honor gravity and retreat. When she came away from him, he watched her—spent, but not. She calmly blew on the strange white orb that pulsed in her palm for a few seconds and then it stopped. She hung it in the air just a few inches above his head and smiled. He was almost too exhausted to be curious, but still was.

"That's one," she murmured, and blanketed him. "Eleven more to go until your planets are properly aligned."

Oh . . . shit . . . he couldn't breathe as her satiny skin fused to his. The instant her mound slid over his length, he wept. He wasn't even in her, but it felt just as good.

Her kiss became a sea of untold pleasure as he willingly drowned in her mouth. Each gasp she released across his tongue sent a new tide all through him. Every slowly undulating motion of her pelvis set off depth charges he didn't even know he owned. But she was relentless as she continued collecting small orbs in different glowing colors, refusing to allow him to enter her or bite her. When she rolled over on her back, he thought she might show him mercy—but she didn't. She just pulled him against her, tapped into his spinal fluids with a touch, and took his back out with ecstasy prisms one vertebra at a time.

He heard his voice from outside his own body, "Baby . . . please . . . *por favor, compasion.*"

She didn't have a heart. Master destroyer of a man's sanity, she was. Her hands covered the base of his spine and he saw stars. She didn't seem to care that he was trembling and sobbing or calling her name. She just smiled and ignored him, allowing her pinky ring to glide over his clenched ass, then gently force its way through a barrier that arched his back. He bit her on impact. Entered her with a hard slide. All language went void in the blackout. Vanishing point was his destination, or bust.

Every cell in his body began to deconstruct when she arched and moaned. Her voice hit a decibel that shattered his skeleton. He felt her hard climax contract around him then send shock-wave vibrations through the tiny gold ring that teased his outer rim. Carnal velocity stripped a gear and his mind right along with it. She'd never . . . He was almost pure mist, and then he heard her moan again. She'd cried out something about creation point, wherever that was, he didn't care. "Oh, God, yes!" *Baby, take me with you . . .*

Every planet she'd aligned in a ring around his head began to slowly split open. His new world would not be built until she willed it so. Translucent surfaces cracked, pouring primordial ooze from multiple internal eruptions. Lava. He was burning up! Gold sweat singeing sand. Lightning strikes within pulsing pleasure orbs. Hot mist. Steam plumes rose from his tears building pressure. Earthquake convulsions, but still he couldn't cum. His mind fractured. His heart stopped.

"I got you, baby, *just breathe,*" she whispered.

And he did.

Instantly, a powerful vacuum suction to her universe drew him from his evaporated state. V-point eclipsed. He teetered on the outskirts of reality too ecstasy dazed to even cry out. His heart started. It skipped across her new oceans and formed land. Within seconds, twelve cataclysmic releases thundered against one another like heavily laden dominoes, then slammed him back into his own flesh and reconstructed him one cell at a time. He was clay for her to mold.

Blinding, rapid bands of color vibrated sound trebles through his system. His lids fluttered. Pinpoints of light created new stars behind them. Release implosions collided, choking him as his lungs fought the new density of pure pleasure. Then twelve patient and closely aligned heavenly bodies erupted and fused into one scorching mushroom cloud that centered in his groin. He almost swallowed his own tongue.

For a moment, everything went still. He had no body. He was weightless energy. There was no sound. There was no time. No past, present, or future. He just was. Then everything hit him at once— supernova—he hollered her name and was made man.

He wasn't sure how long he was out, only that if he could ever walk again he was healed. When he finally opened his eyes, he was lying in a ring of wet sand dampened from his own sweat. She lazily petted his chest and kissed him softly. He looked up at the sky, unable to move, then slowly rolled over still within her. There were no words. What she'd given him was beyond a religious experience.

"You all right?" she whispered and dropped her head to his chest.

He closed his eyes and shook his head no. He'd never be the same.

"You want some water," she whispered. "I can get that."

He didn't doubt it. She was creation itself. There was nothing in his male mind to cope with what she had just done to him. No registers of information that lingered from his Council-level experience of being on a vamp throne could touch it. This thing she did from the Light . . . uh– uh . . . she had to take the Caduceus back. It was a dangerous weapon. He was still trembling from its effects.

"I only did it because I love you," she whispered, brushing his mouth.

He kept his eyes closed, didn't have anything left within him to even lift his eyelids. It was all he could do to breathe.

"You wanna go again?" she murmured, tracing a nipple.

"Take it back," he finally whispered. "Baby, please, take it back."

"It only works that strong because I love you . . . that's what gives it all the juice." She kissed his wet temple and then the side of his face as new tears spilled from beneath his shut lids. "Without that, everything else is just technique."

"You stopped my heart," he murmured.

"Yeah, but I restarted it, didn't I?"

He nodded with his eyes still closed, sucking in huge inhales. "I've never . . ."

"Good,'cause neither have I. So now we're even."

"I'm sorry, baby," he murmured, trying without success to lift his arm to caress her cheek.

"I know. So am I. Forgive me?"

He nodded. "Oh, yeah . . . I don't even remember what we were fighting about."

He felt a long, satisfied sigh of relief exit her body as he cradled her to him. He stroked her back, sending all the love he'd ever owned for her within the caress, and could feel the muscles under her skin vibrate and move to the touch.

"I'll protect your heart," she whispered against his chest with her eyes closed as his hand slid down her back to rest against her Neteru mark.

"With all that I own, all that I am, I promise you, baby, I'll protect yours," he murmured into the crown of her hair as her silent tears wet his chest. "I'm so glad you chose me . . . because I would die without you."

He felt the sob before it exited her body, but as he brought his hands over her hips and up her back to hug her, he froze. Where there should have been skin, delicate feathers grazed his fingers. Her shoulder blades were gone, massive wings had grown right out of them. His eyes opened wide. She was still nestled against him weeping with joy. The ocean's breeze was blocked by enormous white wings that slowly wrapped around him. A silvery sheen covered each fragile feather. He glanced around, wondering if they'd both died and gone to Heaven. But it was still night outside; the surf rolled in and out uninterrupted.

"Baby," he croaked, his voice failing into a panicked whisper. "You have wings."

Damali lifted her head to stare into his eyes, questioning.

"Your eyes are solid silver," he said, unable to stop staring into her transformed irises.

She glanced at his sides and saw the feathers. Tears streamed down her face. "Those aren't mine; they're yours." She began crying hard in earnest, near hysteria, her words choppy and thick. "You took me someplace I've never . . . baby, not even the vanishing point felt like this."

"They're yours, *tresora*," he said, his voice cracking with emotion. "They're growing right out of your shoulders . . . dear God, you're a healing angel."

"I'm a what?" she said, pulling back as he began to cry hard, and crouched above him on her hands and knees.

He just looked up at her and sobbed harder, briefly touching her face and allowing his hand to fall away to the sand. "Marry me . . . I promise I won't mess up."

She kissed his forehead, total alarm racing through her as she rolled her shoulders and saw that the wings unfurling from beneath him were owned by her.

"Every prayer you sent up was answered with the quickness," he choked, looking at her in reverent awe. "The Covenant came to me, because of you. The fires of Hell never singed you . . . the woman in Tibet even gave you tears from your kind . . . oh, baby, warrior angels were ready to take my head because of you . . . now I know why!" He sat up and placed his face in his hands and bawled. "Ausar was about to mount up the Neteru kings with Hannibal leading the charge to go get you in Nod, now I understand what the man was talking about. And I bit you . . . I *bit* you? Almost made you fall from grace? Oh shit . . . was I crazy?"

Part of her needed to stand and back away from him just to take it all in. The other half of her was paralyzed. She'd never seen Carlos so undone. Had never even fathomed the possibility. She flexed her shoulders, mesmerized by the breeze that grew from them as the sand stirred. Now she knew inside her soul why she had trouble shape-shifting into hideous things and could only do feathered birds with ease . . . everything else hurt. Just like vindictive behavior hurt . . . but loving him and her family so deeply felt so right . . . like loving the world of flawed human existence felt so natural.

Her fingers trembled as they reached out to touch his hair. "I love you," was all she could say at the moment. A slow dawning awareness filled her. Cain knew it; he'd called her that . . . an angel. Said he could feel something within her, just under the surface of her skin. Oh, Lord . . .

"I asked for a sign from On High, and the signs were there all along," Carlos whispered, now staring at her and wiping his face as he shook his head. "Total forgiveness, complete understanding, able to move the elements of the universe and produce life even from dead seed at vanishing point . . . all wrapped within a heavenly body, the voice of an angel. Able to raise the dead, heal. I should have known, but instead I couldn't cope with your potential, and it was even further beyond my comprehension. I should have known. I don't even deserve you. How can I even touch you or—"

"Shush," she murmured as she came to him, held him, and kissed him tenderly, and then she enfolded him within her wings. The gentle action set off a new torrent of sobs from him as she stroked his back and gently rocked him against her. "But I would have never found out what was locked inside me without you. Marry me."

EPILOGUE

It was a small chapel wedding in the place named *the peace,* La Paz. White flowers from roses to orchids and lilies covered the pews and turned hallowed ground into an indoor garden. The paperwork could wait; all Guardians were in full attendance as witnesses to the sacred union. Father Patrick could barely get the words of the ceremony out as he peered at Damali, wiping his eyes.

The moment she came into view on Shabazz's arm, Carlos held on to Jose's shoulder for support. But he couldn't take his eyes off his soon-to-be bride.

She wore a simple, strapless silk white sheath, nothing about her neck except a platinum choker that housed all the stones she'd collected. Her smoky Egyptian eyes held tears behind her floor-length veil, threatening to spill over the rims of kohl set off with the barest hint of silver shadow. Her lips, virgin pale pink, quivered ever so slightly. Her hands trembled as they clutched a profusion of white roses and wildflowers, her hair set high upon her head in silver bands, pearl teardrops at her delicate earlobes . . . her best girlfriend dissolved in hiccupping sobs as she flanked her.

He didn't even look at his best man, Jose, as he accepted the twelve-carat blue-white heart diamond surrounded by platinum that he'd found just for her to replace the one lodged in his soul. Just for her . . . anything for her. She was *his wife.* Had taken the worst of him and brought out the best of him. Father Patrick had asked him a question, and he jerked his attention back to the ceremony.

"Huh, oh, yeah, I definitely do."

Chuckles wafted through the chapel, and even Father Patrick smiled.

The elderly cleric let out a fatherly sigh and turned to Damali. Sweat crept between Carlos's shoulder blades, making the tux feel like second skin.

He couldn't get the image of wings sprouting from her back out of his mind. Wouldn't touch her again until they did the thing right. Couldn't. Wasn't trying to tempt fate ever again. But when she handed off her flowers and gave him her hand, quietly repeated words that he was too awed to hear, and softly said, "I do," he nearly passed out.

He was a married man. Just like that. It had happened so fast. His angel had made his deepest wish come true. He had to take two deep breaths to steady himself as he lifted her fragile veil. She was *his*, had made the choice. No man could put that asunder. No forces of evil, come what may, she was his even beyond the grave. Heaven had not even intervened to stop it, and it was done on hallowed ground. He willed himself not to cry in front of his boyz, wishing Yonnie and Tara could have been there, too. But he was done waiting. Although he now waited for the words that seemed to take an eternity for the old priest to say, before claiming his bride's mouth.

"I now pronounce you man and wife."

They both briefly closed their eyes. Marjorie and Marlene started crying. He could hear backs getting slapped as brothers broke out in jubilation somewhere far off in his mind.

There was only one voice he could hear; only one pair of eyes he could see . . . only one mouth that he slowly lowered his to. Only one pair of arms held him gently; only one heart beat against his chest and crushed his boutonniere. There was only one place he wanted to be— alone, with her. There was only one whisper he wanted to hear, hers. Only one person he wanted to give his all.

Food, music, champagne, fruit, and a cake topped with flowers . . . the team could have it and party until dawn. A reception would require his maximum endurance.

Her mind opened to his. *Just for a little while, okay?*

He nodded as she drew out of the kiss. *Anything you want, baby, as long as you let me feed you fresh mango and pineapple in bed.*

She kissed him again. *That and more . . . you can turn off your silver and I'll go gold with you.*

He had to remember that he was in a church. Rather than say another mental word, he tucked away her dear promise, simply nodded, and joined in the celebration with the team.

A private villa on the beach, not a lair, was what she deserved, and what he'd found just for his bride. The surf pounded beyond the deck, sea breeze blew sheers away from sliding glass doors. Fresh fruit and champagne on a silver tray waited patiently by the bed as she balanced the top of the wedding cake in her hands and laughed out loud as he lifted her over the threshold.

"I'm smashing the cake," she squealed, giggling, as he swept her up and nuzzled her neck.

"So," he chuckled, pacing toward the bedroom on a mission. "It's gonna get messed up anyway when we eat it."

"We're supposed to save it for a year," she said, still laughing as he stood beside the high four-poster plantation bed and his expression became serious.

"I don't want to wait for anything anymore," he said quietly, and kissed her softly as he deposited her against white silk and rose petals. He stood back and looked at her as she cradled the cake topper, willing himself not to use any special vamp powers except love when he was with her from now on.

"All right," she said softly as she gazed up at him, and then pushed the cake onto the nightstand, watching him slowly remove his bow tie. She slid her finger across a bit of the icing on the side of the dessert and she popped it into her mouth, playing. But his stone-serious expression stole her mirth and replaced it with a slow smolder as he loosened the knot at his neck.

It was something about the way he did it that made her breath hitch. He just pulled one end of the bow tie and slid the fabric away from his collar, then unfastened one jewel-black onyx stud at a time while staring at her in pure silver. When he dropped his jacket, she thought she'd faint. Men could do a seven-veils dance as well as any woman, and her husband was giving her a deep appreciation of that fact.

Her husband . . . she repeated the title in her mind on a soft chant . . . thank you, thank you, thank you, for once, something had gone so right . . . *Her husband*. He'd made her Mrs. Carlos Rivera, and that was so much better than anything he'd transformed her into thus far.

She slid her hands behind her back and unzipped her dress, but he shook his head no.

"I want to do that," he whispered. "You're my gift, let me unwrap it."

Now she really couldn't breathe. He'd said it so low, with such quiet intensity that it drew a physical contraction from her. So she waited, watching him part with his clothes, late-afternoon sun kissing his bronze skin until she became jealous of the solar rays.

He'd left a pool of black-and-white fabric at his feet, and she had to sit on her hands not to reach out to him; his eyes told her—don't move. If this was his first command as her husband, she'd gladly obey.

When he came to her, she leaned in to kiss him, but he smiled and kissed her calf instead, taking off her shoes. A gentle shove backward landed her in rose petals. Warm hands slid under her and slowly worked against gown fastenings then peeled fabric away from her skin in maddening increments. He was still the master. Damali closed her eyes.

Breathless and naked, she waited for him to blanket her. But he reached for a mango and a small paring knife and lay beside her, totally focused on the fruit. She didn't say a word. Her mind was on fire with anticipation. She watched his hands intently as though in a spell. He wielded the silver blade with care, creating a small slit at the top of the fruit and scoring down the side of it in a slow lateral drag, removing the dripping skin the same excruciating way he'd removed her clothes.

Sweet nectar ran through his fingers and down his wrists, splattering the silver tray, and she watched it ooze pressing her knees together, feeling as wet as the ripe fruit.

Her lips parted on their own when he cut a thick wedge and put half of it in his mouth. Even though he'd told her not to move, she couldn't help it. She was drawn to his mouth just to claim a small bite. Their teeth gently collided as he allowed her to pull away a bit of mango with a kiss.

"Want some champagne?" he murmured, not waiting for her to respond as he reached for the bottle and popped the cork.

She shook her head but accepted the filled crystal flute. She didn't want anything unless he was gonna pour it over himself so she could lick it off. But she acquiesced to his pace and took a sip from her glass. He rewarded her patience with a piece of pineapple chunk between his sucrose soaked fingers, which she sucked slowly, savoring him more than the fruit.

That made him briefly close his eyes; she could only hope that it would make him hurry up. Seeing his lids go to half-mast had made her nearly drop her glass as she leaned back on her elbows. When he took her champagne flute from her and sipped the contents slowly, then winced, her pulse spiked. *Put the glass down . . .*

He smiled. "Want another piece of mango?"

She closed her eyes and let her head fall back. "No," she whispered. "I just want you."

"It's so sweet though," he said, putting a piece halfway in his mouth and crouching above her on his hands and knees.

She leaned up to capture it with a kiss, but he made it miss her mouth and drip on her chin. He dragged it down her throat, stopped at the V in her neck, kissed her deeply there, and then continued on a mind-bending path with the slick, sticky fiber. She gasped as he let it wet the hot place between her breasts, press down her torso, and leave a small puddle of juice in her navel. But as he pulled it further down her body, her legs parted on their own. Then he stopped, kissed her briefly, pulled the mango into his mouth to chew, and swallow it.

"You had your temporary mark renewed for me," he whispered against her.

All she could do was nod.

"And I've created such a mess," he said in a warm rush of sweet air that lifted her hips. "Lemme go clean up."

She opened her eyes, nearly panicked. He couldn't get out of bed to wash up. "I don't care."

He met her gaze with a sly smile and slowly unwrapped the silver bands holding up her hair. Soft velvet locks filled his sticky hands and he didn't care; he'd wash her hair for her later. Her crown should never be obstructed when he was making love to her—ever. It was the source of her inspiration, and he definitely wanted her inspired today.

Sadly, he hadn't even had time to buy her a wedding gift; he'd been in such a hurry to marry her . . . however . . . his wife deserved pearls. Carlos smiled. Yeah, a few Neteru powers were at his disposal, and what better way to let her know how profoundly appreciated she had always been—pearls . . .

Briefly kissing the crown of her head, he rested his cheek against it for a moment, releasing a sigh so he could pace himself. He was many things, but a fool wasn't one of them. Ausar had said to put his household in order, feed her, and work his way from the top down—and he was the kind of brother that only had to be told once. Yeah, he got it. The look on his bride's face was worth it all, even though he was losing his mind he wanted her so badly.

Her gentle caress down his sides almost made him give up his mission, but no, she was so worth it. This time when he kissed the crown of her head, he allowed every dream they'd shared to enter it until the place he attended warmed under his lips. He collected the bead of pleasure that emitted from that place onto his tongue and saved it like a pearl beneath it. His forehead rested against hers, trusting her with his very life and all his darkest secrets as he offered her the unconditional key to his mental black box until the heat exchange caused them both to gasp. Pearl one.

Slowly he pulled away and watched a tiny, silvery version of her Sankofa light beneath her skin. It flickered suddenly to become his symbol in gold, and then went back to hers in the same hue before it vanished . . . but not before he deeply kissed her there and collected another precious pearled bead of her desire sheen from her forehead. Pearl two.

He ignored her mouth, and found the beginning of his sticky mango trail at her chin, rewarded by her arch, which allowed him to savor her throat as her head dug into the satiny pillows. The sight of her symbol rising and changing at her throat chakra was beginning to make him forget his task. He kissed that place deeply, suckling her voice to the surface and then told her the blatant truth. Pearl three . . . and he'd string them together and deliver them in a way that she'd never forget.

" 'Mali, I love you so much, it hurts."

But he couldn't stop there, no, not there, not when she'd told him without words how much she needed him right now. So he collected another fragile bead of her want from her delicate throat, rolling it under his tongue in utter fascination until she moaned through tears. However, he paid particular attention to her sacred heart bridge . . . the one he'd almost damaged beyond repair and gave her the depths of everything within him while indulging his hands on her breasts. Pearl four.

Her quick pants were nearly his undoing as her body warmed suddenly and the surface of her skin dampened with silvery gold. But he demanded her solid gold promise, therefore, in his mind, she wasn't ready enough yet.

Salt tears, rose petals, mango, champagne, pineapple, and her filled his nose as he stayed on the path of righteous pleasure, collecting pearls from her belly, taking back each indignity and filling her with pure love until she moaned. Her deep alto response thundered within his groin and he was unsure whether or not he could even attend to her valley. He stopped at his tattoo that covered her mound and inhaled sharply; control was fading fast. She was *his wife;* arched under his hold, trembled for him—he could wait.

Pearl seven . . . and they all needed to be strung out.

He kissed her slowly until she openly wept and went limp. Although no musician, he knew how to use sound. This was all for her. He released a low, bass line moan into her causing a magnificent soprano response. *Yeah.*

The symbol she wore just for him went from supernatural silver to solid gold then white-hot. He collected that, too, and put it under his tongue, then slowly opened her to weave a lazy figure eight of pleasure around her bud and rim, releasing beads to wait for him to enter with each pass.

Her graceful fingers were in his hair and her voice carved at his scrotum, but this was *his wife* . . . never again would she have reason to doubt him or want anyone else.

"Baby, put it in," she whispered between her teeth.

"Uh-uh," he murmured into her sensitive folds, catching another orgasm and holding it in-state with his tongue. "You promised me pure gold."

"I'm there," she nearly shrieked when he allowed each unbroken bead to roll off his tongue to wait just inside her flooded door.

"You sure?" he murmured, further teasing her with the vibration of sound, but had to stop playing as she thrashed and clutched the sheets.

Yeah . . . he was beyond gold, going platinum, as she writhed soaked with perspiration. When he covered her slowly, he watched her pores leak the divine energy from every pulse point, every place he'd ever nicked her, each chakra quickly transitioning blur of light beneath her buttery smooth skin—his symbol, her symbol and back again, her system so fired on that he entered her hard.

She hit a note that shattered the flutes on the nightstand; champagne was everywhere. Wait; how? He was just a man.

The sound of her voice sent trebles and cymbals up his spine, elicited a low register he didn't know he owned. Her immediate acapella reaction created an offbeat syncopated rhythm; she returned thrusts twice for his every one while the beads of ecstasy he'd planted and strung began to quickly burst.

He didn't know the phenomenon was connected to him or had tangled him in it. This was supposed to just be for her, but they were one. Wasn't prepared for the psychic disturbance or the fast, hot, elongated molten melody that dredged his sac in spasmodic sound waves.

Every promise he'd made to himself evaporated—he'd sworn to God he'd never bite her again, not his angel. But nature was nature, and *oh God, she felt so good.*

Fangs dropped on their own accord, the sudden strike was impossible to hold back. Mango and pineapple and champagne and her. Sweet blood, *sweet Jesus,* her arch was lightning liquid fire. He couldn't stop cuming. White feathers and white rose petals stuck to his mango-drenched hands, his gold-sweat-doused chest, her hair between his fingers, her satin skin in his palms, afraid to break a wing but unable to stop moving between her legs. *Baby, forgive me, but you feel so damned good!*

Vertigo spiralled down, the earth dropped out beneath him. A hard roll and his stomach was practically in his mouth from the sudden change in direction. His head jerked, sought the pillows, dug into them as she kept moving, drawing broken pleasure beads through his shaft embedded in molten seed. Her straddle was a vise, doing her like this one, too, but he couldn't even stop when she'd presented wings.

She was *his wife,* she was *his wife,* Lord, she was his wife!

He forced himself to be a witness and opened his eyes. Sunlight was behind her; the halo effect rimmed her in a brilliant afternoon glare of pink and orange. Her head was thrown back. A trickle of golden blood trailed from her neck, splattering a six-foot white wingspan, every chakra burning gold with his symbol, her movements quicksilver until he had to close his eyes or die from lack of breathing.

Carry for me, baby . . . carry my child.

Yes!

When the last bead burst, he couldn't retract fangs, just heaved hard in a pleasure seizure as she bit him and made white light blind him behind his shut lids. Her name got all tangled up with the Almighty's, then became hers again, no separation, no beginning or end, as his sanity temporarily slipped into another dimension. He could now define infinity.

She collapsed against him, winded, sobbing, trembling, and all he could do was hold her.

"You are my husband," she finally whispered.

He just nodded for a moment, trying to catch his breath. He still had fangs in his mouth.

She pulled back to kiss him, he turned his head to give her his cheek and chuckled.

"I can't make 'em go down." He ran his tongue over his teeth and nicked it.

She grabbed his jaw firmly and kissed him hard, nicking her lip. "I love you. I don't care."

"I don't think we were supposed to do this," he said, slowly recovering.

She laughed and laid her head on his chest. "Have we ever done what we're supposed to do?"

"No," he said, a rumbling chuckle of satisfaction vibrating beneath his Adam's apple as he stroked her wings. "But I think we just made somebody new."

"Ya think?" she laughed softly, nipping his chest.

Then they both became very still. They pulled back and looked at each other at the same time, their words nearly colliding.

"You've got fangs, I've got wings," she said, her eyes containing new awareness.

"I know," he said, partially sitting up. "Uh . . . you think, baby, that could pose a problem? Not trying to be funny . . . but, uhmmm . . . you think we shoulda told at least Marlene?"

She offered him a sheepish smile. "Nah . . . if we woulda told anybody about the wings, they would have made us wait to get married until they could get an answer, yada, yada, yada. Did you wanna wait?"

He shook his head no. "Not in a million years. But if I'm part human, part Neteru, and uh, have a little bad boy in me . . . and you're the same, with a lotta good girl in you—"

"It'll be all right," she said, sweeping his mouth with a tender kiss. "Besides," she said with a shrug, "don't we always make it up as we go along?"

"Yeah," he murmured, allowing his hands to revel in the feel of her skin as he held her hips. He motioned toward the dresser. "Didn't exactly see that wedding present get delivered, so I guess it can't be all bad. Musta happened when everything went white light." He laughed quietly and closed his eyes. Man, if the older brother had seen all that . . .

"The sword of *Ausar*?"

She almost jumped up to go get it, but he couldn't allow her body to unsheathe his when it felt so good.

"That must be a good sign, right?" she said, her voice hopeful yet still carrying a note of concern.

"Either that or Ausar figured I'd *really* need it now."

Carlos just laughed and kept his eyes closed, too content to figure it all out at the moment. Bottom line was, she was *his wife*!

Turn the page for a sneak peek at the next Vampire Huntress Legend novel.

THE WICKED

COMING IN FEBRUARY 2007

Wracked with agony, Cain sat naked at the edge of the sensation pool in his bedchamber, his legs dangling in the ether as he clutched silk sheets to his chest. Anything that would bring her to him, even if it was just her scent. He began slowly rocking back and forth, his hands trembling as he lowered his face to the fabric again with his eyes tightly shut, and then inhaled Damali's ripening essence. Her scent was set ablaze in his mind, fevered by the oil of Hathor she'd trailed. He winced and shuddered, the denial unbearable, the incarceration a suffering he'd never known.

Bitter tears rolled down his cheeks while decimating memories turned his saliva thick in his mouth. *She was his universe, the potential bearer of his empire!* Every breath he took felt as though his Neteru blade was piercing his heart. He could almost taste blood from the phantom wound she'd left.

Cain licked his chaffed, dry lips, remembering Damali's mouth upon his. A shiver almost arched his back. The desire to hold her had become a need, then an obsession, until it produced an incomparable ache. Just the memory of her touch, her sun-fired skin, her ecstasy-producing bite, her deep moans of pleasure, her incredible voice set to song . . . all of it was like a knife that carved at his groin and filled his sac with mind-numbing, unspent seed that could not be spilled in this sensationless realm.

But tasting her blood had made him feel it down to his marrow. The peristaltic drive to release inside her without a way to ejaculate now tortured his mind to near madness.

"Devastation . . ." he murmured into the soft fabric that had been filled with her sweat, "How could you allow him to manipulate you this way?"

Feminine wetness that had overflowed from her valley entered his nose and clung to his palate, a razor of memory whittling his regal pride to sawdust. His apexing would last a month. Cain struggled to breathe as the reality wore on.

Days ago he'd abandoned the frenzied attempt to make love to her telepathically, to find relief in his desperate mounting against the bedding, his hands, the sheets, *anything* she'd touched to no avail. Her vibrations had ceased; his thrusts against inanimate objects were futile, a teasing reminder that Damali was truly gone. All he had left to cling to was her delirium-producing scent and what remained of their last encounter in his mind. Even that was slowly vaporizing, as though she was being erased from his realm and his tortured psyche one memory cell at a time . . . leaving only the burn for her in its wake.

He couldn't conjure her in visions or connect to her astrally. The orgasm would crest and then die away, leaving him unfulfilled in a heat of raw desire. Everything in his chamber had soaked up the sound of his suffering, every lusty groan, every hot gasp, each time he'd wailed her name, and it now reverberated to taunt him with the knowledge · that there would be endless days and nights until his solo apex finally ebbed.

"Damali . . ." A sob choked off his words as he nuzzled the sheets remembering her voice, her caress, the way she'd reached for him and had arched under his hold, a plea in her eyes to love her hard. "I would have given you the world, and so much more . . ."

Seven brutal days of suffering had lacerated his soul. Her blood had been a sweet tonic that still burned inside his veins. "Do not banish me!" he bellowed, throwing his head back as his fangs ripped his gums. Seven long, hard days and endless nights . . .

It was to be twelve days of mourning peace with Damali in his arms during a war hiatus that had also been reserved for his oldest friend. Everything had been so perfectly orchestrated, the strategy sound. The cease-fire had been established to quell civil unrest in his empire, and yet he was more bereft over the loss of Damali than the death of Zehiradangra.

His pool now remained eerily silent; Damali's vibrations blocked to his communion. Her voice was as unreachable as a distant star, dead to him, the flicker of its light only a resonance from the past.

"I loved you so," he whispered against the tear-dampened linens. "Come back to me . . . I beg you with all that is within me. Do not forsake me, angel . . . queen of all that I know."

The sensation tank remained still as Cain's agonized wails echoed off the white marble lair walls. The gold-and-silver mortar and every conductive metal object radiated pain so acutely that he reached his hand out and touched the glasslike blue surface of the ether with his fingertips. His pride in ruins, broken, he would settle for knowing her whereabouts even through the vibrations of another man.

Carlos had befouled his lair, his pool. Cain closed his eyes. Just to know where Damali was, he would link to his Neteru brother who also shared his vampire lineage. He had to know. Seven days was more than he could bear. Her absence had become a viral infection that fevered his mind, drove him to obsession, and had made his body ache with a craving worse than blood hunger.

But the moment he honed his focus to Carlos, Cain drew his hand back as though he'd been burned. The sheets fell away from him as he backed away from the pool shaking his head, and insanity crept across his mind.

"No," he whispered, disbelief robbing his lungs of air. He went to his hands and knees, splaying both palms against the pool's surface, tilting his head, watching, listening—he had to understand. She *couldn't have* done this.

On his feet in an instant, Cain's body transformed into a ripping battle bulk. A war cry filled his chest and he released it like sudden thunder. Lightning arched from each digit on his hands. His eyes went silver, gold, and then black.

"Transgressor! Betrayer! Befouler! Be damned!" he roared, immediately materializing armor to cover his nakedness and his blade of Ausar in his fist.

Capillaries burst in his temples, blood was in his eyes. "Married? You blotted her from my world by a treacherous act of matrimony? In a church? In the Light? *You*—on hallowed ground? I will behead you and make her a widow!"

With one long lightning bolt that cracked and singed the air as it ejected from the tip of his blade, every marble bench along the edge of the Olympic-sized pool overturned and exploded into rubble. The four-poster, solid gold, king-sized bed flipped over and melted, starting a blaze behind him. With a wave of Cain's massive arm, eight-foot marble vases hurled against the wall, shattering into shards of marble as though made of glass. Pillars began to crumble. His guard sphinxes came alive at the front entrance and rushed in to assist him, only to be summarily beheaded, leaving confused, stricken expressions in their glassy eyes that their master had harmed them.

The high, vaulted ceiling began to give way, but Cain stood in the midst of the destruction so enraged that he would not even shield himself from falling marble, boulders, and debris as he decimated his cliffside lair.

"You manipulated her to murder my father, Dante! You took my father's throne in Hell, stole his empire, and then threw it back in his face! You robbed me of my oldest friend after seducing her. You beset the Neteru Council of Kings against me to seal me in Nod with their shields of Heru! You come to my lair and desecrate my home. You steal my music, my nightingale, after you kept her from composing for one year—my Damali, the detriment of my soul! You break my mother's heart by causing me to cross into your world to seek the voice that I'd longed for."

Cain's eyes narrowed to enraged slits. "Because of you, my world is gone and my kingdom is under civil unrest! Then you betray my beloved's heart, take her body, and marry her away from me? Are you insane? Do you believe there will be no redress? I will have justice, Rivera!"

Pure fury roiled through Cain like a dark tornado, spiking adrenaline to rage in blackout proportions. In a sharp pivot with both hands on his broad sword, Cain sliced at a standing column, and then froze as the blade of Ausar shattered in his grip.

"Noooo . . . Imposter . . ." he whispered in utter disbelief, looking at the blade handle in his hand and then down at the broken steel at his feet. "For *millennia* you have deceived me? My mother's people . . . those of the Light?" Cain threw his head back and roared. "What game is this, Adam? Did you also deceive Ausar? What conspiracy is afoot amid the archons—I demand an answer! It is my due!"

Immediately Cain's eyes sought the horizon through the yawning hole in the destroyed lair roof, and his gaze tore around the multiple golden shields of Heru that still covered and sealed the thinning barrier between the Land of Nod and earth.

"I believed . . ." Cain's voice quieted as he raked his fingers through his locks, incredulous. He stared at the blade on the floor that should have cut through stone, tears rising and then burning away with renewed anger.

The Neteru Council of Kings had betrayed him? Had given him a replica of the actual blade, and had given the real mark of royalty to Carlos Rivera, over him? Rivera—a man not made a Neteru by birthright through Eve, but rather through a late elevation? A man bitten and made a vampire, not sired from the original royal lineage of Dante and Lucifer? A common drug peddler made king, over him? A man, who had also slain his sibling, lied, stolen, and God knew what else, was allowed to bed the millennium female Neteru, marry her in the Light, and sire? This transgressor, this interloper of dubious heritage had been incarcerated for only a few short years, yet with full conjugal access to Damali, while he'd been locked away in the Land of Nod devoid of carnal sensation *for eons*—when his only offense had been to execute his wearisome brother? *This* was the justice delivered from On High?

"Never!" He spat on the floor in disgust. "Then my father's people shall have me, where my rule will be revered."

Cain was pure motion, his footfalls gaining in velocity until he reached the edge of the ravine. Headlong he tumbled, burning through the energy atmosphere like a flaming arrow to land in the central kingdom square. His furious landing was greeted by the stunned amazement of his subjects, but constituents from the side of Light and the dark drew away from their monarch. Blue-black flames flickered at the edges of Cain's nostrils as he whirred around to gain his bearings. Battle-length fangs had filled his mouth, and the lack of a blade hadn't left him unarmed. More dangerous now than ever, he strode to the shadow wall zone. Patrons of the illicit sensations there scattered at his presence the moment he entered the dank alley.

Trembling with rage, Cain said nothing as he approached the rubbery surface of the wall of seekers. His footfalls thudded with lethal echoes as he outstretched his hands and dug into the flexible divide, plunging his fists into it up to the elbows. His massive hands grasped several faces, twisting and contorting them, causing the entire wall to wail.

"Warlocks, bring me Lilith," he said in a low, thundering tone. "Bring her to this wall that she might seduce modern men of science to run another barrier-shattering experiment. Tell her to open a hole and prepare my father's throne for me in Hell!"

Harpies genuflected. Level Six vampire messengers cowered against stalagmites and stalactites, and then fell to the floor prostrate before Cain's passage. The Sea of Perpetual Agony ceased its cries and went silent. The molten, bubbling lava in the pit calmed as a slow glacier sealed over it as Cain stormed over the bridge toward the Vampire Council Chambers. Ice slicked the cavern floor behind him; the halting breaths of the bats and messengers came out in strangled puffs of frigid air.

The huge black marble doors leading to the throne room creaked open on frozen hinges. Ice weighed the golden, fanged knockers as the doors struggled to respond to Cain's royal entry, but seemed incapable of doing so fast enough to avoid being kicked off their hinges, each door exploding at the assault. With every footfall that Cain landed on the black marble floor, the blood veins in it oozed to a halt beneath his furious steps, icy fingers choking off the flow of life within it and spreading out in a frosted glaze behind him.

Lilith stood up from the pentagram-shaped ruling table that had been running with fresh blood. From her peripheral vision she watched it ice over into a shining, ruby, still resin. Her fingers and palm stuck to the golden goblet she clutched in her hand as she watched Cain stand in the center of the floor breathing fire and ice, his golden armor turning black at the edges until the hue of pure darkness overtook it all.

"Your throne awaits, Your Eminence," she said, the chilly air making her words come out in visible white puffs. Going to one knee with her head lowered and respectfully motioning Cain toward his father's old throne, her tone was reverent. "Hell has frozen over, sire . . . it is your time to rule."

Cain did not speak as he approached the old Chairman's throne, but he stopped to look at the last vampire's name that had been etched into the high, black marble back of it. "Imposter!" he bellowed, punching the top section of the throne away to rid it of Carlos Rivera's name before abruptly turning to claim his legacy.

He sat quickly, his back straight, his jaw set hard, and closed his eyes. Tears of familiarity wet his lashes as satisfaction and knowing wafted through his cells. Dante's virile image was the first impression that careened through his mind, and just as quickly he saw his mother as a young, ripening virgin in Eden, and then watched his father uncoil in muscular fluidity to shape-shift from an enormous black serpent to take the first Neteru ever made.

"I will avenge you, Father," Cain murmured thickly as eons of vampiric information poured into his consciousness.

Profound pleasure began to burn away his skin as his vertebrae knotted and became welded to the throne. Huge bat wings with a twenty-foot span ripped through his shoulders and his spine elongated to tear flesh away from his back to permit a razor-sharp, scaled, spaded tail to exit.

Cain simply steeled his jaw and gripped the armrests harder against the excruciating transition. *This* was power. He drew in a wincing breath and kept his eyes tightly shut. *This* was of his line. His father's people. He would not cry out as the metal armor he wore fused to his skin becoming one with it to leave him naked.

The transformation hurt so good that it caused him to throw his head back as talons and twelve-inch fangs ripped through his nail beds and gums. He could feel his pupils dilate beneath his lids, and his inner vision showed him the gold bar that they'd become, now set in black orbs. Perfection . . . he had his grandfather's eyes . . . his father's fangs . . . his mother's tolerance to daylight . . . and power within the dark realms unlimited. He was a fucking king! He would slay the pure Light male Neteru!

Every deviant carnal act that had ever been committed on the planet imploded within Cain's groin simultaneously with the power of every evil that existed. His body convulsed and shuddered. But still he would not cry out, even panting, sweat leaking from his pores like black rain. No. Years . . . millennia of abstinence, pain profound for his kind, had been endured. He was a birthright monarch and would not cry out at his dark coronation or dishonor his father by a show of weakness. Not in the throne that his father had ruled from since the dawn of time! Not in the throne that had broken Rivera's spirit into two entities! He would crush that bastard's memory from the throne of royal vampire lineage!

The moment the top of the throne reconstructed and the smell of sulfuric scorch emblazoned Cain's name within it, Lilith mounted him, adding to the exquisite torture of it all.

He savagely bit into her shoulder, still refusing to cry out until his transformation was complete. Her pleasure shriek made him tear his mouth away from her flesh to gasp as her spaded tail twined with his, slashing at the newly scaled flesh. The sensation of wet, hot, writhing female sheathing him, combined with the heart-seizing ecstasy emanating from the throne, finally caused him to arch while she rode him hard. Lilith's siphon as she dug her nails into the thick ropes of muscles in his shoulders dredged a slow, rumbling groan up from his diaphragm.

His wingspan instantly eclipsed hers as the leathery appendages beat in unison to each lunging thrust. Lifting her high into the vaulted ceiling in hovering flight above the throne, his talons tore at her ass, his mouth devouring her forked tongue until it bled black blood. Messenger bats swarmed around them, squealing in frenzied, airborne mating. Cain reached down, gripping Lilith's waist with one arm, his fingers craning as he pulled knowledge since the dawn of time up and out of the throne to him.

Torches blew out as he amassed power in a high-pitched, turbine whine of suction toward him. He lit the cavern with lunar eclipses from the first-world skies to better witness it all. Thunder and lightning sent black prisms to rain rocks down to the marble floor fifty feet below. Sound, sent in shock waves from Babylon, reverberated off the stone walls and he caught each note in his fist while still pumping against Lilith's nearly limp body, forcing the vibrations into her vertebrae one note at a time before allowing them to explode her disks in falling dominoes of pleasure.

Her shrieks of ecstasy drew him to her throat; his black laser sight on her jugular summoned the dead vein up to the surface of her skin as he wound her raven hair around his clawed fist, yanked her head back, snapped her neck, and fed amid her orgasmic wails. Descending in a vanishing point spiral of pure black vapor, he crash-landed with her splayed in the center of the pentagram-shaped table.

He was convulsing so hard against her that he couldn't control his thrusts. It had been so long, vanishing point a fantasy denied so completely that he was barely conscious when his body spewed every drop of agony his tortured scrotum held. Cuming in painful jags, he hollered until he was breathless. He grabbed the base of his shaft to try to slow the ejaculation, but was forced to yank his hand away when the throb along his entire length felt like it would split him.

Lilith's voice hit radar-destroying decibels that sent the bats in the crags in all directions, their disoriented flight patterns crashing them into the walls. Teeming vermin spilled over the ledges in search of a haven to avoid the sonar she'd released. Her damaged womb filled with thick, wriggling, maggoty life as he threw his head back and climaxed hard against her again.

"I'm not sterile like Dante," he said in a ragged whisper into her ear through his fangs, sending his Neteru apex scent into her nose and mouth with a punishing kiss. He broke away from her mouth, gulping air. "Sire the day heir that it might walk at my side as my son!"

"I can't," Lilith wailed, another orgasm ripping a gasp from her throat.

Cain looked down at her, snarled, and backhand slapped her, bloodying her nose. "I said sire for me! Treacherous liar! You used to give birth to one hundred original demons a day—"

"The female Neteru gored my womb with an Isis blade," Lilith wailed, her black, Bedouin eyes ablaze with both fear and raw lust. She licked Cain's Adam's apple and wrapped her legs tighter around his waist. "Neteru, second to none ever created, my dark sovereign . . . I will find you a vessel just as I wrested you from Nod," Lilith moaned, closing her eyes as her head dropped back. "Just V-point fuck me as you apex and we can discuss it later. Hit me again—harder."

Winded from the feed and frustrated by Lilith's dead womb, Cain stood with her spent body still clinging to his torso, her legs and tail wrapped around his waist. Lodged deep within her, he slammed her against the council table, splattering blood everywhere. Her strike was a blinding bolt of black current that made him cum again so hard that initially no sound exited his throat. The seizure Lilith's bite produced was like none he'd ever known, and yet he needed more.

Her body was almost a rag of fatigued limbs, but driven by impulse, he extracted himself from her wickedly delicious pelvic hold and flipped her over onto her stomach.

"Your womb is dead, therefore the orifice leading to it is no longer of use to me," Cain snarled close to her ear. He entered her hard, sodomizing her with rage, dripping black sweat against her bruised spine as she moaned and writhed beneath him.

"Tell me your every wish," she cried out between gasps of pleasure. "Your grandfather will be so proud—just ask it and I will deliver it!"

"Raise the master vampire I request from the Sea of Perpetual Agony," Cain said, his voice echoing when a seizure of pleasure overtook him.

His head dropped back, his long, dark locks sweeping his ass as his deep lunges against Lilith increased in force. He cried out, unable to conceal the years of unfed desire with her blood polluting his system. It felt so good he didn't even care that he might bleed her out and fuck her to death. But he needed her direct access to the Ultimate Dark Power of their realms in order to raise the exterminated. She was already midway between dark mist and pure vapor. Her voluptuous body was beginning to make him see double. The deal had to be finalized but his cells had begun to deconstruct with hers again to the tonal frequency of the vibrating Babylonian chants in the cavern. Unable to scale back the velocity or stop moving, he sent hot flash images of Sodom and Gomorrah into her skull, nearly fracturing it with a brutal mind thrust.

"Cain! Name your terms," she cried out, reaching backward and trying to hold onto his hips with her talons. Black tears streamed down her face and her breathing staggered as she tried to turn to score his jugular.

The need to release had put tears in his eyes, and he held her heavy, pendulous breasts, vaporizing millisecond by millisecond as he spoke through his teeth. "The one not beheaded but felled by an Isis," Cain panted in Dananu, flattening Lilith against the table harder and pulling back from the edge of a V-point spiral. "My armies will slaughter Guardian teams worldwide with every setting sun. My hybrids will terrorize their days with bloodshed and chaos that knows no bounds! *I* will create the darkest night!"

"Yes! Anything—your scent, your voice . . . oh, great Darkness . . . your body—*I am damned for you, lover!*" Lilith shrieked near hysterics, sputtering black blood from her injuries, her talons digging deep grooves into the marble surface as her tail slashed at him wildly. "*Anything,* when you have surpassed even Dante's carnal abilities like this!" She dropped her head back and offered her jugular, craning her neck. "Do it, now!"

He abruptly withdrew from her with a groan that was sliced by her sharp gasp. Frustration caused her to hiss at him when he spun her to face him, and the sound sent a shiver down his spine that closed his eyes to half-mast.

"Just because I've been in Nod for a very long time, did you think you could take advantage of my celibacy, Lilith?" Cain's hand went to her throat as her eyes widened. "Do you know how many entities there are from here to the surface that I could fuck before worrying about you, bitch?" He leaned into her with a dangerous warning in his low, rumbling tone. "After all the centuries devoid of sensation, do you think I would give a damn if it is a she-wolf on Level Five, or an Amanthra serpent from above that? A succubus, poltergeist, I do not care as long as it brings pleasure! Do you not yet realize that I am Cain, son of Dante, grandson of Lucifer?"

His black gaze locked with hers as he slowly anchored his tail to her waist.

"*I* run this council, Lilith, unlike Dante who had to succumb to your rank as his father's Level Seven wife—but you have been stripped of that military privilege," Cain whispered in a slow, even warning. "As a being impervious to the sun, not a dead made-from-the-bite vampire—I was made all that I am *from seed. I* already have a waiting army and an empire and do not need to go through the laborious task of making vampires one by one, as in Dante's time. But be very sure that you understand that you do not even have a seat on this council, yet. You are a familiar to do council bidding, just like you are for my grandfather . . . attempt a coup, and even he will not be able to save you."

"You saw the betrayal in Dante's throne . . ." she whispered, mesmerized, her hand reverently tracing Cain's cheek. "In the *first sitting* you received something buried so deeply within Dante's shame that it should have taken *years* to acquire?" Lilith's voice dropped to a low, quaking decibel. Her whisper was so gentle that the chamber went dead silent. "Fuck me again now, before I faint. I beg you."

Cain simply stared at her for a moment. There was no fraud in her eyes or her voice. Lilith's arousal spiked so radically beneath him in earnest that it was becoming increasingly difficult to negotiate with her. The fact that she was so twisted that the fear of his reprisal had sent a new slickness of desire between her thighs made him tremble. Easing her backward against the ruling table, he kept a dark current protecting his throat to frustrate her strike.

"Do we have a deal on multiple levels?" His eyes slid shut as he brutally entered her and nipped her bottom lip.

"Yes," she whispered on a thick swallow and raked her nails down his stone-cut chest. "Take off the collar . . . please. I *must* strike you."

"Do you want to spiral up through the levels, or take your chances with a knock on your husband's chamber door?" Cain whispered in her ear, nipping it and holding her tighter with his tail.

"Please, spiral up," she said, looking frantic. "Lately—"

"He's been stomping your traitorous ass into a black puddle," Cain said chuckling, and then placed both hands on the table at either side of her hips.

Instantly the Vampire Council table developed a fissure and split in two. Cain's wings opened, Lilith screamed and slapped his face hard enough to draw blood. He smiled, reared back, and severed the vein in her throat as he opened the Harpies' chasm in the floor, then dragged her over the precipice dissolving into a V-point mist spiral headed for Lucifer's door.

It was an act so brazen that even the Harpies they whirled past shuddered and tried to hide, knowing they'd be collateral damage in a rampage. The caverns cleared. Roaring flames from the bottomless pit hissed and spit at the molecular violation. Damned souls retreated in cowering waves, cringing away from the speeding intrusion. The scorching heat forced him to move against her faster, each cell bonding and breaking into hers at the atomic pleasure level, becoming one with the dense plumes of sulfur. What a way to die!

Lilith's orgasmic wails and deep talon gouges into his back added to the increased velocity toward the bottom of the pit. He couldn't slow down. Adrenaline and insanity had him in its grip. Pleasure had made him both blind and deaf, but he was anything but mute. Her sex felt so good that his moan rent the scorching air. The low sonic boom resonance of his voice began to implode the cavern in crumbling splinters that fell inward behind them. Two seconds short of an extinction wish, he pulled up, reversed polarity, and sent them both crashing through the backside of the council table to disturb the orgy of bats again.

He came hard in a black torrent of ecstasy so perverse that he could only close his eyes as the images roiled through his mind with hers. Panting, his movements against her abated slowly and he kept both hands at either side of her skull while in the air, daring her to move by telepathy until he'd normalized. If she had just been Damali, it would have been perfect. Cain opened his eyes, temporarily sated but disgusted. Just the thought of Rivera having his Neteru through an apex made him want blood.

"Bring me the one vampire, the one master of masters that will carve out Rivera's soul to see risen again," Cain said between thundering breaths singed with flames.

"Just tell me, Your Eminence. I shall immediately take up your petition with my husband and convince him of your needs . . . just come to me like this again. Please. I beg you," she said, a sob catching the words spoken in Dananu in her throat.

"We have a truce. Avenge me, and what you did to Dante will be dismissed. I will see you often until my apex wanes. That is a promise . . . perhaps more like a vow." Cain righted the table and lowered them to rest on it, his giant, leathery wings thudding against the now-still chamber air.

The sound of slow, strolling hooves made Cain jerk his attention toward the battered chamber doors. The echo of calm, steady applause entered the Vampire Council throne room.

"Well done, Grandson," a deep, melodic, baritone voice whispered in a murderous tone from the shadows beyond. "With a throne ascension like that, there is no need to go through my wife as an intermediary, although you can at your leisure, since she seems to amuse you."

Lilith cringed and buried her face against Cain's chest, her terrified grip tightening on his arms. "Don't provoke him," she whispered through her teeth when Cain lifted his chin. "I begged you to spiral us upward!"

"She'll do while I apex," Cain said, shrugging out of Lilith's hold and nonchalantly pulling out of her body. "Of greater importance, Your Majesty . . . let us decide how we might best rule the world."

Lilith gasped and closed her eyes, making her body very small behind Cain's hulking form.

A long sigh filled with amusement echoed in response. Each eclipse that had lit the chamber with thin rims of blue moonlight went out, creating pure darkness.

"Tell me the name and I shall consider your request to raise him. We are royal family. Heirs of the world, so to speak. If you can handle the job, you can rule it."

A low, mellow chuckle filled with heat began to melt the ice-crusted floor. "But do not *ever* freeze over Hell again without my permission . . . I will allow this one transgression, given your Neteru arrogance from your mother's side and the insanity induced by your apexing condition. We don't see that much down here. It does intrigue me to witness it bloom on one of my thrones—even Dante never had that in him . . . and I must admit that I've never seen it turn so thoroughly, boldly dark as quickly as you have taken it. My compliments on the way you sire, as well." The sound of hooves began to retreat. "Well done. Yes . . . done outrageously enough to entertain me this evening. Therefore, tell me the name you seek from my prisons and we shall bargain."

Cain smiled, knowing the melodic, sinister voice had relented. He nodded and reinserted himself into Lilith's body with a shuddering wince. She covered her mouth to silence the pleasure gasp that threatened to bring her husband back into chambers less amused.

"Fallon Nuit," Cain called out in a tone of authority, moving against Lilith as he stared down into her stricken eyes.

"Nice move . . . very, very nice," a sinister voice thundered in the distance with another round of slow applause. "Done. You *do* take after our side of the family, after all. Vengeance served—*ice* cold. Great voice, too, kid. Excellent set of pipes and fantastic projection." Rumbling laughter with a hint of implied danger in it made the bats seek shelter again. "Think about what you want to give me, later."

Both male entities chuckled.

Cain closed his eyes, threw his head back, and groaned softly, intensifying his thrusts as Lilith arched with a shiver. "Done."

1. What do you think about Damali's struggle choosing between Carlos and Cain?

2. Ultimately in this saga, each Guardian has a personal hurdle to address or overcome for the good of the group. How necessary and realistic is it to relegate one's own deeply private issues to the background, as each member of the Neteru Guardian team does? In addition, discuss how the Neteru King and Queen Council members were forced to do this in some ways.

3. How is it possible for a person to be both honorable and dishonorable, like Cain? Discuss other real-life people who have acted both honorably and dishonorably.

4. Discuss Marlene and Carlos's battle before the team—her "purge process" of getting to Carlos's inner core and taking him to the rock. Were there other ways for her to identify with him? What has been the best way when you have had to do it?

5. What do you think about Juanita's role in all of this and her ultimate discovery?

6. What lessons did both Neterus learn this time that could be helpful in the future?

7. What effects do you think Damali's newfound powers will have in future battles?

8. What do you think the new paradigm between Carlos and Damali will do to other members of the team?

9. Which "newbie" Guardians do you think will step up and begin to evolve into their powers next? How?

10. What new threat do you envision attacking the team? How will evil come for them next?

11. With this new twist in Damali and Carlos's relationship, what role might the Covenant play? What role do you envision for the Covenant in Carlos's friendship with Yonnie, a vampire?

12. What temptations could easily befall the members of the Guardian squad in the same way both Damali and Carlos have been "tested" over the years? Who do you think is most at risk?

A Reading Group Guide

St. Martin's Griffin

CPSIA information can be obtained at www.ICGtesting.com
Printed in the USA
LVOW10s2224110713

342564LV00003B/155/P